Simul

The sequel to Momenticon

By Andrew Caldecott

ROTHERWEIRD TRILOGY

Rotherweird
Wyntertide
Lost Acre

MOMENTICON DUOLOGY

Momenticon
Simul

Simul

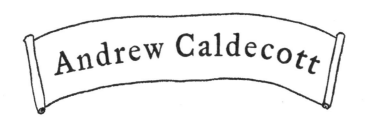

Andrew Caldecott

Illustrated by
Nick May

Jo Fletcher
BOOKS

First published in Great Britain in 2024 by

Jo Fletcher
BOOKS

Jo Fletcher Books
an imprint of
Quercus Editions Ltd
Carmelite House
50 Victoria Embankment
London EC4Y 0DZ

An Hachette UK company

A CIP catalogue record for this book is available
from the British Library

HB ISBN 978 1 52941 547 6
TPB ISBN 978 1 52941 548 3
Ebook ISBN 978 1 52941 550 6

10 9 8 7 6 5 4 3 2 1

Typeset by CC Book Production
Printed and bound in Great Britain by Clays Ltd, Elcograf S.p.A.

Papers used by Jo Fletcher Books are from well-managed forests and other responsible sources.

To Rebecca, Will and Elkie

CONTENTS

LIST OF ILLUSTRATIONS

by Nick May

Endpaper illustration by Nicola Howell Hawley

The College of Novelties.
Endpapers

AUTHOR'S NOTE

Simul is a sequel and its story will make little sense unless the first volume, *Momenticon*, has been read first.

There is a Glossary and *dramatis personae* at the back of this volume which contains major spoilers for those who have not yet read *Momenticon*.

Part I of *Simul* is retrospective and ends roughly where *Momenticon* begins. Parts II to IV take the story to its conclusion.

I
ORIGINS

I

An Unwanted Message

Every seat is taken at the long oval table. Cards, perfectly aligned on the green baize cloth, declare the ministerial post of each chair's occupant. Outside, a yellowish mist clings to the windowpanes. The Prime Minister glares at the Secretary of State for the Environment.

'Logging in the Amazon! Since when are we Brazilians? What the hell is it doing here?'

'It's the UN's Rainforest Day; we can say we discussed it.'

'Right. Discussed. Next: Chancellor?'

At that moment, a semi-transparent young woman in a short skirt appears in the centre of the Cabinet table.

'Hi! I'm Triv. As a minor royal grabs the headlines for wearing the same dress twice, and *I'm a Celebrity . . . Get Me Out of Here!* starts its fortieth series in the Amazon jungle, the following birds of brilliance are lost forever to Brazil and the world: Spix's macaw, the Alagoas foliage-gleaner, the cryptic treehunter—'

The Prime Minister's fist slams the tabletop. Water glasses dance.

'Get that woman out of here!'

Some, mostly men, leer and fantasise; others stare at their shoes. Security steps into the breach.

'I'm afraid she's virtual, Prime Minister.'

'Who's doing this?'

'Tempestas, Prime Minister. You may recall a similar stunt in the Oval office last month.'

'Get the Attorney General. I want an injunction *now*. And find us another room.'

One junior minister whispers to another, 'To think he gave Lord Vane his peerage.'

With a suggestive swing of the hips, Triv moves from her liturgy for the vanished to a farewell song as the Cabinet file out:

> 'In the Final Chance Saloon
> Mere survival is a boon,
> So ready for the horror
> Which undid poor Gomorrah:
> For, baby, she's coming soon.'

2

Audiences

Down the passage in Tiriel's Tower, men and women on plastic chairs and the Tempestas payroll map the progress of the corrosive storms sweeping away the last remnants of the old world, but here in Lord Vane's study, news arrives, and orders leave, on paper. He is deeply radical and yet deeply conservative. One such order has brought his only son's young governess, Nancy Baldwin, to the door. She knocks.

'In!' bellows Lord Vane, who does not wait for the door to close before delivering his diatribe: 'Why is that boy simpering over art books?'

'I was asked to give him an education,' replies Miss Baldwin gamely. Stocky in build, with a plain but resolute face, she stands her ground physically as she does in argument.

'He is heir to the world's last kingdom, not a student of daubs and scribblings.'

The boy, thirteen today, stands awkwardly to one side of his father's large, ornate desk, hands behind his back. 'It's only two hours a week,' he interjects quietly.

'You speak when you're spoken to,' snaps Lord Vane in a voice which cows most opposition.

But the boy has learnt courage from Miss Baldwin.

'She teaches me Machiavelli too,' he says.

'Does she, now? *It is better to be feared than loved, if you cannot be both.* Do you teach that, Miss Baldwin?'

The boy interrupts a second time.

'*Two impulses drive us: love or fear.* Isn't that the choice we rulers have to make?'

Lord Vane rises from his equally ornate chair. He approaches his son, as if to strike him. Instead, he spins round to face Miss Baldwin once more.

'From now on, he'll be taught by the Master of the Weather-Watchers.'

The boy's head sinks low to his chest.

'Mr Jaggard is no teacher,' says Miss Baldwin.

'Why do you say that?'

'He is not a man who shares.'

'He will if I tell him to.'

'And he revels in our tragedy.'

'*Our* tragedy? You mean *theirs*! If the world had listened, if the world had acted, most could – would – have survived. More to the point, Jaggard has a clever son about the same age. They'll get on famously.'

Clever, indeed, she thinks, but slippery as an eel and not her idea of a good influence.

Lord Vane softens, and that is his reputation: generous, once he has had his way. 'I'm not dismissing you, of course. You can help young Potts with the library databases.' He turns back to his son. 'But no art books for you, now or ever.'

Next in is a fresh-faced Peregrine Mander.

'Ah, young Mander! Is the art of the old world logged and recorded?' asks Lord Vane, sitting down again at his magnificent pedestal desk.

'Hardly all of it, my Lord, but what I hope is the *crème de la crème*.'

'Your postcard idea was genius. No galleries to turn people soft, but a space-efficient record of our wasted craftsmanship.'

'I'm pleased you approve, my Lord.'

'Just keep my son away from them. Arty-farties are unfit to govern.'

'I have limited experience on that topic,' replies Mander cautiously.

'Miss Baldwin says you've mastered the Matter-Rearranger.'

'You never master the culinary arts, you merely develop them.'

Lord Vane smiles rarely these days, but he does now.

'I have to say, Mander, you speak like a man in his sixties.'

'I'll take that as a compliment, my Lord.'

'Good, because I've a proposal. I need a fetcher and carrier. Someone to make mealtimes a pleasure. Someone trustworthy, to keep an eye. Are you up for it?'

Mander nods gently as Lord Vane encourages him.

'I want you to stand out and be respected. So, how about the traditional kit?'

'Which tradition is that, my Lord?'

'Personal service.'

'Ah, the gentleman's gentleman.' Mander mulls, but briefly. 'I shall visit the Tempestas' tailor this very afternoon.'

In Mander's complex mind, it is rare for an offer to seem instantly right, but this one does. He will be inside the citadel of power, yet will pose no threat in his white tie and tails. The dress and deferential language of the butler will make him near invisible, but, boy, he will *listen*. And, in his own way, he will act. Lord Vane has no idea what a promotion this is.

'So, you're game?'

Game he is, and *game* is the word.

'I trust I'll not disappoint, my Lord.'

'That's settled, then. I feel this will be a long and fruitful relationship. Keep an eye on my son, too. We can't have a wimp for an heir.'

Two satisfactory audiences, from Lord Vane's perspective: objectives accomplished without conflict. But the next may be more testing.

A young outlier waltzes in, no respectful pause at the threshold like the others. She looks a maverick too: one eyebrow higher than the other, a nose which tilts slightly to the right, a quizzical lopsided smile. At least the eyes are the same colour. They say she is a sponge for detail and mistress of the colourful phrase.

'I trust you are pleased with your appointment, Miss Crike?'

'Tickled pink.'

Tickled pink is not how his patronage is usually greeted. *I'm very grateful, your Lordship* would be a start.

He gives her a prompt: '*The Official History of Tempestas*. That's quite a subject and quite a privilege. The library has a whole shelf set aside.'

Crike eyes the old fox. She could write the official version right now. Tempestas warned like an Old Testament prophet. Humanity closed its ears and paid in fire and brimstone. Think Sodom and Gomorrah.

'What is an *official* history?' she asks.

'A narrative provided by those who know. Mr Venbar and Mr Jaggard will give you whatever time you need. As will I, of course.'

'An excellent start,' replies Miss Crike, lingering over the last syllable.

'The best historian in your year, I'm told.'

'My university had spires, meadows, quads laid to grass and a river. All dust now. Nothing like loss to strengthen your sense of history.'

Lord Vane softens, though less sure, this time, that he has got his way. 'I went to a university like yours. I know how you feel. I've even remembered my college in my will.'

Hilda Crike bobs, more an acknowledgement than a curtsey, and withdraws.

So, Crike the spy and Crike the actress are born, for history is about what *truly* happened: a task for stealth and subterfuge. She might even get a chance to remedy whatever faults the truth reveals. She is ambitious to shape history as well as record it.

On reaching the library, an oddity strikes her. How can Lord Vane donate to a college which no longer exists?

3
Last Words

Hilda Crike pores over the weather-watchers' charts and their reports to Lord Vane. She has burnt the midnight oil mastering the vagaries of the weather, both cause and effect. The more she learns, the more she suspects Tiriel's Tower of presenting design as accident, but there are gaps which only Lord Vane can fill, and he has been critically ill for weeks now.

Peregrine Mander taps her shoulder. She is the only one he addresses with any trace of familiarity. He has, like a chameleon, turned into a fictional gentleman's gentleman. Potts is Mr Potts; Baldwin is Miss Baldwin.

'Miss Hilly, you are wanted. The celestial plane awaits his Lordship.'

She follows him up the great staircase to the private quarters with head bowed. For all his sternness, she has grown fond of Lord Vane.

He lies in a four-poster bed, head propped on a jigsaw of pillows. His arms lie over the sheet, his skin peeling like rice paper beneath a nightshirt as white as a shroud.

Mander busies himself with his master's brow. Beside the bed, a young woman kneads a mix of plaster of Paris, wax and dough-like gel. Lord Vane's son sits, motionless in a corner, head in hands.

The dying man retains his humour.

'She's to strike while the iron is hot,' he says with a nod in the young woman's direction. His chest grumbles like pebbles shaken in a jar. The voice wavers, but he still hits the consonants hard and is easily understood.

'Save your breath, my Lord,' whispers Mander.

Lord Vane ignores the advice. Why else bring her here?

'Is your *History* done, Miss Crike?'

'Yes, my Lord.'

'But you have questions, surely. Now's the time. It is not my brain which fails.'

Lord Vane gives Mander a glance. Their communication is close to telepathic. He gestures for the woman preparing the death mask to leave. To Crike's surprise, Lord Vane's son follows her out.

'Ask away,' he says.

Speaking, Crike knows, aggravates the pain. He wants candour, not flattery.

'I believe the weather-watchers misled you,' Crike says. 'I've made quite a study of meteorology. They may not have created the murk, but they exploited it for their own purposes. Mr Venbar would neither confirm nor deny.'

Lord Vane's eyelids open and close like shutters, the way an owl blinks.

'Watch the Jaggards for me,' he mumbles. 'Father and son.'

His right hand rises centimetres above the sheet and sinks. Ask again, the gesture says.

'You once told me you remembered your college in your will. But there is no record of any such place.'

Lord Vane's reaction surprises even Mander. He rises from his pillows like Lazarus.

'*Arbor spirantia*,' he says. 'My mortal sin . . . to give . . . to give to him . . . Absolve, please absolve me.'

Crike, on instinct, kisses him on the forehead.

'Resurrection . . . resurrection . . . remember Simul,' stammers

Lord Vane, before sinking back, seemingly at peace for his confession. The stertorous breathing gently fails. Mander closes his eyes and readmits the son and heir.

'It's time,' he says to him, 'my Lord.'

4

A Wake

The coffin, on its wheeled bier, runs down a gentle slope through the chitin shield and into the murk. There is no grand mausoleum. Only the first Lord Vane's forbidding death mask, floating in a niche in the study, reminds his heir of the burdens of rule.

Rows of Tempestas' workers stand in silence. There are outliers and a sprinkling of northerners too.

Mander has substituted a black tie for the white, but otherwise there is no change in his attire. Beside him, the second Lord Vane's stern expression hides his thoughts. Grief mixes with a sense of liberation and opportunity. His father delivered deep winter. He must usher mankind into spring.

Jaggard, father and son, stand in front of them. The son is already an assistant weather-watcher.

There is no sentimental music, not even a drumbeat. Mander crosses himself before walking over to his new master.

'My Lord, it's traditional to hold a wake for the departed. To toast the past and talk of the future. I have cleared your Lordship's study and invited those you may find useful.'

'Like those dreadful Jaggards?'

'One must engage with the powerful, so they'll be there. But I've also dabbled in future potential, if you get my meaning.'

Lord Vane does. How else to rule? You choose your lieutenants, and not only the old guard with all their baggage.

'People I can trust?'

'Or people who need watching.' The transition is seamless. The butler's manner has not changed one iota between serving father and son. Mander extends an old-fashioned arm, as if he were making way for a woman. 'You lead, I follow,' he says.

The new Lord Vane wonders quite how true that is, or indeed ever was.

Photographs from the late Lord Vane's life adorn the study's walls: the baby who looks like any other; the youthful adventurer-cum-naturalist; the activist years; the founding of Tempestas and the weather-watchers; in full flow, rebuking the world and its leaders; the building of Tiriel's Tower; prophecies come true in scenes of levelled cities and apocalypse; and, dotted among them, intimate and incongruous family snapshots.

Fifty-odd guests browse the walls and raise their glasses when the new Lord Vane enters. He goes first to a young man, about his age. Squat and bull-headed, he stands alone, dressed in ash grey.

'Lord Sine – our lives march in step. I was sorry to hear about your father.'

'What is there to be sorry about? Death is a natural process. We resume with the talents our forbears bequeathed.'

'Indeed. How goes Genrich?'

'A better model of man is on the way.'

'Better in what way?'

'A streamlined brain: no art, no self-indulgence, no small talk.'

'And no challenge to your orders?' replies Lord Vane good-humouredly.

'They'll work for each other's survival,' replies the master geneticist.

'Will you still take in outliers?'

'Only exceptional ones, if any are left.'

Lord Vane beckons Oblivious Potts over. 'Mr Potts, you once told me we humans are genetically ninety-nine per cent identical. Meet a young man who plays with the one per cent. Mr Potts, Lord Sine; Lord Sine, Mr Potts.'

'That one per cent can do an awful lot of damage,' says Potts.

Having started with duty, Lord Vane moves on to pleasure. Miss Baldwin, his childhood tutor, is gossiping with Miss Crike in the far corner.

'We're bemoaning the fact that your father, though photographed to death, was never painted,' says Crike.

'He disliked artists,' says Miss Baldwin, 'and art. There isn't a paintbrush in the building. Or an art book.'

'A point I make in my *History*.' Miss Crike nods. 'Your father and the late Lord Sine had more in common than meets the eye.'

At that moment, a desire to beat his own path seizes Lord Vane. Whatever the cause, there is a lightning strike. Half-memories of painted buildings dance in his head. His father's legacy – the Tempestas Dome and its replicas of lost fauna – give way to a grander vision.

'We must uncover the sky,' he says.

'How, exactly?' asks Crike, intrigued.

'Technology got us into this mess. Technology can get us out of it.'

He suffers a second lightning strike in as many minutes. A young woman stands at the door in conversation with young Jaggard and is not relishing the experience. Lord Vane has never seen her before. Mander appears, as if by magic.

'Allow me to fill your glasses, ladies, before I whisk his Lordship away to meet the unusual Miss Miranda.'

The two women share a wink. *Unusual.* Mander knows how to bait a line. Lord Vane leaves them with an instruction.

'Remember today, Miss Crike, for the next volume of your *History*. At my father's wake, I said we would uncover the sky.'

Mander shimmies across the floor with his new master in tow. 'This is Miss Miranda,' he says, 'from the Tempestas Dome. You share an interest in colour and texture. And nobody works harder than Miss Miranda.'

Mander slides away.

She wears black trousers, a black shirt and a black-and-green checked jacket. Her face is a near-perfect oval, as in one of those paintings which his father denied him all those years ago.

'Black for death and green for resurrection,' she explains.

He is wary of beauty for beauty's sake, but her smile mesmerises. It contrives to be both respectful and mischievous.

'What's your interest in colour and texture?' he stammers. 'For me, it's paintings.'

'For me, jewels and jewellery.' She pauses. 'Don't ask. I'll bore you.'

Only then does he see that her earrings match the streak of purple in her eyes. Amethyst, he thinks. 'I'll be the judge of that.'

'Everyone has their stone. Take your Lo—' She stops. 'Apologies, my Lord, I was about to be presumptuous.'

Not presumptuous, he thinks, *calculated*. But he cannot resist. He is netted.

'Go on.'

'Diamonds are for showmen, so they won't do. Nor rubies – you're not the fiery type.'

He feels an edge of disappointment, but the game goes on.

'Nor are you cold enough for sapphires or devious enough for emeralds. I'd go for a semi-precious stone. They're every bit as deep, but less swanky.' She is playing with him. 'Onyx,' she says. 'The best form: dark chocolate with an eye of white. It's a layered stone, and the core is mysterious.'

Decades later, when mechanical horsemen are spearing him to death on a pond in Winterdorf, these two lightning strikes at his father's wake are the memories he clings to as the ice closes: a vision of a painted town made real, and an indefinable woman. Both have shaped his rule for good and ill.

5

A Second Minor Oddity

On a whim, Crike leaves the wake for the library, where she retrieves the deed box containing the first Lord Vane's private papers, although there is little that is private about most of them: no letters, no diaries, no personal reflections, just invitations and articles wrapped in colour-coded ribbons. At the bottom, tied in string, she discovers a receipt for a portrait in oils, endorsed in his handwriting: *Excellent for the C of N, but never again – all that stillness.* She smiles. A compulsive pacer, he would have been a lousy sitter. But, if excellent, why has the portrait vanished? What is the C of N?

The same bundle contains building invoices from before the Fall: for period stone and doors; architectural designs of a double square, chapel and cloisters; and a conveyance of a substantial parcel of land. Its location has been erased.

She shrugs.

You think you're done; then another mystery wriggles into view.

6

The New Boy

Gilbert Spire is thirty-three, but he does not feel it. He languishes in anti-sceptic surroundings; he has a number rather than a name; and the work – gene splicing – is as distasteful as the name of his new employer, Genrich. Gone are the home comforts, wife, daughter and library, and, in their place, solitary quarters as pinched as a monastic cell.

Yet DNA is the heart of life, and he has a curious disposition. He is proficient in finding favour, and the cerebral toad in charge, the second Lord Sine, appears to enjoy his company.

'Might I see Genrich's early research?' he asks Lord Sine, after months of hard labour.

'Why would you want to do that?'

'Early research isn't always wasted research,' he replies. 'And, as your father spared my family, I thought a show of reciprocal interest was called for.'

Lord Sine finds Spire's quaint nostalgia amusing.

'In your leisure hours, if you must.'

Leisure hours! At Genrich! In the company of near-identical workaholics with no humour and no outside interests! God pray they never bring his daughter here.

The archives inhabit dingy corridors deep underground. He ferrets away through databank after databank. Endless lists of unproductive mixing and matching yield nothing. Nature is Spire's subject of choice, not man. On a whim, he uses the search facility. In a sea of technical terms and human genomes, he finds a rogue entry: the word *arbor*, Latin for 'tree', with a cross reference which leads him to a stack of boxes which house discarded genetic matter.

All are numbered and lettered, save one – a rectangular strongbox, which, unlike the others, is secured by a complex dial-lock. The *Highly Classified* marking is a red rag to Spire.

He tries various combinations until the simplest works. After entering *arbor* and the reference number, the lid flies open.

The data disc inside records numerous attempts to merge a base cellulose material with other cellulose matter.

Inside the box are two smaller containers. One has various tiny trays, now empty, marked with the Latin names of well-known trees. The other is also empty, save for a printed label marked *Arbor*. Both containers are twisted and peppered with holes. At the bottom of the box lies a single piece of paper.

This box holds the surviving material from roots and cuttings given to me by the first Lord Vane on my fortieth birthday with a challenge: create a seed or reproduce a plant which fruits. One genome is unknown. Lord Vane claimed it came from a tree, now extinct, famed for its healing qualities. It was a trap. Do not attempt the task under any circumstances. Still less attempt disposal.

> *Department XI; Chairman's personal classified Order 113.*

Spire is intrigued. If the material were truly dangerous, disposal would be the obvious solution; and the empty trays suggest disposal. Yet that course has been expressly prohibited. A second conundrum connects to the first. An organisation as fastidious as Genrich would never seal dangerous material in damaged boxes, nor would they preserve, still less seal, empty trays.

Spire removes the two inner boxes to find in the corner of the container a tiny black object, little bigger than an apple pip. If it is a seed, the accompanying note makes little sense. Why give instructions not to attempt a task which has already been completed?

Unless . . . a bizarre interaction within the box has created the seed – a solution which would explain both the empty trays and the damage.

He seals the tiny seed in a bottle and secures the bottle in the original strongbox.

Over the ensuing weeks, he studies the seed's unique chemical and molecular structure. But his late-night research does not pass unnoticed. He is summoned by Lord Sine.

'My other workers do their hours diligently and then retire to chess or sleep. You work and then scrabble about in the past. What's so enthralling about my father's old papers?'

'I suspect you know already.'

'I've examined the data disc which so intrigues you. What use can a futile attempt at creating a plant of some kind be to anyone?'

'Your Lordship's knowledge of genetics surpasses mine. I can only say the structures are most unusual.'

'What if they are? Plants can't reason. We have Matter-Rearrangers for food. There's no sunlight from which to seek shade. The murk has poisoned the earth and the air. You're wasting time and reducing your energy for real work. And that level-one strongbox is hardly apposite for such mundane material.'

'Your father worked on it.'

'Each generation should be wiser than its predecessor. The fact my father wasted his time is no reason for you to follow suit.'

'It's my equivalent of chess.'

Uncharacteristically, Lord Sine concedes. In truth, he too is mildly interested in the organism's structural novelty.

'If you must, but once a week only, and not beyond midnight. I want you fresh. I'll be watching. And be sure to report anything unusual.'

7

A Fateful Encounter

After a Praesidium meeting, the Vanes return to their quarters in the Genrich Dome. It is a night of storms so intense that they can hear the rain thrashing on the Dome's chitin shield.

The second Lord Vane and his wife are playing cards. She has made the sitting room stylish but cosy. In shared tastes, the marriage has been a success; less so in other ways.

'We look like a pair of dotards, whiling away our final days.'

No children, she means, and by implication not enough passion. She has a hundred ways of saying it.

'We're doing our best.'

'You could talk to Lord Sine.'

'As could you.'

The outside door is struck – unprecedented at this hour, with the curfew in force.

'I'll go,' says Lady Vane, drawn by the vigour of the knock. *Give me adventure.*

And the doorway does. A man, their age, stands tall. He exudes energy.

'I'm so terribly sorry, but it's the weather. I couldn't sit in my white box a second longer. I had to hear the storm and, having heard it, I craved company – *real* company.'

Only then does the visitor pause, taking in the beauty of Miranda Vane and her surroundings, more like his old home than the Genrich Dome.

'Might I ask who you are?' says Lord Vane, as intrigued as his wife. 'You're not the average Genrich worker.'

'Did I not say?'

'You didn't,' says Lady Vane. 'Even though your opening speech was all about you.'

'Gilbert Spire. A lucky outlier spared by Genrich.'

'What are you doing here?' asks Lord Vane.

'I work for Lord Sine. But, look, you're missing a mother and a father of a tempest, up there. Live theatre, with special effects! We can access the service hatch without anybody noticing. They're all tucked up in their identical beds.'

He looks and sounds like a schoolboy proposing truancy.

'We can hear it down here,' says Lady Vane.

'That's just a muffled echo. You can't *feel* it.' He taps his chest and turns to Lord Vane. 'Come on, you're the weatherman.'

Lord Vane smiles as he throws down his cards. 'I had a losing hand, anyway.'

Spire takes them into a gloomy passage on the floor below, produces a screwdriver, unscrews a near-invisible panel in a column and disappears up a ladder, past a forest of wires. Lord and Lady Vane look at each other. A new force has entered their lives. Lady Vane makes a mental note. He is the first man not to call her husband 'his Lordship'. She senses a rare gift of instant friendship, if not more. They follow him up – and up.

The visitor is right. The muffled version below is an anaemic shadow. The Dome sheers from bright orange to pitch black as the lightning comes and goes, while shuddering with every deafening blast of thunder. The rain is not constant. It thrashes and swirls across the Dome's protective skin. Rivulets of water, caught in the glare, give the impression that the chitin is melting. Spire opens his arms as if drinking in this elemental violence.

'Explorer's weather!' he shouts above the din. 'Imagine being in a balloon!'

'I'd rather not,' cries Lady Vane, but his brio is infectious. She gives herself to the storm.

'Perfect timing,' adds Spire. 'It's right above us!'

Eventually, senses sated, they retreat to the Vanes' rooms.

'That was quite something,' says Lord Vane.

'And we aren't even damp!' enthuses Spire.

'Perhaps you cooked it up for your entrance?' says Lady Vane.

'Darling, really,' chunters her husband.

Mander enters, as ever omniscient. He carries three glasses and a jug of green liquid on a silver tray.

'This is young Mander – well, he's young in spirit. He looked after my father and now he looks after me.'

'I gather you've been sampling the atmospherics, Mr Spire,' says Mander, with a click of the heels.

'Mander sees and hears more than ordinary mortals,' explains Lord Vane.

Mander waves away the compliment. 'It's no more brilliant than the hollow in the conjuror's hat. We have a security camera, and I've a way of accessing Genrich's databanks, including recent arrivals. Unsurprisingly, you match your photograph, Mr Spire. Child's play. I call this drink Meadowsweet, after the breath mown stalks exhale – or did.'

The pleasantries subside as Spire reveals his deeper self. He talks of glaciers, volcanic activity and polar conditions, and his conviction that they might keep the murk at bay. He talks of tantalum, too – the world's disappearing essential.

'I plan to explore the unknown, out there.'

'In what?' asks Lady Vane. 'Journeys are rationed, these days.'

'There's no need to ration the forces of Nature. I've been studying old-world Airluggers, and there are two moored at the Tempestas Dome.'

'Now we know why he's here – to cadge a lift,' says Lady Vane.

Lord Vane does not register that his wife is playing the game she played with him when first they met, that special brand of teasing which is born of attraction.

'Nothing so ambitious. I'd just like to give one of them an overhaul. You know, like a boy with his boat.'

Lady Vane slips in her first question with real purpose: 'Don't you have a family? Wouldn't seeing them be a better idea?'

'It's not permitted, hence my thirst for diversion.'

He notices the twist of amethyst in her eyes, and that she has noticed him noticing. He is suddenly fearful of where this might lead.

'But you work here, for Genrich,' Lord Vane points out.

'Lord Sine gives me five days off for every three weeks on. Yes, I know, it seems out of character. But the statisticians tell him outliers work better that way, and for once they're right. Just let me restore one for you.'

'You'll be on your hands and knees,' says Lady Vane.

Lord Vane has been won over by their excursion on the roof. He feels an urge to reward his visitor. As a child, he had explored both vessels under Mander's vigilant eye.

'The *Fram* is in better condition than the *Aeolus*. The ship's wood is sound, and the instruments are intact. Spit, polish and a little carpentry is all that's required. Such vessels should not be lost to history.'

Lady Vane awards Spire a winning smile. 'On condition we get a guided tour. I might even patch an airbag or two.'

'I look forward to showing you round,' replies Spire, raising his glass.

8

Fall from Grace

The flesh is weak, but so too is the spirit. Spire is adventurous, but not, by nature, disloyal. He fights the attraction, but the amethyst eyes win. Lady Vane comes to the *Fram* to stitch and mend. Looking back, he is unsure who seduced whom. Mutual combustion might be a fairer description. Their encounters are irregular, and always in the cabin of the *Fram*, but the passion is such that he lives in the moment. He could summon the faces of his wife and daughter with clarity early in his time at Genrich; now, they are a shadowy presence at the margins of his life.

Guilt strikes deeper in the company of Lord Vane, whom he likes and admires. Lord Vane talks of his wife effusively and asks for a thumbnail sketch of Spire's family. 'If only they were here. Give it time, and I'll intercede with Lord Sine,' he says.

At Genrich, Spire immerses himself in his work and at night chases down the true character of the peculiar seed from the first Lord Sine's strongbox.

9

Lightning from a Clear Sky

At last, the gods smile on the second Lord Vane, or so he feels. His son takes his first steps; his wife is beautiful and cares; a device to uncover the sky approaches completion; Jaggard senior has died, leaving only the son, now the new Master of the Weather-Watchers, to deal with.

Only one cloud remains: a unique request from the new Master to see him in Tiriel's Tower on a most urgent and private matter. The father always came to him, but the son insists that there are special reasons.

'It's so good of you to come, your Lordship,' says the man at the gate, with a bow. 'An honour.'

Lord Vane faces a long spiral staircase, with several landings, rising to the rod at the tower's summit, which gives the weather-watchers their extraordinary power.

'Apologies for the climb, my Lord, but we take our exercise here, and the absence of lifts and escalators saves energy.'

'If my baby son can walk, so can I,' replies Lord Vane.

They climb through two landings. On the third, his escort knocks, opens the door and admits Lord Vane to the Master's chambers. Jaggard wears his everyday robes of office, sombre but sumptuous. He offers Lord Vane a glass with an amber liquid lapping over cubes of ice. They are near contemporaries, but chalk and cheese as characters.

'Alcohol,' Jaggard says, 'from a stash in an outlier's dwelling. We keep it for when needs must.'

Lord Vane relaxes. 'You mean we've something to celebrate!'

Jaggard grimaces. 'It eases the shock of unexpected news. I would never drag you here otherwise. It's about Gilbert Spire.'

Lord Vane has an unpleasant intuition that Jaggard, despite the long face, is enjoying this. 'You dislike him, which is no surprise,' he says. 'He's impulsive; you're methodical. He's an explorer; you like the security of your tower. He takes risks you wouldn't even consider.'

Jaggard takes up the theme. 'Oh, yes – and he's humorous, a good mimic, a born raconteur with the charm of the devil. Women cannot resist him. All these things that I am not. But he lacks a core quality.' He pauses. 'One I have in abundance.'

The elaborate décor in Jaggard's chambers surprises Lord Vane, so out of keeping is it with the rest of the tower and his assessment of Jaggard as a puritan personality. An ochre and blue rug with a hexagonal motif covers most of the floor. Light-stones sit in carved wood sconces. An oil painting, gleaned from an outlier's house, portrays a simple cottage in a rocky landscape at night, with a storm above it. Lightning zigzags the sky. Elsewhere, there are old prints: one of natural disasters captioned in French, featuring *tremblement de terre*, *eruption d'un volcan*, and *inondation*, and another a rich variety of magnified snowflakes, whose hexagonal shapes match the carpet. Jaggard's seat is more throne than chair, and a trio of tailor's dummies display his more flamboyant robes of office. A wall rack holds a row of conductor sticks.

He fumbles to retrieve Jaggard's question. 'Sorry, I was admiring the room. You were saying one of your many qualities has eluded Mr Spire?'

'Loyalty.'

'That's quite a charge to make.'

'Personal loyalty.'

'Gil works for Lord Sine because he has to. Genrich saved his family, and he feels obliged to repay the debt.' He pauses. His defence of his friend is inadequate. 'His family are effectively hostages, for God's sake.'

'May I ask why, my Lord, you think he's loyal to his family? He doesn't visit them.'

'Lord Sine would not allow it.'

'Spire has a wife and daughter. He never talks of them. Wouldn't you, marooned in the Genrich Dome, far from home, mention them now and then?' Jaggard pauses, his face reddening like a prosecutor carried away with his case. 'I'd hazard a guess, my Lord, that you don't even know their names.'

Lord Vane sips the drink, lets the potency of it swill over tongue and throat. Jaggard sips too, but in a different way, with relish.

'He lives in the moment,' says Lord Vane. 'He's not one to dwell on those who aren't here.' The alcohol works through Lord Vane's bloodstream and fuels his temper. He stands up. 'Have I come all this way to be told what I already know? My best friend is imperfect. *So?*'

'I just thought you should see these.'

Jaggard opens a drawer and smooths out on his desk two pieces of paper, filled with slim coloured rectangles, lines and tiny boxes.

'What are they?'

'DNA profiles. Spire's, yours, your son's and Lady Vane's. Two make a perfect match for a third. But there's an odd man out.'

Lord Vane reels as if physically struck. 'What do you mean? What are you saying?'

Jaggard's forefinger stabs at the paper. 'You're the odd man out.'

'No!' he bellows. 'They wouldn't. They couldn't have.'

He slumps into a chair. Jaggard refills his glass and adds fresh ice.

'I've had my suspicions for some time. You're too generous, my Lord. Spire is a ruthless, self-interested charmer.'

'How the hell did you get these? How do I know this isn't a set-up?'

'A set-up by whom?'

Lord Vane doesn't answer. Lord Sine, obviously.

'When and where do they . . . get together?'

'I'm no *voyeur*, my Lord. I assume it happens when you and Mander are away. Or when he visits the Tempestas Dome. I don't blame Lady Miranda. She was seduced.'

'And how would you know?'

'Who do you think decorated this room? Yes, I was as surprised as you are. Lady Vane has never been an admirer of mine, more's the pity, but she offered to liven up my quarters when you were engaged at the Genrich Dome. Spire takes his vacations here to work on that wretched Airlugger. Conversely, she redecorated your rooms in the Genrich Dome when you were busy here. Then there was the occasion when I walked in on them . . .' Jaggard wrings his hands as he speaks.

Lord Vane stands up. Enough is enough. This is becoming crude.

'What will you do?' asks Jaggard.

'You tell nobody about this. Nobody.'

'Of course not, my Lord. I repeat: *my* loyalty is absolute. In the eyes of the world, Cosmo will remain your son and heir, and Lady Vane your loyal wife.'

10

Confession and Penance

'Anything to say?'

The two friends face each other in Lord Vane's reception room in the Genrich Dome. Lord Vane has demanded a bottle of the amber liquid ministered by Jaggard. He pours them each a glass. For once, Mander is not here, so there is no ice.

Spire bows his head. 'I can't say about the boy, but otherwise I'm guilty as charged. I can only ask your forgiveness.'

'But you'd do it again. I know you would.'

'Those are the sins which most need forgiveness.' Spire pauses. 'Exile is the only way. Put me beyond temptation. I shall seek out the ends of the Earth. I shall serve you and Tempestas until death do us part. I'm convinced there are safe havens in the polar wastes.'

'You're asking for this Airlugger. Even now.'

'I'm pleading.' He takes a crumpled envelope from his pocket. 'This is my advice and farewell to Lady Miranda. It's unsealed, so you can read it if you wish. It's as much about your strengths as my weaknesses.'

Lord Vane struggles not to show his agony. 'You have no crew.'

'Many outliers work for Lord Sine. Some will join me. Think of them as prisoners who want to escape.' Spire pauses, takes a swig of the whisky. 'They know – and will know – nothing about this.'

Lord Vane feels himself the loser in every way: his 'son', his marriage, his best friend who wishes to roam free in his selfishness, leaving the debris behind.

'You could return to your wife and daughter.'

'My wife is the most intuitive person I know. I couldn't hide being out of love. That would damage her irreparably.' Then comes Spire's peculiar honesty. 'Which would damage me irreparably. As would staying here. *Whereas . . .*'

Lord Vane feels himself at a crossroads. He loves his friend. He loves his wife. He loves the son who is not his. He knows that hatred is the flipside of passion gone astray. He can see how infidelity can sour all it touches *if you let it*. A painting from an art book banned in his youth trips into his head: Giorgio de Chirico's *Prodigal Son*. One man, white as a statue, in formal clothes, addresses a cavalier rake with an exaggerated codpiece and flamboyant clothes. He and Spire may be the same age, but the parallel otherwise holds. He downs the whisky in a single swallow to dull the grief.

'You have your Airlugger. I wish you and your crew well.'

He has, for once, diminished Spire's swagger. The would-be explorer downs his glass and moves to embrace him. As in the painting, Lord Vane rests an arm on Spire's right shoulder.

'I have forgiveness?' asks Spire, astonished.

'You have a chance to atone. Be gone in a week.'

It is little time, but fortunate timing. His would-be crew have saved their holidays for just such an eventuality. The *Fram* is in perfect working order.

In this maelstrom, Spire cannot resist one minor act of rebellion against Genrich. The first Lord Sine had ordered no disposal of the strange seed given to him by the first Lord Vane. Why? What did he fear? Lord Sine also ordered that nobody take up Lord Vane's challenge. What did those two commands have in common? In this agony of his own making, he sees a sinister potential answer.

In the Genrich Dome's cargo hold, he collects a thimbleful of murk-infected sand from the bodywork of a Scurrier. In the privacy of his room, he pours the sand into the bottle which holds the seed. An instant explosion shatters the bottle like a grenade. The tiny seed devours the sand and expands in a startling burst of energy. Only a white innocuous dust remains, with a seed now the size of a misshapen pebble.

Maybe it was a trap, after all. He deposits the seed with the original papers and the damaged containers in the strongbox and leaves it in his room. A devil-may-care mood has seized him. He knows the box will be discovered. He will entrust its contents to Genrich. He retains only the leatherbound notebook which records his nocturnal researches and entitles it *Arbor Spirantia*.

Shipshape

It is a fitting departure for a disgraced exile: dead of night, with not a single person on the gantry to wave farewell. He has a crew of five, all men. He does not want that temptation again. They share his excitement. The sailbags of the *Fram*, stained ochre with chitin paint, have been refurbished – as has everything else – by years of hard labour. The planks and the brass deck fittings have been polished to a shine. The diapason has been retuned. Inside the hull, the materials for matter rearrangement are stored to the maximum. In his pocket, Spire clasps the compass he has designed to protect them from the weather-watchers, whose strike he expects soon after their departure. That is one of his many regrets, leaving the Vanes to Jaggard's tender mercies.

'Free the mooring line!' Spire bellows.

At his insistence, the crew have studied plans of every inch of the ship in their tiny white rooms in the Genrich Dome, when vacations allowed. Now, they scurry and beaver away like school-boys on the ultimate awayday.

Spire is energised too. He would be an Argonaut from myth, except he does not know whether this golden fleece he dreams of – a fresh-air paradise, rich in natural fauna – exists. And Jason set sail as an untarnished hero, whereas Spire leaves only wreckage behind.

He looks down the gantry at the *Fram*'s twin, *Aeolus*, decrepit and neglected, sails like rags and masts and spars greyed by lack of investment. Choices. This ship, that ship; this lover, that lover, no lover.

Beneath his feet, the deck itself comes to life, heaving and lifting.

They are away. A chance to discover and a chance to atone.

I 2

An Accuser Accused

Jaggard had watched the *Fram* slip through the shield and into the night. The traitor's course would be easy to plot. He will give them three days before unleashing a storm which no vessel of wood and canvas could withstand.

Now, at his study desk, his musings on the avenues which Spire's absence has opened up are interrupted by a young female weather-watcher. She is nervous.

'Master, Lady Vane is on her way up.'

'Lady Vane? *Here?* What about?'

The question is for appearances. He can guess.

'She hasn't said a word. She looks . . .' She fumbles for the word; the Master hates panic in his minions. 'Unamused,' she adds finally.

'Point her to my door and disappear.'

The young woman does so.

Lady Vane does not storm in. She walks with a steady step and closes the door. Hatred for those you once loved has fire as its element; whereas hatred for those you have always disliked has ice.

'You gave me your solemn promise,' she says. 'In return, I decorated your rooms. I promoted your various causes.'

'Miranda—'

'Lady Vane, to you.'

'*You* gave a much more solemn promise to Lord Vane. In sickness and in health, for better, for worse, all that jazz. He meant it, so imagine how he feels.'

'My husband was happy. I was happy. Gil was happy. With ignorance in the right places, anything can work.'

'But I was not happy. I watch the one woman' – it is his turn to fumble for a word which is less than the truth – 'the only woman I've ever respected falling for an oily opportunist.'

Oily? Coming from him? The man is repulsive! Lady Vane, for once, sheds guile for frontal attack.

'I've long searched for a word to do you justice. *Repressed* is too weak; *frustrated* too workaday. *Self-seeking* is true, but who isn't? *Desiccated* is my adjective of choice. Any warmth, any red blood, any affection, honesty or humour has long dried up, if you ever had any. You're a husk sustained only by limitless ambition.'

She does not like the look in his face. She sees not rage, but desire. She moves for the door, but he gets there first and deftly locks it. There is excitement in his voice.

'That sounds like encouragement to prove myself, and I shall happily oblige. After all, I've waited long enough. Let it be a lesson in deference, if not in love. Spire is not the only fish in the sea.'

'How dare you!'

He hits her hard in the stomach, as his right hand moves to his belt.

13

Alternative Thinking

A chilling inertia has seized the Vane household in the year since Gilbert Spire's unexplained departure. Not even the arrival of a daughter, Cassie, has dispelled it, and Cosmo Vane, despite a precocious brilliance, is a cruel boy who despises everyone save for his mother. Restored to her old position as tutor, but now to the next generation, Miss Baldwin takes her professional concerns to Mander. They take a night-time walk in the make-believe countryside of the Tempestas Dome.

'I've tried everything,' says Miss Baldwin, 'I really have.'

'He has not worked out as he should. He is not in his father's image,' observes Mander gravely.

'What can we do? Another dose of failed leadership, and mankind really will be done.'

'My money is on a well-chosen outlier or two. We could plot them a course. If they pass whatever tests we set, we might give history a nudge on the shoulder. But now is too early.'

Miss Baldwin is so used to hearing Mander in butler-speak that she is taken aback by his directness.

'Take the late lamented Gilbert Spire,' he continues. 'He has a daughter little older than young Master Vane. According to Genrich's file, their house has a library, which is surely a good sign. Genrich will bring her in when she's of age. Lord Sine bemoans the loss of her father as much as we do. A candidate, wouldn't you say? She might bring Cosmo to heel, or . . . who knows?'

'Mander, what are you up to?'

'I am not alone in this venture. Miss Crike and Mr Potts are like-minded. And other changes are afoot at last. His Lordship has had unexpected news from an unexpected quarter.'

'And where is that?'

'*Far away, far away, in the land where the Jumblies live* . . .' chortles Mander. 'I'll make sure you're invited to the launch, now you're one of us.'

'Launch!'

'Lord Vane has rediscovered his mission in life. There are exciting times ahead, Miss Baldwin. We have a beacon to steer by.'

14

A Trial Run

Genrich's workers are so absorbed in their work, and so attuned to the comings and goings of the second Lord Vane's private craft, that they take no notice of a new addition: a cylindrical structure standing proud of the fuselage like a conning tower.

As his vessel slips into the murk, Lord Vane paces. His companion witnesses to this experiment are Mander, acting as pilot, Miss Crike and Miss Baldwin, to whom he had first made the pledge of *uncovering the sky*, and Jaggard. Lady Vane declined the invitation. The children are in need of attention. Lord Vane drums his fingers on the window.

'We need to be well clear of Genrich, Mander. I don't want a Scurrier crashing the party. As for our own people, this must be a surprise.'

Miss Crike smiles inwardly. The first Lord Vane would have said *my* own people. And he would never have thought of bestowing a new benefit as a surprise, as if it were Christmas. Deep in the second Lord Vane, the child lives on. She likes him for this fragility.

'Avoid the Genrich tantalum mines,' replies the butler, 'and we'll be fine, your Lordship. That's all they care about.'

'I hope this won't put my tower out of work,' growls Jaggard. The remark is not jocular.

'Quite the contrary, Master. With no chitin to protect us, we'll need you all the more.' Lord Vane pauses. 'If it works.'

'At your command,' says Mander, swivelling on his pilot's chair.

'Open sesame!' says Lord Vane grandly.

A faint hum above their heads is without effect at first, but slowly, like a steaming kettle filmed in reverse, the vapour is drawn to the beacon and absorbed. The murk thins, and the ground beside the craft opens to view.

'We're beside a riverbed,' observes Miss Baldwin. 'You can see the curve and the shale.'

'Now, there's a curious thing,' adds Miss Crike. 'The murk reduces man-made buildings to dust, but not natural rock.'

Jaggard reacts as if stung. 'That's a chemical question and frankly beyond your pay grade.'

'I know your job, Mr Jaggard, but it appears you don't know mine. I'm a historian. I have to be a linguist, a student of fashion, a chronicler, and even a chemist if a particular puzzle demands it.'

Lord Vane decides to change the subject. He turns to Mander. 'Open the roof blinds.'

All heads tilt upwards as the screens retract. They gape. As in a religious painting, the beacon has opened a widening circular hole in the murk, where a sickle moon hangs among a coterie of stars.

'Now, that's a rarity,' says Miss Crike. 'A political promise actually delivered. *I will uncover the sky*, he said at his father's wake, and so it is.'

'Large beacons will clear several square miles. Imagine, by day, we'll have sun and shade to play with,' enthuses Lord Vane.

'I don't follow,' says Jaggard coldly. 'The Earth is dead. What's the point?'

'Name me your favourite painting of a town. Ladies?'

Miss Baldwin did not hesitate. 'No contest. Bruegel's *Hunters in the Snow*.'

'Describe it.'

'It's a whole world.'

'Describe it.'

'Snow. Cosy dwellings. Municipal houses. Crows. Trees. A river gripped by ice. Ordinary people living ordinary lives, and at play: sleighs, skates, ball games.'

'And the ordinary afflictions,' adds Mander. 'Old women carrying faggots of wood, a house with a chimney fire. The shape of the river is oddly not unlike this one.'

Lord Vane's head spins with images. But he needs detail, exactness. 'Do we have the image?'

'That will take some getting,' replied Mander. 'But you can leave it to me, my Lord. I may have a postcard.'

Only Crike frets over this new technology. She makes it her business to know all that passes of note in the Tempestas Dome, and she has never seen or heard of anyone working on such a device. What other secrets have the Vanes withheld?

15

At a Loose End

'I'm only two years younger than Cosmo. He gets to do everything, but I get to do nothing.'

It is not a whine, just a statement of fact.

'He's imaginative,' replies Lady Vane coldly. 'He makes his own projects.'

'So, I'm not imaginative?'

'Let's say you're a mite predictable.'

'What did you do at my age?'

'I prepared.'

'Meaning what?'

'I prepared my path. I prospected ahead. I learnt skills.'

Cassie Vane reflects. She feels both cossetted and neglected, lonely but privileged. But her mother is right: she must find her own way to break free.

'I shall study functionality.'

'You can't do that here.'

'I shall work twice as hard with Miss Baldwin and spend every other month in our own Dome.'

'Making clockwork birds fly?'

'Whatever I'm good at.'

'Let's see how long that lasts,' replies Lady Vane tartly.

What a clever idea, she would have said to Cosmo. Such is favouritism.

Cassie Vane finds a new life in the functionality corner shop in the Tempestas Dome. They treat her like any other apprentice, despite her youth and background, but not for long. In a matter of months, their master, a bizarre-looking middle-aged man named Jinx, discovers he has a fellow genius on his hands.

On her workbench, he discovers a clutch of beetles, but imaginary ones, not the imitations of old-world insects which they make for the Tempestas Dome's false countryside.

'Are they just decorative?' he asks.

'Oh, no – they do what they're told.' Cassie plays with a small box, and two insects fly up and land perfectly. 'The special ones are my eyes and ears,' she adds, without a hint of conceit.

'I see,' he says.

'So do they, and so do I,' she replies.

16

A Birthday

Lady Vane has opened two of her three presents. The first two
have been plundered from outliers' homes: a golden silk dressing
gown from her husband, embroidered with dragons, and an old
master drawing of the martyrdom of Saint Sebastian from her son,
beautifully rendered, if gruesome.

Her husband has already left. Cosmo follows with a dismissive
nod at his sister's final gift.

'It's not even a real species,' he says.

Cassie Vane sits quite still and watches intently as her mother
opens the tiny box.

'It's charming,' says Lady Vane to her daughter, with a forced
smile and little enthusiasm, holding the brooch between thumb
and forefinger.

'It's useful,' says Cassie quietly.

'To keep a scarf in place, maybe. If it had a pin, which it hasn't.'

The brooch is a fly, barely larger than life size. Mechanical insects
inhabit the Tempestas orchard, and, as Cassie works in functionality,
the present's surprise value is negligible.

Cassie Vane removes from her pocket a pair of crude glasses
with smoky lenses.

'Try these,' she says.

'Really not my taste, thank you. In fact, Cassie, they're hideous.
You must be more discerning.'

'Would you like to see how tidy my bedroom is?'

'Cassie, stop it. You're being childish.'

'I meant from here.'

'Very, very childish.'

Then, it happens. The brooch takes flight, wings aquiver, worms its way through the door's keyhole and disappears.

'*Now* will you try my glasses?'

Her mother's expression transforms from irritated disinterest to that predatory, focused look with which she greets any opportunity for self-advancement. She grabs the glasses. The lenses play like a miniature cinema. She is in Cassie's bedroom. A large birthday message has been propped on the pillow.

'How do you control it?'

'Here.' Cassie hands over a small control.

Mesmerised, Lady Vane plays with the fly.

'Its power isn't limitless. Like the real thing, it has to rest sometimes. But, of course, it's not much use surveying what you already know. Give it to someone you want to keep an eye on.'

Cassie is confident where this little device will end up. Her mother hates Master Jaggard for reasons which, to Cassie, are obscure, save that he is decidedly creepy. More to the point, the weather-watchers are powerful, and Cassie herself wants to keep an eye. Lady Vane is taking the fly, in both senses.

'No doubt Jinx made it. He's so very talented.'

'A secret one-off, just for you,' replies Cassie, without adding that Jinx had said he'd never seen anything like it.

Lady Vane, now radiant, awards her daughter a peck on one cheek by way of reward.

Cassie retreats, passing the fly in the passage which leads to her bedroom. 'Don't let me down, little Musca,' she says. *Musca domestica*: the extinct common house fly. It seems a good name for it and its other airborne brethren.

She flings herself on her bed. Even when performing well, she is given little shrift and no credit. As for appearance, her mother is beautiful and her brother is striking – indeed, handsome to many. They enter a room, and heads turn. Cassie is just plain.

She wrestles with her conscience, having not told her mother the whole truth. She will be watching what her mother watches. She remembers a remark by one of her few confidantes, old Miss Crike: *To be wrongly dismissed as of no consequence confers a peculiar freedom. You can build your hand unseen. I speak from experience. One day, Cassie, the world will look up to you. At least, I hope so.*

Her mind turns to more practical matters.

What to manufacture next? Pincered beetles, perhaps?

17

Two Lords a-Waiting

The second Lord Vane rarely visits his rooms in the Genrich Dome, other than for Praesidium meetings. The memory of Gilbert Spire is too painful. But today he is here on private business. He and his teenage son, Cosmo, are on their way to visit Lord Sine.

How Lord Sine's domain has changed in recent years. There have always been scientists, but with their individual idiosyncrasies. Now, it is an ants' nest: everyone identical in temperament and outlook, all devoted to the common cause. He remembers his exchange with the second Lord Sine at his father's wake and wonders why his presence has been requested. Everything and everyone appear to work, if joylessly. He turns to Cosmo, who has never met Lord Sine before.

'Don't be provoked, his creatures are not like us.'

'They'd make a great army, but lousy generals,' replies Cosmo.

'Just the kind of thought you should keep to yourself.'

'Spoilsport.'

He never quite knows whether his son is being playful or insolent. Their escort strides ahead like a clockwork soldier. Mander trails Lord Vane and his son like a shadow.

Lord Sine admits them to his chamber. Age has not softened his ugliness. The jowl is more pronounced, and his hands have grown podgier. He does not mince words.

'I have a small problem. As you will have observed, our new generation is a model of efficiency.'

That is the word, thinks Lord Vane – *model*. They are built like a kit.

'However, in recent months,' continues Lord Sine, 'they have acquired what I believe you call *angst*. Sleep is impaired. Secondary symptoms are appearing. Some are even incapacitated. Physically, they are, of course, perfect.'

'Forgive me, Lord Sine, that cannot be right. The mind is physiological. Like the body, it needs a sound exercise regime.'

'They get exercise all day long,' snaps Lord Sine. 'The right kind and plenty of it.'

'Your regime lacks any variety. Your new model has surplus energy which needs to be earthed—'

'He means they need entertainment,' interrupts Cosmo.

Lord Sine grinds his teeth. 'The pursuit of entertainment destroyed the old world. We have our chess. That is quite enough.'

Lord Vane clenches his fists as his teenage son takes over.

'I am easily bored, which is why mind games are my thing. I've a device called a weaver. It can create pills which deliver a thought package to the mind. I've a particular game in development.'

Lord Vane has long wondered where his son disappears to. Now, he knows.

'Game?' Lord Sine spits out the word, but Cosmo is undaunted.

'Hide-and-seek on a landscaped chess board. It's based on a book. Allow me a guinea pig or two – your worst cases. What do you lose?'

'It sounds a good offer,' adds Lord Vane.

Mander merely stands, hands behind his back, watching and listening.

'I'll need facilities here, and . . . I'd like to go through your outsider profiles, just the unusual ones,' continues Cosmo.

'Might I ask why?' asks Lord Sine.

'There's a rare talent I'm looking for. It might help share the load. If I might be permitted to consult your outlier profiles . . .'

'Lady Vane and I can stay on here for a time, to oversee matters,' adds Lord Vane.

Lord Sine considers. He is intrigued by Cosmo Vane, sharp as a pin and a potential ally perhaps, and the boy is right. He has nothing to lose, even if this solution, invading the mind with trivia, is inimical to his deep-rooted conviction of what mankind should be.

'You will have what you ask for. Meantime, might I see this book you talk of?'

'I doubt it's your idea of a good read,' says Cosmo.

'That's why it interests me.'

'See to it, Mander,' says Lord Vane.

They shake hands and part company.

Alone at his desk, Lord Sine reflects. He loathes imperfection in his creatures. His scavengers are leprous and short-lived, but that is an acceptable price for inhaling the murk and surviving. They gather chitin and tantalum. They have purpose. But Genrich's highest workers should not fall below the highest standards.

Conclusion: despite this agreement, he must start again, which means disposing of the current model. Their capacity for obedience will not extend to self-destruction.

A dark stratagem forms. Young Vane's game could do the needful. Tether their minds and lead them to destruction. But how and where?

Genocide is a game for foreign soil. The Tempestas Dome is where it must be done, and, thanks to Jaggard, he has a special offer in mind for Lord Vane – one which will bring him to the table.

Two days later, number 17 arrives with a package.

'Unwrap it,' says Lord Sine.

Number 17 does so. His cuticles are raw, like so many others. The emerging objects are so crude, he chuckles: the space they take up, the weight, the immunity to word search or amendment. Old-fashioned books – two of them! Some fool has lavished hours decorating their spines. Even the titles exude cheapness and vanity: *Adventures in Wonderland* and *Through the Looking-Glass*.

'Extraordinary.'

'Absurd,' agrees 17. 'Pointless and absurd.'

If you can see that, why are you ill? Lord Sine screams inside, but he says, 'Is Master Vane's laboratory set up?'

'We are mass-producing his weavers. They are a remarkable construct.'

'I judge on results,' replies Lord Sine coldly, dismissing 17 with a flick of his forefinger.

He can barely bring himself to handle such a ridiculous anachronism. A book, in the Genrich Dome!

'You're a pygmy,' Lord Sine says aloud to the absent Lord Vane, as he flips open the cover.

In two pen-and-ink drawings, a young girl in antiquated costume shuffles *through* a mirror above a mantlepiece. In the mirror room, chess pieces walk, two by two, in earnest conversation: bishops talking to bishops, knights to knights, the Red King to the Red Queen and so on. He flicks forward to two identical schoolboys with a sinister, adult air. Pages later, an extraordinary mammal with tusks converses with a human holding a carpenter's hammer. There is verse, but it's gibberish. Yet, the more he looks and reads, the more he wonders how the human mind could fashion such nonsense and such pictures. He senses the nonsense is so brilliantly nonsensical, and the pictures so in tune with it, that they might hide an elusive truth. He paces the room, returns to the book, paces again, repeats the process. Strip away the stodgy period dialogue, and he senses a razor-sharp intelligence at work.

A path to revenge comes to mind – one which will also showcase his skills. He will mobilise his now-underused birthing pools to construct characters from these books, and they will serve him. Planting the books' topography into a trivial mind game will be nothing compared to the real beings he will produce. The identical twins will be baby-faced assassins. The madman with the hat will be his envoy. He might even attempt the Jabberwock and his diminutive executioner.

He has had excellent reports on his new Goliath model: a military giant, for use in clean air, with a chameleon's gift for invisibility. Tempestas will fall before long.

18

A Payment on Account

In the Tempestas Dome, the Northerners' Chief Engineer faces Lord Vane over the latter's desk. He wears a guarded expression.

'The work on Winterdorf nears completion, my Lord, but there is a snag. Tempestas is behind on payment, and we have expended much time and material.'

'Rest assured, we always pay our debts,' replies Lord Vane. This is true. The second Lord Vane is a man of his word, but tantalum, the currency of the contract, is running low. 'We have a new seam, but it will take a little time to mine it,' he adds. This is also true, but engineers respect figures, and a contract is a contract.

Mander sidles from the gloom. 'A payment on account by way of interest might ease the pain, my Lord. These Northerners are artists as well as artisans, and, if I may be so bold, this old-world masterpiece would cut quite a dash in their main chamber.'

Mander tenders a postcard to the Chief Engineer as if it were an object of enormous value. He adds the painting's dimensions.

'In its way, it is beyond price. You will note the two men stripped to the waste are planing a floor to the smoothest of shines with vigour and skill. *Raboteurs* is from an old-world language, but perhaps "Northerners" is the best translation in ours.'

Lord Vane wonders at Mander's peculiar gift for service. For months, he does the humdrum tasks in respectful silence, but, come a crisis, he steps in as if his mind builds potency in those quieter periods. Lord Vane glances at the postcard. He knows nothing of the painting or how Mander has acquired it.

'Would that do?' he asks.

The Engineer knows he cannot take tantalum they do not have, and that his ruling body respects initiative. 'Can I take the original with me?'

Lord Vane tilts his head towards Mander. 'It will be packed and loaded before you can say "Caillebotte" – odd name for an artist, wouldn't you say?'

'And the debt of tantalum remains?' asks the Engineer.

Mander returns the nod to his master.

'This is by way of interest only. Six months will yield your dues in full,' says Lord Vane.

The Engineer shakes Lord Vane's hand. 'Done, then,' he says.

Years ahead, this impromptu transaction will yield an unexpected dividend.

19

Opening Gambit

The mutilated body lies spreadeagled on the floor, horribly at odds with the gentle view through the window, of the snowbound foothills leading to Winterdorf. Every drawer, chest and pocket has been rifled, every jar and bottle broken. The longcase clock has been dismembered and the floorboards lifted. A once-cosy room resembles a shipwreck.

The identical twins rub their identical knives on their identical trousers and jump up and down with rage.

'Nothing, nothing, nothing!'

'Not one, not one, not one!'

They begin to cry, bawling like babies and mopping their eyes with identical handkerchiefs, until a knock on the door interrupts their syncopated tantrum. The visitor does not wait for permission to enter. The door opens. He stands, framed in silhouette, against an early-evening sky. He is slightly stooped. Bandy legs separate the tails of his jacket, but his clothing is immaculate, from the white bow tie to the epaulettes on his shoulders, from the white tights to the buckled shoes which shine like liquorice.

'It's the frog footman!' cries Dum.

'He looks fishy to me,' says Dee.

The visitor proffers a stiff cream envelope sealed with red wax.

'An invitation!' shouts Dum, clapping his podgy hands, before snatching the envelope and slicing it open with his knife. He reads the stiff white card twice, cheeks blowing out and in like a bellows.

'Read, read, read! Share, share, share!' shrieks Dee.

Dum reads the formal script with mounting incredulity: '*Alice invites . . . me first and you second . . . to a prizegiving . . . Dress: School Uniform . . . Place: Far Away . . . Transport: Outside, west 627 paces . . . Prize: An Outsize Pillbox, gift-wrapped and well filled.*'

'Momenticons?'

'Wonderland momenticons,' says the footman. 'You will find Alice changed in appearance, though not in voice.' He hands over a small grainy photograph.

The twins shake their heads.

Dee jabs at the footman with his dagger. 'We don't like impractical jokes.'

'That's all made up, cos it's too good to be true,' adds Dum. 'We've been looking for her everywhere.'

'Wrong,' says the footman, firmly but gently. 'It's too good to be false. You couldn't make it up.'

'What's the prize for?' asks Dum.

'Getting there,' replies the footman.

'What's the transport?' asks Dee.

'Airlugger Mark I, *Aeolus* by name – all yours, if you accept. The bearings are already entered.'

Dum kicks the prostrate body beside his feet. 'He tried giving us directions.'

'Our marching orders,' adds Dee with a giggle.

'So, I take it you're turning down this most special of invitations – despite the absence of any previous engagement. That makes you write-offs, and requires me to summon the crow to end your chapter.' Pause. '*Or . . .*'

The knife arms drop at mention of the crow.

'How do you know about that bird?' stammers Dum.

'We all have to croak some time.'

Another pause.

'*Or . . . ?*' they ask in unison.

'You graciously accept, you step outside, you discover the

Airlugger is real, you board, you find a few momenticons in the cabin to ease your passage.'

With an explosion of excitement, the twins sheath their knives in their waistbands, pick up the black bag at their feet and tumble outside. Their voices fade westwards as they bound down the slope to the *Aeolus*.

Mander surveys the wreckage and crosses himself. He will have to tell Lord Vane about the loss of the Airlugger with the alleviating news that the psychotic twins have gone with it.

He will not tell Lord Vane that the great game has begun, and that the keys to his kingdom will be at stake.

II

(This part resumes where *Momenticon* ends)

JOURNEYS

I

Turdus Torquatus

'I'm too effing old for this,' shrilled Oblivious Potts as he wrenched the gyrocopter's joystick yet again. His three pursuers were in a craft that resembled his own, which he had acquired second-hand from Fogg and Niobe, who had stolen it from outside the Black Circus. The enemy's sentinel crows and his own mechanical birds had eliminated each other. He faced a simple dogfight with odds against.

He looked at the compass in the grip of his knees. He had not visited the Northerners for decades. Hopefully they had retained the decency which had marked them out in the old days. A harpoon glanced off his shield. Before long, Cosmo's pilots would shatter his rotors or his shield, or both.

With death so close, he marvelled at his speed of thought, despite the ducking and diving. Multitasking at his age! If only his old flame, Crike, were here to see him playing deadly dodgems while weighing deeper questions.

Where were the four young he had launched in the *Aeolus*? Had they made it to Deception Island? Had they found a way to resist Cosmo Vane, Jaggard and Lord Sine?

The cocooning effect of shield and murk abruptly shattered. Potts flung his free arm across his eyes to shade them from the blinding light of the afternoon sun as the craft's chitin bubble rose in response. A chill wind slapped his cheeks. The mountainside towered above him, a jagged landscape of outcrops and ravines, flecked with splashes of snow.

As a young man, he had walked here from the old Tempestas headquarters, following a hazardous but thrilling path over the ice ridges, down to the great hidden oak door which marked the entrance to their subterranean town. He had made friends there. But rulers come and go, and cultural change is inevitable.

Careering along, he could see no sign of welcome. But what did it matter?! Revelling in the fresh air and the straw-green of real grass, he forgot his pursuers.

But not for long. A bolt scythed through a rotor blade, sending his craft into a lurching downward glide. Potts steered through the rocky spires, as above him an extraordinary contraption emerged – a large, wheeled platform, laden with ballistae and a giant bow. His stricken gyrocopter slowed, allowing Potts to bring it to rest in a gully. He clambered out in time to see his pursuers shattered by balls of rock propelled with uncanny accuracy from the platform, which, its work done, receded back into the mountain.

His craft was beyond repair. The shield had sundered on landing and the rotor blade sagged over the fuselage like a broken limb.

By some quirk of nature, this domain had escaped the murk. In the distance, a small wood of evergreen trees occupied a lower slope. He ambled between the rocks, finding grass of Parnassus, sprigs of heather and one slope rich in blayberries. A dark-plumaged bird watched him sample the fruit.

'Afternoon, vicar,' said Potts, responding to the white collar on the bird's otherwise black neck and chest. 'I know you – you're an old-world bird, a connoisseur of rugged extremes, beetles and juniper berries. Your eggs mix the colours of earth and sky. *Turdus torquatus*, the ring ouzel.'

Sure enough, on the scree above him stood isolated clumps of juniper, with their telltale berrylike seed cases. Potts continued to share his knowledge with the ouzel.

'They're gymnosperms, vicar,' said Potts. 'They have seeds, but no flowers or fruit.'

The bird stood close, flicking its long tail, before flying to a further rock, returning and repeating the process.

'You want me to follow you?'

The bird clearly did. It flew ahead, checked back, flew ahead again. Other ouzels rose and kept their distance. On his last visit, Potts had skipped up the slopes like an ibex, but now his wiry legs found it punishing work. Time's arrow.

The ouzel halted on a huge rock just below the snow line.

'What now?' Potts asked.

The light was fading fast, and the cold had turned cruel. The bird disappeared into a patch of heather. Potts' feet caught a mild tremor accompanied by a faint rumble deep in the earth. An arched door, in the lee of the rock, invisible from above and below, swung open. A cage of squared wire cables held its outer surface of earth, rock and grass in place.

Stone stairs guided Potts to an empty circular cavern. Light-stones hung high in the roof. On the wall above, a series of cogs and pulleys swung the door back into place. The silence of a funeral vault engulfed him. There was no welcoming committee, avid for news of the wider world. He stood alone.

The ouzel's trisyllabic note echoed down the ghostly hall. Potts turned. A single woman opened a door and walked towards him.

'I'm glad you made it,' she said. 'We're ultra-cautious in these dark days.'

In late middle age, but well preserved and lean, she wore practical clothes without ostentation. Her silver hair was cut to the nape of her neck. Only the medallion at her throat testified to the highest office.

'We have more elaborate gates than this,' she said. 'But opening them attracts attention.'

Potts made an instant judgement: he was not being welcomed for the pleasures of a fireside chat. 'Anything I can do to help?'

'That remains to be seen.' She gave him an appraising look.

'It's harsh on the mountain in winter, unless you're like him.' She nodded at the bird. 'You'll be tired, but time is not on our side. I'm Hesper, by the way, Elector for the next five years, having served two already.'

Her manner reflected her looks: unostentatious, pragmatic, and just the right side of brusque.

They descended through a maze of passages to a thoroughfare as wide as a street, with magnificent columns of oak. From tunnels off it drifted snatches of convivial conversation. It was a Sunday. Even now, even here in the deeps, the traditional day of rest survived.

A row of doors, each distinctively carved, faced them.

'That's the one we want,' she said, pointing to the least imposing. As they strode through, she confirmed what Potts had already suspected. 'I'm avoiding my own people, because your expertise is known and I don't want panic. It only takes one idiot with an over-fertile imagination. We have a most peculiar problem.'

She ushered him into a cosy room. Bookshelves lined the walls. A rug, with floral motifs in warm shades of blue, grey and russet, covered most of the floor. Local landscapes in oils decorated the walls. A laid fire occupied a generous hearth beneath an equally generous chimney.

'You have wood, too!' Potts blushed at the triteness of his observation. 'Of course you do. How else could Winterdorf be built? I meant, enough wood to burn.'

'The first Lord Vane collected timber in vast quantities, and most of it is stored deep under these mountains. An open fire is a luxury reserved for visitors or the heart of winter.' She rang a small bell. A young man entered. 'Wine with bread and honey for our guest. *But* his presence here is not for general consumption.'

Bread and honey! He was being treated.

'A machine brought down my pursuers. I haven't thanked you.'

'Outrageous Fortune is our pride and joy.'

Potts laughed at the allusion to Hamlet's line: *The slings and arrows of outrageous fortune.* The machine had delivered both. Hesper did not laugh with him. She stooped and lit the fire. The wood released a soothing resinous smell. She ushered him to the table, removed a small box from her pocket and laid out the contents: two flies of identical size and shape, distinguished by the colour of their thorax – one red and one blue. From a side table she produced tweezers, a tiny scalpel and a magnifying glass.

'Don't hold back. We have other specimens.'

Potts examined the flies from above and then from below, flipping each one over on to its back.

'They're built like *Calliphoridae*,' said Potts, 'but bigger.'

'The blowfly family, that's what my people said.'

'But the jaws are different, and indeed they're different from each other.' With a delicate touch, Potts sliced with the tip of the scalpel, peered, and reflected. 'Do you have Zelig on *Insects*, second volume?'

She tapped a book on the table. 'Already consulted. There's nothing like them.'

So, Potts thought, *I have the floor.*

'Both are asexual. The red has a single sting like a retractable blade; the blue has oversize mandibles chiselled like the edge of a saw. And they have minimal chitin protection. They'd need clear air to survive for any length of time. So they must live here or wherever there are beacons.'

'Keep going,' said Hesper, with an encouraging smile.

Potts returned to the magnifying glass. 'Unless my arse is my elbow, they're from a common home. Like drones and worker bees. Of course, worker bees are female but do not reproduce. There must be a queen somewhere.'

'They came in on a freak storm, and we've found no sign of a nest. They don't look like mechanicals.'

Potts pursed his lips. 'Because they aren't. We made a rich variety of insects in the Tempestas Dome, but they were replicas of known species. These are natural insects. I'd blame Lord Sine, but he only plays with human genes. What's known about their behaviour?'

'The red one with the extended sting is a killer, and I mean a killer. We lost two men. The sting is not a defence mechanism. It's hard, sharp as razor and designed to kill people. It went for the eyes, and then burrowed. The blue one consumes metal. It attacked one of our outer doors.'

The bread and wine arrived. Despite the grisly implications, intellectual curiosity had revived Potts, and the first sip of the richly layered blayberry wine prompted an insight.

He put down the scalpel and eyeglass.

'It's not the work of the second Lord Vane, for I would know. His son, Cosmo Vane, is clever, but preoccupied with gadgets to manipulate the mind. He shows no interest in nature, and I tried teaching him.'

'Cassie Vane?'

Potts paused. 'Now, there's a dark horse. She's as precocious as her brother, but you wouldn't know it. She made a mechanical insect brooch for her mother's birthday. It could see, record and transmit. A remarkable device, but still a mechanical replica. And she's no geneticist.'

Hesper aligned the corpses on the table.

'I call them *The Assassin* and *The Demolisher*,' she said, as if they were tarot cards. 'I'm sure they have a shared strategic purpose.'

A dark possibility struck Potts.

'We destroyed Nature. Maybe Nature is returning in kind.' He took a mouthful of bread. It tasted of the herbs of the mountainside.

Hesper looked grim. 'The Vanes and the Sines and the Jaggards will come for us and our resources sooner or later. But I fear these little creatures more. Insects were here before us, and they'll be here after us if we're not careful.'

'They've no art and no love,' said Potts wistfully.

'But efficiency in spades,' countered Hesper.

2

After the Battle

Niobe, the miner's daughter, stood in awe in the cavern beneath Spire's mountain hut on Deception Island. Fogg watched her from the top step of a long flight cut in the rock. In the eerie luminosity of their light-stones, the cathedral-like space felt like a sanctuary from the horrors outside.

'Enough for everyone,' he said, before adding an instant qualification: 'And enough to bring every predator going.'

Niobe spoke without turning. 'Let be. A spent mine is among the saddest sights in the world. They're stripped clean – or rather dirty – like a burgled palace.'

Niobe's father had died in a tantalum mine, and she had been there. He had named her after tantalum's sister metal, niobium.

'Shouldn't we be helping, out there?' Fogg said, pointing upwards.

Freed from her trance, Niobe sprinted back up the steps.

'Of course, we should. Don't stand there, Fogg – get on with it.'

Outside, the lower slopes were still wreathed in steam from the collision between the sea and the magma released by Spire's explosives. By luck or design, the blown chamber had been small. The town's chimneys poked through the fog, and overhead the sun's disc was visible. On the mountainside, groups clustered around the fallen. None of Lord Sine's toves had survived. Modelled to breathe the murk, they had no answer to the freshness of the island's air. In death, their carcases looked pathetic, their skin disfigured by sores, faces twisted as if they were victims of gas.

'Over there!' cried Fogg.

Carlo, Spire's friend and leader of the community, was issuing directions and calling in stragglers. Above him, near the ridge, the *Aeolus* lay on its side like a beached whale. They clambered across the scree to join him.

'Everyone is either untouched or dead,' said Carlo fiercely. Most around him looked in shock. Many were in tears. 'Thanks to those *monstruosidades*, we've lost women and children, good people, torn to pieces. Who the hell created them?' He kicked one of the toves with his boot.

'A geneticist called Lord Sine,' replied Fogg, adding hastily, 'We've never met him.'

'Well, go deal with him.'

'We should help here first,' said Niobe.

'That *is* helping here. Arrogant people like that never admit defeat. They'll be back. As, no doubt, will that boy who thinks himself emperor of all. Go check your ship. We'll help repair her, once we've buried our dead.'

They did not stay long at the *Aeolus*. The hull had been holed amidships, but the masts, sails and instruments were intact. Lady Vane's maidservant, who had failed to control the craft in the face of the blast, lay dead on the deck, with a broken neck. Fogg and Niobe carried her body down. A rising wind cleared the acrid air, and by evening the descent to the town began. A stack of solidified lava – slightly crooked, like an accusing finger – blocked the harbour mouth. The houses were streaked with black but had survived. Spire had done his calculations well.

The community's single mechanical digger gouged out a communal grave on the beach. In the coming days, they would build an imposing cairn with a Latin carving on its largest rock: *Inventi sumus* (we have discovered).

Well away, beneath a forbidding cliff, they burnt the corpses of the toves. The flames had a greenish tinge, and the burial party wore scarves tight across their noses and mouths.

Four days later, a storm blew in, clearing trees and plants of soot.

Five days later, the penguins returned, and, with them, a semblance of restored morale. Repairing the *Aeolus* also provided a welcome diversion from the sapping force of grief.

A week later, the Airlugger was ready to launch, replenished with real food and drink. Carlo and his wife sat between Fogg and Niobe at a farewell supper. With the table cleared, the community left them to talk.

'We Spanish have a saying: *To forget a wrong is the best revenge.* But I'm with your *Príncipe* Hamlet: *Revenge should have no bounds.*'

'This Lord Sine should be spitted like a pig,' added Carlo's wife, thumping the table, with eyes ablaze.

'We'll avenge you,' cried Niobe.

'Hold on, hold on,' cautioned Fogg. 'We don't have any bearings to go anywhere.'

Carlo stood up, after refilling their glasses with apple brandy.

'Strategy is using what you know. *Uno*, the monsters and the pretty boy were, how you say, in league. They work together. Find one, you find the other. *Dos*, Señor Spire, bless his soul, said you and the *Aeolus* were the answer. He said it, when he was sober, so it means something. *Tres*, you are, like Catalina and me, bigger together than apart. I have hope. *Cuatro*, Señor Spire said his daughter has something they all want. Señor Spire was rarely wrong. As you're their friends, maybe they'll find you to find her. *Cinco*, the pretty boy's craft is not as nimble as yours, but it's faster.'

'It's all our fault. If we hadn't come . . .' said Niobe.

'The pretty boy came before you did,' said Carlo.

'And the woman with the airs and graces,' added Catalina.

Carlo ducked his head. 'We have been spoilt by all these years in paradise. We'd forgotten what *Homo sapiens* is really like.'

'*A veces*,' said Catalina.

'Sometimes,' translated Carlo, before standing up, glass in hand.

'We need a *gesto* – a gesture to lift our spirits. You will launch at dusk tomorrow. We will all be there.'

Niobe launched an initiative of her own. 'Carlo, you knew Mr Spire better than anyone. Tomorrow morning, we want to show you a secret. It means another long climb.'

'There are no secrets on this island. I assume you mean his mountain hut. We don't go there, we respect his privacy.'

'He liked to leave clues. Isn't that right, Fogg?' said Niobe.

'He liked to steer,' mumbled Fogg.

That night, in their cabin, Fogg upbraided her.

'Niobe, why tell Carlo about the hut?'

'He knew already.'

'You didn't know that, and he hasn't been there. He'll find the mine.'

'It isn't a mine; it's a cavern. It becomes a mine when man interferes.'

'Quite.'

'Look, Fogg, I go on instinct. We can't win this alone. We have to share information, and I trust him. I trust his wife too.'

Fogg reflected. Maybe she was right. Maybe he was forgetting the backstory. Carlo and his community had welcomed Spire and allowed his wayward genius to flourish. God knows what Carlo might know which they did not. But he did not want to encourage her impulsiveness.

'It's done now. Let's see what we learn.' He paused. 'You didn't share the thought with me first. That's what I mind.'

She kissed him.

'I'm a spur-of-the-moment person. You like to reflect. Sometimes, you get it right. Sometimes, I do. That's how it should be. A partnership.'

'Right enough,' mumbled Fogg, 'this time.'

'You're sulking.'

'We're indebted to these people. And I don't see how we can repay them, faced with Cosmo, Jaggard, Lady Vane, Lord Sine and all their ghastly minions.'

'Celebrate the fact. Having truly wicked enemies gives us something useful to do.'

The following morning, the weather changed, and they were grateful for it. Snow flurries covered the splashes of blood and the shreds of clothing snared on the rocks.

'Cosy,' was Carlo's first reaction, as Fogg shook the light-stones and brought Spire's retreat to life. His brow furrowed. 'A Morse-code machine?'

Fogg explained: 'For friends from his old life. I've met most of them. They're trustworthy. Or were. One, at least, is dead.' Fogg still had nightmares about Miss Baldwin plummeting from the gyrocopter into the burning circus tent, jeered to her death by Cosmo Vane.

Carlo picked up the two books on the table. 'Now, this is interesting. Arensen on *Glaciers* is an old-world classic, but Cuttle? I've never heard of him, nor of *arbor spirantia*, and I'm a botanist. Hello!' Carlo was excited, now. He sat at the table and flipped through the pages. 'These are plant genomes. With Gil's manuscript all over them. Some I recognise.'

'Where's Benedict when you need him?!' hissed Niobe.

'You said this Lord Sine was a geneticist,' Carlo added.

Fogg again explained: 'He runs a company called Genrich, and Gil worked for them for a time. Though not from choice.'

'Genrich, Gene rich; it figures. Frankly, I disapprove. Nature does a perfectly good job, left to her own devices.'

Carlo appeared keen to escape outside. He put down the book and led the way back. The tantalum cavern remained a secret.

On the day of their departure, the weather again obliged. Wisps of high cirrus furrowed the sky, and a gentle but steady wind held the *Aeolus* firm on her moorings. The windbags filled and emptied as lungs might on a leisurely stroll. The island's community had, for the first time, abandoned mourning black for more colourful clothes.

'Fight like a bear and fly like a hawk,' said Carlo, shaking the hands of Fogg and Niobe in turn beside the rope ladder.

'And drink like a fish,' added Catalina, who had supervised the provisioning.

They ascended, hauled up the ladder and weighed anchor. The diapason hummed as the vessel rose. The spectators waved and cheered. Even Hector, the albatross, swept across the bows of his old home as if to wish them well.

They had been on Deception Island for little more than a week, but the days had been so rich in incident, pleasurable and tragic, that it felt like a month or more. When the Airlugger slipped back into the murk, and their ocean view was lost, the dip in their morale was correspondingly severe.

Fogg tried out bearings from Spire's notes on the compass device in the cabin, but the hands were locked. Likewise, the wheel would not set to any of its pre-fixed numbers.

Niobe refused to be downcast. 'I bet Spire has set a course. Spire did a tour of the craft, remember? Out of curiosity, he said, but past form suggests otherwise.'

'She doesn't feel as if she's drifting,' said Fogg. 'There's a consistent tack. South-south-west-ish. It could be anywhere.'

Niobe grimaced. 'Into the belly of the beast,' she said.

3
Fool's Mate

A not dissimilar conversation about locked wheels and frozen compasses was taking place on the deck of *Aeolus*' sister ship, the *Fram*, on her journey through the murk. This had been Morag's father's craft since his flight from the Tempestas Dome, and he had ordered them aboard when the attack on Deception Island began. Morag and Benedict agreed that he must have applied his mind to where his own ship would take them.

Benedict commenced his interpretation of *where* with his favourite word: 'Logic suggests it's somewhere he's been. A weak spot in the enemy's armoury, perhaps.'

'Dad wasn't a human abacus like you, Benedict. He was a risk-taker, a player of the tables. Forget weak spots. That's where intelligent enemies like Cosmo and Lord Sine expect you to go.' Morag still found talking about her father in the past tense distressing. Day and night, her memory, unasked, replayed the exploding column of fiery water engulfing him. 'I did make my peace with him, didn't I?'

Benedict nodded.

'Say it, Benedict, please. He would have felt forgiven?'

'You made peace with him during that walk along the beach. No question.'

'Sorry. I'm not usually in the market for reassurance.'

Benedict moved on. 'Simul,' he said. 'That's where he'd send us. It's how Deception Island came to be what it is.'

'Simul? What's that?'

'Carlo let it slip to Niobe.'

'Who told you, but you didn't tell me.'

'You were understandably preoccupied.'

The exchange brought Morag to her senses. She had to stop wallowing in grief's cloying waters. Her father had died at a time and for a purpose of his choosing; he had achieved atonement, a luxury given to few. She must move on.

'Well, I'm not preoccupied now,' she responded tartly.

'Niobe got little more than the name. Apparently, an Airlugger from Simul would visit the island from time to time, carrying old life for rebirth. Your father must have known what and where it was.'

'Even if it's a place, why send us there?'

'He's hardly going to send us to Cosmo or Lord Sine. His only homes were Deception Island, which we've just left, and the *Fram*, where we are now.'

'Talk about stating the blindingly obvious.'

Benedict continued unabashed: 'That leaves some other place which is not too dangerous and might help the community's survival. It's my best bet, on what we know.'

Morag looked at Benedict. She loved his calmness, but worried about the price for being so remorselessly rational. She tried him out on a different problem: 'During our walk on the beach, Dad said something really odd. I asked him how he and Lady Vane had been found out. He said Jaggard had discovered the affair, which is no surprise, but then added: *accidentally on purpose*. I took him to mean he allowed Jaggard to expose them. Why on earth would he do that? Lord Vane was his oldest friend. Lady Vane was his lover.'

Cavall loped up to Benedict as if he had a contribution to make. Benedict patted his head. Morag could only smile. Just her luck to have an automated Winterdorf dog and a pre-programmed human for company.

'Work,' said Benedict.

'I'm losing you.'

'Your father was working for Lord Sine. So, we're talking genetic work, as in that book in his hut.'

'He would never do a project he didn't believe in.'

'I agree.'

She watched Benedict weighing her intervention.

'But suppose he set out to investigate something with potential for good, but stumbled on something malign. He would need a reason to get away from Genrich. But Genrich must believe this reason, or they'd suspect a discovery of value and follow it up. Couple that with guilt at betraying his best friend . . .'

Morag thought back to her first meeting with Lord Sine. He would have bought adultery as the reason for her father's exile. He would probably have relished it.

'It's a viable theory,' she conceded. 'Worryingly viable. But why did Lord Sine join the Vanes' assault on the island?'

'Your father had your special gift, didn't he? Going back into paintings – and that means back in time. A freakish power – Lord Sine would want to harness and develop it.' Unease was creeping into Benedict's face at the talk of genetics.

'Thanks, Benedict – that really cheers me up, as I have it too.'

Benedict suddenly rushed to the cabin and returned with a chess set.

Morag turned away. 'No. Absolutely not. You can process a thousand combinations, while I'm trying to remember what the moves are.'

'I've been deprived of the pleasure of learning. Allow me the pleasure of learning how to teach.'

'Patronise me, and that's it.'

'Deal. Let's start with fool's mate.'

4

Black to Move

As the only Airlugger II in existence, the *Ceres* was blessed with much that its primitive forbears lacked: servants' quarters, a second mast, more windbags for greater propulsion, and luxury cabins. Yet, in one department, at this particular time, it could not compete.

'I can't believe we didn't plunder their produce,' said Lady Vane, pushing the Rearranger's paste around her gilded plate. 'Once you've tasted a real apple . . .'

'*Our* produce, not theirs,' corrected Cosmo.

'Possession is nine-tenths of the law, darling boy.'

'We had no time to possess anything, thanks to that treacherous lover of yours.'

Lady Vane rose to her feet. She had thought herself impervious to emotional pain. She had not forgiven Spire for preferring his community, for thinking his ship and exploration mattered more than she did. She had found his self-immolation satisfying, despite the pleasures of the night before. But now his absence gnawed, that magnificent dynamism lost forever. Only one answer: find a replacement. Somewhere among male outliers there must be a man who would satisfy her. *Surely.*

'We must assume Lord Sine knows of this defeat and will be displeased. That is the most immediate problem. Those giants on that submersible suggest he knew your strategy and planned accordingly.' She eyed her son. Great men admit mistakes and learn from them.

Cosmo twirled his knife through his fingers. 'It will not happen again. And I have designed a little diversion to reinvigorate the men.'

A grudging recognition of defeat is some progress, thought Lady Vane.

'Let me deal with Lord Sine,' she said.

'You barely know him,' replied Cosmo petulantly, his contrition ebbing away.

'And you do?'

'He's not so clever. Anyway, we were undone by your lover's local knowledge, which neither of us could have foreseen.'

'While we're on the subject of unknown quantities, what do you know about that mysterious young man? Benedict, I think his name was.'

'He turned up with Father at Winterdorf, then scarpered with the Spire girl as soon as things got interesting. I've never seen him before.'

'How very peculiar. The lith says he's quick on his feet. And we know he's quick-witted.'

'Don't confuse wit with knowledge. He's a swat, a quiz machine who likes to show off. He needs bringing down to earth.'

The shard of purple in the young man's irises, which exactly matched her own, Lady Vane chose not to mention. Cosmo had overlooked the resemblance between the Spire girl's gift and his own. With luck, he had overlooked Benedict's physical resemblance too. Unknown cousins, recessive genes – she had toyed with all the possibilities and found no answer. She had to know the truth.

'It's not a good idea to dispose of everyone who shows talent,' she said gently.

'It's not a good idea to lecture me.'

Lady Vane ignored the rebuke. 'What's certain is that nothing loses a war faster than bickering generals. We have to sift what we know. We need Lord Sine. We know he wants a Spire for some reason and that there's only one of them left. So, our priority is to track her down. She's in Gil's craft, remember? He would have set a course. And I've a hunch what it is.'

'A course to where?'

'The weather-watchers have discovered an oasis of clear air, miles from anywhere.'

Cosmo's eyes narrowed. 'Bollocks! Mr Jaggard tells me everything. He's never mentioned such a place.'

Lady Vane slipped on a pair of dark glasses. Through them, she could see what the golden beetle, her birthday present from her daughter, could see in Jaggard's chamber. A large map hung on the wall, to which this new feature had recently been added.

'Darling boy, it's becoming a fault. You underestimated Gil, now you underestimate me. Believe me, Jaggard has a new map with open spaces marked. All have beacons, save for Deception Island, the Northerners' mountain and this place.'

'How do you know?'

'Why does that matter?'

Cosmo eyed his mother. She had never lied to him.

'What's in this space?' he asked.

'I've no idea. But Gil was an explorer. He hunted down clear air. He wouldn't deliver his daughter to us or to Lord Sine, now, would he?'

'I rule, Mother. You should consult.'

'I think that's what I'm doing.'

Cosmo snapped his fingers in irritation. 'Never visit an unknown destination without muscle,' he barked.

Lady Vane smiled. 'That's why I've arranged a rendezvous with those carriers you sent ahead, the day after tomorrow. Women as well as men, in case we need flexible management.'

'*My* carrier.'

'Don't be so sensitive, dear. I presented the order as coming from you.' The Airlugger swayed as a current caught them. Lady

Vane placed her knife and fork neatly together. 'Was it your idea to kill Lord Vane?'

'It was necessary.'

'That wasn't my question.'

'I discussed our great company's drift into sentimentality and pretty paintings. We saw no alternative.'

'We?'

'Jaggard and I, who else?'

'Why not imprisonment?'

'A magnet for rebellion.'

'You thought it inappropriate to consult your mother?'

'You lived apart and showed no sign of missing each other. I factored that in.'

'As it happens, I do miss him.' She paused, conscious she was on treacherous ground. 'In the old world, parricide was a crime against Nature.'

'Matricide didn't bother bees in the old world. Everyone loved bees. Nature's workers! Why would parricide bother me? I shall run a better hive.'

'Would killing me bother you?'

'Mother, really! That is offensive.'

'If matricide doesn't bother bees, why should it bother you?'

Cosmo ignored the rhetorical question, stood up and bellowed towards the servants' quarters, 'Take these plates away! Can't you see we've finished?'

Everyone was against him. So be it. Everyone would pay.

5

The Vorpal Swordsman

Lord Sine still held the illustration in his head: the Jabberwock at the edge of a forest, and the young man, little more than a boy, poised to behead the monster. The two antagonists had been his most satisfying creations, even if the Hatter, whom he desperately missed, had been the most amusing. He called the baby-faced assassin Beamish, mindful of the lines:

> *And hast thou slain the Jabberwock?*
> *Come to my arms, my beamish boy!*

When plans went awry, he sought the company of Beamish. They shared a ruthless view of life and its dispensability.

'It must be disappointing,' said Beamish, referring to the destruction of the Goliaths and the Hatter at Deception Island.

Lord Sine's assassin stood well short of his creator's shoulder, but he was otherwise perfectly formed: flowing curls, light brown with a touch of gold in the light; a baby face and a slim, agile body. He wore, as ever, a blue jacket with pockets embroidered in gold, and carried a double-handed sword strapped to his back.

'It was a humiliating defeat,' admitted Lord Sine. 'To outwit the new Lord Vane only to be bested by an outsider! The wretched Spire had been in the sea a long time. Why didn't they see him? Why wasn't there a lookout?'

'If you'd sent me, and not the Hatter . . .'

Lord Sine glanced at the Morse-code message from the Hatter, sent minutes before his destruction. It could not have been more bullish: the submersible had surfaced in the bay; the scavengers were ashore; the unarmed locals were in flight and there for the picking; the cocksure Cosmo Vane had arrived and was watching on; the Goliaths would shortly wade ashore to finish the job.

'Maybe I will, next time,' said Lord Sine.

'How did you discover this island?' asked Beamish.

'A man called Jaggard is the lead weather-watcher in Winterdorf. Lord Vane thinks he serves him, but he serves me.' Lord Sine pushed three pieces of paper across his desk. 'First, he reports an island with clear air near the Antarctic peninsula. Two days later, he tells me Cosmo Vane is heading there. Then, he mentions the Spires are there too. They were of particular interest to me. The surviving daughter still is.'

'Why so?'

'Their genome is freakish. She has a peculiar gift.'

'Where is this Spire girl now?'

'She's pursued by the new Lord Vane, whom you may not have met. The young man has a certain energy, and his craft is superior to hers. He'll catch her sooner or later, then he'll come to me.'

'Why would he do that?'

'That's not an intelligent question. Cosmo Vane has humdrum soldiers. I make special ones.'

Beamish noted the plural with displeasure and said, 'I would not trust this Jaggard.' His voice was gentle, barely broken, but it carried. Strength in a small frame, like the man himself.

'Jaggard wants to rule Tempestas. Only I can get him there. Of course, if and when that happens, I will cease to trust him.'

Beamish blurted a question with a peculiar urgency: 'Where's the Jabberwock?'

'Dear boy, that would be telling.'

'He'd better be alive. It's my destiny to kill him. It is written.'

Lord Sine's new quarters bore no resemblance to the Genrich Dome. A flurry of workers were adding the finishing touches to a country house in the classical style, with a modern emphasis on light and space. Outside, a garden with garish blooms was taking shape.

His study boasted antique old-world lamps, chairs and a desk, all seized from outlier homes. Steps rose to a semicircular platform dominated by a large circular pedestal table and nine chairs of the same period.

'First things first,' said Lord Sine.

He led Beamish down a long passage into a low-lit chamber filled with display cases. He stood at the entrance and explained, 'While Tempestas plundered worthless works of art, we assembled scientific artefacts.'

They walked through a maze of manuscripts, scientific instruments and personal memorabilia, each methodically labelled.

'This is a favourite,' continued Lord Sine. He opened a modest rectangular blue box. 'It's an old-fashioned writing implement. They called them fountain pens, for reasons lost to time. Loyal to the watery motif, this is a Waterman.' He handed it to Beamish. The barrel was slim. Lord Sine moved to the next case. 'That nib wrote those calculations.'

Their complexity had once stretched the greatest minds, but in the here and now they were little more than advanced school text. Beamish recognised them instantly.

'Einstein, feeling his way to relativity,' he said.

'I have Newton's quill, too. Now *their* genetic material would be worth working with, don't you agree?'

'How do we get hold of it?'

Lord Sine, noting the mildly disrespectful *we*, glided past the question. Not an answer to share, not with an assassin. 'I've a solution in mind. I shall gather all the disciplines that matter: a chemist, an AI expert, a geneticist, a natural scientist, a climatologist, an engineer and so on. Only new technology and focused rule can rescue the human race.'

'I trust you'll have room for an enforcer,' replied Beamish.

As if on cue, the lith, Lord Sine's personal bodyguard, appeared.

'What is it?' asked Lord Sine.

'The craft you sent to bury the strongbox. There has been no response.'

'They should be back by now.'

'They landed without mishap. But, within hours, their life supports failed. They had chitin suits, all the equipment. And there's more, my Lord. Retrieved data from the craft says the air suddenly cleared. There are puzzling signs of other life. But the crew are not responding.'

Dead, in a word.

Lord Sine weighed the risks. The material in the strongbox had been highly unstable, with an extraordinary capacity for cellular reproduction. His father had worked on it, and so had Spire. Could a mere organic growth threaten his plans for a new generation of mankind?

He had no wish to lose his smartest Wonderland creation, but he needed to know. He turned to Beamish. 'There's an old-world expression: *earning your spurs.*'

'Reconnaissance falls short of my talents,' replied Beamish pompously.

'Really?' Lord Sine paused for effect. 'With the crew were the remaining Wonderland creatures.'

'You mean ... including the Jabberwock?' Beamish's fingers

twitched towards the pommel of his sword. 'That's not reconnaissance, that's doing what's ordained.'

'Be sure to report back,' said Lord Sine. 'I don't want you going the way of the Hatter.'

'Hatters are for tea parties; Beamish is for battle. Fear not.'

6

Discovered Check and More

'I resign,' said Benedict, toppling his king.

'Don't patronise. You've two escape squares and you're ahead on material.'

'It's mate in five. Hat's off! Brilliant play.' He sounded genuinely impressed.

She blushed. 'In *five*? Show me.'

He did. 'See? My king has nowhere to go, whatever I do.'

'Sod you, Benedict. You've just mated yourself. I'd never have seen it.'

'Your knight sacrifice took me by surprise.'

Weeks in, such was her improvement that she could test Benedict, when the board was right. His calculations always put material advantage before position. The sacrifice was his Achilles heel. He never did it and never imagined that she would.

'You're too risk-averse, Benedict.'

She spoke with feeling. He would tousle her hair and rub the small of her back, but never ventured further with a move towards real intimacy. She assumed he feared rejection – too rational to register her encouraging signals. Frustration simmered. Maybe it would be different on land or in adversity. Cruising through murk to an unknown destination hardly stirred the passions.

Benedict stood up and pointed. 'What's that glow, out there?'

She did not catch it, at first.

'We're heading for it,' added Benedict.

Morag rushed to the prow. The murk was thinning from a rich

soupy ochre to the pallor of a dying man; nothing like the hard-edged contrast which the beacons created. The *Fram* was heading for afternoon sunlight.

'There's green down there.' Morag opened her arms in wonder: this was not the false grass of Winterdorf and the Tempestas Dome, but verdant meadowland. 'It's been cut,' she shrilled, 'which means it grows! This place must be Simul.'

The *Fram*, ever obedient to the logged directions, settled over the meadow.

Beyond lay an intricate arrangement of yellow stone buildings: a generous chapel, spires, quads and gardens beyond an ornate iron fence. A flinty wall with battlements and towers encircled the gardens. Here and there, stone grotesques peered down, some with metal spouts embedded in their mouths. The whole wore an unmistakable aura of learning and study.

Benedict delivered his judgement from the prow: 'It's Cotswold stone. The general style is late perpendicular. The wall is thirteenth century in the old reckoning. The smallest quad is a cloister for spiritual reflection. The larger building is a chapel.'

Morag had a fleeting memory of Fogg at his worst. 'You sound like a tourist guide,' she said.

But one detail jarred. A narrow stone passage led to a modest oak door, which did not fit with the meadow or the grandeur of the buildings. A suspicion dawned. This institution, whatever it was, had lost its surrounding town.

Once anchored and down, they ran their fingers through the fresh-cut grass. The vegetal fragrance was intoxicating. Morag could only stand still and inhale.

As they headed for the entrance, she looked for beacons, but found none. What was keeping the murk at bay? They passed a vineyard, a hop garden and a cluster of beehives.

The oak door at the end of the stone passage swung open

and released a woman in white. She carried no weapons. Morag dithered over how to respond. Walking on felt confrontational; merely stopping felt weak. She held her ground and waved. Benedict, equally at sea, followed suit.

In her late forties, the woman wore no make-up and no jewellery. Her hair, more dark than grey, was tied back in a bun.

'Who are you and why are you here?' She had a pleasant voice. The delivery was no-nonsense but wary.

'I'm Morag, and this is my companion, Benedict.'

'That is Mr Spire's craft. Is he with you?'

'My father is dead.'

The woman shook her head. 'What a terrible loss.' Her voice faltered. 'To you and to us. I'm so sorry.' After a moment, she regained her composure. 'Where and how did he die?'

'He sacrificed himself in defence of a faraway place called Deception Island. A successful defence, thanks to him.' Mention of the island had caused no surprise. 'We think he set our course here.'

'You weren't followed?'

Benedict spoke for the first time: 'We left the island with another craft, an Airlugger II, commanded by the third Lord Vane and his mother. We regard them as hostile, but we haven't seen them since.'

At the word *hostile*, the woman smiled.

'I'm Professor Blenkiron. Long-distance travel in the murk leaves a distinctive pallor. Let's see if we can remove it.' She turned and gestured to the walls. 'Welcome to the College of Novelties.'

Three statues stood guard over the door, set in niches. Morag and Benedict followed Blenkiron into the main quad, with its grass centre and a yellow-pink gravel surround. Gloom into light. A black painted lantern on an elaborate iron support headed the entrance on the inside. At the opposite end of the quad, a second arch opened into an area leading to the black railings and gardens which they had seen from the air. Ahead and to the left, an external stone staircase led up to a great hall with grand windows. Every first-floor window had an attractive stone decoration above, alternating between a semicircular and a triangular motif. The island of grass in the middle had been immaculately kept.

They turned a sharp right and headed up a narrow staircase. Blenkiron knocked on the first-floor door, which promptly opened.

'Warden, this is Morag Spire, Gil's daughter, and her companion, Benedict. They came in the Airlugger. I'm afraid there was an attack on Deception Island, and Gil died in its defence.'

The Warden wore a grey suit and a drab tie, with – incongruously – a pair of plush, crimson slippers. He had a face, whose one striking feature was its lack of feature: blandness personified. Average height, average girth, average everything. His hair was cropped short. He greeted the news of Spire's death with a grimace and then a moment of reflection.

'Your father wouldn't want us to mope. He'd want our memories of him to energise, don't you agree?' His eyes sparkled and fingers flexed, as if a switch had been thrown.

'I'm Mr Polychronis. You may find *Warden* less of a mouthful. We supplied your father with seed and birds' eggs, and he'd update us on current affairs. He'd stay a few days and be off back to his island. Paradise, he called it.'

'What learning did you share?' asked Morag innocently.

A curious figure entered the room. The middle-aged man wore a short black jacket and a tie over a cream-coloured shirt. He carried a tray with a plate of scones, a jar of honey, five teacups and saucers, and a teapot. His oversized head looked as though it might tumble to the floor.

'This is Platchet, our Head Porter and general factotum. You may have met his uncle, Peregrine Mander.'

'Mint and nettle,' said Platchet, tapping the teapot with a spoon. 'Watch the flour on the scones – it can ambush with a sneeze.'

Polychronis turned to graver matters: 'The first and second Lord Vanes respected our privacy. Can we expect the same of the third?'

Morag regarded Cosmo as her brief, being her kith and kin, whether she liked it or not. 'We've no reason to believe he knows of your existence,' she replied. 'But I can say Cosmo Vane detests the slightest whiff of independence.'

'Hence the assault on Deception Island?' asked Polychronis. 'Tell us more.'

Polychronis, Platchet and Blenkiron listened without interruption, heads dipping as she reached the climax.

'Not unlike Hannibal's masterpiece at Cannae,' observed Polychronis. 'You draw the enemy in, and then you strike. Your father would play it out with the salt and pepper pots. If he were here, he'd ask whether plants, trees and birds survived.'

This time, Benedict answered: 'The magma chamber was tiny and the volcanic plume of narrow compass. By the time we left, the penguins were back.'

'And the songbirds?' asked Polychronis.

'Likewise.'

Polychronis stood. 'Eat up, and I'll show you the library.'

On their way across the quad, Polychronis waxed lyrical.

'You'll be wondering where the rest of us are. Well, we work the outer fields. We research. We gather seed and birds' eggs. We believe in a healthy mind in a healthy body.' Polychronis pointed out an unusually large grassy mound in the centre of the gardens. Steps had been set into its facing slope. 'That's our place of exercise. Forty-seven steps, up and down, up and down. And you have to jump clear of the prime numbers or start again.'

'What about Simul?' Morag asked.

She detected a flicker of wariness in his otherwise relaxed demeanour.

'It's a craft we use for reconnaissance,' Polychronis replied.

They ascended an open stone staircase on the left, and passed through an outer lobby into a grand single-storey room, with walls panelled to a third of their height and an oak-beam roof.

Arched, uncurtained, stone-framed windows admitted natural light. White square tiles with black diamonds at the corners covered so much of the floor as was visible. Yet, despite these impressive features, the hall was dominated by bookcases with a maze of passages between them. Almost all the books were bound in black or white.

'Once a refectory and now the library.'

Polychronis avoided the narrow aisles and followed a straight passage on the left, beneath the windows. They emerged at the other end of the hall, facing a solitary portrait.

Morag poked Benedict's shoulder.

'The first Lord Vane, our founder,' Polychronis explained.

The Vane traits were unmistakable. He sat in a magnificent chair, elbow propped on a carved arm, head leaning on the palm of his hand, with two fingers resting on his right cheek: the pose of a pensive man. No wonder the death mask had so impressed Fogg. The canvas oozed personality.

'This is a library of record, but also of judgement,' explained Polychronis. 'You'll see white volumes and black, each lettered and numbered. They correlate. Series A1–5, for example, extols the virtues of the internal combustion engine and its various descendants. Their equivalent black volumes expose the evils caused by the same invention. Of course, some inventions stand alone; others breed like rabbits. It helps us assess whether our more recent inventions merit suppression or use. That has been mankind's greatest failure: the assumption that all that is new is progress. Communication systems are a case in point. The occasional purple volumes list our own inventions, and the amber volumes their downsides. For example, we designed the beacons. They provide clean air, but make our long-term existence dependent on tantalum. I have nightmares about the Tantalum Wars!'

'Yet, you have no beacons.'

'Yes and no,' he replied.

Evasive, for once, thought Morag, but why would such an obvious topic be delicate territory?

They made the journey back across the quad. Stars shone through a broken sky.

'The dead with their lanterns,' whispered Polychronis.

Lighter conversation came with supper – a vegetarian salad conjured by Platchet. Afterwards, Platchet produced an ornate green decanter surrounded by undersize glasses, like pupils in dutiful attention.

'Mint julep,' declared the Warden, 'our comfort and our inspiration. Pull the stopper, Benedict, and inhale. But be wary of how much you imbibe. Mint julep has its own black volume, I can tell you.'

After clearing the plates and glasses, Platchet said to the Warden, 'I've allotted our esteemed guests adjoining rooms in the garden quad.'

'Excellent. You escort them, Platchet; I need exercise.'

Platchet pointed out various architectural flourishes on the way. On the stairs to their rooms, he turned and said over his shoulder, 'My uncle, Mr Mander, sends his felicitations to Miss Spire. He is delighted to learn you have progressed this far, despite the obstacles.' At the top of the stairs, he opened a door. 'You have interconnecting bedrooms, a cosy study and bathroom. You're here on the top floor of the outer wing of the garden quad and are blessed with one of the college's better views. I recommend the dressing gowns in the hanging cupboard. It can be chilly at night. Breakfast is late, by old-world standards. Nine thirty, in the Warden's lodgings. I offer eggs in all their old-world varieties. The doors in college self-lock at night and reopen at seven.'

He bowed, as Mander might have done, and retreated down the stairs.

'Once in the bloodstream,' Benedict declared, his speech a little slurred, 'alcohol reaches almost every cell in the body. Expect me to be more animated in speech and movement.'

'Benedict, this is not news. I'm all for self-discovery, but can we concentrate on what on earth is going on. Why did my father send us here? Why is the air clean when there isn't a beacon to be seen? This isn't an Antarctic exception. Why is Mander following my every move? Where is everyone else in this peculiar place?'

'Up and down that Mound,' said Benedict, peering through the window at the gardens. 'And I would add this question: why does Platchet recommend dressing gowns when it's pleasantly warm inside?'

'Only explorers find answers,' replied Morag, only to discover that the outer door was already locked. 'If you can't go out or down, try up,' she added.

Benedict peered at the wing opposite. 'There's no roofline above the crenellations. The pitch must be gentle.'

'There!' cried Morag, pointing at the ceiling. A prod with a broom released a trapdoor and an attached collapsible ladder. 'Go check those dressing gowns,' she added.

The roof space above was wide, but cramped height-wise – a forest of short timbers mired in gloom. In the distance, she could make out a faint shaft of light. She crawled towards it – painful work, with the hard joists scuffing her knees and her back bowed.

The light source was a crack in a narrow, slatted door set into the roof. She fumbled for a handle, found a bolt and drew it. Fresh air dispelled the resinous smell of the roof's interior. She gasped in discomfort as her back straightened. A frisky breeze was driving ribbons of cloud across a waning moon. Without it, she doubted the door would have been visible. Luck, for the moment, was with them.

She peered over the parapet. Nothing but dark windows and closed oak doors peered back. She let her ears do the searching. A screech ripped through the silence; an owl was abroad. They must have small rodents too. What a remarkable anachronism this place was!

A single chime struck the quarter hour – quarter to midnight.

A faint clicking noise came from the opposite side of the quad, followed by another, further away, then more. To her ear, the notes were not identical, but similar. Latches and locks, she decided, on different doors, opened by different people, with differing strengths and energy.

To her left, a student appeared and ascended the steps on the Mound, jumping every now and again, before disappearing over the other side and then reappearing. An oddity, if all the doors were truly locked.

'Productive pockets,' said Benedict. 'I mean dressing-gown pockets.'

With his greater height and girth, Benedict had not enjoyed the crawl, but he didn't complain beyond rubbing his knees. He held out two unusually long dressing-gown cords, as thick as ropes, which he joined together.

'They call it the double fisherman,' he whispered. 'Two lines into one.'

'Thanks, I'm sure that extra titbit will be useful,' replied Morag with a grin.

'Someone has to haul the rope back up, or you'll be rumbled in no time.'

'You're not coming with me, then?'

'Aren't two explorers in different places likely to be more productive than two in the same place?'

'That's settled, then,' she replied.

They hurried along the gully, turned left across the archway to the main quad, right into the main quad's parapet, and then crossed another roof division to the outside wall. The flirtatious moon dallied enough to reveal occasional gowned figures sauntering through the cultivated land.

'Meet back here when the clock strikes five?' suggested Benedict. She gave him a peck on the cheek. 'Deal,' she said.

He took no liberties with the brickwork, tying the single rope round his waist and playing the anchor role as Morag abseiled down.

Benedict hauled it back, offered a single wave and was gone.

She felt a tweak from her father's spirit, and her grandmother's too. Spires explore. Spires go it alone.

Nature's details cheered her on her way: the dew, the gossamer patchwork of spiderwebs, another shriek from the hunting owl. But they also intrigued. How had this temperate place escaped the murk's deadly embrace? God's acre.

Benedict noted the spring in his companion's step as she moved away. Fogg had talked of her independence of spirit, and he respected it, but he had his own urges too. The answer to the college's immunity had to lie within its immediate environs and not outside. He had his task, and only one quad remained unseen: the cloister. He backtracked to the interior parapet, continued, turned left and then right, over the Warden's lodgings. An oak door closed off the cloister's narrow ground-level entrance, and he rejected risking a descent on the off chance it might not be locked. A challenging route took him to the cloister roof.

More than the quads or the rooms or the gardens, the cloister exuded a mystical sense of repose, an invitation to reflect and find clarity: a bower for a perfectionist. Maybe the solitary bench was reserved for Mr Polychronis.

In the far right-hand corner, a spectacular single tree was already in blossom, its leaves a seductive silvery grey, its branches elegant. The fragrance had a bittersweet tang.

Benedict was about to retreat, when he had an unpleasant experience. His loaded databanks rendered every plant, bird and cloud identifiable in the blink of an eye.

But not this one.

He rummaged like a frustrated burglar through flowers, bark, shape and leaf. No returns.

He had been caught out!

Might this tree explain the clean air? Uncharacteristically, he ceased to calculate risk. He slid down the steep-hipped roof, fastened the rope to the guttering and descended. The guttering buckled, and the rope and Benedict fell to the ground. He scrambled to his feet and wiped his knees, no harm done save that he was stranded. But so what? All that mattered was resolving the riddle.

At ground level, the tree was even more imposing. A small iron nameplate had been spiked in the earth. He had to kneel to decipher it in the moonlight.

The Boojum Tree.

Pull the other one, thought Benedict. A Boojum is a phenomenon in the physics of superfluidity. It made no sense. He sensed another yawning gap in his knowledge.

Back to reason. Examine the exhibit. Observe. Analyse.

The process only aggravated his unease.

Scent comes from petals, and those of the Boojum tree were peculiarly coloured – a rich pink and carmine. The flowers had no stamens. No male reproductive organ. Asexual reproduction in plants is not uncommon. A deep personal discomfort afflicted him. Was he like the tree, unique but asexual?

He walked up to the trunk and recoiled a pace or two.

On one leading branch, amber tears smeared the bark at its base, slicks of a hardened orange sap, like dried blood. Old wounds, but the bark had been sliced and gouged. Torture, of a kind.

Not a single leaf covered the ground, although the tree looked deciduous. An assiduous gardener perhaps, but he doubted it. Uncollected spent flowers littered the grass, the recent and the long dead.

Theory: the Boojum tree's blossom exhaled a scent which dispelled the murk. Its flowers created no seed, but for compensation came and went all year round. Man had tried to replicate the tree, hence the tissue extractions, but, for whatever reason, the experiments had failed.

On this hypothesis, the college had been built around the tree, funded by, and as a tribute to, its most distinguished modern alumnus, the first Lord Vane, and was a replica of whatever institution he had attended in the old world. Hence the portrait.

Arbor spirantia.

The breathing tree.

Or Spire's tree? He sensed that Morag's father was connected here, as he was with so much else.

Benedict felt submerged in deep forces which, despite his vast knowledge, he was ill-equipped to face. He sat down on the bench, head in hands, and pondered his inadequacy.

This is as close to temperate old-world countryside as one can get, reflected Morag. Moths stumbled across beds of lavender and a bat jigged crazily above her head. From her vantage point beyond the main gate, she could see that the college sat at the centre of a circular island of clean air, a few miles in circumference, suggesting that the cleansing agent lay within the building precincts.

The cultivated areas had been methodically organised. Small wooden cabins held trays of seed, meticulously labelled. Some way off, a more substantial shadow marked a long, low cottage. A single light glowed from an upstairs window like a distant lantern. Those responsible for this husbandry must live there.

Near the edge of the murk, Morag resolved one mystery – or so she thought. A small wooden tantalum-driven craft, with room for only two pilots, rested hull-down in the long grass. The cockpit doors were locked, but the prow bore the carved name *Simul*. So, *Simul* was not a place, just a craft. But hadn't Carlo told Niobe that an Airlugger had brought seed and birds' eggs to Deception Island? And what about the Warden's unease when she had quizzed him about *Simul*? She reassessed. She was a stranger, and the College of Novelties doubtless had its own share of secrets. She would be wary too, in Polychronis' position.

She set off towards the cottage, but did not get far. A large double-masted Airlugger, instantly recognisable as the *Ceres*, broke clear of the murk and anchored close to the college. The main gate opened, and two lanterns bobbed through: Polychronis and Professor Blenkiron. They must have observed the *Ceres* before she had. Morag saw no point in evasion. The moored *Aeolus* was a telltale. She ran across the meadow and joined the Warden.

Further powered craft emerged from the murk. One landed; the others circled.

'That's Lady Vane's Airlugger,' Morag said, breathless after the run. 'The one I mentioned.'

'As hostile, if I remember correctly,' replied Polychronis, who seemed more intrigued than alarmed.

'The new Lord Vane needs careful handling. Seriously.'

'Secular rulers always do.' Polychronis pointed with a wry smile at the huge figure descending the ladder from the *Ceres*. 'Now, that's not a species I know,' he added.

'He's a lith – as in monolith – from Lord Sine's toybox. More brawn than brains.'

Cosmo Vane, and a handful of soldiers on a separate rope, followed the giant. Lady Vane came last. Cosmo did not wait for his mother.

'I do hope that young man isn't as pleased with himself as he looks,' said Polychronis. 'Let them come to us. By the way, I don't bow to uninvited guests.'

Morag warmed to the Warden. Unfavourable first impressions – a dry-as-dust don in slippers – had been misleading. His intellect was laced with wit and cased in steel.

'*You*, again!' Cosmo growled at Morag. 'What is this fucking place? And who's this relic?'

Polychronis offered neither hand nor smile. 'The name is Lupin Polychronis. Welcome to the College of Novelties. Your grandfather built it, and we have served his precepts ever since.'

'Well, now you serve me.'

Despite the bravado, Cosmo looked ill at ease. Morag knew why. He liked to control *everything*. An unfamiliar place, and a greeting without deference, nettled.

'This is the third Lord Vane,' said Morag.

'Indeed,' said Mr Polychronis neutrally. 'Welcome to the college, your Lordship.'

'What does this place do? Why is it free of the murk?'

'Which question would you like me to answer first?'

'My guard will tear you limb from limb, if you don't answer both. *Now.*'

'Who could resist such a charming invitation?' replied Mr Polychronis. 'In accordance with that crude advice which novelists have rammed down their throats, I shall show before I tell. Follow me.'

Polychronis led the way to the nearest cabin.

'We cultivate seed and we're blessed with pollinators. Bees, birds, moths, wasps and butterflies. Eggs, larvae or chrysalises, as the science dictates. And one mammal. Any guesses?'

Cosmo glared.

'Bats!' cried Mr Polychronis. 'We also produce vegetables and eggs to equip our resourceful cook. For good measure, we have a library recording the inventions of the old and new worlds, with their attendant virtues and vices.'

Cosmo Vane, already looking bored, waved a dismissive hand. 'You're ignoring my second question, Pollycock. Why's your air so horribly clean?'

'Now, that's a mystery. We were founded by your grandfather at the time of the Fall, so I hoped you might know.'

'Where are the rest of you?'

'They exercise, about now.' Polychronis pointed towards the gardens. 'We call it the Mound. Up and down is just the ticket.'

Cosmo spun round to face Morag. 'And you, my life's bad penny – what brought you here?'

Morag plumped for the truth. 'We came in my father's Airlugger. Mr Polychronis was showing me around when you arrived.'

Lady Vane ghosted forward, as ever a picture of elegance.

'And where is Miss Spire's companion? The one they call Benedict?'

Polychronis answered: 'I last saw him in the cloister. He appeared to be contemplating the meaning of life.'

'Not for long, he isn't,' said Cosmo. 'He and Miss Spire are coming with us.' He turned to his men. 'We'll overnight here, after you've gathered all we need. Don't hold back. Meantime, Pollycock, I want a tour of my inheritance.'

Benedict woke with his head on the arm of the cloister bench. He never had dreams; his mind merely shut down. While others admired his encyclopaedic knowledge, he was discovering the cost. He felt exhausted, by the end of a day. Worse, he feared his formidable store of data was beginning to corrupt as new knowledge and experience arrived. Answers appeared more slowly. Twice, now, he had been unable to summon a detail which he knew was there.

He swung his legs back to the ground and peered up at the moonlit Boojum tree. Despite the dark and the chill, the blossom had made no effort to close.

'Good evening,' said a woman's silky voice. Lady Vane glided through the cloister's entrance. She wore a fine yellow monochrome scarf, practical trousers, boots and a green woollen overcoat. 'We meet again.'

Benedict had no clue what to say or do. For all her elegance, Lady Vane would have happily left Deception Island to the tender mercies of Lord Sine's scavengers and then her son's troops. She had abandoned her lover to his fate. But one quality defied analysis: *presence*.

She walked slowly past him and sank to her knees to read the tree's nameplate. She rose and wiped her eyes with a handkerchief, before tucking it back into her sleeve.

'He could recite that poem by heart,' she said. 'Gil chose that name, I've not the slightest doubt. *For the snark was a Boojum, you see*.' She examined a leaf, tilted her head to a flower.

'It's dioecious,' said Benedict.

'Is it, now?' said Lady Vane, raising an exquisite eyebrow.

'It has only female flowers. *Carpellate* is the word.'

'And where's the Boojum's lover?'

'Not here, as far as I can see.'

'Poor, lonely Boojum.' She sat down on the bench.

Benedict uneasily obeyed her invitation to follow suit.

'Di-o-ec-ious seems an unnecessary mouthful,' she said. 'And brand new, to me.'

'It's Greek for "two houses". Holly is a much-cited example.'

'How old are you?' she asked casually.

The one question he could never answer slid away into the dark.

'I don't count the days,' he mumbled.

She playfully tapped his nearest shoulder with her hand. 'You must have had one hell of a tutor.'

Benedict could not articulate the new sensation engulfing him. Morag had been his saviour and companion, but Lady Vane's company stimulated him. Leave aside her past behaviour; at this moment, on this bench, under a ragged moon, he was at ease.

Harsh truths welled up, and he could not suppress them. 'I had no tutor and no childhood,' he said.

Lady Vane's face changed. Her playfulness receded. 'You mean you were maltreated? Who by? Where? I want to know, Benedict. Please tell me.'

'I mean I had *no* childhood.'

Lady Vane leant back and eyed the sky. 'Isn't it odd we give these remote shards of light names?'

'And enlist them for our legends,' added Benedict.

'Yes.'

He knew Lady Vane was biding her time, that the killing question would come, but he made no effort to leave.

'What's that one?' she asked.

'Mizar.'

'My father was an amateur astronomer. My interest in the precious stones underground was a reaction to his affection for the heavens. I recall my first lesson: the pointers to the north star in Ursa Major. All rather absurd, as by then we couldn't see sun or moon.' She paused and struck: 'What's your first memory?'

During their many weeks on an Airlugger, Morag had never asked him that. Perhaps deliberately. He flexed the fingers of his right hand – once, twice, three times. Lady Vane chuckled. To his surprise, a chuckle with warmth.

'My husband had that exact gesture, when I asked him a probing question. You may not believe me, but I loved him. There are many different kinds of love, you know, and their values should not be weighed. They're incomparable. Look! One of those pieces of junk the old world launched into orbit.' She pointed at a tiny white ball crawling across the sky.

Too fast for a planet. No twinkle, so not a star.

'Cosmos 1703,' said Benedict.

Lady Vane moved from a chuckle to a laugh. 'Come on, you can't know that.'

'It was launched on 22 November 1985, in the old chronology, by a power then known as Soviet Russia.'

'All right, if you know that, you must know your first memory. Or at least the one you think was the first.' Another playful tap, on his knee this time. 'You have the floor.'

As if on cue, the moon hid her face behind a ribbon of cloud.

'I am in a craft.' Benedict bowed his head, still living in the moment.

'What kind of craft? Whose craft?'

'I don't know yet.'

'Who's there with you?'

'That I don't know either. I'm strapped to a bed and blindfolded.'

'This is your *first* memory?'

Benedict ignored the question. 'Data flood my subconscious, untethered and meaningless, until I have a question to cling to. *Leave the blindfold on*, says a voice. *If he's as smart as they say, he'll manage it.* What is a blindfold? Answers come and self-sort: an aid to meditation or execution or sensory deprivation or enhancement or kidnapping or magic tricks or the amusement of children. Why is it being used on me? Sub-answer: I haven't a clue.'

Wracked by the memory, Benedict shudders.

Lady Vane holds his hand. 'Go on.'

'The flight lasts four hours, seventeen minutes. I am unstrapped. They walk me eighteen metres to a downward ladder. Its position tells me it is a Scurrier IV. Scurriers are run by Genrich, on whom I also have a file. My immediate surroundings, though I cannot see them, are taking shape. My feet land on a frangible surface and sink. I have never known cold. It bites at my cheeks and hands. I have been dressed: shoes, socks, shirt, synthetic jersey and coat. The temperature is minus two degrees centigrade. Hands spin me around. I decide this is either a child's game or an attempt to disorientate and slow the blindfold's release. Am I a child? Too strong, too tall, too aware, the data tell me. And yet I have no experience of growth. I hear the Scurrier recede. My hands read the knot; it is a triple bowline. I unscramble it. Quite a moment. Utter darkness, to the dazzle of sun on snow.'

Again, Benedict stopped. He had witnessed Fogg facing up to painful memories. The agony of forced recollection was quite new to him.

'They left an arrow carved in the snow's crust,' he continued. 'I followed it.'

'How long ago was this?'

'Five days before your husband's death.'

Lady Vane rose to her feet and stepped back to the nearest cloister arch, where her tone changed as she asked, 'How do you know that?'

'I was there when he died. He was the first person I ever saw and the second I ever heard. He was on a horse, alone in the snow. He greeted me and led me to Winterdorf. He gave me quarters and could not have been kinder.'

Benedict had lost his usual fluency. Morag had worked out his origins, but had not pressed him as to the how, when or why.

'My husband was the welcoming sort. But, surely, he was taken aback. It's a small world, nowadays. Strangers don't appear from nowhere.'

'*Welcome, Benedict*, were his very first words, followed by, *I was expecting you.*'

'He knew your name?'

'No, he gave me my name: Benedict, the one who is blessed. Hyperbole, to put it mildly.'

'That means' – Lady Vane rubbed her forefinger round the stone tracery, as if to tease out the mystery – 'he knew you had no name. That suggests he knew you had no childhood, and that your name was his to give. That, in turn . . .' She took a step towards him as the moon obligingly unveiled. 'Do you ever look in the mirror?'

'I prefer not to.'

A pause. Her voice turned from inquisitive to practical: 'When we're alone, please call me Miranda; I would like that. More seriously, Benedict, you're in danger.'

'So were the innocents on Deception Island.'

Lady Vane bristled. 'Gil was no innocent.'

'I wasn't referring to him.'

Lady Vane's moral sense, once a guiding light, had shrunk to near total eclipse from sexual frustration, exclusion from her husband's policies, boredom, disappointment in – and fear of – Cosmo, and a desire to preserve her position, not to mention prolonged exposure to the deference and cynicism which court life cultivates. This quietly spoken rebuke from a young man, who she now realised must be her biological son, struck a nerve. The dormant spirit of a decent younger self stirred. Perhaps the cloister, with its atmosphere of reflection and penitence, contributed.

'I'm not ducking your point, Benedict. I see its force. I'll answer another time. My worry is the here and now. Cosmo does not tolerate rivals, and he thinks you're of the blood.'

She paused. Thin ice was singing beneath her feet. *Does he know what I've guessed?*

'And, who knows, he might be right,' she continued. 'He killed his father. He would kill me, if that were necessary, which makes your prospects slim. There's your unguarded Airlugger out there. For God's sake, take it now.'

Benedict rounded on her. 'You don't understand loyalty, do you? I don't think you understand love either. I think I got that coldness from you.'

So, he does know.

'Maybe I gave you a smidgen of warmth,' she said. 'After all, you're all nature and no nurture. But I still care. I truly do. If you won't take the Airlugger, let me do the talking with Cosmo. Let . . .' She halted. A maternal desire to defend him gave way to a more ambitious agenda, and she started again.

'Benedict, you're the child Lord Vane and I should have had. You're the one true heir. From your father, you have artistic sensibility and a capacity for kindness. From me, you have aspirations, high standards and a horribly low boredom threshold, with, I regret to say, an ability to be devious when necessary. But all this data from Lord Sine swamps the richness beneath, what makes you *you*. Find and release the talents you've been bequeathed. You are a Vane. You are born to rule.'

In Benedict's psyche, an atavistic spirit stirred. He was not born to entertain, to deliver obscure facts, to correct and inform – a process which might enlighten others, but never enlightened him. Maybe he *was* born to rule.

But he had no chance to respond.

The intrusion of a swirl of people had a sacrilegious impact, barging in on the tree, the moon and the two voices trying to get at the truth.

'Who have we here?!' Cosmo Vane strode to the fore, followed by a phalanx of soldiers. 'If it isn't the know-all from that primitive island.' He spun round to face his mother. 'Why are you communing with this rebel?'

'He has unusual talents. He could be of service, Cosmo.'

'He and his companions were insolent when last we met, in case you've forgotten. I've a mind to hurl him from the battlements *pour décourager les autres.*'

'He'd shine in that Black Circus I hear so much about,' suggested Lady Vane gently.

'No, that would be *déjà vu*. It was bad enough having Fogg give us the slip. But you're right: that bulging brain must be put to the test. I've just the place.' Cosmo yawned. 'Mother, I've just seen the most pointless library ever, and that Pollycock person gets on my nerves. We're leaving tonight.' He turned and bellowed, 'Piety!'

She stepped forward from the shadows.

'You're staying on. I'm leaving you and a detachment of soldiers as backup. Suss out this place. Clean air doesn't come from fancy stonework.'

'Will do,' replied Piety quietly.

Cosmo turned to the lith. 'Secure brainbox and the Spire woman in the hold. Hurry up the provisioning. I want to be gone within the hour.' He addressed his final *envoi* to everyone present. 'This place belonged to my grandfather. Now, it belongs to me.'

Lady Vane did not intervene in Benedict's departure with the lith, nor did Benedict object.

'Show the way,' he said to the giant.

The lith gave him a hard look, remembering their tussle at Deception Island. 'Nobody bests me twice,' he growled.

'I admit I was lucky,' Benedict whispered back, 'but lightning can strike twice.' Satisfaction pinkened his cheeks. This mild riposte had come from him, not his databank. Maybe he was turning into a real person.

He looked over his shoulder. Something had happened to Lady Vane too, if only in the eyes. Maybe that was his work, too.

He had had quite an evening.

Morag emerged from the press and joined the lith, after awarding Polychronis a farewell wave and a smile.

Lady Vane trudged back to her craft. What had she done in her life which could truly be called rewarding? What adult chapter on her deathbed could be revisited with pride? True, she had loved her husband and Gilbert Spire in very different ways, but her motives had hardly been selfless. Such grief as she had felt for their premature deaths had been more for her own loss.

Benedict represented what might have been: a son, and the only child of a once-happy marriage, who had looks, talent and an outlook on life which was positive but moderate. He had stood up to her too, which she respected.

Preserving him from danger was a worthwhile cause, and altruistic, since it would threaten her too. A maternal protective spirit, barely experienced with Cosmo or Cassie, began to glow: a last ember amid so much ash.

Piety watched the chitin shields of the Vanes' craft and its cumbersome escorts close as the murk reclaimed them. Administering *The*

Garden of Earthly Delights in Cosmo's absence had been stimulating, even if the town's name was an overstatement.

Under her tutelage, the repertoire at the Black Circus had increased in grotesquery, while banishing cruelty in favour of make-believe violence. Audience participation had not suffered in consequence. Her affection for studded leather clothes and black make-up did not make her a sadist. Equally, it did not make her a traitor to Cosmo. She had politely declined an invitation to discuss 'matters of mutual interest' from Jaggard, head of the weather-watchers and temporary ruler of Winterdorf. She did not trust him.

In truth, she was adrift, in search of new loyalties.

She inhaled: not the air of beacon country. A faint vegetal tang, quite alien to her senses, spoke of a new power – or, rather, an old power revived. The unfamiliar fragrance implied new colours, living creatures and adventure. Here, and here alone, Nature was stirring.

A figure emerged from behind her.

'I'm the Warden, Lupin Polychronis. Your retinue must be tired. Twelve men and five women, at a quick count. We've plenty of accommodation, and Platchet can cater for an army. Breakfast at nine thirty?'

His tone struck home more than his words; it was relaxed, without side, and eloquent as to what divided this place from all others.

It was free of fear.

The gift came, she felt, from the whole: stones, arches, tree, the quads with their gentle intersecting balance, and the serried ranks of books.

Nor did the place feel dry. You could hold a gothic party here. You could express yourself however you liked. You could have weird costume, high wires, trick cyclists, off-beat music – and the stones, the arches, the college's soul would take no issue. Nor, she suspected, would Mr Polychronis. Only violence of action or thought would offend this sanctuary.

She decided to keep to a favourite motto: treat the unfamiliar as an invitation to explore.

'Breakfast then is fine,' she said. 'Provided I have a guided tour afterwards.'

7

Arbor Spirantia

On the *Aeolus*, meanwhile, sustained exposure to the murk had sapped even Niobe's resilient spirit; so much so that, as another night fell, Niobe ferreted out the last bottle of apple brandy and filled their glasses to the brim. Cavall sat beside them, as was his habit when the light failed.

'When it's gone, it's gone,' said Fogg.

'Drift,' said Niobe. 'Is there anything worse?'

'How about drift without me for company?'

She kissed Fogg. 'Orphans both,' she said.

The dynamic between them had subtly changed. Fogg now provided the light relief. On their journey, he had worked his way through the paintings of the Museum Dome, as in his performance at the White Circus.

'Let's face it,' said Fogg, sipping the dregs of the precious brew, 'I might be wrong. Maybe Gil never reset anything. Maybe he only programmed *The Fram*. I'm not his daughter, after all.'

'You were his godson in all but name. He loved you, Fogg. He knew how the invasion of the island would play out. He planned ahead. We may be heading for our doom, but we're certainly heading somewhere.'

'I've recorded our speed, direction and the number of days. We've just about equalled the journey out to Deception Island. It must be spring, wherever we are.'

'Benedict would tell us which penguin was hatching when.'

'And the colour of the eggs.'

They both stood up. A juddering sound came from all sides.

'It's the shield,' said Fogg.

'A star. I saw a star!' Niobe peered up. Murk again. 'I promise I did.'

'It's thinning,' cried Fogg. The shield rose an inch or two, fell back, and manically repeated the process every other second. 'Prepare for turbulence!' But none came. 'This can't be a beacon.'

As Niobe looked down at a sprawling forest, all twisted limbs and luxurious leaves, various inhabitants peered up at the floating ship. The largest wore a buttoned beige waistcoat over a green scaly chest, and orange-brown woollen leg-mittens with holes to accommodate his hooked claws. Leathery wings folded into his back. A worm-coloured tail wended between the trees. The creature's mind had been so constructed that any outlandish image, and the wood housed many, conjured verse which made no sense. It fitted, because he and his surroundings were equally nonsensical.

He was monstrous, unique, a creature with no mate, the first and last of his kind, the word made flesh. All this he knew. What purpose could a jabberwock have, unless this strange craft could deliver it?

In a deep, gravelly voice, he serenaded the celestial boat with mast and sails:

> 'High above I see a ship,
> Which confuses brine with air,
> Like a cat which barks,
> Or water which sparks,
> Or an unascending stair.
>
> 'Crewmen twirl their shrimping nets:
> The cook favours sparrow pie,
> Unstudied in fowl,
> They hoot like an owl,
> And only catch cumuli.

'Puffed-up waves of grey or white
Can break above or below.
They play with the moon
Like a catchy tune
And even weep falling snow.'

Loneliness had driven him to rhyme. He joined his claws and prayed that the crew would descend and fearlessly make his acquaintance.

Fogg joined Niobe on the ship's rail as the air turned still and the *Aeolus* came to a halt.

'That's not from any painting I know,' he said, 'and I can't see a beacon anywhere.'

'I thought I heard a voice, and – don't laugh – the words *sparrow pie*.'

'Anything's possible,' replied Fogg – and, in the light of recent events, he meant it.

Not for the first time, he wished they had Benedict on hand. The trees did not resemble the elegant species which adorned impressionist canvases, nor the bare, fingered varieties from the winter scenes in earlier works. Natural, but unnatural.

'I'm not going down there now,' announced Niobe. 'Nor are you.'

'What? A miner, afraid of the dark?!'

'We're going to finish that bottle, and I'm going to explain, Mr Fogg, what you're missing.'

'God, I'm an idiot! We can have a closer look without going down. Stay there!'

Fogg retrieved the Long Eye from the cabin.

'Ladies first,' he said with mock gallantry.

'Sod off! Your object, you go first.'

'Actually, it's Morag's, and I must return it.'

'Fogg, cut the politesse and get on with it.'

He peered down. The Long Eye filtered out darkness, and the canopy dominated the view. Close up, it looked like a single tree at the forest edge, with a trail of vigorous shrubs in its wake.

'Blossom already,' he said, handing the Long Eye to Niobe.

She played with the stops on the telescope's side.

'What month are we now?' she asked.

'Mid March, I guess.'

'I think,' said Niobe, 'the blossom comes and goes all year. That's why the air is clean.'

'This is a temperate zone, not the Antarctic. This means we can start again everywhere. Nature has evolved and come to our rescue.'

'Don't be so sure.' '

'All right, misery guts, back to the last bottle, and you can explain.'

They remained at the ship's rail. Niobe poured the last of the rich dark caramel liquid into their glasses with scrupulous fairness.

'All right, what am I missing?' asked Fogg.

'It's only a theory.'

Fogg grinned. 'And?'

'It goes like this. Gil works for Lord Sine. In the Genrich Dome, he encounters Lady Vane. They have a passionate affair, more than a passing fling. It matters to both of them. That's my reading. You saw them together, Fogg. Anyway, while at play with Lady Vane, he researches a tree for Lord Sine. That explains the volume in his mountain retreat. *Arbor Spirantia* is a pun of sorts. A plant that breathes clean air, and also Spire's tree, a tree discovered by him.'

'How do you know he did the work *then*?'

'It's a complex genetic analysis. Gil had no instruments on the *Fram* or Deception Island, and I assume he had none at home. That means he did the work when he was with Genrich. Yet he doesn't hand his findings over to Lord Sine or anyone else. Not to Carlo, not to the second Lord Vane, not even to Potts. That suggests this tree, for all its miraculous properties, has a hideous downside.'

'Hold on, that's quite a leap.'

'Gil needs an excuse to end the research which will convince Lord Sine and not alert Lord Vane to his discovery. So, somehow – and this is speculation – he allows the affair to be discovered. He is banished by Lord Vane. Lord Sine thinks that's the reason. He escapes the mess – and so, by chance, he rescues you.'

'How did the tree get here? How did it multiply like this?'

'Maybe that's what worried him.' She peered at the glow of the *Fram*'s deck lights.

'This place can't be Simul. Not a bird or insect to be seen, and there was no sign of this vegetation on Deception Island.'

The tree tossed, as if in the grip of a nightmare.

Fogg stood up. 'Hear?' He couldn't find a word for the noise – a rustling with a groaning sound beneath. 'Now, that is odd,' he said. 'We have peace below and turmoil at the edge.'

'This tree is spreading, colonising. That should be a good thing, but it doesn't *feel* that way.'

Fogg gave the forest a final sweep, and caught, closer to, a splash of a different colour. 'There's a structure of some kind down there. At least, I think there is.'

Niobe had, from experience, a practical bent when it came to dark, covered spaces. 'Tomorrow, we take a compass bearing from here. Or we'll have nothing to go on at ground level.'

That night, entwined in one of the *Fram*'s ungenerous bunks, with the rare pleasure of a porthole open to the night sky, Niobe revealed a limit to her wanderlust.

'I'd like somewhere which gives me a sense of belonging. No more than that. It doesn't have to be somewhere I own, just a rock to settle on. We were always moving from mine to mine.'

'I wonder which is worse: losing a home you can never return to, or never having one in the first place.'

'I know which,' she replied.

Fogg missed his paintings as one might a family. He worried over the humidity, even misalignment, and suffered a recurring nightmare about canvas-consuming mice. But Niobe had nothing to cling to, not even wreckage.

'We have a mission, then,' he said, tousling her hair.

'It's not as simple as that. I also hate sameness, as in that dreadful school. They're trapped inside me, these two different voices. They don't exactly yell at each other, but they never agree.'

'That's because they're not truly opposed,' said Fogg. 'You need a wide sweep to your life, but an anchorage to come back to.'

That had been his parents' life – forever exploring, but with the base, their cosy room and the camaraderie to return to.

Niobe's body eased a little. She seemed content with the answer.

Two words sung in her head, over and over, as she drifted into sleep – fresh, but with an oddity bordering on the sinister.

Sparrow pie.

8

The White Queen's Breakfast

Dawn on Deception Island had had a straightforward brilliance, with the glare of sun on snow and ice, and the lap of the sea. Here, the play of the morning sun on the forest's umbrella had a more nuanced quality.

The Long Eye, perversely, was far more effective in failing light, and the structure Fogg had glimpsed the previous evening now proved hard to locate. A faintly discoloured area, like a dent in the canopy, fitted their best recollection. Fogg took a compass bearing.

They hesitated at the ship's rail. They could not both descend without leaving the ladder attached, yet neither had any intention of letting the other explore alone. Any agile creature below would be able to seize the vessel unopposed.

Leaving Cavall behind was an option, but the dog had become increasingly responsive to sophisticated commands. They judged him more use as a scout on the ground.

So Cavall led the way, head facing the forest, his prehensile toes as sure in their grip as human hands. He struggled with the canopy before disappearing, only to re-emerge backwards with an encouraging wag of the tail, before vanishing once more.

The large leaves had pliable stalks and the branches a whippy elegance. The blossom was plentiful.

'The flowers have no stamens,' said Fogg, 'and no sign of any fruit either.'

Branches from the different trees had been fighting for light and supremacy. They coiled around each other to the point of strangulation. Beneath the leaves, a thick, tangled layer, some of it dead wood, resisted their progress. The ladder lacked the length to reach the ground. Cavall's jaws had created a gap in the canopy, but they still had to work.

The forest floor had a springiness which Deception Island's rock had never had. Luminosity, too. Tiny pools of sunlight danced across the earth, the crumbling surface of which was pierced at intervals by new shoots. The forest had an uncomfortable feel, as if the growth was sentient and hostile.

'Wow,' said Niobe. 'These trees must clean the earth, too. What are they?'

'I haven't an earthly,' said Fogg. 'But, through the Long Eye last night, one tree looked much taller than the others.'

Cavall trotted back, turned on the spot and trotted away again.

'Hound on the scent,' said Niobe.

Fogg read out the bearing for the break in the canopy. Cavall tilted his head and trotted off once more.

He did not return.

'That was a mistake,' said Fogg, but a gentle singsong voice quickly disabused him.

'Dear dog, we're late for breakfast and quite lost *again*.'

In a clearing stood an elderly woman in a white pleated dress, with a loose bag over her shoulder: Tenniel's White Queen, just as Morag had described her. She stood in a circle of sunlight, like an actress caught in a spotlight. She was patting Cavall on the head as they approached.

'Nice dogs have nice masters. It's one of those masts you can cling to. But we do so like to look our best for breakfast, and we've lost our bun.'

'You've lost your *what*?' said Niobe.

'My bun, dear. It should be here, but it isn't.' The White Queen patted the nape of her neck.

This is too peculiar, thought Fogg, life imitating art so exactly.

Near her feet lay a hairbrush, just as in Tenniel's picture. He picked it up.

'This is my friend, Niobe, your Majesty. She'll do the needful.'

'Majesty? When did I ever have majesty?'

'What's a bun?' Niobe whispered to Fogg.

'It's a hairstyle. Knot it together and tie it back.'

'I have pins and needles. But the point is,' said the White Queen, 'you can see it, and I can't. But I know when it's gone.'

She was short and pale. Her features shared her gentleness of voice: small mouth and eyes, a delicate chin.

Niobe worked the silver hair as Fogg made the introductions.

Bun restored, the Queen turned decisive. 'That way to breakfast!' she announced, and strode off.

The structure in the forest turned out to be a grounded Genrich carrier. Vigorous shoots had grown through the fuselage. Its side had been opened out and flattened to create decking. Wooden seats had been removed from the craft, as had two wooden tables, which had been joined together. To one side, a third held a Genrich Matter-Rearranger.

A knight in white armour busied at laying the table. The spurs on his feet tinkled like a glockenspiel, and his greaves and breastplate gave his gait a cumbersome quality. With the whiskery moustache, flying white hair and inquisitive eyes, he resembled an inventor more than a warrior. At least he was human. A White Rabbit, little shorter than the knight, had lopsided features – from ears of disparate width and length to a mouth with unaligned teeth – in sharp contrast to his immaculately tailored jacket and fly collar. He held up a pocket watch.

'It should go slower when we're being serious,' he said.

'And what if my idea of serious is different from yours?' asked the White Knight.

'Two more places!' commanded the White Queen gently, but with authority. 'This is Mr Fogg and Miss Niobe.'

The White Knight clicked his heels, bowed and set about rear-ranging the table. The White Rabbit peered at them briefly and returned to his watch.

'And a nice dog,' added the White Queen, 'with manners.'

Cavall did not respond to the compliment. He stood stock-still in front of a strange, cylindrical, orange-pink pipe, which curved back into the undergrowth at the edge of the clearing. Niobe ran across and tugged it gently.

She had turned on a music machine! A mellifluous singing voice echoed from the gloom.

> 'If one were two, and two were three,
> Would iron chains enslave the free,
> Would the weather change,
> The new normal be strange,
> And would aardvarks swim in the sea?

> 'If half past noon were ten to one,
> Would the finished be just begun,
> Would the midnight hour
> Fade like a shower,
> And would moonshine tan like the sun?'

The *sparrow pie* voice from the night before! Niobe took a pace forward, then three hurried paces back, as the pipe retracted and a huge scaly leg emerged, and then another. The Jabberwock shambled on to the veranda, its dark leathery wings folded away.

'I'm the one who's meant to make an entrance,' complained the White Queen.

Fogg gawped. It was the spitting image of Tenniel's monster.

The White Queen stepped up and did the introductions. 'This is Jolyon Abberwock. Jabberwock or, when pressed for time, Mr J to his friends.'

'Jolly-on is a dreadful misnomer,' muttered the White Rabbit. 'He's irredeemably gloomy.'

'If only he bottled his good memories for a rainy day,' said the Knight. 'That's the key. I only ever won one battle, but it lives with me. The defeats I consign to history.'

The monster bowed, head to his mittened, clawed toes.

'You sing very well,' said Niobe.

'Much obliged,' said Mr J. 'Applause is the mulch we artists feed off.'

The White Knight distributed a golden-coloured fruit, which was delicious, unfamiliar and restorative.

'Can I ask a question?' asked Niobe, downing her spoon.

'As long as it has an answer,' said the White Rabbit.

'Where exactly do you all come from? I imagine you can answer that.'

Their hosts looked at each other with a pained expression.

'Oh dear, I'm wrong again,' said the White Rabbit, chiding himself. 'A question with an answer can be crueller than a question without one.'

The Knight stood up and clacked his mailed gloves together. 'Spruce up! Miss Niobe should be rewarded for showing interest.' He paused before adding, 'White walls.'

'Barred windows,' said the Jabberwock.

'Pools of salty water,' said the White Rabbit.

'Sacs with rubbery skin,' said the White Queen.

'Scanners and weavers,' said the Knight.

'Him,' said the Jabberwock.

'*Him*? What do you mean, *him*?' queried the Knight.

'I think we've got the picture,' said Fogg. 'You come from the Genrich Dome. Lord Sine made you in his birthing pools. Just like the Hatter and the schoolboys.'

'Not forgetting the beamish boy, who'll have my head.'

'Is he here?' asked Fogg, looking round.

'Obviously not,' said the White Rabbit, 'or we'd have a headless Mr J.'

'Time for tea,' said the White Queen diplomatically. 'The leaves may be shiny, but they're quite aromatic.' She placed a large home-made copper kettle on the fire and distributed cups. 'It's difficult being out of a book. You've limited room for manoeuvre.'

The White Knight produced more slices of fruit and filled their cups with a rich, purple liquid.

Niobe gave Fogg a look. *Your turn*, it said. Fogg took the cue.

'I was wondering about the carrier's crew. Did they survive? How did the forest start? How did you survive? Where does this delicious fruit and juice come from?'

'This is all terribly serious,' said the White Rabbit, pursing his lips. 'My watch will go slow, and breakfast will take forever.'

The White Knight stuck out his chin and delivered the narrative like a military despatch: 'Matter-Rearranger is the craft. It lands *here*. Murk all about. And we're in the back. Let's say the clink. That's us, *here*.' The Knight trotted a glass along the table. 'We can see Genrich personnel through the porthole, *there*, carrying a reinforced steel coffer outside. They're wearing weather armour. Chitin suits, in a word.'

'Two words,' whispered the White Rabbit.

The Knight savaged the interruption: 'There's nothing worse in the soldier's canon than being held up by friendly fire.'

'Soldier on,' said the White Queen.

'The crew do not come back. Night falls and we hear screams. Near dawn, the craft heaves like a ship at sea. Through our port-holes, the air is clearing. Shoots sprout and sunder our cell. Nearby, a tree grows like the beanstalk of legend. We emerge. Where there was murk, there is *mist*. We do a recce, Mr J and I, while her Majesty tidies up, and the fourth in our quartet consults his chronometer. Mr J finds the master tree. *Here*. It can move like a man on stilts when it wants to.' The Knight marked a spot some way from the far side of the craft with his glove. 'At the base of the tree, the coffer is twisted, broken and empty. The crew have been strangled by saplings. Twigs protrude from their eyes and encircle their legs.'

'So, why haven't the trees strangled you?' asked Fogg.

'I don't know how he did it, but Mr J wound his neck and his tail around the trunk; ever since, we've been left alone,' explained the White Knight.

In that telepathic way lovers sometimes have, Fogg and Niobe both felt ill at ease. Something was being held back.

'Can we see this tree?' asked Fogg.

Silence descended.

'Those who eat pork shouldn't traipse straight off to the pigsty,' said the White Rabbit, grabbing his watch and nibbling his last slice of fruit, 'if ever at all.'

'Still less the abattoir,' added the Knight.

'I'll take you,' said the Jabberwock, rising from his haunches.

Spurs clinked. The Rabbit shook his watch and held it to his ear. The Queen fiddled with her hair.

The Jabberwock gestured with a crooked claw and shambled off into the trees, singing as he went.

'Saunter through the shadows
To where the sad rose grows,
Where occasional light
Delivers fruit and blight
And leaves us comatose.'

Fogg, Niobe and Cavall followed. It made an odd procession, the Jabberwock's neck rounding the trees before his body did, and his tail snaking behind like an afterthought.

It took twenty minutes to reach the master tree, as Niobe named it. Its girth was already substantial, and the branches reached high into the sky, supported by a complex tangle of aerial roots. Most striking was the absence of fruit, so abundant elsewhere, save for one, oversized, discoloured fruit, hanging from an equally distorted branch with reddish, pitted bark.

'Good and evil?' muttered Niobe.

Cavall pawed at a pile of twisted chitin suits at the edge of the clearing; there was a mound of earth beside them.

'The good Knight buried the poor souls,' explained the Jabberwock.

'Such an odd timeline,' said Niobe. 'The crew carry out the coffer. We assume they've come to bury it, because it's dangerous. And then they're killed before they can even make it back to the craft.'

The Jabberwock looked flustered. 'We must be going, we really must.'

'What's that?' asked Fogg.

The rotten fruit swayed, as if caught by a breeze, only the air was quite still.

'There's a fly on the rotten fruit,' said Niobe.

The Jabberwock now looked doubly flustered.

'More than one,' added Niobe, 'and not on it, they're emerging from it.'

'How do you get back to your craft?' asked the Jabberwock urgently.

'There's a ladder,' replied Fogg.

'What's it made of?'

'Steel chains.'

'You must have a chitin shield.'

'It closes when it meets the murk, but it's open now,' explained Fogg.

Snap! They had forgotten Cavall. The metallic crack of his jaws closing on a fly turned all their heads.

'On my back, now!' cried the Jabberwock. 'You won't outrun them.'

Now they saw the urgency, as more and more blue-coloured flies emerged to focus their attention on Cavall. Puffs of metal exploded from Cavall's head as he bit and snapped at his attackers.

'Don't wait for the flesh-eaters – you're next!' shrilled the Jabberwock.

They clambered on his back, Fogg clinging to the scaly neck, Niobe grasping Fogg's waist, while hauling Cavall on board with her free hand.

'Hold on for dear life!' cried the Jabberwock. 'I need a run-up!'

He careered into the wood and around several trees, before gathering speed back to the clearing. His wings, hitherto tucked into his flanks, spread wide. He bounded across the clearing and leapt through branches, fruit and blossom into clear air. Fogg's arm muscles could barely take the strain. Ahead, the *Aeolus* was drifting up and away. The anchor chain dangled free without its anchor, and the ladder was disintegrating before their eyes, under attack from a swarm of blue flies.

The Jabberwock's wingbeats delivered speed and smoothness. Worries evaporated. He would deliver them on deck, the chitin would close and they would be away.

But . . .

The flies had a crowd intelligence. The swarm surged from the *Aeolus'* sundered cables, back to the Jabberwock and, more particularly, Cavall. For a moment, the air seethed with insects. Niobe felt the dog unclamp his teeth. He fell, paws outstretched, into the undergrowth, where he ran on to distract the attackers. The swarm zigzagged across the forest in pursuit.

Fogg cried out a new alarm. They had forgotten the flesh-eaters. A cloud of red flies was closing in from behind.

The Jabberwock turned about and slammed his wings shut, squashing the first wave. As his stained wings reopened, a new problem dawned. If the *Aeolus* reached the murk before they reached the *Aeolus*, the shield would close and they would be doomed. The Jabberwock found a new gear, wings clacking open and shut at a hectic pace. Speed increased; smoothness was lost. One especially violent lurch would have cast them into space, were it not for the Jabberwock's beige waistcoat, the buttons of which held despite the strain.

Even so, metres short, the red cloud caught them.

Fogg and Niobe flailed as the insects swarmed around their faces and stabbed at their protecting arms. At this moment of crisis, Fogg's guardian golden beetle came to their aid. With astonishing speed and agility, its tiny feet and claws drove their assailants back. Half maddened, half disorientated by its unfamiliarity, they pursued the beetle away from the craft, allowing the Jabberwock to land on deck, just in time.

Fogg raced to the controls and yelled the familiar commands: 'One and five, one turn!'

The sacks breathed in and out, like lungs revived, and the *Aeolus* hurtled into the murk.

'Amidships!' he yelled to the Jabberwock, who curled his tail about the mast and closed his wings.

On meeting the murk, the shield closed. From the stern, they watched the flesh-eaters succumb to the beetle's fighting prowess, until the blue flies, having reduced Cavall to powder, swarmed up from the forest floor and the odds reversed. Against them, the beetle stood no chance.

9

A Room with a View

The rim of the sun reddened the thatch on Cassie Vane's house, that perfect replica of John Constable's *Cottage in a Cornfield*. The mechanical donkey stood by the five-bar gate, as it always did; the corn stood true to the canvas, near ripe, as it always was. Only the clouds had the audacity to differ.

This aura of exterior calm deceived. In her workroom, Cassie screamed as her beautiful beetle exploded and the screen went blank. She had lost her eyes and ears. She could no longer protect young Fogg, the only man who had shown her true affection. She stood up and flicked her fingers in frustration.

She had refused to let his intimacy with Niobe disturb her. She had forsworn physical involvement with men. Her mother's passions had brought nothing but tragedy in their wake.

She surveyed the pieces on the irregular board on a table beside her. A craftsman in the square at the old Tempestas Dome had carved them for her. A little out of date now, but the resemblances held true.

At least she still had Morag Spire's beetle. Cosmo, Benedict and her mother occupied the same square because she knew from the beetle that they were together on the *Ceres*. She also had access to Jaggard's rooms in Tiriel's Tower, thanks to the present she had given her mother.

On an adjacent table rested the lost pieces, mostly good people: among them, 147, also known as Hernia; the second Lord Vane; her own tutor, Miss Baldwin; and Gilbert Spire. And one piece stood beside them, whereabouts unknown: Peregrine Mander, her equal as an observer, and perhaps as a player too. He was forever turning up when you least expected him.

The board brought home the complexity of causation. Outcomes in conflict are rarely linear.

10

Unwriting the Written

They might as well have killed an albatross, such was the prevailing despondency on the *Aeolus*. The White Queen's breakfast had provided an entertaining interlude, but Cavall's demise depressed them, as did the tree's apparent hatred for mankind and all its works. They had no known destination to look forward to or prepare for.

But they were light-heartedness personified beside the Jabberwock. He barely moved from his central station by the mainmast and rarely spoke. When he did, he versified his own doom:

> *'There I stood by the tulgey wood*
> *And tendered my neck like a swan,*
> *With one vicious hack*
> *And a snicker-snack,*
> *My sputtering life-light was gone.'*

'He thinks death is imminent, because it's written,' explained Fogg. '*And with his head he went galumphing back* is not a nice line to read about yourself.'

'Who beheads him?' asked Niobe in outrage. She had quickly grown fond of the Jabberwock, a standout minority of one and therefore a kindred spirit.

'Well, in the book, his executioner is more disturbing than anyone. He's minuscule but cocksure—'

'A *him*. No surprise there!'

'With hair like a Botticelli—'

'Botty who?'

'He's a painter, Niobe.'

'Just describe, Fogg. We simple minds don't want the fancy stuff.'

'Fine features and crinkly hair, beautifully brushed. Like this.' Fogg drew the diminutive warrior in pencil on the back of the Airlugger logbook. 'This is the beamish nephew from behind. He holds his sword with both hands behind his right shoulder. The sword is as tall as he is. He wears red leggings and a blue surcoat with golden pockets.'

'You mean he's privileged, with a nauseating sense of entitlement.'

The Jabberwock, still alone by the mast, was muttering wistfully to himself.

'This has to stop,' she said.

'You'll make it worse,' cautioned Fogg.

'He's in a rut and he needs rescuing. Watch me.' She slipped down behind him.

The Jabberwock was singing a new mournful song:

> 'That which is written is written,
> For our stories must end as they're told:
> By rogues, princesses are smitten,
> Magicians turn silver to gold,
> And all the fabled monsters tend
> To die to make a happy end.'

'What drivel!' said Niobe.

'Your end isn't fixed in black and white.'

'Nor is yours. *That* Jabberwock is a creation; you're real – you make your own way.'

'The beamish boy is every bit as real. He's psychotic – and don't be fooled by appearances. He's built to kill.'

Niobe looked deep into the Jabberwock's eyes. He was not

making this up, which complicated matters. 'What's written can be unwritten. You must learn to fight.'

'People are such wonderful constructs. I don't see the point of damaging them. I'd rather be damaged.'

Another problem: the Jabberwock was a pacifist.

'You mean you'd rather have your head cut off?'

The Jabberwock put his head in his claws. Whatever the moral niceties, he was doomed, so why bother?

'Self-defence is not aggression, it's survival,' explained Niobe. 'You defend yourself when the White Rabbit is annoying. If someone comes at you with a sword, do the same. Meet words with words, and steel with steel. *Have at you!*'

She prodded him with her fist and kept prodding, but the Jabberwock was not to be provoked.

AIPT,* still fixed to the foredeck, made the breakthrough. 'You're wasting your time, Miss Niobe. A creature with such a distorted neck knows nothing about exercise. Note how his cranial cavity is too small for the rest of him. As for those floppy antennae, what do they contribute to anything? He's all hiss and no bite.'

The Jabberwock jumped to attention. He retracted his neck like a coiling snake and hissed in AIPT's direction. 'I'm stupid, am I? You wind in the neck, you ignoramus, to reduce the target. The rest, like everything in life, is timing.'

Niobe saw a slim window of opportunity. Push too hard, and he would relapse.

'Broom handles!' she cried. 'They can't hurt anyone.'

She rushed back to the cabin and de-handled two brooms.

'*En garde!*'

The Jabberwock parried with ease.

'See!' he cried.

---

* ARTIFICIAL INTELLIGENCE PHYSICAL TRAINER

'A child could parry *that*,' replied AIPT.

'Do your worst,' the Jabberwock snapped at Niobe, now infuriated.

Like an old-world pirate film, they parried and thrust their way along the deck and back. The Jabberwock performed with grace and speed until Niobe, unthinking, raised her handle in both hands over her right shoulder, as in the illustration. The monster froze.

'Do it! Despatch me, Beamish!' he cried in horror, extending his neck to receive the fatal blow.

Niobe stepped back, hands on hips. 'You do not surrender to a ridiculous man with a ridiculous name. And you don't surrender to me until I've disarmed you.'

'The pen is mightier than the sword,' replied the Jabberwock sagely.

'Tell that to the massacred innocents,' countered AIPT.

Fogg had been listening with mounting incredulity. AIPT's catch-phrases hitherto had focused on his and his friends' abs and pelvic-floor muscles, except for that morning in the Museum Dome, when his great adventure had started. The voice had a familiar lilt, which he could not place.

'The machine has a point,' said Fogg.

The Jabberwock considered the subtle philosophies in play, the imagined and the real, sense and nonsense. He still felt a prisoner of fate, but a little less under its thumb.

'How do I parry that particular blow?' he asked nervously.

'Every thrust has its parry. Right arm, up and across, claws forward, and your wing in reserve.' Niobe spoke gently. 'Take your time.'

'As the White Rabbit would say,' added Fogg.

Days passed. The broom handles changed hands. Niobe taught Fogg. The Jabberwock taught Fogg. Niobe and the Jabberwock taught each other. Fogg taught neither Niobe nor the Jabberwock, and AIPT switched loyalties.

'To think, Mr Fogg, you were my pupil. Where's the speed and finesse?'

'I never had either,' Fogg screamed.

Niobe slumped. Men, ever in need of a boost!

All the while, the *Aeolus* cruised on, its new destination unknown, save that the craft had chosen 10, a lever hitherto unused, and ignored any contrary instruction.

11

Stopwatch

Mid-morning, two days behind the *Aeolus*, Beamish landed his small craft beside a huge tree in a spreading area of clear air, on his reconnaissance mission for Lord Sine. From above, he had marked the position of the Scurrier and its makeshift veranda. He had identified the White Queen and the White Knight lounging in their equally makeshift chairs. He had no wish to engage with either: both were has-beens.

He stood and surveyed.

Facts: an old-world tree bears golden fruit, but one exception is bloated, discoloured and hangs from an aberrant branch; shrubs of the same species, in blossom, surround the tree, and beneath it five graves yield, when probed, skeletons strangled by aerial roots.

Deductions: the blossom cleared the air; the tree had erupted from the fissile genetic material which the crew had been sent to bury; the fruit-laden tree had spawned the rest, leaving free space for its own branches, and had disposed of the crew in that first explosion of energy.

Unresolved: who or what had picked the skeletons clean, to the whiteness of pure chalk.

Beamish freed the vorpal blade. Danger had its own sickly-sweet smell, and he caught it now. He had never seen a living insect before. He knew their life cycle, but had never heard of flies inhabiting dead fruit. Yet now they emerged in numbers. The drying of their wings created a high-pitched hum.

Beamish stepped away from the trunk to the centre of the clearing. He needed space to swing. They hovered briefly, settled, and hovered again. He imagined the crew burying the steel crate, the tree exploding from nowhere, then this horror.

He crouched and waited, but they showed no interest in him, nor in the unusual figure who now shuffled into the clearing.

'I worried for you. My watch was slowing a little, which it doesn't do unless death threatens.' The White Rabbit peered at the ground. 'They don't attack us, but I worried they might attack you.'

Beamish responded with the question with which he greeted everyone, friend or foe: 'Where's the Jabberwock?'

'He left in an Airlugger.'

A surge of rage shook Beamish. 'Fled! How dare you block my destiny!'

'We had no say. Anyway, Mr J is a friend of ours, and you're no friend of his,' replied the White Rabbit.

'I rather envy that watch of yours,' said Beamish. 'It would fit my pocket very nicely.'

'It's not a second-hand watch,' said the White Rabbit, 'though it ticks like one.' He raised the instrument to his ear, and his face contorted with worry. 'It's going ever so slow. It's never done that in my lifetime.'

'It's the sand running out,' said Beamish.

The White Rabbit looked at him. 'You ... you wouldn't,' he squealed.

'I'm a professional. It'll be so quick and so painless.'

And it was. Beamish had to vent his rage at the Jabberwock's escape on someone, and he did like the watch.

Wiping the vorpal blade clean, he pondered his next move. Lord Sine had expressed interest in the surviving Spire. Bring her back, and Lord Sine would surely reveal the whereabouts of his one true quarry.

But where would the Spire girl be? He reached for his Morse-code machine and began to tap. Jaggard the weather-watcher would know.

He set the controls, noting with satisfaction that the metronomic tick of his new acquisition had recovered its normal pace.

Upon the Good Ship *Ceres*

Lady Vane was at her most charming.

'Do come in, Morag, and your friend. Have a seat.'

'Seat' sold the four chairs short, with their plush upholstery, tapestry covers and elaborately carved arms and legs. They were set around a low, circular table like the points of the compass, exactly distanced from one another. A higher, rectangular table tucked into the long wall offered a coded hint perhaps: at this table, we talk as equals. Lady Vane dealt in sophisticated messages.

'This is my vessel,' Lady Vane continued, 'and I make a point of being hospitable, but my son is wary of outsiders.' Opposite her, west to east, sat Benedict, tense and silent. 'However, he does like old-world sustenance. I can't understand why they chose the word *food*. It has an ugly ring, don't you think?'

'*Foda* or *fodjan*,' said Benedict, 'low Germanic words from the mists of time. They're the origins of *fodder* too, which was what animals ate, long ago.'

'Does your knowledgeable friend have a name?' asked Lady Vane.

Morag caught the insincerity. Lady Vane and Benedict had been alone together in the cloister of the College of Novelties. She would have ferreted out his name already. So why cultivate distance between him and her? The fear Cosmo might be listening in? She played along.

'He's called Benedict, meaning "well said" or "blessed".'

Lady Vane smiled. A manservant entered with glasses and a jug brimful of off-green liquid. *Four* glasses: Cosmo would be joining them, in his own time no doubt.

'Not quite Mander, I'm afraid,' said Lady Vane, 'but we do our best.'

Benedict peered at the jug. 'The trick is to separate the juice of the lime from the rest. Old-world kitchens had liquidising machines and sieves. We need to reinvent them. You can make liqueurs with the residue.'

Lady Vane rang a small bell. A manservant lingered in the doorway.

'Take Mr Benedict to the galley, and tell cook to do whatever he says.'

Benedict looked relieved to have escaped his hostess.

Lady Vane turned her attention to Morag. 'I'm sorry about your father.'

Morag raised an eyebrow. Lady Vane had abandoned her father to the tender mercies of Lord Sine's monsters without any attempt at warning or rescue.

Lady Vane leant forward and whispered, 'He preferred me to your mother, and then exile to me. We could have eloped. We could have started a new dynasty.'

Morag could see only one reason for the whisper: Cosmo still did not know who his father was.

'But you did start a new dynasty,' Morag whispered back, before raising her voice: 'So, where are we heading now?'

'My son has some private adventure in mind.'

Cosmo's strong male voice broke the interplay between the two women: 'What do you see in that know-all?'

He had his mother's gift for stealth. He lounged in the doorway, just as he had at his first meeting with Morag, in her room at Infotainment, in the Genrich Dome.

Lady Vane came gently to Benedict's defence. 'Don't be dismissive, dear. A fund of excessive general knowledge can get tiring, but it has its practical side.'

'Where is he, anyway? I've a question for him.'

Lady Vane's bell tinkled once more.

A different man appeared. 'He's brilliant, that Benedict, m'Lady. He's constructed a fruit press. Second rounds will be up, any minute.'

Morag could only admire the subtlety of Lady Vane's moves. First, get Benedict below decks. Then, give him a chance to impress.

'Please make sure he comes with them,' said Lady Vane gently.

Morag watched Cosmo appraising his mother. The dynamic between them appeared to be changing.

'You rather like him,' said Cosmo, as the door closed.

'He's different,' replied Lady Vane.

Morag considered the balance of knowledge. *Cosmo does not know I'm his half-sister, but suspects I know from Fogg that he killed my grandmother. That, and my gift, make me dangerous. Lady Vane privately suspects Benedict's origins. Cosmo is suspicious of Benedict and of his mother's attitude to Benedict. Lady Vane does not know I know who Benedict really is, but Benedict's looks are quite a giveaway. So, what is the question Cosmo wants to ask him?*

The answer came quickly. Benedict appeared with new glasses, a new jug and a new drink, which he served before sitting between Lady Vane and Cosmo. Lady Vane reached for a tapestry. Her needle began to dip and rise.

'A little tart, but not bad,' pronounced Cosmo after his first sip.

'I find the sharpness clarifying,' added Lady Vane.

Cosmo clapped his hands. 'I like clarification too.' His head darted to face Benedict. 'Do tell us who placed that sliver of purple in your eyes. One of your parents must be as distinctive-looking as my mother.'

'It's nothing to do with my parents.'

'Who, then?' asked Cosmo.

'Lord Sine.'

'What do you mean, *Lord Sine*?'

'As you know, Genrich collect talented outsiders. I had an unusually receptive memory. I went to a Genrich school, where someone reported that my face bore a passing resemblance to your own family. I was taken to the Genrich Dome and inspected by Lord Sine. They tranquillised me and, when I woke, my eyes, nose and ears were bandaged over. I cannot describe ...'

The performace was mesmerising. Benedict's eyes watered as if recalling that hideous surgery.

'I don't follow,' said Cosmo. 'Why would Lord Sine—?'

'I regret to say Lord Sine has designs on your kingdom. He is keen to provoke dynastic strife.'

Disappointment tempered Morag's admiration for this tour de force. Benedict had fashioned a plausible story, but that very guile mirrored the dark side of the Vanes. Cassie, with her beetles, had it too. Benedict might once have been the innocent she had fallen for, but he was learning fast and changing. Lady Vane's eyes sparkled with pride: her biological son had passed his test with flying colours.

Cosmo sipped his drink.

'That's just about possible,' he said finally. 'I suggest, Mother, we upgrade their living quarters.'

Then, remarkably, Cosmo turned affable. He discussed food and cooking with Benedict, and his impression of Vermeer's studio with Morag. He even promised her and Benedict a guided tour of their new destination.

'I often reflect on the complexities of causation,' he added grandly. 'Consider this. I deliver a children's book to Lord Sine to explain how Infotainment works. Lo and behold, he brings these illustrated grotesques to life to show how clever he is. Soon after, Tweedledum and Tweedledee deliver an Airlugger to your Museum, and a multitude of narratives start to run. But who sent the twins to you? How much of this is planned and how much random accident? And, if planned, planned by whom and to what end?'

Lady Vane's needle ceased its diving motion. 'Did you say *Museum*?'

Cosmo answered before Morag could muster a reply. 'At the time of the Fall, someone, without permission, built a dome to house mankind's finest art. Morag and the ghastly Fogg were left in charge, if that's the phrase for a museum which has no visitors.'

Nobody was safe from Cosmo, Morag decided. He and his weaver had delved deep into Fogg's memory.

Lady Vane put down her tapestry. 'I would like to see this Museum. Tell me, Morag, about your favourites. My husband, my late husband, and I shared a love of art.'

Cosmo yawned and left the room. In his absence, his mother blossomed. True to her word, she allowed Morag the floor. Lady Vane asked perceptive questions about colours, mood, the texture of the paint and the attitude of the human figures in paintings she had never seen. Benedict contributed dry old-world details, dates and who taught or influenced whom. At times, he could have been Fogg.

As the light failed, Morag and Benedict were led to separate quarters – Morag next to Lady Vane and Benedict next to the lith. A guard stood outside each room, but it was a definite upgrade.

Their first day of relative freedom brought home a simple truth: they all needed diversion.

Lady Vane played skittles against 'the boys', as she called them. Skilful, competitive and not above self-mockery, Lady Vane resurrected an old grief for Morag. No wonder her father's head had been turned. Lady Vane offered more than beauty.

Inevitably, there was chess. Every afternoon, by the clock, the lith set centre-deck a table with two chairs facing across it. Cosmo placed each ivory piece dead centre on its starting square. He then shook hands with Morag and Benedict in turn.

'I always play black, giving you the advantage of the first move. I must play all my moves within three minutes. You have as long as you like, within reason. May the best player win.'

Benedict played the openings efficiently, but he lacked Cosmo's gift for improvisation. Benedict lost the first six games, though not at a canter.

'You should consult your partner,' said Cosmo, on the fourth afternoon, as Benedict tipped over his king once more.

'I have, often. Morag says I have positional sense, but my dislike of losing material means I miss the sacrificial moves.'

'You play all the standard moves, like one of Lord Sine's identicals,' said Cosmo.

'They're standard moves because they're sound,' replied Benedict weakly.

Over the ensuing afternoons, Benedict improved against the better player, as Morag had against Benedict. The unstretched never progress. He even showed flashes of defiance.

'Come on, my Lord, your three minutes are all but up.'

'Yes, yes,' Cosmo would snarl in reply.

But he still avoided defeat.

That afternoon, Lady Vane took out a pack of cards. Morag had never played. Lady Vane's introduction felt like a coded message.

'Spades rule because they're devious and ruthless. Hearts come second because love can make or destroy all. Diamonds are third, the emblem of wealth and all it can buy. Clubs have the power of violence, which one should never underestimate. Of course, these suits can ally as well as fight each other, and different combinations have different effects. Lord Sine would say they are rooted in our genes in subtle combinations. But perhaps he is unduly cynical. Now for the rules of this particular game . . .'

That evening, Benedict and Morag worked a moment of privacy by retiring to their rooms while Cosmo and the crew attended to a problem on deck.

Benedict, leading the way, turned and whispered, 'I had my first dream last night. Crazy and illogical, but a dream all the same.'

Morag felt pleased for him, but anxious that his dreamless nights, another feature deserving of special care, had ceased. Before she could reply, he took her head in his hands and kissed her on the mouth: not quite passionate, but neither tentative, nor clumsy, nor brief. She entwined her hands in his. Above them, the boards creaked with the heavy tread of the approaching lith.

'Whatever befalls us,' he said.

Inexperienced in the grading of physical contact, Morag reached a judgement nonetheless. She loved him for that half-sentence. Long-repressed emotion broke through, and, unbidden, an old-world expression came to her, rich in comfort but also menace: *better to have loved and lost than never to have loved at all.*

'Whatever befalls us,' she muttered to herself.

A few days later, a storm ambushed the *Ceres* in the early hours, with a violent crosswind. Lightning and battering rain quickly followed. A diapason would have screamed, but the straining timbers provided music enough. The Airlugger yawed from side to side, and up and down.

Hurled from her bunk, Morag protected her head in the nick of time. Her door flung open as a mattress fell from the ceiling in the passage outside, held upright with criss-crossed shrouds of rope, like rigging. Yards away, another fell. Such onslaughts must have happened before.

Morag crawled across the heaving floor into the passageway. Hand over hand, she raised herself to a standing position, her back to the mattress, interlocking her feet in the rope for additional security.

From down the passage, Lady Vane, in a silk nightgown, sashayed her way to the neighbouring mattress and anchored herself. She swayed like a bucolic dancer in tune with the music of the storm.

'It's best to be amidships, upright and facing forwards,' she shouted over the groaning timbers.

They stood, side by side. Humidity soared. Sweat spangled their brows and streaked their nightclothes.

Lady Vane's features twisted into a mask of unalloyed hatred. 'It could be that bastard, Jaggard. This certainly wasn't forecast. Good thing your father helped me improve this ship's defences.' She arched her back, as if the storm were a sexual encounter.

'Where is Cosmo taking us? What does he want from us?'

'Sport,' said Lady Vane. 'Usually.'

'Sport where?'

'Not in Winterdorf. Not in that ridiculous Bosch painting, Acheron. Somewhere I don't know, to judge from the compass bearing. But, wherever, be on your guard.' She paused. 'I have only ever loved two men. You're the only daughter of one, and your friend Benedict is the only son of the other. I'll do my best for you both while I can.'

A little later, Lady Vane gave a cryptic response to a question from Morag about Cassie.

'I have suffered in ways you cannot imagine,' she whispered.

Gradually, the random pitch and yaw subsided into a rhythmic, predictable motion, and the timbers eased their protest.

Lady Vane released her hands and swayed her way back down the passage. Morag disengaged too, and the mattresses retracted into the hidden bays between decks. Back in her bunk, she rifled through her recent conversations with Lady Vane and Cosmo. Neither had ever mentioned Cassie. Out of sight, out of mind? Her feet twitched at the memory of those clutching pincers high on the outer surface of the Genrich Dome.

Neglect her at your peril, she said to herself.

13

Landfall

Three days later, at nightfall, the *Ceres* broke into clear sky. Cosmo summoned them on deck as the murk gave way to ribbons of cloud with a smattering of stars between. The wind-bags slowed until they barely breathed at all, as the crew brought the craft in low. The raising of the chitin shield brought a blast of freezing air and cheers from below, where a semicircle of torches sputtered into life.

Luggage appeared, the wind-bags were reefed, and anchors were hurled from the prow and stern for those below to secure.

'Where are we, dear?' Lady Vane asked her son.

'Heorot.'

'Such an odd name.'

'No odder than Winterdorf.'

Lady Vane paused, as if toying with a potential revelation. 'Your father did mention it occasionally as a place he'd go to, but he never went with me.' She glanced at Morag. 'They were difficult times. He needed to get away.'

No buildings could be seen, other than two simple huts nearby and, much further away, a squat, square tower with a flat roof and pied brickwork.

Lady Vane waved a finger at the tower. 'Is that it?'

'That's just an outpost for recreation,' replied Cosmo, before yelling, 'Gangplank!'

Gangplanks, he should have said. Status governed their descent: Lady Vane and Cosmo descended an ornate fixed ladder with a double rail; everyone else clambered down rope ladders, including Lady Vane's maids. Winches lowered the luggage.

Behind the flickering firelight of the torches stood a cluster of craft, like a family of foraging beetles.

A tall man with a luxuriant russet beard and jet dark eyes stepped forward and shook the hand of the new Lord Vane, after bowing to Lady Vane.

'Welcome, my Lord. Heorot awaits you. Lord Sine has delivered—'

Cosmo theatrically put his finger to his lips. 'Come now, Sigurd, we have guests, and guests like surprises.'

Sigurd smiled. 'I hope you do, too, my Lord.' Cosmo's eyes narrowed. 'We've taken in two unexpected visitors.'

'Save them for later; boredom is the eternal enemy,' said Cosmo, before turning to his men. 'For those who may not have had the pleasure, I introduce my mother. My *stylish* mother.'

More clenched fists, more cheers.

The huts housed stairwells leading to lifts, which quickly filled. Evidence, Morag decided, that the second Lord Vane was egalitarian. Lady Vane and Cosmo would have insisted on a more ornate version for them.

The workings featured complex combinations of wheels, cogs, ropes and cylindrical weights carved from rock. Every tooth and groove fitted flush, every weight had been polished to a finish. While Benedict admired the use of fulcra and pivots, Morag reflected on their creators. Rope and wood had been the staple components of the Airluggers; wood and slate of Winterdorf; here, wood, rope and polished rock. Even the nails were wooden. She detected the hand of the Northerners, the craftsmen beneath the Tempestas mountain who, when not working for hire, kept themselves to themselves. *Where did they get their raw materials?* she wondered. *What payment did they seek?*

The lifts made no sound, as if friction were a stranger. They opened into a modest circular cave, leading to a steep gorge.

Occasional chips of globestone glimmered in the gloom, accentuating the prodigious height of the walls. A narrow path snaked down the rock face. Lady Vane summoned her maid and exchanged deck shoes for walking boots.

Cosmo prowled, with Sigurd in his wake, sniffing the air.

'I suggest the guests have a spearman in front and an archer behind,' said Sigurd.

'Don't worry about her Ladyship,' said Cosmo. 'She's a survivor, so long as she's loyal. The lith will guard her back.' He nodded towards Morag and Benedict. 'And split those two up,' he added.

'You behind me,' Sigurd said to Morag, 'and you towards the rear,' he said to Benedict.

The chests were lashed to poles to enable carriage in single file. Cosmo took the lead up the path, snaking its way into the gloom. Sword drawn, he walked at a determined pace.

The subterranean world proved less barren than the surface. Fernlike plants clung to the outcrops, their palmate leaves sprinkled with moisture. A tiny corpse, its bleached skull crushed by a passing foot many years past, was unmistakably avian. An insect scurried through a pool of luminosity into a hole in the rock.

Save for the scuff of their boots and the occasional plink of a pebble tumbling into the abyss, they walked in silence. The air remained clean and moist. Seams of globestone provided just enough light to see by. A rock bridge, high above, united the two sides of the gorge, but the company passed beneath. Puffs of sleet fluttered down, blown through funnels and crannies in the rock. At last, the ascent levelled and widened until it reached a plain, punctuated in all directions by stone columns. The rockscape resembled an impenetrable maze, complicated by a rising mist. Mere coils of smoke at first, the vapour thickened until they could not see their own feet. Cosmo looked uncertain. At every column, a guard would point the way ahead. He could not have been here in a long time, if ever.

Sigurd moved alongside Morag. 'Compasses don't work down

here, and the mist can come without warning. So we crowned a few columns with sculpted heads to make a permanent map. This is the bear who gazes towards the eagle. You quickly learn the sequence.'

Well above the mist, a finely carved bear's head, whiskers and all, peered ahead.

'My father was one of the sculptors, and so was the second Lord Vane. We had true camaraderie, in those days.'

They followed the sculpted heads until Heorot came into view. The glow of its windows and the soaring architecture brought words to mind, all apposite, but none descriptive of the whole: *chalet* for the balconies on every upper floor; *castle* for the crenellations along the roofline and the drawbridge over a stream; *garret* for the bars over the windows – recently added, to judge from their gleam; *mansion* for the double oak entrance doors and the two carved columns on either side; and *lighthouse* for the huge globestone clasped in the hands of a phoenix which topped the edifice.

The door uttered a metallic greeting as the inner workings of an elaborate lock unwound, releasing a bevy of young men and women, who swarmed around the arrivals, gathering baggage and shaking hands.

Lady Vane turned to Morag. 'Odd,' she said, 'that my husband should delve so deep.'

But not so odd, once you entered Heorot's Great Hall, an open atrium many storeys high, overlooked by interior galleries on every floor. Morag had only seen two lit fires in her life – one in the tavern at Winterdorf and the other in the communal dining room on Deception Island. Neither compared with this blazing hearth. The wood had a petrified appearance, and the flames were streaked with green. On the panelled walls hung oil paintings – landscapes, portraits and abstracts – with sculpted heads on brackets between them, not unlike those on the rock columns outside.

Cosmo turned to the servants. 'Put the fancy boy down there and the Spire girl up there.'

Morag gritted her teeth; two floors apart and on opposite sides.

'Put Miss Spire next to me and I'll keep an eye,' said Lady Vane.

Cosmo rounded on the nearest servant. 'And get them clothes for tomorrow, with decent boots.'

'My Lord, it's been a long time.'

Cosmo spun round – not that he needed to; the voice was as distinctive as the dress and posture.

Mander, in full regalia, was proffering a single glass, brimful with a green liquid topped with a light foam. Two others, one orange and another green, remained on the salver. 'Your favourite, my Lord, in memory of old times.' Mander nodded in Morag's direction. 'If it isn't Spire's child . . .'

'Not you again,' barked Cosmo, downing the green liquid. 'What happened to that retirement of yours?'

Cosmo's hardcore supporters tittered.

'Self-service pales, after a time,' replied Mander.

'Well, I'll give you this. Your green sludge is better than the piss on the *Ceres*, so get cracking.'

Mander gave the orange glass to Lady Vane and the green one to Morag.

'How the hell did you get here, Mander?' Cosmo asked.

'Craft of one kind and another.'

Cosmo turned to Sigurd. 'You said two unexpected visitors. Who's the other?'

A weakness, thought Morag, this impatience. Cosmo had asked Mander a penetrating question, but could not be bothered to see it through. Mander shimmied away with the empty glasses.

'We had a problem, my Lord.' Sigurd pointed at the huge lock on the main entrance door. 'We needed an expert, and Mr Jinx was equal to the task. You may remember him from the functionality shop in the old Tempestas Dome.'

Morag did remember. She and Lady Vane had passed Jinx's Emporium in the run-up to the Tempestas party. He had not been at home.

The door beside the fireplace opened to admit the master locksmith. Jinx outdid all the unusual-looking people Morag had met on her travels. A silver thatch of hair framed a face where nothing matched. Eyes, eyebrows, mouth, teeth and ears were all in imbalance. His hands danced, as if their long and elegant fingers were playing an invisible instrument, and he moved with balletic grace.

'My father designed it,' said Jinx, 'but age, alas, catches up with us all. So the regrettable fault with the thirteenth flange should not be laid at his door.' His voice had a singsong quality and the belt at his waist, festooned with microtools of all shapes and sizes, tinkled as he spoke.

'Do you service weapons?' interjected Cosmo.

Jinx hopped from foot to foot. 'Animation, locks, functionality and childish wonder are my stock-in-trade,' he replied. 'Not the toys of death.'

'Fuck childish wonder, our crossbows take an age to load! Get him the needful, find him a table out the back, and get down to it *now*,' ordered Cosmo.

'He entertains, too,' said Sigurd. 'We had a sample last night. Perhaps after we've eaten?'

'What is he – a senile acrobat who farts in tune? Tell him he's one night to prove himself, or he'll be the first trophy on that wall.'

Lady Vane lowered the tension. 'I'd like to put my feet up, and I'm sure Miss Spire feels the same.'

'Dinner at the bell,' declared Sigurd. 'You have a good hour, your Ladyship.'

Lady Vane followed her luggage out, and Morag followed Lady Vane, after giving Benedict a discreet wave.

'My husband made this place in his own image,' said Lady Vane, as they climbed several flights past walls hung with woodcuts and paintings.

Morag's small room had a cosy simplicity: a single bed, a single light, a single clothes hook on the back of the door, all fashioned in wood. On the wall hung a single drawing of a hare, ostensibly by Dürer, but with a caption in a modern hand: *Enlarged from the original*. It was unmistakably Fogg's work. He must have done it during his stay in Lord Vane's quarters in the Genrich Dome. For the first time, she rather missed his stumbling presence.

She dozed until the dinner bell.

Underground plants and fungi made a pungent salad. Mander busied to and fro with drinks of diverse colour and consistency.

Cosmo, his mother and Sigurd sat at a separate table. Morag positioned herself within earshot and heard Sigurd's proposal.

'After the show, my Lord, you could try your luck in the tower – or should I say *skill*. It's a maze, of sorts, which your father created.'

'I've seen the plans. The whole thing needs gingering up. Visit my Circus, and you'd understand.' He paused. 'No worries about tomorrow?'

'Lord Sine's note was clear they'd be ready. You wanted a test, my Lord. I suspect we'll have one.'

Mander bustled up. He bowed deeper to Lady Vane and her son than anyone else.

'Would your Lordship wish to partake of more salad?'

Cosmo thumped his glass on the table. 'I would like five leaves exactly, symmetrically arranged.'

Men nearby cheered and joined in.

'Three for me, in a star shape!'

'Four, perfectly halved!'

Mander treated the orders as if they were just that, fulfilled to the half leaf, each delivered to the right recipient. The abuse he ignored.

'Not for me, thank you,' said Sigurd, when his turn came.

Lady Vane leavened a gesture of refusal with a smile.

Mander's maltreatment ended when Jinx re-entered with a trunk on wheels, inscribed on the top: *Jinx's Emporium*. A miscellany of objects emerged, from telescoped struts to strings of tiny lights and curtains. A miniature theatre took shape like an old-world Punch and Judy show. A rack of instruments in different shapes and sizes appeared from a smaller trunk. They looked like ear trumpets.

'Speaking horns,' announced Jinx, before dragging this second box behind the theatre and then disappearing himself.

'I'm not a child, Jinx. This better be good,' shouted Cosmo.

Mander reappeared and cleared the tables.

The theatre's curtains quivered, and a thunderous alien voice declared, 'The Jinx Emporium presents *The First Labour of Heracles*.'

Cosmo's men looked at Cosmo for a lead.

Cosmo looked at Sigurd and nodded. 'Good start! Good subject!' he bayed.

Morag had never heard Cosmo bestow an unqualified compliment before, and she wondered why. His men drummed the floor with their feet, and the curtains parted.

Tiny points of light twinkled between ribbons of cloud which sedately eased their way across the backcloth. In the foreground, a shield, sword, club, bow and quiver rested against each other. Alongside slept a man, whose heavy bearded face suggested great size.

A child, minuscule by comparison, entered with an adult sense of purpose. His painted papier-mâché face and curly hair had a cherubic quality. The giant did not stir. The boy addressed the hero through his dreams.

'You tell the gods you crave fame to last to the world's end. As the oracle told you, you have twelve tasks to complete, and with them will come immortality. Prepare to meet the first, and know his golden hide turns the arrow and the spear.'

Half-light gave way to sunrise. The giant stirred, gathered his equipment and set off. The backcloth scrolled, moving the hero from bare ground to rocks, to scrub and on to tall spearheaded grass.

They heard the beast before they saw him – a roar so loud and feral that a maid dropped her tray. The backcloth stilled as Jinx's Nemean lion rose from the undergrowth.

Heedless of the boy's advice, Heracles fired arrows, which bounced off the lion's hide. The beast leapt, and Heracles discarded his bow for his club, but its swinging arc likewise had no effect. Man and beast rolled over. Legs braced, Heracles hauled himself back to his feet. The lion's claws scored crimson stripes in Heracles' side, but, with an acrobatic wrestler's spin, the hero reversed his postion and seized the beast from behind in a stranglehold. A speaking horn delivered a crescendo of deafening roars.

The lion's neck audibly snapped, and its great body went limp. The giant skinned the carcase with one of the lion's claws and marched offstage with the skin about his bloodied shoulders like a cloak.

Darkness brought the boy's return. He buried his hands in the innards of the beast and extracted five brilliant lights. A celestial ladder appeared, which the boy ascended. He picked out the constellation of Leo with punctilious care; immortality for killer and victim alike.

The curtain came down without cheers or abuse; instead, there was a complimentary silence, which Cosmo broke with the tersest of announcements.

'Tomorrow, it's our turn to shine. Down at the bell. Guests – and relations – over thirty are exempted.'

'Such magic is rare, these days,' Lady Vane said to Jinx.

'Legerdemain and technical know-how are not magic. If only they were.'

'You persuaded us to suspend belief,' replied Lady Vane.

'I'd say *disbelief*, your Ladyship. Children exercise this muscle all the time, for so much is new to them. We adults get mired in the familiar, and our sense of wonder wastes away. Talking of youth, how is my most brilliant pupil?'

Lady Vane looked nonplussed.

'Your daughter, my Lady.'

'Oh, she keeps herself to herself,' replied Lady Vane brusquely, before turning to Morag. 'Up we go.'

Lying on her bed, Morag pondered the complexities. Under the second Lord Vane, Heorot had been a place of art, diversion and civilised discourse. Now, Cosmo was out to exorcise these agreeable ghosts and impose his own vision. But what ideal was he pursuing? Male camaraderie and a cult of himself as hero? If only Cassie would stride in and return Heorot to its gentler past.

Morag tried the door, already locked. She tiptoed to the small window. Not so far away, a globestone lantern, strong enough to illuminate the surrounding columns, was on the move. Not for the first time, she cursed the loss of the Long Eye.

She lay on the bed again, hands cupped behind her head. She had stumbled aimlessly from square to square, from the golden forest with its frozen hunt to Cassie's cottage, to Winterdorf, to Deception Island and the College of Novelties, and, now, to Heorot. Death, or the threat of death, had been her constant companion.

She dreamt of an island, dry and bleached like the dust of decayed bones. Offshore waves combed, and brilliant seabirds soared and dived just for the hell of it. But no wave broke and the island's solitary tree, dead and outstretched like a beggar's hand, remained untenanted. If only one brilliant bird of passage would alight; if only one white horse would canter ashore.

Down in the Great Hall, Cosmo dismissed the servants and turned to Jinx, whose theatre had all but returned to the two trunks.

'I make a study of the weaknesses of my more talented subjects,' said Cosmo. 'You know yours, I assume.'

'A love of fine gems is no vice,' replied Jinx.

'And a collection without a ruby is no collection.'

'I've a chip or two.'

'Rubies don't chip. You need a diamond even to scratch them.'

'I was referring to their size and quality. Poorly cut and of mediocre colour.'

'Then you'll appreciate this.' Cosmo opened the palm of his hand.

'A star ruby,' Jinx muttered breathlessly.

'The rarest and most valuable, cut in the cabochon style.' Cosmo held the stone close to the fire. 'It has a tiny, brilliant orange flaw, right at its centre. Meaning it's natural.'

'The work of millions of years,' stuttered Jinx, wide-eyed.

'And the work of a minute to pass on.' He tossed the stone into the air and caught it again. 'It's called the Heart of the Mountain.' Cosmo paused, allowing the stone to work its magic. 'All I need is the location of Lady Vane's private estate.'

Jinx's incredulity showed, so mundane was the labour. 'Surely you know.'

'I wouldn't ask if I did. People only enter her domain in her craft, and she guards the coordinates. The place is too small for the weather-watchers to locate, and she's very choosy about visitors. But, in these precarious times, I feel a filial obligation to keep an eye.'

'And if Lady Vane doesn't take me there?'

Cosmo grinned and closed his palm. 'No dice.' He paused. 'But I think she will.'

14

Piety's Dilemma

It had been a hard sell.

'I don't see the point of them,' Polychronis had declared as they strolled around the main quad in the College of Novelties.

'The point of parties is pleasure.'

'How long do they last?'

'As long as you want them to.'

'What kind of pleasure?'

The wretched man seemed as black and white as his wretched books. Good and bad had to be weighed to the last ounce. She ticked off the ingredients by flicking the forefinger of her right hand over the fingers of her left, one by one.

'In the white book, we have music old and new, inconsequential conversation, observing others at play, best food and drink, peacock clothing, if that's your thing.' She reversed hands. 'No hatred, a chance for love or sex, unarranged encounters, unexpected discoveries.'

'And the black book?'

Polychronis was so literal-minded that Piety gave it to him straight.

'You get stuck with a bore. You store up a hangover. Or, worst of all, the festival spirit eludes you. But I'm sure you wouldn't let that happen.'

But he would, she thought. Polychronis wore a pained here-we-go-again expression, as if parties had brought mankind to its knees.

'Oh, yes, and the clearing up,' she added with a smile. 'But you can delegate that.'

Another gulp from Polychronis. 'That's not my style, nor the college's. We all muck in.'

Piety tried another route: 'You don't have a book on parties. Consider it an experiment. Your students and my guards are in favour, and I'll do the organising. I could make it an order, but I'd rather not.'

Polychronis' face brightened, as if he'd stumbled on a benefit hitherto overlooked. 'All right, but three hours max, and we stop at ten *sharp*.'

Piety felt a shift in the sands. Was Polychronis playing a game? Was there more to him and the college than met the eye?

Word travelled fast. The promise of festivities drew into view the college's full community from the warren of staircases and the humbler dwellings beyond the college wall. Numbers swelled to such a degree that Piety would have worried that her force could be overwhelmed by the inmates, had armed confrontation not been so obviously foreign to their make-up.

A committee was formed. Musicians were chosen. Candles were collected and their positions decided. As to costume, Piety removed the distinction between occupied and occupiers. All would be unidentifiable.

'The college has paper and coloured ink in abundance,' she declared. 'We shall mask ourselves in papier mâché.'

To her surprise, Polychronis joined in, busying himself with the lighting and the acoustics for outdoor music, and even releasing a liberal supply of mint julep.

'A warm glow is what we're after,' he informed the committee.

The college's occupants fashioned masks of old-world life forms, and Piety's contingent, men and women, followed suit.

On the night in question, the weather behaved, candles blazed and musicians struck up in the garden quad. Drink flowed, and conversation with it.

Piety, wearing the gauzy wings of a praying mantis, found

Polychronis standing alone at the base of the Mound. His mask, an owl, was askew.

'So this is a party!' Polychronis took a sip of mint julep and broke into song:

> *'Grant me the spume of the whale,*
> *The squawk of a cross macaw,*
> *The pangolin's nose,*
> *The sloth's six toes,*
> *A tumbling sea and a shore.*
> *Rid me of reefs of plastic,*
> *The breath of carriage and car,*
> *Let's trip the light fantastic*
> *And watch a voyaging star . . .'*

That fool Potts, in Winterdorf, had sung similar anthems to the lost. Spilt milk, in Piety's view, and about as much use as Simul's scattering of bird life. But the warmth of his rich, melodious baritone did strike a chord. Polychronis, the man she had judged him to be, could not have owned it or sung with such feeling. Still, he remained an unobservant fool. The true reason for the party was, of course, diversion.

'Forgive me,' she said, 'party planners have constant duties. I'll be back.'

She made her way to the library, which was conveniently empty and unlocked. It had to hold more than judgements on the past. The rows of bookshelves had no obvious scheme alphabetically or by subject matter.

She searched for buttons, levers or switches without success. In frustration, she punched a shelf of white books on the pluses of nuclear fission. It spun on its axis and black books appeared on the other side addressing the negatives, from fissile waste to the perils of mass destruction.

She retraced her steps. The change had opened up a new passageway. The next bookcase to spin opened another new path, which led deeper into the maze. Trial and error revealed that only cases with books of one colour revolved, and they did so alternately. After twelve further rotations, she found herself facing a solid door, the first since the library entrance.

Despite the fortified frame and two elaborate keyholes, it was unlocked.

She tiptoed into a square room. A table at the centre had chairs at each side, and its surface was occupied by sheets of paper, a microscope and tweezers. Scientific instruments covered the wall shelves.

Bzz. Bzzzz. Bzzz.

The pitch fluctuated between irregular pauses.

She traced the noise to an opaque smoked-glass container. She held it up and turned it round. Inside, a shadow moved as if drawn to the ceiling light.

Intrigued, she unscrewed the lid. A tiny old-world creature flew straight at her face. The insect jabbed at her cheek and the bridge of her nose – not pinpricks, but slicing bites. She flailed with her hands as blood flowed, and stumbled back, scattering test tubes on the floor. The insect switched to her hands. *My eyes*, she thought. *It's after my eyes.* The whine of its wings had a ferocious intensity.

She faced an impossible dilemma: remove her hands and expose her eyes, or cover her eyes and have her hands reduced to bloody stumps. She screamed.

Snap!

Silence.

'You had only to ask,' said a familiar voice. Polychronis opened the book in which he had sandwiched her attacker. A splash of scarlet, like a Rorschach drawing, disfigured two facing pages. 'They blind and then they burrow,' he added.

'Yuk,' stammered Piety, but her mind raced. She had lived too long in danger's shadow to miss the obvious inference. 'That was a well-timed entry.'

'You should have mentioned espionage opportunities in your list of party pluses,' replied Mr Polychronis. 'Here.'

She accepted his offer of a handkerchief. 'You wanted me to get this far. You wanted me to discover this room.'

'I didn't want you to open the jar.' Polychronis moved to a drawer and extracted a roll of bandage and a tin of safety pins.

Enraged by her own folly, Piety lost her temper. 'You're not answering the question. You'd do well to remember who's in charge, here. I could have you—'

'Hung, drawn and quartered? Reduced to ash? Crucified?'

Piety bit her lip. Cosmo had inflicted such cruelties, and she had done nothing to stop him. The image of the elderly Miss Baldwin falling to her death, and the Dark Circus' ringmaster pierced with arrows, still troubled her sleep.

'But I'll happily answer your question,' Polychronis continued. 'Misapplied ambition will be the end of us all. I brought you here in the hope you might keep an eye on your master's plans.'

'There are no secrets between me and Lord Vane.'

'Hence your value to us.'

'I meant I keep nothing from him.'

'I don't believe you. Those who live in fear always have secrets.'

Piety changed the subject. 'What was that thing and where did it come from? And why's it *your* secret?'

'It's – it was – an insect.'

'Were all old-world insects like that?'

Polychronis shook his head. 'This is a new-world insect of our making.' He pulled up a chair for himself and another for Piety.

She sat down, still dabbing her face. 'Oh dear, not a lecture,' she said.

Polychronis persevered. 'The first Lord Vane built the college after discovering a tree which kept the murk at bay.'

Piety could not resist the urge to impress her rescuer: 'You mean the tree in your cloister.'

'He intended its progeny to clear the air in stages. Paradise regained, in other words. But – disaster – the tree proved infertile. So, Lord Vane turned to Lord Sine, who subjected grafts and cuttings to all manner of gene-splicing without success. But something went wrong. The resulting vegetal matter absorbed other genetic material in storage and turned rogue. It made a seed of itself, which Gilbert Spire discovered in a secure coffer when working for Genrich. Only it wasn't secure, and now it's out there, on the rampage. Good news if you like clean air, bad if you dislike insects dedicated to our extinction. They come from one particular fruit, by the way, ready-made. Question: what would the present Lord Vane do with these creatures?'

'Weaponise them,' replied Piety without thinking.

'I agree,' said Polychronis, retrieving a tube of ointment from the drawer. 'A college invention – a salve which heals, disinfects, and hides the scar. A black volume under *Medicines* records the downside: the staple ingredient is the seed of a very rare plant.'

Piety surprised herself by making a moral choice. 'Just the face wound, then.'

Polychronis bandaged her fingers and applied the salve, which instantly stemmed the bleeding and cooled the ravaged skin.

'Where did you get your charming specimen?'

'See – I knew you'd be a perfect double agent. You ask the right questions.'

'And the answer is?'

Polychronis hesitated. To trust or not to trust? He slapped the dome of his forehead, as if that might provide the answer.

'We have a craft,' he said. '*Simul*, by name – built by the Northerners, long ago, in their favoured materials. A two-seater, made of wood and glass. It chanced on a patch of clear air above a forest in flower before being attacked by a swarm of flies. The blue ones attacked the craft; the red tried to get at the pilots. We brought back a few specimens, one or two alive. There was a single dominant tree, with the ability to move at speed. It's all very concerning. But *gather ye rosebuds while ye may . . .*' Polychronis stood up. 'Now, what was it you said I mustn't do? Lose the party spirit. To the dance!'

Polychronis delivered one last surprise. When the assembled quintet slipped into old-world traditional jazz, he pulled terrible faces and waved his arms as if in agony. But his feet! They flickered out and in, heel to toe and toe to heel, knees flexing and unflexing in perfect time. Extraordinary to tell – the prosaic Polychronis had rhythm!

When the music slowed, Polychronis and Piety did not hold each other close, but their bodies bumped together from time to time, and not entirely by accident.

That night, Piety sat in front of her Morse-code machine and agonised. *Suss out this place* had been her instruction. Duty before sentiment, she decided.

Tap, tap-tap, tap . . .

Her expert fingers reported all – the tree in the cloister, the rampant growth as a by-product of Genrich's and Spire's research, the gift of clear air, the bane of the murderous flies, the college's research in the library's inner sanctum, and the fact that, whether teachers or dons, the community was more numerous than it had previously appeared.

The response was prompt and in Cosmo's staccato style:

How did they get these specimens?

In a craft.

How? These flies consume metal.

She bit her lip. She had missed a point of importance.

The college has a craft made of wood and glass. It must be immune to the flies.

Cosmo's reply was brutally short:

Forget tantalum.

To Piety, this sounded crazy – so crazy, she tapped before thinking.

Forget tantalum?

That rare mineral had dominated their lives for so long.

We enter a new world. The murk goes. Solar energy is back, save that this plant faces off against us. We're all destroyed or I rule.

In the early hours, she woke and went to her window. The party's debris had been cleared. An inmate or two, anonymous in long black gowns, continued to exercise on the Mound on the quarter hour – up, the double leaps, out of sight, and then back. Moonlight bathed the gardens.

You cannot serve two masters. She had made the coward's choice. A single tear slipped down her cheek, not a tear of sorrow or rage, but of disappointment with herself – a deeper wound than any insect could inflict.

15

The Sixth Labour

In Heorot, Lady Vane, Jinx and Mander ignored the first morning bell, following Cosmo's announcement of their exclusion from the expedition the previous evening, but three of Cosmo's men were also absent, among them a wiry figure with a weaselly face.

Everyone else was present, including the lith. One side table held food, mostly from Rearrangers. Armour and weapons littered the other tables. Sigurd handed Morag and Benedict breast- and backplates and assisted with the straps.

'Cumbersome, but lifesavers,' he said, 'and take gloves, too. Only hands can protect the eyes.'

'So, we *are* going?' asked Morag.

'His Lordship insists.'

'Without weapons?' intervened Benedict.

Also Cosmo's orders, Sigurd's answering shrug implied, though it did not necessarily suggest that he approved of them.

Benedict merely grinned.

'And the enemy?' asked Morag.

'You know how his Lordship likes surprises,' said Sigurd, 'but I fear there will be casualties.'

'If need be, we'll arm ourselves from the fallen,' said Benedict.

'Just keep close,' replied Sigurd sternly.

Benedict's mock-heroic stance disturbed Morag. He had rallied the defenders during the brief siege of Winterdorf, but without this new look of martial enthusiasm. She caught a smile, but not directed at her – rather, it was intended for a maid who brushed against his rear as she passed. Had he moved his hip towards her? Morag could not be sure. She rebuked herself. She had never known jealousy and did not intend to succumb now. She had no rights over him. He had to be won, *if* he was worth winning. That question had not hitherto troubled her, but it did now.

'Go for leather to cover the rest of you,' continued Sigurd.

'Don't patronise me,' Morag replied testily.

He tossed her a helmet, dark as ebony, and so heavy that she buckled on catching it.

'Wear that for ten minutes, and you'll have a stiff neck and a raging headache – handicaps you don't need.' He took back the helmet and handed her a leather cap. 'Steel strips hide beneath the padding. I myself prefer its flexibility, but his Lordship goes for the classical touch.'

Sigurd pointed across the hall, where Cosmo was donning weapons and armour worthy of a royal burial hoard. Cosmo called out the name of each piece as if summoning wayward children: *Lacero* (a spear), *Aegis* (a shield with a boar's head in the centre), *Falco* (a short bow), *Jarn* (his gauntlets) and *Orvar* (his armour). His short sword he modestly addressed as *Cosmo*, as if to fashion a new legend. The equipment worn by others, ordinary by comparison, shared sufficient stylistic features to mark its wearers as his followers.

Benedict handed Morag a pair of thick leather gloves.

'They're a tight fit, but a firm grip matters in battle,' he said, like a seasoned veteran.

'And you wear a leather helmet,' she responded tartly.

All around, men were arming themselves. The fire had died, and a chill air steamed their breath. Cosmo did not linger. He raised his sword, pointed and led the way out across the bridge.

Beyond stood three lightly built two-wheeled chariots. The centre one, higher, wider and more ornate, accommodated Cosmo and two attendants bearing his armour and shield. Sigurd, with his more modest spear and long sword, took the right-hand chariot with Benedict and Morag. On the left, the lith's chariot had been piled high with equipment, the purpose of which was obscure. Two of the more heavily built men, each in lighter armour, drew each chariot. Of the others, the more nimble occupied either wing, like skirmishers in a battle from antiquity. Three men, well spaced out, trotted in front with globestone lanterns aloft.

Cosmo raised an arm.

'Silence all the way. These caverns carry sound, and we need to get close before they see or hear us. Any creature constructed by Lord Sine will be intelligent and designed to wipe us out. They're his proxies, and this is a battle with him as well as them. Spears must protect the bowmen, not swords. If you need them, we're in trouble.'

Morag shook her head in disgust. Cosmo Vane had placed this order to feed his own legend. Also, but for her father's intervention, Lord Sine would have bested him at Deception Island. Defeating this challenge was designed to impress, if not to restore parity.

The chariot men leant forward and set off at a trot, despite their burdens. The flanking soldiers kept pace. The shadows came and went as the lantern bearers passed through the forest of columns. Morag was glad of the chariot; AIPT had promoted flexibility more than stamina. She memorised the carved faces and their sequence, just in case. Despite the mandated silence, the crunch of boots and the mild squeak of chariot wheels still carried an echo. They passed the defile path which had brought them here and entered new territory.

Occasional eddies of snow still puffed down, leaving haphazard splashes of white. *Like guano from a gigantic bird*, thought Morag, only for the simile to turn real.

Cosmo's chariot wheel turned on a white patch of a different consistency. He called a halt to examine the deposit. Its cones and jagged spikes had set like concrete. Sigurd's chariot pulled up alongside. He dismounted, snapped off a spike and wiped a finger along its length.

'It must be them. We placed the eggs half a mile or so from here.' Cosmo gestured a lantern bearer forward.

'Take a spearman and check for more, but not too far forward, and don't run.'

The pair advanced almost to the point of disappearance and then halted, before returning to report.

'There are many more stains and a jagged fissure not far from where we stopped,' said the lantern bearer. 'It looks deep.'

'How far?'

'A hundred metres at most,' said the spearman.

'But nothing moving,' added the lantern bearer. The two men spoke alternately, like a rehearsed double act.

'How wide is the fissure?' asked Cosmo.

'Too wide to leap,' replied the lantern bearer.

'Too wide to bridge with a deconstructed chariot?' asked Sigurd.

'That would be my guess,' replied the spearman. 'We thought we heard hissing,' he added, 'but it could be one of those random winds you get down here.'

'From below the fissure?' asked Cosmo.

'From the darkness beyond,' said the lantern bearer.

'I said they were intelligent beings. Close ranks and form up. No chariots from here. Seventy metres from the fissure, we stop and send in our scarer.'

A bull of a man, one of Cosmo's chariot haulers laid out the pile of accoutrements from the lith's chariot and, with the aid of others, transformed himself into a creature of iron, encased in armour from head to foot. His helmet's eye holes had long spikes for protection. In each hand, he held a pair of wooden boards tied together with cord.

From the other side of the ravine, foul-smelling ribbons of vapour snaked towards them.

They trudged forward in a crescent formation, with Cosmo alone in the lead, shield held in front, spear to the side, with the iron man just behind him. The fissure cut through the floor. From a distance, its uneven course resembled a dark river, and the reconnaissance report had been accurate – too broad to cross or bridge. The hissing had a gurgling undersound, and the white blotches on the cavern floor grew in number and dimension. Several had not set, and smeared their boots.

'That hissing noise isn't the wind,' observed Cosmo. 'Let's stir the bastards up.'

They halted halfway to the fissure. The vapour thickened into mist. The iron man stumbled on alone, chiming like a blacksmith, until the deafening clack of his giant castanets took over, his arms jerking up and down. He shuffled on at a snail's pace to a few steps from the edge of the ravine. His arms went limp; the boards clattered to the ground. The hissing turned into a cacophony of shrieks of no clear origin. He could see what they could not.

'Forward!' cried Cosmo.

For once, Cosmo's command lacked precision. At what pace should they advance? They looked to him for a lead. He crouched, shield in front and spear levelled, and moved forward as quickly as his crabbed posture allowed. Whatever else, Cosmo did not lack courage. Ahead, the iron man drifted in and out of focus as the mist thickened and thinned.

The reborn Stymphalian birds, the sixth labour of Heracles, skimmed into view like ghosts. Avian beyond doubt, the V-shaped leathery wings, the elongated beaks and the boney eye-sockets conjured a prehistoric model which Morag felt she should have foreseen. The splashes of guano had not contained a single feather. The birds floated towards them, nine in number, long legs trailing behind, reminding Morag of storks from old-world natural-history books, but their chests had no precedent, glowing as if they had each swallowed a fragment of the moon. Wing tip to wing tip, minimising the target, they broke formation only metres from the iron man, who abandoned his boards and turned to retreat.

Cosmo rushed forward, but the archers hesitated for fear of killing their comrade with their corrosive-tipped arrows.

'Let him fend for himself!' yelled Cosmo, but the order came too late.

Two of the birds landed beside the armoured giant. As nimble on the ground as in the air, despite their size, they hustled him with their beaks and wings towards the edge of the ravine. He flailed with his arms to no avail. Before Cosmo could reach him, he had toppled in. They heard a scream and the crash of armour on the rocks below. The whole flock soared high, before plummeting into the gorge with wings tucked in and beaks thrust down like spearheads.

His stricken armour rang out. Cosmo and his men rushed to the lip. Coils of mist now threaded between outcrops of rock, one of which, far below, had caught the iron man's body. The circling glow of the birds by the corpse winked like distant lanterns. The fall had been precipitous, the gorge so deep that its floor remained invisible.

'Two arrows each, in sequence,' ordered Cosmo. 'They're not to be wasted on the same target, and aim for the lights.'

'They're ravenous, remember, and have had no flesh until now,' muttered Sigurd. 'Once they've finished down there, we'll be next.'

The shrieking subsided as the birds savaged the iron man's carcase, after snapping off his armour's straps.

'They're checking out his anatomy and armour,' said the lith with a macabre smile, prompting Morag to remember that the lith, too, had been a gift from Lord Sine. How his creations had shaped their world!

A clear target proved elusive in the foggy gloom, with only the lights from the chests of the birds milling around the corpse to aim for. The swirling eddies of air added to the challenge. But strike they did.

'Two down,' cried Cosmo, 'but hold your fire for when they come back.'

Wise advice, as their quivers were already half empty. Many poisoned arrows had missed or passed through the wings without inflicting serious damage.

The gothic scene disgusted Morag. These birds had been constructed to live off meat, and faced slaughter to indulge no more than Cosmo's desire for trophies. She mourned the wasted valour of the iron man, sacrificed in the same cause. Beside her, Benedict had acquired a spear and adopted one of the clapperboards as a makeshift shield.

Six birds rose, spreading out far and wide before gliding back out of bowshot. They had learnt quickly.

'Shield wall!' bellowed Cosmo. 'The closer they bunch, the easier they'll be to hit.'

They formed a tight square, a spear pointing outward in the centre of each side, three upward spears in the middle with the bowmen.

'Let me out when I give the order!' added Cosmo, drawing his sword. 'And jab with those spears, don't throw them.'

Cosmo was giving his quarry due respect, and they returned the compliment, skimming fast over their heads from different directions in a reconnoitring sweep. Then, disturbingly, they disappeared from view.

The rock columns were denser here and provided more cover. From the spaces between them, fresh clouds of foul-smelling mist rolled towards the military party, accompanied by the familiar hissing noise. Several men spluttered and coughed.

'They're creating this damned fog,' observed Cosmo, moving his troops to the most open space he could find, a good fifty metres from the edge of the gorge.

'If I might make an observation,' said Morag, still in the centre of the square of men.

'Get on with it, then,' replied Cosmo gruffly.

'Six flew over and two died in the chasm, but there were nine to begin with. That leaves one outstanding, and I think it's larger than the others.'

Cosmo, for once, did not question her judgement. 'They're hoping we face out from the gorge,' he said. 'The one still down there is waiting to attack from the rear. Pretend we're fooled, and face out towards the columns.'

'Is this wise?' asked Sigurd.

'And sing,' said Cosmo. 'Sing anything, and be sure to sing the way you're facing. Don't look back.'

And they did. Morag sensed a tactical battle by proxy between Lord Sine and Cosmo. Lord Sine had endowed his creatures with intellect as well as brawn.

Cosmo abandoned his shield, seized his bow and crawled towards the lip of the gorge, then rose to his knees and notched an arrow. He had been right. The voices had fooled the waiting bird, which now rose from the gorge. Eyes fixed on the wall of men, it sailed high and dived towards them. As if in slow motion, Cosmo stood, drew, aimed and fired. The bird's maned crest, which the others lacked, marked it as their leader. At the last minute, it jinked, and Cosmo's arrow passed through its left shoulder, smashing the scapula and bringing it to ground. Despite the handicap, the bird sidestepped Cosmo's second shot and charged straight at him. Cosmo discarded his bow, seized his shield and couched his spear, but the bird bowled him over before Cosmo could throw it. Now at close quarters, he exchanged sword for spear, blocking the bird's stabbing motions with the shield.

'Keep your line!' bellowed Cosmo, sensing another trap.

Beyond, out of their self-created mist, the other six birds charged on foot. One fell to arrows and one to a spear from Sigurd, full in the chest, but the other four broke the defensive line and struck two dead with jabs between helmet and breastplate, the weakness they had identified from the iron man's armour.

Inexplicably to Morag, she appeared to be the focus of their attack. In consequence, the men bunched around her.

'She's the childbearer, that's why they're after her,' mumbled Benedict. His early air of martial self-confidence had deserted him. His lips worked, as if striving to bring a wind instrument to life, and he moved like a man in shock.

One of the four birds backed away, took off, turned in a tight circle and plummeted into the vanguard; another man down, but the bird fell too, impaled on a spear.

A short way back, for the birds' assault had driven them closer to the abyss, Cosmo had slashed the leading bird's second wing to ribbons, but its iron beak deflected any frontal blow and, between parries, pummelled his shield. Cosmo was tiring, his guard slipping by the minute. Soon, his neck would be exposed.

Despite his crimes, a half-sisterly urge seized Morag. She picked a spear off the ground, broke from the press and ran towards him. As the bird's head turned to face her, Cosmo lunged upwards into its throat. Behind them, Benedict and Sigurd brought down another, and the last pair, now leaderless, took off and dived into the gorge and out of sight.

They sank to their knees, the ground slick with a curdling of red and green blood.

Morag thought back to Jinx's magical show. This was the reality: several eviscerated men, seven mangled creatures defending their territory, and no boy to ascend a ladder to preserve the event for posterity. Indeed, no applause, until the lith broke an uncertain silence by raising his right arm and cheering. The other men followed.

'The singing was a masterstroke,' said Sigurd.

Cosmo nodded in acknowledgement, before hacking the head off the birds' leader.

'Heorot thanks you for your courage,' he said. 'This head is for the trophy wall, as are the names of our fallen. Strip the other dead birds clean, toe to crown. The meat looks edible, once drained of blood, and we must feast tonight. One chariot will carry the meat home, another will take our comrades. We'll bury them in the small caves in the wall of Heorot's moat. This isn't woman's work, so the Spire girl and Bene-whatever-his-name-is can try their luck elsewhere. Get your men to take them to the tower, Sigurd. They won't need weapons there.'

Sigurd selected two men.

'Perhaps I should accompany them,' intervened the lith. 'Two of those creatures are still loose, and they could leave the ravine without us knowing.'

'Let me,' said Sigurd.

'No,' replied Cosmo, 'we need you, and this is work for my bodyguard.'

A rehearsed move, thought Morag, and the casual dismissal enraged her. She had saved Cosmo's life, after all, and Benedict had fought hard.

'They never gave an inch,' interjected Sigurd gently.

'Not bad for beginners,' replied Cosmo. 'Now, off you go. It's time to see what they're made of up top, and we've butchers' work to do.'

16

The Tower of No Return

'Where are we going?' asked Morag, as soon as they were beyond Cosmo's hearing.

'The Tower of No Return,' replied the lith.

'Our old master's tower. The name is a jest, of sorts,' said the man on the left. 'We got past three puzzles, didn't we?'

His companion nodded.

'Do you two have names?' asked Morag.

'Volpone,' said the one on the left.

'Horsa,' said the one on the right.

Morag welcomed this shard of humour with a grin.

'How many floors?' asked Benedict.

'Too many to count,' said Horsa. 'Anyway, it's not the floors you have to worry about, it's the obstacles, when you can see them.'

'Less cackle, more speed,' grunted the lith.

After the din of conflict, the quiet worked like balm. Morag flexed her arms and legs. Bruises were showing, but generally the company's wounds had been either light or fatal.

Benedict broke his silence: 'Most battles are avoidable, and few achieve the object they were fought for, but there can be a just fight. But this wasn't one of them.'

'You over-philosophise,' replied the lith. 'Act passive and you get crushed. A soldier without experience is not a soldier, he's an armed man. That's all you need to know.'

Silence returned until the lith jabbed his spear towards a huge rock stack, as wide as a house. 'There,' he announced.

It did not remotely resemble the finished structure of dressed stone which had caught their eye above ground when the *Ceres* landed. The windowless exterior appeared to be a natural formation, conspicuous among the others only for its size.

Close up, idiosyncrasies emerged. Clusters of question marks had been chiselled into the rock at intervals up to head height. Higher up, occasional bricks shared the colour and consistency of the natural rock. The stone had been lightly dressed into distinct faces.

'It's obviously hollow,' said Benedict.

'Was it always?' Morag asked.

The lith shrugged. 'What does the past matter? You'll be facing the present.'

'Hollow as a flute, my father said,' Volpone confirmed, 'and, in the wind, she would sing.'

He left the stationary chariot and walked up to the column, which Benedict was already examining. He jabbed at the question marks, which flipped round and disappeared when pressed, only for another to appear elsewhere.

'We had only a few to deal with, and widely spread. They seem to have multiplied.'

'Touch them in the right sequence and the entrance will surely appear,' whispered Benedict to himself.

Morag's nostrils puckered. A trace, faint but unmistakable, of Lady Vane's scent lingered in the air. A maze of footprints patterned the dust. Most had a masculine tread, but, close by, a set of light toe and ankle prints made a perfect match for Lady Vane's boots. Morag felt an urge to distract.

'Did you come here with the second Lord Vane?' she asked Horsa and Volpone.

The lith shook his head in irritation as Volpone, the more articulate of the two, opened up.

'Of course, never without him. A challenging pleasure dome, his

Lordship used to call it. Between times, we'd sculpt, paint, map and record the vegetation. There wasn't a sword in the place.'

'Why build it here?'

'Good question, miss, good question. Far from the madding crowd, is my guess. My father said his Lordship had a wound which needed healing.'

Again, her father's ghost slipped into view. Another consequence of his affair with Lady Vane to add to a growing list. How wrong the lith was to dismiss the past as irrelevant.

Benedict's mind was elsewhere. 'We count the column's faces and then count how many groups of tiles there are,' he suggested.

Only the lith declined to join in. After cross-checking, they agreed on nine for both.

'Right,' added Benedict, the pitch of his voice elevated by the excitement of a cryptic challenge. 'Now, we search for a group with ten question marks. My guess is there'll only be one, and the rest will have nine.'

And so there was. Each question mark in the group of ten, when pressed, removed another group, leaving just one, which removed itself. The column grumbled, revealing a door of polished wood with the Tempestas sigil at its centre. Benedict pushed and it slid open.

'That's our job done,' said the lith, in the tone of an order.

Volpone shook Morag's hand with a faint bow.

'Thanks for everything,' said Morag.

'If they've changed the outside, the inside might be tougher too. Best be on your toes. As I said, we never got beyond the third puzzle, but half the puzzle is spotting the puzzles.'

Volpone added a sidelong glance at Benedict, who was already peering into the dark beyond the doorway. Morag caught a subtext: *This friend of yours, the lookalike Vane, is a threat to my new master, so beware.*

'How do we get back to Heorot?' Morag asked as the chariot turned away.

The lith offered a rare smile, more knowing than amused. 'In there, new ways open, and old ways close,' he hissed, striking the chariot floor with the base of his spear.

Like horses to a whip, Volpone and Horsa bent their backs, and the chariot disappeared at pace into the gloom.

Benedict edged his way forward. There are shades of darkness. Here, it smothered all. Morag could not see Benedict, but footsteps and voice placed him only a yard or so ahead.

'There's a flat surface ahead, blocking the way. It has a locking mechanism. My guess is we need light to get through.'

Morag's frustration boiled over. 'What's the point of all this?'

'So speaks the maker of momenticons, the world's last great distraction,' replied Benedict. 'Anyway, we haven't a choice. Keep calm, engage your brain and enjoy.' The obstacle's surface sounded like wood, to judge from the drumming of Benedict's fingers. 'There were ten questions in the crucial group,' he continued. 'Think of a word for *light* with ten letters.'

'That's too crude, Benedict. You need a word for *let there be light*. So, why not *illuminate*! Ten letters, as asked.'

High above, a sonorous male voice thundered like a divine intervention: 'You have only to ask.'

The light arrived in stages, theatrically managed. First, juxtaposed black and white floor tiles began to glow on a multitude of levels; then, the stairs, which seemed to be everywhere, also pied on over- and undersides and often turning back on themselves; then, wall lights illuminating each of the many landings. Narrow suspended canals ended in waterfalls, only for the water to double back somehow. In places, ladders replaced stairs. Other incongruous details emerged, from small boats on the narrow canals to turrets with walkways between them. The curved roof rose to a cupola, which bestowed a sunny artificial glow, adding a further interplay of light and shadow.

They had entered at ground level, facing two raised landings linked by ladders. In the centre stood a further series of landings which reached much higher, almost to the cupola itself.

The mundane obstacle in front of them caught their attention last, so mesmerising was the overhead view. A hinged counter, as in a shop or bar, ran across the entrance. On it rested a porcelain bowl, decorated with an old-world cat. Inside the bowl were nine polished wooden balls, all small, but of varying size and colour.

Benedict had been right about the lock. A simple double bolt yielded easily. Beyond the barrier, a low wall surrounded a square pond with square stepping stones at irregular intervals, blocking the way to a moored boat on a raised canal. Beyond the canal, the first ladder beckoned.

The unbroken diagonal line of eight stepping stones, from the left-hand corner to the right, looked inviting – perhaps *too* inviting.

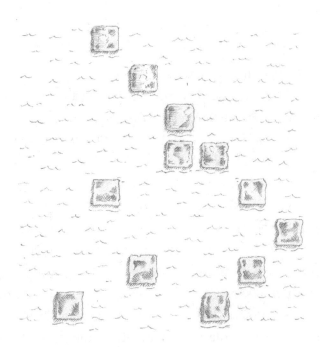

They both hesitated.

'What's the point of those balls?' asked Morag.

Benedict rolled one in the palm of his hand. 'A cat has nine lives, and there's one set of nine between us.'

'*Lives* – literally or figuratively?'

By way of an answer, Benedict tossed one on to the corner stepping stone, which disappeared beneath the surface. The ball floated briefly, before dissolving in a puff of vapour.

'Acid! So now we know for sure. It's Cosmo's version we're playing.' Benedict peered at the stepping stones. 'Imagine the pond divided into squares like a chess board, eight by eight. And imagine the stones are the only squares we can occupy. But some are lethal traps.'

'Right,' said Morag, dealing out the remaining wooden balls equally between them. 'Odds are, we're gonna need every one of these.'

The semi-divine voice which had greeted them spoke again: 'One life spent. The way is dubbed to avoid a bish.'

'I'm not sure I can take this know-it-all's running commentary. Him up there, and you down here. Talk about being between a rock and hard place.'

'Him against me,' replied Benedict.

Morag ground her grazed fingers into her thighs. *Him against me.* She might as well not exist.

In his head, Benedict devised a grid of the pond, placed the stones on the grid, including the one which had sunk, and applied his theory to separate the false friends from the true.

'*The way is dubbed,*' continued Benedict. 'We start on the knight's square and keep to knight's moves thereafter: two to the side and one forward, or two forward or back and one to the side. We avoid the bish, meaning the bishop's more direct route is fatal.'

'Story of my life,' whispered Morag.

'Our good knight joins the bishop's line on the seventh rank, which we must take to be safe, but then he jumps to the other side. We avoid the eighth-rank stone. Overall, the jumps, like a knight, are a touch crooked, so be careful.'

'Well, Cosmo wouldn't make it easy, would he?'

Benedict made the first leap comfortably, and the second so as to leave space for Morag.

'Your legs are shorter than mine, so you'll have to launch from the lip.'

Morag gritted her teeth. 'Fuck off, Benedict, all right? I do know my own legs.'

She removed her shoes, held one in each hand and took the one-pace run-up which the square allowed. She tottered on landing, but made it. She silently thanked AIPT for her new-found flexibility.

'Hold it!' cried Benedict. 'He'll penalise any repeat moves. Go left and not right on joining the diagonal.'

The glare from Morag brought silence, but she did as he suggested and, two leaps later, joined him on the far side.* Beneath their feet the floor rose, bringing them level to the canal, the walls of which were too narrow to walk. The ascent had been silent and smooth, a tribute to the quality of the engineering.

'Just think of the effort invested in this place. God knows how Volpone solved three,' Morag grumbled.

'He had a different host, with a different game.'

'Do you think he's watching us suffer? Cosmo, I mean.'

Benedict ignored the question. A small coracle, just big enough for two, bobbed up and down on the canal in front of them. The current flowed unhelpfully towards them. As Benedict clambered in, the semi-divine presence intervened again in a rich singing voice:

> 'Row, row, row the boat,
> Gently down the stream,
> Merrily, merrily, merrily, merrily,
> Life is but a dream.'

'Well, that's straightforward,' said Benedict. 'We have to paddle.'

'If you think I'm going to dabble my hands in that brine . . .' She took a ball from her pocket.

---

* THE SOLUTION TO THE STEPPING-STONE PUZZLE CAN BE FOUND ON PAGE 354.

'Don't waste it. The coracle couldn't survive in the acid. It's a mind game. Keep your cool.'

Annoyingly, he was right. The water, this time, was unadulterated and refreshing, but the harder they paddled, the stronger the current ran against them.

'We could just wade across.'

'Please don't. So far, the advice from on high has been cryptic, but true.'

'I begin to wonder who's the biggest know-all, you or him up there.'

Benedict smiled. 'The world is illusional. Water flows uphill; stairs descend, but finish higher up. In fact . . .' He paused. 'We should paddle with the current, *down* the stream, as the man says.' They did so, and, bizarrely, the coracle drifted in reverse, upstream, to the far side.

'Contrariwise,' muttered Morag, in memory of the psychotic twins, Dum and Dee.

But she had lost concentration. Five circular paving stones ran from the landing stage to a waiting ladder – four incised with the grinning mask of comedy and one in the centre with the drooping mouth of tragedy. Being in the stern seat, Morag disembarked first and could not resist the ladder as the nearest take-off point to the next landing.

As her feet struck tragedy's mask, it accelerated sharply upwards, turning as it went. Morag had to jump on the spot, so as not to be spun into space, arms out wide to keep balance. It halted its upward progress thirty feet up, where the rotation finally ceased.

'Shit,' she screamed.

'*Merrily, merrily, merrily, merrily* . . . I did say,' uttered the semi-divine voice in a patronising tone. 'Four merry stones to choose from and you land on the glum one. But you can still bow out in style, if you're quick.'

'We'll find a way,' said Benedict, but his examination of the column revealed only a raised green thread, as on a screw, curling its way up.

A chip from Morag's pedestal fell, reducing her standing room even further. *If you're quick.* She could see the curling green thread with tiny leaves attached, reminiscent of Cassie Vane's clematis. She manoeuvred herself so she lay flat across the stone and could reach it. The stem had to be Tempestas' work; only the texture betrayed its artificiality. At the top of the stem, a single five-petalled flower faced her. It had anthers, but a circular hole where the style should be. *Bow out in style.* Thank God her father had taught her the parts of old-world plants. She fumbled in her pocket. Another chip fell, and another, giving the reduced stone a jagged edge which bit into her stomach.

'What are you doing?' brayed Benedict from below. 'It's disintegrating!'

She ignored him. She checked her four balls against the hole. The smallest wooden 'life' fitted the cavity perfectly. She released the ball and heard it scurry down the stem through where the style would have been. Gears activated, cogs kicked in, and the column descended back to ground level.

'What was it you said, Benedict, about keeping calm and engaging your brain?'

'I stand corrected,' he said gracefully.

They ascended the first ladder to a bare chequerboard landing and continued on up the second to the next floor without difficulty – a rarity, in this twisted place. No collapsing rungs or electric currents, and nothing from the voice. A banister rail held flowerpot trays. Morag recognised imitation plants from the woods at the edge of the Tempestas Dome. Invisible from below, the platform also housed a miscellany of model fauna in what appeared to be grey stone-like pumice: a pigeon, a huge butterfly, a rat sneaking along the rail, a kitten and, slithering through the plants, a snake. Morag stroked the kitten. A light dust stained her hands.

'We're still marooned at the edge of the tower,' said Benedict. 'We have to work our way to the central stack.'

Morag could only agree. They had reached the maximum height of their sequence of landings. The central platforms started not far below them, supported at ground level by a forest of spiked stilts rising from an island. The surrounding water had the grey-green hue of the toxic pond which had provided their first conundrum. The gap between them and the nearest central platform was unbridgeable without assistance – and the voice declined to offer any.

'Just when you want a clue, he goes word-shy,' protested Morag, hoping to provoke the unseen presence.

No luck, silence.

'Is it the plants or the creatures, or neither?' asked Benedict.

'I don't think your quizmaster would sink as low as a repeat answer. It's not the plants, which leaves the creatures or something else.'

But what else? She could see no other candidate. On close examination, each creature offered a small circular cavity, but of slightly varying sizes, which appeared to match the variations in their surviving 'lives'.

'He's offering a lazy way out. Use up our lives on guesswork, and we'll be in trouble later.' Morag had another flash of inspiration. 'Lord Sine never loaded you with children's games, did he?'

'Children play chess, Morag.'

'I mean simpler games, which turn on luck. Like *snakes* and ladders.'

'Sorry?'

'It's a board game. All turns on the throw of a dice. Ladders take you up, snakes take you down. It fits. We've come up, and we want to go down. Easy peasy.' She checked the hole in the tip of the snake's tail against her remaining lives. 'One of yours, I'm afraid – unless it's the one you threw in the pond.'

Benedict smiled. 'Or the one you used to get back. Anyway, I have a duplicate.'

'That's not an answer and you know it. We may need two of the same.'

'We may, we may not.'

Benedict did have the perfect fit. As the ball slipped through the hole, they both recoiled. In a puff of dust, the snake unwound itself, revealing a brilliant green skin stamped with contiguous ochre diamond shapes along its back. A black forked tongue flickered, as if smelling the air.

'Don't worry, it isn't real,' stammered Morag without conviction.

'It certainly isn't. No snake could do that.'

The false reptile, the end of its tail locked around the banister rail, extended itself further and further into space until it reached the balustrade of the nearest landing on the central stack. Having secured its head, it tautened to form – in effect, a rope bridge.

'Creatures from Jinx's Emporium can do anything,' muttered Morag.

She climbed on to the rail and swung herself, hand over hand, along the serpent's body to its head. The skin, though cold and smooth, was not unduly slippery and held firm. Benedict gingerly followed. The snake, its mouth now frozen in a rictus grin, remained impassive.

'We've done it!' cried Benedict.

The new platform was bare of decoration. Two spiral staircases, their steps alternately black and white, curled up to the next level.

Morag broached a more delicate mystery: 'I forgot to tell you. Lady Vane has been here in the last hour or two. Well, not here exactly, but outside.'

'She frets. I'm all she has left,' Benedict replied nonchalantly.

All she has left, as if Cassie Vane did not exist.

A clack like the beat of a metronome interrupted Morag's train of thought.

Above them, a square box on a tall pole had opened to reveal an old-world clock with Roman numerals, a single black hand, like an accusing finger, and a lit white dial – but it was half a dial, thirty minutes only. The slither behind where the hand had moved had already turned black.

'We've twenty-nine minutes before darkness maroons us,' she said.

Benedict did not dissent. He climbed up the staircase nearest him, only for its spiral to descend. The faster Benedict climbed, the faster the staircase reversed. Morag tried the second staircase, with the same outcome.

'We have to synchronise the two somehow,' shouted Morag. 'Otherwise there would only be one, and they're identical, and for once all white and no black.' She was now acclimatised to the quizmaster's set of mind. Pent-up frustration burst through. 'Come on! We're almost there!'

The voice broke its extended silence: 'See the way to scale up.'
Clack.

They had consumed another five precious minutes.

'Is this another childish game?'

Play. Scale. C for see.

Morag shouted back, 'They're notes! The scale of C has no black notes.'

Benedict tried, but again the staircase countered every effort at ascent.

'No, no,' said Morag. 'As I said, there are two staircases for a reason. You go for your first step, I go for my second. Then you for your third, one after the other.'

Their feet touched the steps in sequence, like a pianist's fingers playing the keys. Any inexactness of timing brought both spirals back to their starting point. Mastering the art consumed another seven minutes.

The next landing was bare, save for a series of poles of varying heights and circumference, which supported nothing. Directly above, a wheel in the cupola held a rope ladder, fully wound and tantalisingly out of reach. Either side of it, hinged skylights hinted at access to the tower's roof and escape.

The voice uttered its last clue: 'The Overture to Wonderland.'

Clack.

Eleven minutes left.

A burst of song echoed through the tower – birdsong, but oddly disjointed. The bird on the flowerpot landing had shed its dust. Now bottle-green in plumage, it skimmed past them.

'Isn't Wonderland your department?' asked Benedict anxiously.

It had been. She and Cosmo had created momenticons to assuage the anxieties of the Genrich workers before the cull.

Clack.

Two more minutes gone.

Overture to Wonderland, the voice had said. An overture precedes the main show. She dragged her memory back to the Tempestas party. It seemed an age ago, now. There had been music at the moment of the cull, when Genrich's drugged unfortunates had wandered into the murk in search of Alice's lost crown.

But what music? A grotesque memory, long suppressed, burst through. At the party's murderous climax, an organist had played a nursery rhyme. Morag rearranged the bird's song in her head.

> *Baa, baa, black sheep,*
> *Have you any wool?*

'They're not poles, they're organ pipes,' she said. 'Different sizes for different notes, and I bet they're hollow at the top.'

'Drop in our remaining lives, and the pipes will play,' said Benedict, clapping his hands.

Clack.

Eight minutes left.

They sorted the balls to match the pipes and clambered up. Once activated, each pipe cleared its throat and released a sonorous organ blast. On the last insertion, they joined together and played the nursery tune.

High above their heads, the wheel unwound.

Benedict stretched out an arm. 'You solved it, you go first.'

She did not have to climb. The wheel wound back, raising her and the ladder to a ledge beneath the left-hand skylight. It then moved right, collecting Benedict and delivering him to the opposite skylight. Across the vertiginous space, they exchanged triumphal salutes, punching the air.

Clack.

Three minutes to open the skylights and exit.

Only then did she see the seashell. It stood on a slim stand, proud of the cornice and well within reach. Spikes rose from its back, as if in fright: a porcupine of the sea. The plinth bore one word: *Noli*. Morag recognised the word from a painting in the Museum Dome.

An image came: a garden bathed in dawn light, with a woman half-kneeling before a benign, bearded man, whose right arm is raised in gentle admonishment. Behind him stands an open tomb. On one of his nightly soliloquies, Fogg had explained. It is the Son of God, back from the dead, and, being now of another world, he warns a friend, *Noli me tangere* – 'Do not touch me.'

She twisted round. Benedict, ever curious, stood stooped on his tiny platform over the equivalent plinth on the other side.

'No!' she screamed. 'Don't touch!'

As Benedict reached and raised the shell in his hand like a diver's prize, the platform collapsed beneath him. Morag watched in horror as he tumbled like a stricken bird on to a square of vicious spikes at ground level.

Clack.

Darkness.

Will, sense and feeling deserted her. Numbed by shock, her fingers loosened their grip on the skylight.

17

Rescue Party

Lady Vane, her maid alongside, watched the light bob and diminish as the chariot wended its way back to Heorot.

'Now!' she cried. Her servant unwrapped their own globe-light and they ran to the tower. Both were dressed for travel: boots, trousers, cloaks. The rest of their luggage they had left behind to allay suspicion.

They arrived breathless.

'Did you see the door?' Lady Vane asked frantically. 'They were playing around with those little panels.'

'We were on the blind side, my Lady, when they went in.'

Lady Vane stamped the ground in frustration. 'Why didn't I declare myself earlier!'

'The lith?'

The lith's intimidating presence had indeed been the reason. The bodyguard resisted all blandishments, Cosmo's creature through and through. Lady Vane prowled around the huge column, patting it from time to time, as if it might open on her command.

'We wait,' she replied.

'We cannot get in, and we cannot go back. We could return to your craft, my Lady, and head home. The chasm path can't be far away.'

'We wait,' repeated Lady Vane frostily.

The maid did not ask for what or for whom. In this mood, Lady Vane did not brook questions, let alone challenge.

More than an hour passed. Lady Vane continued to circle the

rock column, uttering the same sentences every time she passed her servant:

'They're fools, they should never have gone in.'

'Impetuous boy!'

And, finally . . .

'He promised he'd come.'

Finally, from far away, a beam of light, narrow but strong and slowly closing, settled on the faces of the two women before dancing over the column like a roving eye.

'And I always keep my promises,' shouted a man's voice from the same direction.

'You took your time,' Lady Vane cried back.

The minutes passed, and the beam gave way to a gentler, less focused light, as Jinx's distinctive figure shuffled into view. He gripped a long staff in his right hand and dragged his wheeled silver trunk in his left. A heavy backpack induced a mild stoop. On his head, a bizarre helmet sprouted a variety of lights on stalks, which waggled like antennae.

'I have my house on my back, and, like the snail, it makes for slow going,' came the reply.

'They went in,' said Lady Vane.

'Of course they did. You wouldn't come all this way and not go in.'

'I fear for him,' said Lady Vane urgently.

'The tower's puzzles strain the mind, but that's all.'

'I don't share your optimism. Please, get us in.'

'You can't get in from here, not until they're out.'

'I'm *sorry*?'

The maid watched her mistress's frustration mount. She disliked her obsession with this mysterious wunderkind, Benedict – a man with no known past. He was not Lady Vane's son, yet she treated him as if he were and increasingly neglected Cosmo. She liked those she served to serve the right people.

'Anyone inside can give up and get out. But nobody outside

can join them. It would spoil the challenge. Imagine the vulgar shouting: *Do this, do that, try the other!*'

'You just said we can't get in from *here*. Is there another way?'

Jinx hesitated. 'The Tower of No Return guards its secrets, but, for my old master's widow, we might stretch the rules.'

'Hurry! Hurry!' said Lady Vane, but Jinx merely fluttered a hand. The stalks on his helmet swivelled this way and that. New beams cast a magenta glow over the cavern floor, quartering the ground like searchlights. A red line appeared in the dust as the beams teased out the rectangular shape of a metal lid. Jinx jettisoned his trunk and backpack, and, with the aid of an oddly shaped implement, raised the disguised cover to reveal a flight of steps. His lights reverted to a more normal colour and reduced to two – one forward and one back to assist his companions.

Jinx descended to a passage clogged with pistons, cogs and tantalum rods, clearly a man who knew his way. He undid a wheel-lock and admitted them to a rectangular chamber. Mechanical creatures of various kinds occupied racks on one long wall. On the other, a forest of levers surrounded a desk facing a throne-like chair. Charts hung on hooks, one above the other. A cursory glance suggested that each represented a different sequence of puzzles in the tower beyond.

Jinx located another door. 'Open sesame!' he said, playing with a single dial on the adjacent wall until the door yielded to a simple push.

They entered the tower on the ground floor. Jinx's swirling lights magnified the confusion of the multiple stairwells, waterways and platforms, before settling on the cupola.

He pointed. 'A skylight is open. That means they made it.'

The announcement had barely settled when a whimper of helpless agony, faint but horrifying, jerked their heads downwards.

'There!' cried Lady Vane.

Jinx hurried across to join her. Benedict's body lay impaled on a nest of spikes at the edge of the central stack. Arms, legs, one hand and an ugly wound to the side of his head dripped blood. His eyes were closed and his lips quivered.

Lady Vane froze, as if this were her doing, and Jinx took control. First, he gave orders to the maid.

'Give me your cloak and go back to the control room. There's a first-aid box in the left-hand drawer of the desk.'

'My poor boy, my poor boy,' mumbled Lady Vane.

'It's truly remarkable,' said Jinx dispassionately. 'He landed in such a way that the vitals are untouched, and his master hand too. Luckily the spikes widen towards the base, or even that would not have saved him.' He cut the maid's cloak into strips. 'To staunch the blood when we raise him,' he said, 'and I'll have to retrieve my trunk, but first . . .'

The maid returned. Jinx extracted two sprays from a plastic box. The first, he applied to the wounds. 'An anaesthetic and a coagulant,' he explained. 'Hold his head still, please, my Lady; we don't want it falling back.' He squeezed the second spray into Benedict's face, his body visibly relaxed. 'Knock out,' said Jinx. 'Now, stay with him here and keep head and body still.'

Jinx wended his way back through the concealed door.

Lady Vane uttered only four words, as if passing sentence: 'Bloody Cosmo's bloody doing.'

Jinx returned with a stretcher improvised from the struts of his travelling theatre. He and the maidservant raised the unconscious Benedict from the spikes and laid him there. Lady Vane bound the wounds, and Jinx led the way back to the control room and on to a lift.

'This was the builders' shaft,' he said.

The lift took them, via another concealed cover, to the upper surface between the tower and the *Ceres*' landing place.

'We haven't seen the Spire girl,' commented the maidservant.

Lady Vane waved the subject aside. 'Who cares about her? She left him to die.'

Whether by telepathy or sharp eyes, the remaining crew on the *Ceres* noticed their mistress early. Male servants took the stretcher.

'Gently, gently,' implored Lady Vane.

On arrival at the ship, Jinx assembled two davits which allowed the stretcher to be raised like a lifeboat and eased through the window of Lady Vane's quarters.

'We cannot linger here,' she told her crew. 'It's time to head home.'

Her orders elicited a restrained cheer. In minutes, the vessel had weighed anchor.

Below decks, Lady Vane's cabin resembled a hospital ward. Kettles steamed; bandages came and went; the pungent aroma of Jinx's mysterious sprays filled the air.

She and Jinx stood on either side of the patient, who lay in the maid's bed. His breathing had stabilised.

'We cannot keep him under much longer,' said Jinx. 'He needs to activate his mind, whatever the pain.'

'Will he walk again? Will he be able to hold anything?'

Jinx took a step back, as if insulted, and retorted:

> 'Humpty Dumpty sat on a wall,
> Humpty Dumpty had a great fall.
> All the king's horses and all the king's men
> Could not put Humpty together again.
> But Jinx's toolkit was an unknown then.

He'll sprint like an old-world gazelle and grip like a giant, when I'm through with those joints,' he added. 'And I'm not being frivolous. I never jest about creative work.' He paused, shifting on his feet. 'The only question is . . . my recompense.'

'We've abolished money, Mr Jinx. All work for all, but then I suppose you aren't after money. What's it to be, this time?'

'An onyx, in the usual form – black, with a band of white – would be most satisfactory.'

Lady Vane made jewellery, the one creative skill she excelled at. She had gathered stones from the abandoned homes of outliers and the deeper tantalum mines. Years ago, she had shown her collection to Jinx, and it had galvanised him. Thereafter, Jinx had set about collecting precious stones like an old-world jackdaw – not for use, but for cherishing. The habit unsettled Lady Vane. Acquisitive people invariably had hidden agendas.

The onyx had sentimental value. She had matched the stone to her husband-to-be on their first meeting.

'It's at home,' she said.

'That's fine, and only when he walks – if he doesn't, I deserve nothing.'

The night brought little sleep. Benedict never settled, tossing and turning with distressing cries of pain which Lady Vane could not stem. In the broken periods of quiet, she revised her condemnation of Morag Spire.

Until the arrival of Jinx's helmet, the tower would have been swathed in darkness, and Benedict had fallen a long way. Had darkness engulfed them both at the summit? Would they not have ascended the tower together? Had Morag been stranded there with no choice but escape? Consistent with that scenario, the open skylight had not been above Benedict's body. If Morag had escaped, where was she now? The anchored craft had not decreased in number. Some other fate had befallen her.

Lady Vane shook her head and reached for the sponge. She had enough to worry about without adding her late lover's daughter to the list.

18

Out of the Frying Pan

On Benedict's fall into darkness, Morag had thought of joining him, but then a bloody-minded refusal to be beaten by Cosmo took over. Her fingers found the skylight bolt and she clambered out.

Out of the frying pan and into the fire was her instant judgement. On the roof, the weaselly man and two more of Cosmo's retinue leered at her with daggers drawn. A lantern propped on the battlement bathed the scene in a sepulchral glow.

The burliest of the three spoke first: 'You took your time. Where's your fancy Dan?'

She did not reply.

'He flew down,' cackled the weaselly man, who had an unpleasant habit of sniffing after every phrase. 'He fell for a shell.' *Sniff*. 'And your heartfelt desire is to join him.' *Sniff*.

Morag acted on a favourite saying: when Lady Luck deserts you, play the tables and buy time for her return.

'Guess what I have in my pocket?' she said.

All three laughed.

'A handkerchief to stem the blood.'

'Or snivel into.'

'To surrender with,' added the weasel, who clearly thought his suggestion the best. 'A waste of a handkerchief, as we don't take prisoners.'

'A momenticon, *actually*.' Morag raised the single pill to prove it.

'Looking-glass creatures won't save you now,' scoffed the weasel man. *Sniff*.

'She's playing for time,' added the burly man.

The weasel man shook his head. 'Poor Alice has run out of squares.' *Sniff.*

Tick . . . tick . . . tick . . .

Faint, but clear and regular, the sound came from the opposite side of the tower's roof. The trio glanced over their shoulders, while keeping their blades to the front.

Over the parapet climbed a miniature young man or adolescent boy, no more than four and a half feet tall, carrying a sword of the same height. He wore a blue tunic with a golden hem and pockets with criss-cross stitching. He wore shoes suggestive of stealth, red leggings, and armoured protection on his elbows. Chestnut hair ran down to his waist, straight at first, but then richly curled. A grappling iron snagged the battlement behind him.

Morag instantly recognised him. He had been with Lord Sine at the Tempestas party, and he came straight from a book.

'She comes with me,' said the apparition.

'Who the fuck is *me*?' asked the burly man.

The apparition opened his arms theatrically. 'The name is Beamish, and I should be greeted with the following anthem:

> *'And hast thou slain the Jabberwock?*
> *Come to my arms, my beamish boy!*
> *O frabjous day! Callooh! Callay!*
> *He chortled in his joy.'*

He continued in a voice whose pitch matched his boyish features: 'As I say, she's coming with me, so let her through.'

The weasel man and the burly one laughed.

'Grease your blades, boys, it's women-and-children-first day!' *Sniff.*

The third man did not laugh.

'Hold on, didn't he just say he's the bloke who killed the Jab—'

'Finish them!' shrilled the weasel man, lunging at Morag, who jumped back and sideways on to the parapet, which truly was her last square.

One moment Beamish stood, right hand resting on the pommel of his sword, the next he was poetry in motion. In a single balletic sequence, he leapt and spun, slashed left, slashed right, and ended by running the weasel man through, his longsword flourished like an épée and his left hand cocked behind him like a practised fencer.

'What must a man do to find a decent challenge, these days?' protested Beamish, gesturing to the grappling iron as if opening a door for her.

Confronted by three fast-filling pools of blood from two throats expertly cut and a heart pierced through, Morag saw little point in resistance.

Descriptions for Beamish applied as well to his craft: unique, sleek, spruce, undersize, quick and smooth of movement. The passenger seat had obligingly been designed for people of ordinary size. A transparent shield encased Morag, with an aperture to facilitate conversation. Beamish's sword hung from hooks attached to the ceiling. Morag had already guessed their destination.

'Lord Sine said he would find me, when the time was ripe.'

Beamish ignored the remark and did not speak until they had returned to the murk. 'I hope you noticed my use of the flunge, the *trompement* and the *passata-sotto*. Few are so privileged.'

Fencing moves, clearly. Beamish was not a modest man, and she had learnt that immodest men had to be fed to keep them onside.

'The *trompement* caught my eye especially.'

Beamish accepted this compliment to his genius with a nod, as they passed over the clutch of craft assembled near the lift entrance.

'Who owns the large one?' he asked.

'Lady Vane, of course.' Morag added the *of course* as a riposte of her own.

Beamish's voice acquired a new urgency. 'Was there – *is* there – a monster on board?'

'If you mean Cosmo Vane, yes.'

'I mean' – Beamish's eyes blazed – 'the Jabberwock. He's the only creature worthy of my blade. I shall dispatch him with a *ridoppio*.' He grimaced. 'When I can find him.'

'If he'd been on board, I think I'd have remembered. *The jaws that bite, the claws that catch.*'

Beamish turned oddly petulant. 'You think you're Alice, the queen bee, but you're not. You don't control anything. Just because I only have one page in the book, and you're everywhere, doesn't make you memorable.'

'You're quite right, but also quite wrong, Mr Beamish. I don't control anything, I'm not Alice, and nor do I think that I am. But it's the Jabberwock people remember.'

'Nonsense,' spluttered Beamish. 'They remember the monster-slayers, men like Perseus, Beowulf, Saint George and *me*.'

This litany of names from times and cultures Beamish could not have known reminded her of Benedict. Her near-perpetual companion in recent months had fallen to his death, alone and in darkness, but she could only summon a dull numbness. She wanted to grieve; she wanted her face to contort as Cassie's had done in the cornfield on hearing of her father's death. But nothing. Maybe there had to be a letting go first.

Oblivious, Beamish rattled on: 'When I skewer the real-life Jabberwock, I'll be a legend – you'll see.'

The boast passed Morag by, and she slept, only to be woken by a vicious jolt. Outside, the murk was thinning from dense cloud to mist.

'You slept for hours,' said Beamish, as if it were a sign of weakness.

Morag ignored the barb. 'Were you expecting turbulence?' she asked.

'I never *expect* anything,' he said grandly, but he looked puzzled. 'It's not a wind, it's an updraught.'

Another judder rammed her forehead against the shield which separated them. Obligingly, Beamish lowered it.

'I never deliver damaged goods,' he explained. Beamish consulted his watch. 'It may be mid-morning, but there's a view when there shouldn't be.'

The mist was indeed thinning, and ribbons of blue appeared like cuts through cloth.

Morag peered down. 'Good God!' she cried. 'There's greenery down there, and it's consuming the murk. It's salvation, Mr Beamish.' In her mind's eye, Simul's creatures, restored to life, wandered over a new sunlit landscape.

Beamish cut the image short with a shake of his chestnut locks. 'No, Miss Spire, it's extinction.'

By now, the ribbon effect had reversed, with the clear sky dominant and the murk reduced to straggly vapour trails.

'Can't you see?' exclaimed Morag. 'The leaves are sucking in the poison and the carbon, and their roots must be doing the same to the earth. We can start again and avoid all the old mistakes.'

'The vegetation has parasites which will suck you dry,' said Beamish. 'My blade would see them off, but little else.'

'Parasites?' parroted Morag.

Again, Beamish consulted his watch. 'You have a minute to admire the tulgey wood.'

The craft swung round, briefly returned to the murk, dived back into the clear air and dipped to give Morag the promised close-up view.

Rich cream-white blossom bobbed in the clear air, interspersed with golden globes of fruit. Leaves fluttered, green above and silvery grey beneath. The foliage looked familiar.

A modest but near-identical space separated each smaller tree from its neighbours, as if some central intelligence were dictating the pattern of growth. They appeared to spread by underground runners. Yet the flowers dominated, a flamboyant statement of nature's beauty. Morag hunted through her near-photographic memory for the illustrations of flowering trees and shrubs in her grandmother's library, but nothing matched.

In the distance, a tree, far larger than the others, was on the move. Unlike the lesser trees, it had no golden fruit. But, it had a counterweight: a huge, very different fruit, mottled black on an oversized, twisted branch with reddish bark.

Suddenly, as a random sprawl of cards might self-organise to make a hand, disparate threads came together. The foliage mirrored that of the Boojum tree in the College of Novelties. Her father, while at Genrich, had worked on a dangerous tree and named it *arbor spirantia*, a characteristic pun on respiration and his own contribution. *Nature's verdict on mankind*, he had said. His records, replete with warnings, had been preserved in his cave on Deception Island. But, if Lord Sine's laboratories had transformed this magnificent, flowerless tree into one which could generate a rampaging growth to consume the murk, where lay the danger?

Beamish glanced at his watch and banked the craft away for another pass.

He tipped the craft to bring Morag's window even closer to the distorted, dark fruit on the moving tree.

The scabrous skin twitched as blue-headed insects snipped their way through, wings a-whirr to clear the saliva-like moisture which weighed them down.

'Now!' she yelled.

Beamish accelerated away with a posse of flies in pursuit.

'The blue ones reduce metal to dust,' he explained. 'Only the murk keeps them at bay.'

They reached the murk just in time.

'You said *blue ones*, as if there were others,' replied Morag.

'The red ones follow the blue. They are the flesh-eaters.'

Beamish said nothing more. He raised the partition between them, set a course and closed his eyes.

Morag peered through the vapour. Even when she managed to banish the image of Benedict falling, a sense of hopelessness prevailed. Death behind them, death below them – and, she suspected, death ahead.

19

The Red Queen's Tea Party

Another break to clear sky woke Morag, but this time with the abruptness of a beacon's work. Below, a garden shimmered in mid-afternoon sunlight.

One would have said a *riot* of colour, but for the rigour of the gardener's organising mind. Unfamiliar plants stood in ranks, serried by height, colour and exactness of spacing. Between them curved an emerald-green lawn, its banking and mown stripes just so in line and contour. No intruding weed scarred the surface of lawn or bed. Croquet hoops had been set on a flat section at the far end, in a scene so perfect that Morag imagined a ball struck from anywhere would sail serenely through the chosen hoop.

Beamish landed the craft behind the screen of a flowering hedge. He led the way through a gate to join a winding path.

On they strode, until halted by a no-nonsense voice as shrill as a knife on a blackboard.

'On an inch, left a foot. Have you never heard of Pythagoras?'

Even Beamish, hitherto undaunted by anything, slowed his pace. They edged through a narrow gap between a bank of giant orange lilies.

A late-middle-aged woman in a red dress, her hair tied back in the severest of buns, was directing a bevy of under-gardeners marking out a new bed with wooden pegs. A crown nestled tiara-like above her forehead. Her head jerked towards them like a puppet's.

'And *you*, don't walk on the grass.'

'We're not,' protested Morag.

'Prevention is the best cure, as someone your age should know. And I'm your Highness to you.'

Cosmo had scripted the Red Queen in their momenticon days in the Genrich Dome, but Lord Sine's version rang truer. The peppery monarch was the mirror opposite of the gentle, absent-minded White Queen.

'Where is Lord Sine?' asked Beamish.

'Frittering,' she replied.

'I asked *where* he was.'

'Lucky you, then,' replied the Queen, 'getting more than you bargained for.'

Ignoring her own command, she marched across the grass, before jerking her head back.

'A Queen can move in all directions,' she cried. 'You're my wake and my train, so not too far away or I'll lose you, and not too close or I'll flatten your toes. Chop, chop!'

Beamish, sword slung across his back, obeyed, and Morag followed suit. The path uncoiled to end in a two-storey house, the portico, sash windows and pleasing dimensions of which bore no relation to Lord Sine's ascetic quarters in the Genrich Dome.

Lord Sine sat in a stylish blue canvas deckchair on the veranda, poring over a weather map. He had lost weight, and his sallow complexion had burnished, almost to bronze, but the oversize bullet-head remained. To Morag, he was still a human toad, *Bufo bufo*, if now a sprightlier version. He was also the man whose machinations had contributed to the death of her father and many others.

'Well?' said Lord Sine to Beamish, acknowledging Morag's presence with little more than a nod.

'The borogrove is rampant. It will consume you all.' Beamish explained the fruit, the flies, the surging growth and the cleansing of the air. He also spoke of a crashed craft and dead pilots.

'What did these flies attack exactly?'

'The red like flesh. The blue like metal.'

'Only metal? Not wood or glass?'

Beamish reflected. 'So it seems.'

'That explains Mr Jaggard's news. It all fits neatly into place.' Lord Sine stroked his chin and changed subjects. 'And how are my Wonderlanders?'

'The Rabbit had a terminal accident. The rest are their usual irritating selves.'

Lord Sine turned to Morag. 'The borogrove was your father's doing.'

'Your father and the first Lord Vane set the ball rolling,' countered Morag.

'A proper gardener would sort it out,' interrupted the Queen. 'The old ways are the best. Chop, chop!'

Beamish suddenly exploded in righteous indignation. 'Where the hell is the Jabberwock?'

'Searching for a wood to whiffle through, most likely,' answered Lord Sine casually.

'We all go back to our roots,' added the Queen.

'He runs and runs. He would deny me my destiny.'

The Queen's admonishing finger switched to Lord Sine. 'You're wearing odd socks again. If it's to charm, you fail. If it's accidental, you're pathetic. You will wear matching anklewear for my party.'

'Party?' stuttered Lord Sine.

The Queen inhaled prodigiously, as if preparing to deliver a trumpet voluntary. The words flowed like a waterfall: 'Baron Palm, the Baroness de Snoy, the Comte de Chambord and the Comte de Paris, the Countesses of Oxford and Chandon-Moët, the Dukes of Bordeaux, Cambridge and Wellington, the Duchesses of Brabant, Grammont and Nemours, the Empereur du Maroc and the Empress Josephine . . .'

Morag was recasting the Red Queen as a deranged snob, when Lord Sine called a halt.

'She's referring to her roses. We have the picture, my dear, and we don't need the whole catalogue. As you might say, prune a little. Chop, chop.'

Visibly miffed, the Queen hunched her shoulders and finished with a flourish, 'And the Grossherzogin Feodora von Sachsen ... among *others* ... invite you to tea for four, at four, in our rose garden and nowhere else.' And she flounced off, followed by an equally disgruntled Beamish.

'Do you ever have any affection for your creatures?'

To her surprise, Lord Sine winced at the question. 'The Vane model I was pleased with.'

'He's called Benedict.'

'A good name. I really think he was blessed. I hoped he might inherit. He would have made an interesting opponent and even breeding stock.'

Morag bristled. He spoke of Benedict as if he were a test-tube pet. 'He's the one Genrich creation who really wasn't yours at all.'

'I gave him his knowledge, if not his character,' acknowledged Lord Sine. 'Is he alive, or has young Vane killed him already?'

Morag looked away. 'He fell,' she said.

Suddenly, despite the fact that Lord Sine had launched the attack on Deception Island and been privy to the genocide at the Tempestas party, he became her confessor. Someone had to be told. Beamish thought only of himself, and Lord Sine, she felt, had warmed a little since their last encounter. She opened up and recounted the recent chapters of her story. When she reached Heorot and the Stymphalian birds, Lord Sine asked for a detailed account.

'So, young Vane survived them. Vexing, as the Queen would say.' He gestured to Morag to continue.

She described their progress through the Tower of No Return to the shell on the shelf marked *Noli*. Lord Sine listened intently as Morag's sentences began to break up. His reaction surprised her.

'Believe it or not, I too have discovered grief. The Hatter, you see, was my exact opposite. He had a true sense of the absurd.

He saw through the charade of life. He was my ambassador, and I miss him terribly.' Lord Sine paused. 'Long ago, a boy of extraordinary ugliness arrived in the world. His head was so bulbous as to be barely human. His father meant him to be perfect, but one design flaw followed another. He lost all his hair. His body . . . well, words fail me. The boy was spared the bullying such handicaps usually bring, because his father ruled the roost. The boy admired his father, but from a distance. It's hard to love someone you continually disappoint. The boy grew up into someone who craved respect and was determined to leave his mark on the world.'

Typical of Lord Sine to dress up his life story in the third person, thought Morag, as she identified a glaring gap in the narrative.

'What about the boy's mother?'

'He never knew if he had one.'

'Like most of your creatures, I suppose.'

Lord Sine nodded. 'You're entitled to be harsh. I've made mistakes. Your father bested both me and Lord Vane. That's why I now employ outliers. I'm looking to find a saviour, and I'd like you to be part of it, but not yet. You must be tired. The water is hot and the linen is clean. The Queen likes her creature comforts.'

Lord Sine summoned a young woman from the garden.

'Syphax, be good enough to show Miss Spire to her room.' He turned to Morag. 'Don't forget tea, and please wear what you're given.'

Once free of Lord Sine, Morag turned to her new companion. Her hair, cut in a bob, accentuated the mischief in her eyes.

'You're an outlier,' Morag said.

'We're all outliers, apart from visitors and the Wonderland people. We're well looked after, and the work is divine – optimising new life forms. Extraordinary talents lurk in unexpected places.'

Syphax's little speech unsettled Morag. Had she seen her before, minus the haircut, in the Genrich Dome? Was the reference to hidden talents directed at her? Worse, *optimising new life forms* did not suggest Lord Sine had changed his spots.

Syphax opened a door at the rear of the house.

'Be ready at ten to four, sharp,' she said as she left, 'or the Queen will have my head.'

Morag's small room was furnished with a single bed and a small writing desk and chair. On the bed lay a full-length dress and a pair of dark laced shoes. Both had a period feel and fitted perfectly. She would not have looked out of place in an impressionist street scene.

She could not resist a smile at Lord Sine's entrapment by the Red Queen. But maybe her bossiness had softened him. As for Beamish, he would be a dangerous free agent if the Jabberwock were ever disposed of. No wonder they kept him and the monster apart.

And her own role? She was musing on Lord Sine's disturbing statement that she would help him find a saviour for the human race, when a shadow passed her window, followed by a knock on the door.

Before she could respond, Marcus Jaggard walked in, greeting her, as at the Tempestas party, with a leer.

'You look most fetching, Morag.'

'What are you doing here?'

'A little business.' He slipped behind her. 'You've missed a button.' Without asking, he did the fastening, fingers stroking the nape of her neck.

Morag stepped forward to create distance. Jaggard eased himself into the chair.

'When I say *here*, I mean my bedroom, Mr Jaggard.'

'Marcus, please. We're friends, aren't we?'

'Friends! You tried to destroy our ship and everyone on it.'

Jaggard made no attempt to dissemble. 'I didn't appreciate your uses, then.'

'What uses?'

'I don't believe you've grasped the full reach of your talents. For example, you haven't a clue why you're wearing that becoming dress. You're a phenomenon, Morag. We weather-watchers like phenomena.'

'Who are you planning to betray this time?'

'Nobody.' Surprise moments had been a constant companion in recent weeks, but the weather-watcher's next remark surpassed them all. 'I would like Lord Sine to resurrect my father, but there are technical problems, which you might be able to solve.'

'What problems exactly?'

Jaggard visibly bridled. 'Miss Spire, I question you, not vice versa. But we'll meet again soon enough. For now, it's back to Winterdorf and the daily grind.'

With a last lecherous smile, Jaggard left, and, minutes later, Syphax returned.

'I wouldn't breed from him,' she said.

Morag kicked herself. She should not have been surprised by Jaggard's appearance. Lord Sine had been studying a weather map. The pair were up to something.

She followed Syphax to a garden within a garden, where open trellises supported swathes of roses. Their overblown blooms bore little resemblance to the aristocratic forebears listed by the Red Queen. No insects traversed the show, no anthers and no pollen. An extravagant, sexless display. How long, Morag wondered, before *arbor spirantia* engulfed them all?

In the centre of the garden, ironwork chairs of different heights had been set around a table similarly divided into sections, like a sliced cake, each one level with its allotted chair.

'It's a four times table,' said the Queen, who sat on the highest chair, feet dangling off the ground. Various forms of confectionery surrounded her. Everybody else had empty plates beside a cup of steaming, strong tea. She patted the lowest chair. 'You sit here, Morag.'

The Queen flicked her head towards Beamish, who was practising fencing moves. 'He's in a sulk,' she confided, 'because we lost the Jabberwock or the Jabberwock lost us.' She tossed Morag a biscuit, which she dropped. 'Butter fingers!' cried the Queen. 'Have another.'

That now-familiar jag of her head greeted Lord Sine as he shuffled towards them. 'Ah, the *late* Lord Sine . . .' she hissed.

The butt of this threatening welcome took the second-highest seat and a sip of tea.

'Apologies, but I have a mission for Miss Spire.'

'A mission?' said the Queen. 'Who's she converting and to what?'

'If you let me speak, you might find out. She'll be leaving shortly.'

'In a short time or for a short time? Be precise.'

'Both, I hope.'

'Then she'd better have some shortbread,' added the Queen.

Lord Sine leant down to Morag's table and placed a simple black old-world fountain pen in front of her. 'I want you to go where this takes you and bring me back a hair.'

'What sort of hair? Mad in March or curly?' interrupted the Queen.

'She'll know,' replied Lord Sine wearily.

Beamish ceased shadow fencing and came over, demanding to know why Lord Sine's mission had been entrusted to a feeble woman whom he had already rescued once.

These exchanges passed Morag by. The pen was exuding the energy of a late Rembrandt. She recalled Matilda's voice, exhorting her to open her mind to the icon of the hermit, on their last evening together.

She did just that, now, letting the pen's energy take command. She grimaced and disappeared.

'That is unexpectedly quick,' exclaimed Lord Sine.

'Unexpected!' chuntered the Queen. 'Disappearing at tea is beyond rude. She must be from Chester.'

'I think you mean Cheshire,' corrected Lord Sine.

'It comes down to the same thing. A cat's a cat, whatever you call it.'

Lord Sine mulled a familiar dilemma. Arguments were either interminable, or the Queen had to have the last word. He chose the road to peace.

'If you say so,' he mumbled, and turned his mind to more important matters.

'I do say so,' concluded the Queen.

Lord Sine summoned Syphax. 'Matters are drawing to a close. There is much to do.'

What's in a Hair?

Morag knew instantly that this journey was different. On previous visits, including her last to Degas' studio, she had arrived with a sense of transience, but not so here. Either her gift was changing or the pen's distinctive energy had worked the change.

Its pulse drew her down an old-world street, men and women milling about in costumes from the same period as her dress. The chairs of a coffee salon spilt on to the pavement. On one, an abandoned newspaper caught her eye: the *Berner Zeitung*, 12 May 1905. Ahead, an arch crossed the thoroughfare, a large circular clock at its centre. She knew, because her quarry knew, that every other municipal clock, from the station's to the art gallery's to the Town Hall's, was synchronised with this one. She had arrived in a timekept city, and for some reason this fact troubled the owner of the pen.

The clock said 11.47 a.m. A warmish sun dipped in and out of light cumulus. The passers-by conveyed a festival spirit, all in their Sunday best and church done.

She remained invisible, although a dog and an old woman narrowed their eyes as she passed, as if catching a presence. Her destination lay in this very street, Kramgasse, number 49.

She slipped through the closed outer door like a ghost. A black cat edged by her on the stairway. She ascended, and entered an apartment on the third floor. It was decorated with floral wallpaper in low-key colours. A sofa with an antimacassar occupied one wall, a bookcase another. A grandfather clock stood between two tall narrow windows overlooking the street. This room, and those off it, had a stayed elegance, but without ostentation or signs of significant wealth.

He sat at a table in the middle of the room, the iden-
tical fountain pen in one hand and his head resting on the other. He was surrounded by pages of manuscript. Amendments and deletions pointed to work in progress, as did the typewriter, as yet unused, beside him. Few  old-world faces had stayed in the public consciousness, but his had – or, at least, an older version, with the grey hair flying and the moustache. The moustache was already there, untouched by time, and that quizzical walrus look could not have been more distinctive. She was in the company of Albert Einstein, in 1905, his *annus mirabilis*.

The gentle visual concentration of the artist, even Vermeer's more intense approach, paled beside the cascade of complex thoughts which enveloped Morag. Equations came and went, names she had not heard of and the oddest images. A woman on a train, travelling at a constant speed (apparently important), drops a stone without casting it (equally important). A pedestrian on the cutting (she assumes a younger Einstein) watches on. To him, the pebble falls in parabola; to her, in a straight line. Which is the true path? Why does it matter that they both are?

In Matilda's library, Morag had read about, but barely grasped, the astonishing reach of these discoveries in one young man's head – three papers which would, in years ahead, develop atomic power and quantum mechanics, and provoke reworkings of the universal laws relating to space and time.

She belatedly remembered her mission. Could reconstituting

this creative genius assist mankind in its present parlous condition? If not, might a strand of his genetic material provide a bargaining counter with Lord Sine? She pinched two hairs from the leather back of Einstein's chair and wound them round her little finger, only for a new problem to surface. Errand accomplished, she would be of no further use for Lord Sine, save perhaps as a source of genetic material, and she had no wish to share her one claim to be special.

Einstein's revolutionary insights derived as much from everyday observation as complex equations. She tried the same approach and stumbled on a fact whose significance she had quite overlooked. Her father had had no access to Vermeer's *Muse of History* or Cézanne's *Card Players*, but he had journeyed back to their moment of creation to leave his messages.

Einstein's thought about space and time seeded an idea. If an object's stored creative energy could transport her to its past when she was passive, might not the process be reversed if she were active? Suppose, when in the past, she recreated in her head another object's energy, might that take her forward to that object in the present?

Yet, this possible solution had a companion problem. All the memorable paintings she knew hung in the Museum Dome, whose shutdown had prompted her and Fogg to flee. The Museum had become a tomb with no escape.

The Vanes' paintings had been second-rate, purloined from outlier houses, and she could think of no other artistic work with the necessary energy . . . save, perhaps, possibly, one.

The Museum Dome had had a single absentee, a painting by Gustave Caillebotte entitled *Les Raboteurs*, mysteriously marked in the catalogue as *Out on Loan*, with a postcard in its place. The Museum's two other paintings by Caillebotte featured well-dressed passers-by with a dog, crossing an ironwork bridge, and two male canoeists in straw hats, paddling down a river. Fogg had talked (to himself) about how Caillebotte's independent means were reflected in these pleasant but unchallenging subjects. Yet the missing painting had been different, a tribute to the demands of skilled manual labour. Three men, on their knees and naked to the waist, are planing an interior parquet floor. In her nocturnal rambles, she had spent as much time poring over this miniature reproduction as with any of the originals.

But on loan to whom, and why? She had never seen it in the Tempestas buildings or in the Vanes' private quarters, and Genrich frowned on visual art. Even if the Red Queen had an eye, such a menial subject would surely not appeal.

Worth a try, she decided, wherever it might take her.

Shutting out Einstein's thoughts, she focused intensely on the woodworkers, on the painter looking on, catching the light on their bare torsos with his brush, and the boards, the lines of which fanned out like a child's drawing of sunlight.

Despite a sense that her presence in number 49 Kramgasse was loosening, she maintained her concentration.

A moment later, she was gone.

III
COMMON CAUSE

I

In Search of a Mission

Hilda Crike, despite her advanced years, considered herself a secret agent for the forces of good, and the best in the field. But agents need missions, and she had been starved of them since the quartet of young had left and her old comrade, Oblivious Potts, had disappeared. She had gathered intelligence on the flow of Cosmo's enforcers arriving in Winterdorf, the number of craft, the roster of guards, the comings and goings of Cosmo himself, and, of course, the weather-watchers, on the rare occasions they ventured from Tiriel's Tower. But Cosmo had left, and Jaggard's iron hand made intelligence gathering perilous. Worse, unshared intelligence was of no use to anyone. Was there an opposition? And, if so, where? The town had subsided into sullen cooperation with its new rulers.

Not for the first time, she sought inspiration from the battered old-world deed box hidden beneath the floorboards of her front room. It held the research materials for her *Official History of Tempestas*, as commissioned by the first Lord Vane and completed shortly after his death: interviews, original documents and copies taken in her immaculate manuscript. Her disorganised exterior, crafted for camouflage in these difficult times, hid a fiercely incisive mind. The purpose of the exercise was to find in the past the seeds of the future.

She read and reread the notes of her last meaningful interviews with the first Lord Vane. He had played games, laying false trails and half truths, but, in their final encounters, the shadow of mortality had induced greater candour. Fear of eternal retribution can unshackle the lips of the dying.

Three peculiar words stood out. He could hardly have invented them.

Simul: according to the first Lord Vane, the place where his portrait hung and home to Man's last chance to reverse its destruction of Nature. *Resurrection . . . remember Simul*, had been his last words to her, and indeed his last words to anyone. She had no clue where this place might be or what it held.

Arbor Spirantia: a phrase Lord Vane had repeated on his deathbed in a tone of warning. Literally, a breathing tree, but all trees had been lost in the Fall, save for a few unspectacular evergreens on the mountain slopes above the old Tempestas building. Nor did she know of any old-world tree which imperilled anything – rather, the contrary.

She always stumbled, at this point in the reasoning. It made no sense.

She patted Goya's head, a creature from Lord Sine's laboratories, but an old-world dog in her eyes, and inspiration came.

There was a dog which had not barked.

The first Lord Vane had never hinted at the existence of a museum and had been, unlike his son, hostile to art in all its forms. Yet the construction of the Museum Dome must have preceded the Fall. Mander and Potts or Potts' father were the obvious suspects, and its recent occupants, Spire's daughter and Fogg, might have been chosen as curators with greater destinies in mind. But that did not explain the Museum's construction decades earlier. The young Mander's love of art might have been reason enough, but instinct's whisper said something else lurked there, something which still mattered.

Yet, the Museum was now beyond reach. Morag and Fogg had described its shutting down at the time of their enforced departure.

Goya, now prone, twitched as dogs do when dreaming. The animal had a genius for prompts.

She was wrong. A way did exist, but, even if she could wangle access, she would only catch fragments of Fogg's memories of the Museum, and, worse, fragments chosen by him for their blandness. On Fogg's account, he had resisted revealing to Cosmo anything of note. Yet Fogg knew none of the wider history, and she did. His notion of the banal might well include something significant. The Museum sounded an intriguing place and a virtual visit would help fill a missing chapter in her *History of Tempestas*.

Crike, a glass-half-full personality, did not let the difficulties of the enterprise deter her. She packed a suitable disguise, entrusted Goya to a neighbour, picked up a mop and headed for town at dusk, with a spring in her step. She had rediscovered purpose. Too much drift isn't good for a girl, as her late father liked to say.

The invaders' craft, scattered around the outskirts of town, disfigured the purity of Bruegel's vision, as did the visitors' black and purple uniforms.

Crike's study of the guard roster paid off with a familiar face.

'Blimey, if it isn't Miss Mop!' said the guard.

'I'm to clean the craft.'

'At this hour of night?'

'It's dirty, malodorous work, Mr Gallop, and people don't like reminding of their cruder bodily functions. Anyway, I've my reputation to think of.'

'I'm not as dim as I look,' replied Gallop.

'Mercifully,' replied Crike.

'You've no chemicals, no receptacles and no light.'

'Them's in the craft.'

Gallop grinned. 'Word is, those renegades got away, and that Spire girl was made up as your lookalike. I mean, what a choice!'

'Poor soul,' replied Crike. 'I hope it's not permanent.'

Gallop turned his head towards the craft. 'They spoil the view, don't they?'

'Is Lord Vane in town?'

'Whisper is, he's far away.'

That figures, mused Crike, who had known Cosmo since childhood. *He's restless, forever bored, and forever in search of further excess.*

'Whisper also is . . .' continued Gallop, only to hesitate, as if the rumour were too absurd to repeat. 'There's some kind of plant life on the rampage.'

'A *what*?'

'Tavern talk, most likely.'

'How does a plant rampage? What sort of plant?'

Gallop shrugged and returned to the business in hand. 'S'pose I looked thataway, and you darted the other . . . I might be too late to stop you taking off.'

'You'd be putting your life at risk.'

'I doubt that. We fret over every detail. Each clockwork crow we place just so. These arrogant bastards don't care about detail. They don't count the craft. They don't record their comings and goings, they're too busy spying on the likes of us.'

'Gallop, you're a star,' said Crike.

'Bollocks, I never shone at anything. I'm one of those things that come out of the dark, spark for a moment and fizzle to death in the snow. Ooooh, there's a bat.'

Gallop looked to his right, as Crike slipped by. She chose the remotest craft. She jettisoned her mop and, with the aid of a hand mirror and a change of clothes, assumed a very different look: tortoiseshell half-moon spectacles, cream blouse, tweed skirt and, because guards fall for archetypes, blue stockings.

She surveyed the controls. If Potts could master them, any fool could. Simplicity ruled: a joystick, an accelerator drive, launch and land levers, and a panel offering a choice between return and new directions. She chose *Return* and pulled down *Launch*.

The craft lurched upwards, as if caught in a violent thermal. She had missed the floor pedals which operated the stabilisers. Her feet barely reached them. She had to perch, but practice made perfect. The craft levelled before it slid into the murk.

Like most Winterdorfers, Crike had never visited Acheron. She shuddered on breaking into clean air only to face Hieronymus Bosch's vision of Hell. Gouts of fire illuminated dark archways, battlements, glassless windows and bridges over streams of toxic effluent. She passed over the Hindsight Inn, a human head on a bone torso with bare skeletal legs.

The craft followed its preordained course to the landing field, which Fogg had fleetingly described during his stay in her house in Winterdorf. Four in the morning, said the dashboard chronometer, but the field was a hive of activity. Wagons laden with heavy ordnance shuffled from craft to craft. She took in huge harpoons and grappling irons on extended chains. Ladders ran up to troop carriers, huge low-slung shapes with rows of porthole windows. All in all, a vision of imminent war. But against whom? Winterdorf had no defences to speak of and was already under their control.

A middle-aged man, closely shaven, with a businesslike but humourless face, strode up as she climbed down from the cockpit.

'Who the hell are you?'

'I'm from Winterdorf.'

'I can see that. I asked who you were.'

Crike decided a little aggrandisement was needed. She pushed her spectacles back up the bridge of her nose. 'Doctor Hilda Crike.'

'Doctor of what?'

'Electromagnetic energy. I'm responding to an emergency call.'

'From whom?'

'The person in charge of his Lordship's weavers.'

'Piety isn't here.'

Crike seized this fortuitous opening.

'Presumably that's why they sent for me.' She jangled her bag. 'I have my tools and I'm keen to get going.'

'At *this* hour?'

'You wouldn't understand, Mr ... Mr ... ?'

'I wouldn't understand what?'

'Lord Vane waits for no woman. Or man, for that matter.'

The hint of a threat did the trick.

'Get directions from the Inn,' the man said. 'They're open all hours tonight.'

'Your name, officer? I like to give credit where it's due.'

'Hodges, *Sergeant* Hodges.'

She awarded him a glacial smile befitting a doctor of electromagnetic energy, and headed across the landing field, over the rising ground beyond and down to the Hindsight Inn. Fogg's reception had been ribald; hers was not. A generous proportion of the Inn's stock had been requisitioned, to judge from the pyramid of barrels by the Inn's left arm.

'Load 'em vertical,' said a man boasting an epaulette on his shoulder identical to that worn by Sergeant Hodges. His crew obeyed, two to a barrel. The landlord, his dress starkly different, almost colourful, scowled, hand on hip.

'You can't need all of them,' he growled.

'You don't know where we're going. Anyway, you're a patriot, aren't you?'

The landlord mumbled and withdrew up a ladder to the Inn. The sergeant turned to Crike.

'This is man's work, whoever you are. Scram.'

'Sergeant Hodges said I should get directions from here. I've remedial work to do on Lord Vane's weavers, Piety being away.'

'Follow the path, and it's the first tower on the right.'

At the door of the tower, Piety's name worked its magic again. Crike feared the worst when a taciturn guard escorted her to Interrogation Room 1, only to realise that Cosmo questioned suspected dissidents here. She had watched Cosmo Vane inventing weavers as a precocious teenager and had absorbed such technical details as her more limited science could grasp.

Weavers could hunt through the mind for current thoughts and recent memories regarded as significant by the subject, enabling a third party to view them like film. Uninformative sequences could then be deleted, and useful ones retained. Images of clandestine meetings and a few scenes of sabotage confirmed that not everyone in Acheron accepted Cosmo's rule. Fogg's file was one of the most recent and the most substantial. Cosmo had delved deep and long.

She marvelled at Fogg's inner eye and his copyist's gift for retaining fine detail. At first, she saw only paintings, which Fogg must have deployed in an attempt to keep his innermost thoughts secret. But then she saw, as Cosmo must have seen, the momenticon sitting beneath Monet's *Water Lilies* and the vision of Monet in his garden which it had opened up, followed by Morag descending from the Museum ceiling. What a shock that must have been to Cosmo! Morag Vane could catch the energy of a painting, travel there, and later fashion a momenticon to enable others to do the same. Fogg must have realised what he had unwittingly revealed. To prevent further revelations of importance, Fogg had turned to a virtual tour through a maze of landings and ecalators. Cosmo had persevered, and Fogg's daily rituals surfaced next: Fogg exercising with his legs in the air; Fogg telling stories to an audience of none; Fogg sweeping a particular patch of floor; Fogg at the Rearranger; and finally, Fogg by the Visitors' Book, flanked by two identical twins in schoolboy uniforms. She could read the single entry: *Liked the totem poles the best.*

Fogg's dusting had been beneath a totem pole. Why were they there? She had seen no other indigenous artefacts. Then she remembered Fogg's description of a photograph in the old Tempestas library deep in the mountains: an elderly white man in shorts, standing beside a Amazonian Indian in an old-world jungle scene, with a totem pole among the trees. She sensed a parallel history playing out, which connected to the present.

Suppose the subsequent arrival of Fogg and Morag with their

art-focused gifts had distracted from the original purpose of the Museum . . .

Suppose . . .

Where the hell was Potts when she needed him?

2

Back to Biology

Despite scarlet-rimmed eyes, the legacy of prolonged microscope work, Potts had been rejuvenated by a scientific challenge which mattered. Trawling encyclopaedias in his snowbound house beyond Winterdorf for long-lost fauna had been light entertainment, but of no use to anyone else. Assisting the youthful adventurers in their quest for paradise had had purpose, but, for him, it was a walk-on part at best.

He moved his chair to the fire. The warmth and flicker rekindled memories of an old-world childhood. His father's expertise had been dendrology, the study of trees. He had loved them more than any human.

Poor form, his father would say, *that I enjoy fires so much. Imagine an ornithologist who basked before a bonfire of birds.*

Maybe they were phoenixes, he had replied, a precocious seven-year-old who regretted the remark as soon as he said it: too trivial, too show-off.

His father, a hard taskmaster when not away on his travels, frequently rebuked him for being superficial, but not this time. *You're right, boy. Myths carry a smidgen of truth. Suppose there was a terrible tree which could consume us all, but could equally save us, were it fully understood.*

Why is it that a handful of childhood conversations lodge deep in the memory, while most, ostensibly more significant, are lost to time?

Potts had joined his new friends, the ouzels, in acquiring a white bib around the chin. He plucked this wispy white beard in puzzlement.

'Any progress?' Hesper, Elector of the Northerners, was as stealthy in voice as she was in movement. She spoke so gently, her words barely disrupted his thought processes.

'You're right about the flies and their respective functions. The blue have extraordinary mandibles, hard as steel, and the red—'

'Jaws like knives. That's not progress, Oblivious; that's recycling what we already know. I need more. This is too serious and too urgent.'

Put on his mettle, Potts responded, 'All right, let's start with the oddities. They have primitive and limited digestive systems. The red fly cannot digest blood, which suggests it kills for killing's sake. Nor can the blue digest iron or steel. They seem designed to assault man and all his works, but little else. They attack, they die.' He paused. 'But, unlike the mayfly, all the year round.'

'Better,' said Hesper, 'but hardly enough to form a strategy.'

'Oh, I don't know,' said a third voice.

They both spun round. Morag stood opposite the fireplace. Potts did not immediately recognise her.

'We have a time traveller,' he said, gawping at her costume dress.

'This corset's killing me,' Morag replied. 'Does anyone have a pair of loose-fitting trousers?'

'Ah,' exclaimed Potts, 'the painting! That *was* clever.' He turned to Hesper. 'This is Morag Spire. She has a most peculiar gift.'

'I can see that,' replied Hesper, just about controlling her aston-ishment. 'You must be Gil's daughter. Welcome to the town under the mountain.'

Potts introduced Hesper. 'Hesper is the Northerners' Elector, and better than the rest of our rulers put together.'

'Now, now, Mr Potts,' replied Hesper. 'In my experience, disap-pointment always follows praise.' She turned to Morag. 'But I'd love to know how you came here and why. Storm clouds are gathering, and we need all the help we can get.'

Though never a father, Potts had an eye for emotional damage, and he sensed it in Morag now. The ebullience had seeped away; something was broken, a wound in need of attention.

'How are the others?' he asked.

'I haven't seen Fogg or Niobe since Deception Island.'

The absentee spoke volumes. Possibilities hardened into probabilities.

'And Benedict?' he asked gently.

'He . . . I never saw a body.' Morag sank to her knees, and, now among friends, her formidable outer shell shattered. She covered her face with her hands. Her shoulders shook.

Hesper tugged a cord on the fireside wall. 'Blayberry brandy,' she said into the adjacent speaking tube. 'The best, now.'

Potts built the fire and said nothing.

'I'm so sorry,' Morag said, shaking her head. 'How pathetic.'

'Feelings are never pathetic,' said Hesper, sitting Morag down beside the fire. 'We don't see enough of the right kind, these days.'

The drink arrived in minutes – three glasses already poured, the liquid the darkest purple. The taste reminded Morag of Deception Island and her father's death, and it restored her composure.

'I've been on the road,' she said. 'The College of Novelties, Heorot, the Tower of No Return, Lord Sine's new mansion, the Red Queen's garden, and 49 Kramgasse, in the old-world town of Bern.'

Hesper and Potts exchanged glances. Many places, the last four unfamiliar, and the very last bizarre.

'You've a captive audience,' encouraged Potts. 'Let's take them one at a time.'

The narrative process proved as restorative as the drink. Morag kept it chronological, describing characters new to her when they had first appeared: the Boojum tree, Mr Polychronis, Piety, Sigurd, Jinx, the Stymphalian birds, Beamish, the Red Queen, Syphax, and Albert Einstein as a young man. She managed Benedict's fall without wavering.

Here, Potts intervened for the first time. 'Did you see his body?'

'I saw him fall, a long way, too far.'

'And you think Lady Vane had been outside the tower just before you arrived?' queried Potts.

'Her scent is distinctive. You're not saying . . . ?'

'There is hope. No more, no less. Benedict has Lady Vane's eyes, if not more, and why would she risk Cosmo's wrath unless she cared? She is resourceful, too.'

Morag had used Beamish's word for *arbor spirantia*, the borogrove, when describing their narrow escape from its insect life. Hesper waited to the end of the story before returning to this subject.

'Did you have long before these flies emerged?' she asked.

'Minutes only.'

'Could you have grabbed a slice of this rotten fruit in that time?'

'That depends on the texture, but it would be touch and go.'

'It certainly would,' added Potts.

Hesper pronounced a theory – based, she said, on their own records: 'We Northerners built the College of Novelties for the first Lord Vane. That included the cloister, where we planted the Boojum tree. Your father, Mr Potts, delivered the tree and supervised the planting. He described it as the most significant living thing in the place. This was just before the Fall. When the murk came, the tree was already in bloom and protected the college. This new tree sounds like a rogue variant, with its good and deadly fruit.'

'The Boojum tree doesn't fruit at all. Lord Sine tried but failed to create a seed, and I'm afraid my father must take a share of the blame,' said Morag. 'He was too curious to leave well alone.'

Hesper kicked a stray log back into the fire. 'Sooner or later, they'll realise. By *they*, I mean Sine, Vane and Jaggard – the trio from hell. Wood and glass are the two materials the blue insects don't attack, and we're woodworkers and glassworkers, in a town made of wood and glass. Look at the lengths Lords Sine and Vane went to on Deception Island. When the borogrove closes in, they'll take whatever's to hand, and that means us. Bad empires are drawn to resources, and we're sitting on a gold mine.'

Potts paused. 'Stop the borogrove and they might lose interest?' he suggested.

'First things first,' Hesper said, returning to the speaking tube. 'We have a special guest in urgent need of loose-fitting trousers.'

A tiny kindness, but enough to make Morag smile for the first time since the Tower of No Return.

3

A New Player Joins

Cassie had watched her mother's growing fascination with Benedict with mixed feelings. Lady Vane bestowed more affection on him that she ever had on her. Morag's beetle, nestling in the Boojum tree, had relayed the conversation between them, the drift of which was that Cassie was Benedict's biological sister.

The thought unsettled her. She did not have his looks. Nor did she have that chip of amethyst in her irises. Had her mother neglected her because she was plain? Would a deeper understanding heal these wounds or widen them?

She took a step towards the desk, stopped, and took another.

She had, via Morag's golden beetle, witnessed a conversation below deck on the *Ceres* during a freak storm. Her mother had answered a question about her from Morag with these disturbing words: *I too have suffered in ways you cannot imagine.*

The remark had festered long enough. She reached the desk, opened the drawer and removed the letter. The envelope had been sealed on the back with a circle of red wax embossed with the Tempestas sigil. On the front, the writing of a dying man confronted her, each letter painfully formed:

To be opened in the event of my death.

Leaving her father's seal unbroken, she opened the letter along the top with a paper knife. Inside, the words betrayed the same frail anxiety.

My dearest Cassie,

I have loved you as well as a stepfather could, but not well enough. It is your mother's story to tell. I wish you every happiness. Remember how the phoenix rises.

One word screamed from the page.

Stepfather. *Stepfather!*

Not Lord Sine, surely. He would never have fashioned or fathered a face as ordinary as hers. Who, then?

She walked to her bedroom and gazed dispassionately in the mirror. Traces of her mother's beauty lingered in her eyebrows, the bridge of her nose, her high cheekbones and her ears. She blanked them out and focused on the remainder.

Suddenly, fragments of another face peered back – the overthin lips, the jut of the jaw.

She sank to her knees in horror. She was a child of the worst kind of violence, not love. She had been damaged goods from the off.

It had to be him: a man who pursued her mother, a man her mother hated, the kind of man who *would*.

A glacial rage seized her. She returned downstairs to her microtools and set to work.

4

Serendipity

Syphax had pursued scientific truths from adolescence: truths yielded by complex equations, trial and error, and hours of study. Some disappointed; some were revelations; and some were stepping stones to more substantial discoveries. Such single-minded quests had cost her any vestige of a personal life. The one young man in view, and then only sporadically, was Beamish, whose perfect good looks repelled her. Lord Sine and the Red Queen treated her more like a skivvy than a companion.

Take this morning. As instructed, she had sieved through Genrich's long-forgotten hard-copy records of outliers worth preserving. The cull at the Tempestas party had left Lord Sine short-staffed.

But drudge can harvest the unexpected. Some two hours into this task, she turned a page to find her own family name staring back, and, beneath it, the given names of her siblings, parents and a surviving grandparent. Her entry was pleasing enough: *Exceptional scientific gifts, including advanced genetics*, but all the rest had been struck through in red, with a date only weeks after her departure for the Genrich Dome. The bottom of the page recorded in red ink: *Chitin recovered: 13 medium sheets, condition reusable.*

The underlying message could not have been starker. Her family had been eliminated for lack of utility and a need for raw materials.

Suppressed childhood memories bobbed to the surface. Her commitment to Genrich was rooted in a restless intellect, rather than any lack of affection at home. Interesting scientific challenges had blinded her to the worth of what she had left behind and the company's true agenda. These thoughts delivered, in quick succession, regret, guilt and, lastly, a desire for revenge.

Not any ordinary revenge. She must find a punishment to fit the crime.

5

Short and Sharp

'Who let them go?'

Cosmo Vane's retinue, seated at the tables in Heorot's Great Hall, cowered in silence. Only Sigurd spoke up.

'A maid could hardly command Lady Vane to stay,' he said. 'Or Jinx, for that matter.'

'Where's Mander?'

'He left after them, and alone.'

'Well, what do they matter?' cried Cosmo. 'We focus on our next labour. We've a whole wall to fill. How about the Hydra? All those heads?'

Silence. His followers did not fancy another venture into myth-making.

'Come on, have you no spleen?'

A pair of men entered and cut the harangue short.

'Well? Were their bodies in the tower?' Pause. 'Or above it?'

The older of the two replied: 'The spikes at ground level were smeared with blood, but no corpse. The shreds of clothing point to the young man. He must be dead or grievously wounded.' The man pursed his lips.

'Get on with it, if you want to keep your tongue.'

'On the roof, we found the bodies of the three men your Lordship sent. The other footprints belonged to the Spire girl and someone else, someone with very small feet. They were nowhere to be seen.'

'Not natural causes, I assume,' said Cosmo, greeting this setback with uncharacteristic calmness.

'One, a strike to the heart; the other two, to the jugular.'

Cosmo digested the detail. Sigurd watched him intently. He sensed a devious strategy taking shape, one Cosmo would be unlikely to share fully.

'Well, that simplifies matters, as does other intelligence just in. The weather-watchers report spreading tentacles of clear air. Piety informs me that a vigorous new plant has appeared, which lives off the murk.'

This astounding news prompted an outbreak of turning heads and whispers.

Cosmo raised a cautionary hand. 'Lord Sine corroborates the news, but with a twist. The plant is home to flying insects which live off flesh and metal. He talks of a threat, where I see opportunity. But we need wood and glass to take on these flies, and only one place has both in abundance.'

Cosmo took the lith aside and handed him a small piece of paper. 'Destroy when read and go alone.' He then turned to his retinue and assumed his statesmanlike voice: 'We enter a new world. An invasion force is on its way to claim the vital resources we need. Sigurd, take two men and get to Winterdorf, quick as you can. Meantime, I must leave you for more pressing matters.'

Cosmo opened his arms for theatrical effect and vanished.

6

A Challenge

In Winterdorf, Tiriel's Tower thrummed with activity. With the advent of the beacons, the weather-watchers had been marginalised, much to their Master's chagrin. But opportunity comes to those who wait. Jaggard now administered Winterdorf in Cosmo's absence. But that did not explain the voluminous data ascending and descending the winding stair. Maps were being pored over, minute adjustments made. Barometric pressure obeyed the tower's bidding. The stratosphere was going to war.

'Master ... ?'

Jaggard broke away from the huge screen on the wall and glared at the minion. *This is demanding work, you idiot,* was the message. Another minon entered behind the first and fine-tuned the display, a constant process all afternoon.

'You have an unexpected visitor.'

'Don't waste time,' Jaggard snapped. 'Just say who.'

'Lady Vane's daughter. She's in your chamber.'

Jaggard suppressed a rebuke. Never ignore a Vane. They're wily, and the timing troubled him. Cassie Vane had never visited the tower, her late father only once, when he had revealed in private Lady Vane's infidelity with the revolting Spire, and lastly Lady Vane, also only once, if memorably. Now, at a critical juncture, the daughter – a nonentity, by Vane standards – drops by.

Cursing under his breath, Jaggard descended to his rooms. He revised his opinion of Cassie Vane within minutes of entering. She had grown up – lengthened in the leg and, to his lecher's eye, filled out. Her hair, held back, revealed a delicate neck, reminiscent of her mother. She had also acquired a knowing smile.

'Master Jaggard, your tower is like an ants' nest,' she said. 'All this coming and going – to what purpose?'

'The weather changes by the second. Ordinary people don't realise that.'

She gave him an amused look. How could she know today's hectic bustle was untypical?

'They look horribly anxious. Is it going to rain?'

Jaggard felt like slapping the little minx. 'Why are you here?'

'I've never met you, one to one.' She rearranged her legs. Her skirt was shorter than usual. 'My brother wants to marry me off. I'm exploring the field, and you're first up.'

Jaggard gulped. 'Does your brother know you're here?'

'Of course not – he doesn't trust you an inch.'

'Then why am I *first up*?' hissed Jaggard.

'Oh, come on, Mr Jaggard – as a spy.' She settled into a chair, crossed her legs, and smiled.

Jaggard found his cruder senses getting the better of him.

'But we could give him false information,' Cassie continued. 'Or that deadly mix, the half true. But, first things first. The point of a courtship ritual is to impress – so, impress me, Mr Jaggard.'

Jaggard could hardly believe his ears. What had happened to Cassie Vane?

'I'll do more than impress; I'll blow your mind. But on one condition. You're blindfolded until I say. However long it takes.'

Cassie Vane had not allowed for Jaggard seizing the initiative, still less this bizarre demand, but, having started the game, she was determined to finish it. She had lived a convent life; now, she would be an adventurer.

'I've a condition too. You do nothing I do not consent to.'

'I accept. But understand this, Miss Vane: I too have to be

impressed. I need to know you have the courage to face the true majesty of the weather-watchers without flinching.'

Jaggard meant it. Cassie's proposal had real attractions. Such an alliance would legitimise his rule, yet she must serve him, and that meant respecting his power.

'When?' asked Cassie.

'Now.'

'Let's get on with it, then,' she replied.

7

Old Steps Retraced

The murk, ignorance of their destination and the Jabberwock's innate melancholy induced in Fogg and Niobe a sense of suspended animation. From time to time, lovemaking broke the spell, but the relief did not last. They felt like ghosts on the *Marie Celeste*.

A sudden dazzle of sun on snow, therefore, came as a shock, as did the squalls of freezing but fresh air as the shield rose without warning.

Niobe danced on the foredeck and admired her shadow. Mr J opened his wings, extended his scaly neck and inhaled, eyes narrow and shut, as if intoxicated.

Fogg, however, instantly recognised the landscape as the craft, buffeted by crosswinds, swung over a high ridge into a steep and narrow valley.

Below, little had changed. The rickety slide still ran from the balcony down to the square below. The circular lid, which had led to Mander's subterranean island, remained in place. Even Mr Venbar's staff, and the skeletal remains of the two toves who had fought over it, lay where they had fallen on the open ground nearby. He could neither see nor smell any living tove. Hopefully, they had all perished at Deception Island.

'I've been here before,' he shouted down from the bridge to Niobe. 'Those ruined balconies belong to the original Tempestas headquarters.'

He kept to himself his encounter with the ancient Mr Venbar. He could imagine Niobe's wrath on discovering that Venbar and the weather-watchers had exploited an ecological catastrophe to hasten the demise of the old world. They had enough to confront in the present.

The wreckage of the high balconies might have provided an anchorage, but the issue was taken out of Fogg's hands. The craft settled itself in a hollow close to ground level and then shut down.

They disembarked. The lid at the base of the slide had been secured from below, but Mander, Fogg suspected, had moved on, so it did not matter. *Arbor spirantia* would wipe out everyone unless a defence could be found. Spire, bereft of an answer himself, must have delivered them here with that in mind.

Mr J's exhilaration quickly passed. He returned to type with a mournful melody:

> *'Like waves, the empires rise and fall.*
> *Clouds gather just to disappear,*
> *So meet me in the ruined hall*
> *To sing a song of fleeting cheer.'*

'That's enough of that,' said Fogg. 'We need to get up there.' He pointed towards a saddle near the mountaintop, the highest balcony of all. 'That's where the state rooms are, and, more important, the library.'

Niobe shook her head. 'What? *Up* that slide? No thanks.'

Mr J offered his services, but with provisos. 'I can't carry you in my claws; they're too sharp. And I can't hover up there and drop you off; it's too windy.'

'You mean you're too windy,' said Niobe. Her fear of vertigo, natural in a child of caves and mines, quickly gave way to her love of a challenge.

Mr J raised a scaly claw towards the summit, where snow puffed off the ridge like smoke. 'Fliers understand these things. Allow me to demonstrate.' He knelt for his riders, like an old-world camel.

'Give your shoes to Mr J,' Niobe commanded Fogg.

'What?!'

'Just do it.'

Fogg obeyed, and Niobe tied their shoes to the Jabberwock's claws by their laces. They clambered on to his shoulders, as they had near the borogrove with the late lamented Cavall.

About halfway up the slope, the gusts turned vicious, causing Mr J to lose direction whenever he opened his wings wide. If he fully closed them, he fell, the faster for the added weight of his passengers.

He turned to short, sharp wingbeats, tacking gradually upwards, but, the higher they progressed, the more a fatal collision with either rock or ruins threatened. Niobe did not repeat her charge of cowardice. The monster was displaying pluck and skill. She and Fogg merely nodded when Mr J yelled over the storm, 'There – that outcrop is on the lee side. You'll have to take the slide for the rest of the way.'

The monster seized a protruding stanchion with a claw, allowing them to dismount on to a large concrete block beside the slide, but he could not hold the position for long. They watched aghast as he spiralled higher and higher, as if in a violent thermal, reducing to a dot in the azure sky, before plummeting like a banished angel. At the last minute, his wings opened, braking his descent to land on the topmost balcony.

'One up, two to go,' said Fogg to Niobe.

'We did the Dark Circus and we can do this,' yelled Niobe, punching Fogg gently in the shoulder.

Close up, the slide seemed less secure than it had during his harum-scarum escape from the toves, but at least the scooped sides offered shelter and the supporting brackets felt firm.

'We roll on to the slide, then hand over hand, keeping flat. And the black moth goes first,' suggested Fogg, judging that his greater weight would be better placed to hold her than vice versa. She did not demur and set off.

The wisdom of losing their shoes quickly became apparent. Toes, even very cold toes, gripped the surface, sparing the arms the full burden of their body weight.

Niobe's superior fitness and lighter physique opened a growing gap between her and Fogg.

'Not too fast!' he shouted. 'If you fall, I won't be able to stop you.' *Or myself*, he thought, but did not say. But she did not stop and did not turn. Belatedly, Fogg realised this child of the caverns could not face looking back and down. The wind whined between them, harsh and unforgiving. Yet childhood resilience lasts, and, for Fogg, extreme cold was a familiar enemy.

Keep moving was the mantra, yet, even so, by the time Niobe reached Mr J, Fogg was twenty minutes behind. As he toiled on, arm after arm, step after step, he wondered why Tempestas had abandoned this impregnable citadel, leaving only the deranged Mr Venbar behind. Guilt, he decided, being more than the old-world leaders had ever felt for inflicting war and devastation on their peoples and the planet.

The sun had dipped from sight, hardening the skyline into a random assortment of broken teeth. As the temperature plummeted, a tiny bird skipped past, staccato wingbeats managing the wind with aplomb. Its white collar lent it a strange, decapitated look against the snow.

Hands numb and legs stiff, Fogg finally made it to the balcony.

'It gets you in the small of the back,' said Niobe, hauling him up through the hexagonal opening which had allowed Fogg to escape, weeks earlier.

'It got me everywhere,' replied Fogg, unwinding his torso. 'I preferred the downhill experience.'

Mr J delivered another gloomy pronouncement on the cliffs and crags, as snow flurries drifted across in the dying light:

'The lie of the land
Is a lie which kills,
For even high hills
Have their evening.'

'You're facing the wrong way, Mr J,' said Fogg, as he turned.

Ahead, globe-lights glimmered in the first room and through the doorway beyond. On his last visit, Fogg had raced through these chambers in panic. Now, he had time to take in the wooden beds with their adjacent tables. Prints of old-world birds and animals dotted the walls, barely discernible through the dust.

They retrieved their shoes and Fogg led the way. An undeclared detour to avoid Mr Venbar's huge hall with the rod of judgement and whatever remained of his body paid dividends. They emerged halfway up the grand central staircase. Above them, the bust of the first Lord Vane looked down from a plinth, where the staircase divided. Not even the Jabberwock's hypersensitive hearing could catch any sound of pursuit.

'Here, we go down,' said Fogg.

Below them, a succession of marble landings, each with a globe-light above, receded into the gloom. Off one of the most generous lay four doors, their architraves carved with the titles of the room beyond: the Chamber of Maps, the Chamber of Warnings, the Chamber of Cities and the Chamber of Records. As on Fogg's first visit, the brass curlicue handles on the first three would not move, but the door to the Chamber of Records opened freely.

They froze. A wafer-thin line of yellow light marked a second door at the end of a small vestibule, only to be extinguished. The door had been open on Fogg's last visit. The Jabberwock's head coiled up to the door and returned.

'Paper rustling,' he said, as if some academic crime were in progress, his green antennae erect and quivering like hair combed into electricity.

Fogg had become more devil-may-care, more take-what-comes. Whatever or whoever lay beyond the door had to be confronted.

He spoke normally: 'It's what you'd expect from an archive. And, Mr J, if you don't mind, to those unaware of your many virtues, the sight of you in this sepulchral light might be terminal.' He strode forward, opened the door and walked in.

The single occupant, a hunched, slight figure, had retreated to the darkest corner. Globe-lights might be perpetual, but their ghostly glow left pools of darkness. A blade glinted, as the Jabberwock disobeyed orders and slithered into the room, his great fish-eyes all agog.

The blade disappeared, and a familiar cheery voice broke the silence: 'Is that not the fizzog of the Jabberwock?'

'*Mr J* is easier on the tongue,' the monster replied.

Crike abandoned her corner and stepped into the light.

'You look younger,' stammered Fogg, and so she did, in her tidy dress and shirt, with her hair drawn back and her smart spectacles.

Crike merely stroked the base of the Jabberwock's antennae, eliciting an old-world feline purr.

'How did you get here?' asked Niobe suspiciously.

'I crash-landed, on the lee side, where there are hangars of soft snow.'

'And *why* are you here?'

'Look, ducky, I've a better right to ask you that question. I'm Tempestas' official historian, as commissioned by the first Lord Vane. He's the don't-mess-with-me floating plaster head at the top of those stairs. So, this is my patch. All the more so, now present, future and past are busy converging.'

Crike activated a desk lamp, which illuminated the large central table. Photographs littered the surface in a disconnected collage. They had an aged, sepia look. Beside them lay a magnifying glass and Crike's manuscript notes.

'The life and times of Tempestas' first climatologist,' explained

Crike, 'one Oberon Potts: a hard man, not to be confused with his softy of a son, Oblivious. Oberon preferred creepy crawlies and trees to mankind.'

The single photograph which Fogg had found on his first visit was there – the man in colonial shorts, posing beside an Amazonian Indian – but Crike had assembled many more.

'Before the Fall?' asked Niobe.

'Not long before,' replied Crike, revelling in the return of civilised company. She tapped the table. 'Welcome to the Crike School of Counter-Espionage. We each have our own mind's eye, conditioned by our particular baggage. So, tell me what you see when you're ready, one at a time, no conferring. They were taken on an expedition to the Amazon basin.'

Crike's methodology inspired a competitive spirit. Fogg and Niobe peered harder and thought deeper than they would otherwise have done, while sharing Crike's magnifying glass with studied courtesy. Privately, each wondered what the other would be looking for. The Jabberwock was selective and appeared to have an agenda of his own.

Crike did not interfere, retreating to a corner, where she pored over a pile of dull accountancy ledgers and building plans.

Niobe spoke first, after theatrically dropping the magnifying glass on the table.

'It's deplorable, it really is. They take the one seed pod from that native's mystical tree, and then they kill it. Poor man.'

Crike put down her pen. 'Kill it? Are you sure?'

'Of course I'm sure. There are many pictures of the same species of tree, but only one of them flowers *and* fruits. *This* tree.' Niobe's finger stabbed at the photographs in question. 'Note the sole long seed-case in this photograph, *here*, and how, in this one, it's gone, *there*. And look at the leaves. Happy and healthy in the first; drooping and discoloured in the second. I thought you were Tempestas' historian. Why are you surprised? One of those men is a weather-watcher. There's a badge on his jacket. Would they gift an indigenous tribesman control of the skies?' She paused. This time, her finger jabbed at Crike. 'Did the weather-watchers engineer the Fall?'

'The murk came first, but I believe they exploited it. The weather-watcher in the picture is Jaggard senior.'

'Tempestas wanted to teach the world a lesson, and it got out of control,' added Fogg, under his breath. And even that's generous, thought Fogg, remembering Mr Venbar's speech about the rod of judgement.

Niobe spun round. 'How do you know?' she asked fiercely.

'A man called Venbar told me. He was a weather-watcher who stayed behind. I met him in Tiriel's Tower, just down there. He secured my escape before being torn to pieces by toves. It's not an image I wanted to share.'

Niobe continued, 'That stolen seed mothered a rampant form of plant life which breeds killer insects and has the same ambitions as the weather-watcher: wipe us out and inherit the Earth. I can't say I blame it.'

Crike pointed to the pile of ledgers. 'It's more complex than that. The seed went to the College of Novelties, wherever that might be. There, it bloomed and cleared the air, but did not fruit. Lord Vane sought Lord Sine's help. That's how Genrich got their grimy mitts on the tree's genetic material.' She turned to Fogg. 'Tell me what the photographs tell you.'

'Less than they told Niobe,' he replied bashfully. 'But I can add one. I found it on my last visit.' Fogg fumbled in his back pocket, where the photograph had resided ever since. 'It has a unique feature, and I've been a fool. I missed its significance.'

'Just more non-flowering trees – what's unique about that?' queried Niobe, after a glance.

Crike peered over Fogg's shoulder. 'The one at the back isn't a tree. It's a totem pole made from one.'

'Well spotted,' said Fogg, a little taken aback. 'It ended up in the Museum Dome, with the label *Provenance unknown*,' he explained. 'But what matters is – it's finely carved with flowers and fruit. The Museum notes said the wood was unknown. It must be an earlier specimen of our flowering tree – one which also fruited, to judge from the decoration.'

'What possible use is a dead trunk – other than to the locals who venerate it?' chipped in Niobe.

Mr J had so far said nothing. Now, he burst into near nonsensical verse:

> *'Pictures surpass a pretty phrase;*
> *His god is stencilled on his skin.*
> *Gods must give to earn such praise,*
> *Capture their gift if you would win.'*

'Meaning?' asked Crike.

Niobe stamped a foot. 'You won't get more. He's maddening, he just has to be cryptic.'

Fogg stared at the photographs which had attracted Mr J's attention. They all featured the Amazonian Indian, a chieftain, to judge from his elaborate jewellery.

'He's tattooed in gold . . . with insects,' Fogg said. 'Flying insects.'

'That doesn't make sense,' said Crike. 'The insects came later, as we've just been . . . and they're not gold.' She paused. *Unless* . . .

The Jabberwock's mysterious verse raised a bizarre possibility. To share or not to share? So much hung on this most slender of threads. She remained silent as a bird skipped into the room, landed on the Jabberwock's head and burst into song.

'Ouzels do mood music,' said Crike, 'and this one is agitated. We best get moving.'

'Since when did birds give orders?' asked Niobe.

'They're the Northerners' eyes and ears. I'll explain as we go.'

The ouzel led them back to the main staircase and down at pace. Crike's promised commentary was delivered in breathless dribs and drabs.

'The Northerners were not a people, at the start ... just the world's best craftsmen and women ... Recruited by Tempestas, they gathered all the materials they could find before the Fall ... and stored them deep in the mountain ... They built this place, but kept themselves apart ... Outsiders are rarely admitted ... The ouzels are mountain birds ...'

As they descended, the intervals between globe-lights lengthened and the staircase diminished in width and grandeur. They reached a circle of marble set in the floor, surrounded by an elegant grey-white marble colonnade with eight broad identical arches. Beyond, they could see a second colonnade, with the arches doubled in number and reduced in size, and beyond that the dim outline of another circle.

'This must be their fabled Postern Gate. I never believed it existed,' said Crike. 'It's a succession of rotating gateways, which you have to follow in the right sequence to gain admission. Miss one and you've no chance.'

'I think I heard a footstep,' whispered Niobe.

They stopped and peered down the stairs into the gloom.

Nobody else could catch it.

'Heavy and slow,' Niobe added, 'from the depths.' A pause. She looked worried.

As they strove to catch this elusive sound, a deafening crash, as of torn metal, thundered upwards in an explosive blast.

'I can't see a sausage,' said Crike, looking through a miniature telescope which had appeared from her bag as if from nowhere.

'Follow that ouzel,' cried Fogg, 'whatever arch he takes.'

They did, at speed, but there was a problem. As the arches narrowed at the third circle, the Jabberwock could not get through.

He did not hesitate. 'Fate has a different journey for me,' he said. With a bow, he embarked on a final envoi:

> '*May forests honour you with shade,*
> *The Earth be sprung beneath your feet . . .*'

'Scram!' yelled Niobe.

Mr J disappeared the way they had come, back into the gloom. Columns were falling nearer now, and the noise was deafening.

'What the hell! No voice and no body,' cried Fogg.

'Another present from Lord Sine,' gasped Crike.

'Hurry, hurry!' shouted Niobe.

The circles became wider as they advanced, increasing the distance to the next allotted exit. Keeping the ouzel in sight was quite a challenge. Fogg and Niobe half-carried Crike to keep in contact.

Whatever lurked behind showed no interest in them. It merely destroyed as it progressed, not unlike the toves.

The final ring of arches led to a short passage enclosed by an unworked rock wall. Behind them, their invisible stalker continued its rampage.

The ouzel disappeared down a hole, and seconds later a concealed gate opened. They needed no invitation. They rushed in. On the other side, a complex mechanism of pulleys and counterweights closed the gate.

Their rescuers, a man and a woman, made an incongruous pair of guards. Each carried a spear and wore a belt festooned with woodworking tools. The woman carried a birdcage in her other hand, with the ouzel already installed. They looked in shock and not especially friendly.

'Did that monster of yours do this?' asked the woman.

'Certainly not,' said Crike. 'Unusual-looking he may be, but he's a model of restraint.'

Her audience looked dubious, as the gate shuddered and shook. The intruder was piling up rubble. The entry mechanism jerked and fell to the ground.

'He couldn't get through the last arch, so wisely ran,' added Crike. 'I regret to report that whatever is out there is invisible as well as psychotic.'

The man reached for a speaking tube and held it to the gate. 'Hear that! The Postern is immobilised and the Fractal Gate destroyed.' Pause. 'Apparently not. Something else is out there, only we can't bloody see it.' Another pause. 'Yes, the other three are here.' Pause. 'Of course.' He turned to them. 'The Elector wants to see you.'

Only then did they take in the unusual features of the passage ahead. The pit props and ceiling beams had been finely carved. Old-world images abounded from the diverse worlds from which this community's ancestors had been drawn: swags of exotic fruit; domestic wild animals from the tropics and more temperate zones; even the occasional skyscraper, with its hard, vertical geometry. Above them, mobiles constructed from slivers of cut glass and globestone basted the passages in a shimmering light. Underfoot, a mosaic transformed the passage floor into a river, whose waves bent grasses, carried fish and eels, and circumnavigated boulders.

Fogg wondered what Morag would say, if here. To his eye, the whole was a more fulsome tribute to what had been lost than the synthetic fauna with which the second Lord Vane had populated the Tempestas Dome.

Some side caverns held huge piles of felled trees. Others contained furnaces, the chimneys of which conjoined and ran up through the ceiling. A hamlet occupied another, all balconies, exterior staircases and windows of coloured glass. Niobe felt an urge to knock on the nearest door, but she did not get the chance.

A horn sounded, not a personal instrument, but a mechanical

serpent, powered by bellows. The guttural call to arms rang through the entire city. Men and women appeared ahead and behind, dressed for war, but calm and organised. The guards broke into a trot.

'Don't mind me,' said Crike as she lagged behind.

Without a word, the male guard tossed her over his shoulder in a fireman's lift and ran on.

'Ooh, you are strong, young man,' stammered Crike, removing the spectacles from her nose.

They hurried on to a lift-like contraption, which hurtled up a shaft at a forty-five-degree angle, to emerge in a large circular chamber with stairways to a gallery lined with optical devices at regular intervals: an observation room at the mountain's summit, with a view all around. The place heaved with unfamiliar people, but old friends too. In front of strangers, there was little physical embrace. Speech was less restrained.

'Potts!' cried Crike.

'Morag!' cried Fogg.

'Fogg!' cried Morag.

'Potts? Morag?' stuttered Niobe suspiciously, as if this might be a trick.

To Fogg, Morag looked different. The word *weather-beaten* came to mind, and there was no Benedict, he noted.

An imposing woman, her face as warm and resolute as her handshake, greeted them at the top of the gallery steps. Beside her, Potts beamed like a schoolboy. He had trimmed his beard and smartened his appearance. Old fool, Crike thought, she's a good twenty years younger. Potts' introductions added to her irritation.

'Miss Hilda Crike, more resourceful than she looks; Niobe, as resourceful as she looks; and Mr Fogg, who has a gift for surprise.' He paused and waved a deferential hand towards his neighbour. 'Meet the Elector,' he added, 'the ruler of this place, ever enlightened but never despotic.'

'I prefer *orchestrator*,' the Elector replied, 'as all I do is conduct the more challenging passages. Like now. And I prefer my name to my title – Hesper. But let me show you what we're up against.'

Optical devices, which resembled fixed harbour telescopes, fed into the wall, but swivelled freely to widen the view. Crike, resolving not to show her annoyance with Potts, hurried from one to the next, before pronouncing her verdict.

'It's Cosmo's fleet from Acheron. I came from there.' The admission earned quizzical looks from almost everyone. 'I was on a private mission to better acquaint myself with young Fogg and his Museum.'

The Elector ignored Crike's puzzling last sentence. 'Was Lord Vane in Acheron?'

'Not that I saw or heard,' replied Crike.

'When I last saw him, he was in an underground town, far away, with a small retinue,' added Morag.

Hesper shrugged. 'Well, his main force is here, and one thing's for sure: tantalum might have made the world go round in the past, but now it's wood and glass. They're the pirates, and we're the treasure ship, only we have no sails.'

'And now no escape hatch,' said a tall man with a lugubrious voice and bright eyes hooded by the bushiest of eyebrows.

'This is Fabius,' explained Hesper, 'the closest person we have to a general. He is also Master of Pendulums. The destruction of the Fractal Gate is an architectural tragedy, but a strategic irrelevance. Retreat is not a viable option. We'd be abandoning our materials, our homes, our workbenches and our history – all that makes us what we are.'

Niobe jumped back. The observation tube in front of her fell from its socket with a clatter.

'There was a blur,' she said, 'like an incoming missile.'

Potts picked up a fragment of broken glass.

'Check the cavity,' said Hesper. 'If it's not an attack, it's a message.'

Fabius, who did not consider mundane tasks beneath him, shinned up a ladder and inserted a hooked pole into the opening.

'Got him,' he cried, extracting the remains of a mechanical bird, which had impacted the lens with pinpoint accuracy. Wires spilled through its ruptured skin. A small canister, attached to its back, remained intact.

Hesper read the enclosed message to herself and then out loud:

Surrender by midnight and be given terms.
Fight and expect no quarter.

'What terms?' asked Niobe.

'Lord Vane's terms,' said Hesper. 'Subjugation, in a word.'

'And he'll kill you and your leaders,' added Potts. 'It's a no-brainer.'

'Fuck them,' said Fabius, as a second telescope escaped its moorings. Another bird emerged with another message, only its plumage was white.

'Close all the ports on this level,' said Hesper. 'They're horribly well informed.' She nodded towards Fabius. 'Read away. We've no secrets here.'

'*Fight to be rescued.* The writing is unsurprisingly different.'

Silence.

Two contrasting birds and two contradictory messages.

Morag stepped forward. 'I dropped in on Lord Sine, and Jaggard was there. He betrayed the second Lord Vane; he's quite capable of doing the same to the third. I think the second bird is his.'

Fabius stepped off the ladder. 'But the weather-watchers have only a few craft of their own. We're too deep for them to reach us, and, with all the sheltering gullies and ravines, Lord Vane's fleet would be hard to dislodge, meteorologically speaking. I don't see how they could rescue us.'

Hesper surveyed the room. 'When uncertain, let the enemy

move. Meantime, let's show our guests our Operations Room and a more convivial welcome. Follow me.'

'If I may . . .' Crike's voice had upped in volume and determination. 'Might I borrow that excellent bird which saw me in, and return to my craft?'

'And your reason?' asked Hesper.

'I don't think Lord Vane is here or coming here. I think another crisis looms. For which I need Mr Potts' company.'

'Well, Oblivious? A warning from a good historian should not be lightly dismissed.' She gave Crike a cautionary look. 'Despite the lack of detail.'

'Yes, but I . . . you . . . and yours . . . I mean . . .' stammered Potts.

'That's settled, then,' said Hesper firmly. 'Morag, Fogg and Niobe will fortify us with youth; Miss Crike and Mr Potts will deploy their wisdom and experience elsewhere.'

A man with a birdcage appeared and departed with Potts and Crike, as the others followed Hesper back into the depths of the Northerners' city.

8

Fencing Between Friends

'You old goat,' hissed Crike, as she and Potts edged along an icy gully, the ouzel leading the way.

'You mean *mountain* goat. Oblivious Ibex Potts.'

'I mean it's disgusting, fawning over a fifty-year-old at your age.'

'Fifty-six.'

'You make it so revoltingly obvious,' added Crike over her shoulder.

'I like her call and I like her plumage. Why shouldn't I celebrate the fact?'

'You sound like an old-world dirty postcard.'

'Come on, Crikey. You forget you turned me down, all those years ago.'

Crike was about to say she was playing hard to get, and changed her mind, because it was not true. She had valued her independence too much. 'So I did,' was all she could muster.

Crike's description of her landing site as a hangar of snow was apt. The craft was near invisible and the cockpit had frozen over. Their bare hands took time in the biting cold to clear the ice and release the door. That achieved, the ouzel departed.

'I drive,' she said. 'No arguments.'

'Your vehicle,' replied Potts, keen to make peace.

'Passengers first.'

As Potts clambered in, Crike looked out from that forlorn peak. The besieging craft were exchanging brief messages. Sparks of red and green came and went like a far-off firework display. She had faithfully chronicled the history of Tempestas. Her name appeared but once, in minuscule letters on the title page. Her life had run on the periphery of events. She could have stayed with the Northerners as a combatant, were it not for her theory. At times, it seemed fanciful; at other times, the only coherent solution. Historians, she cautioned herself, have an inbuilt tendency to place the claws of the past in the present.

The craft lifted clear in a plume of blasted snow. Crike steered it back over the hidden valley ascended by Fogg, Niobe and the Jabberwock a few hours earlier. The blocking of the Postern Gate ruled out an attack from that quarter, and the craft slid into the murk with no sign of pursuit. On entering the coordinates for the college, taken from the plan in the library, she felt a twinge of guilt. The coordinates might be inaccurate or a trap. The craft's power reserves were an unknown. Most importantly, insofar as she had a strategy, it was dependent on Morag, who might not survive the siege. And she had not explained these risks to Potts. She comforted herself with the thought that the rules of risk-taking must bend in times of war.

'Why am I here?' asked Potts as they levelled out.

'Some reasons you can know; others must wait.'

'I'm listening.'

'Tell me about your father.'

'He was hard on me, my mother and the human race. He was also the most brilliant naturalist of his generation. Tempestas recruited him well before the Fall.'

'Did he know Peregrine Mander?'

'Anyone who knew the first Lord Vane knew Mander. He made himself the gatekeeper without anyone noticing.'

'Could they have plotted together?'

'Plotted what? A night on the town?'

'Calf love has made you facetious, Potts. Might they have prepared a second chance for mankind after the Fall?'

'I doubt it. The first Lord Vane was banking on the Boojum tree, and that came to nothing, as we know.'

'What about Fogg's Museum?'

'My father had no truck with human art. He admired birds' nests and spiderwebs. Mander, on the other hand, regarded art as mankind's saving grace.'

'So, what was Mander doing with your father in the Amazon basin?'

'The weather-watchers spotted a hole in the murk, which led to the Boojum tree's discovery. But Mander had no interest in that. You've tasted his drinks: spices, herbs, roots, fruit. He was always on the lookout for new flavours. In fact, he returned with a new cocktail – the Orinoco. Bloody dynamite!'

'With effects lasting into old age,' muttered Crike. To her, Potts' explanation did not ring true.

'I helped Morag to the Museum,' continued Potts. 'Spire said she would be safe there and out of Lord Sine's clutches. According to him, Mander had set the Museum up decades earlier, at the time of the Fall.'

'You'd never met her before?'

'Mander set a clue in my old library, Pandora's Place, which only Morag could solve. She cracked it and found the craft hidden nearby,' continued Potts. 'As soon as I learnt from Fogg that Spire left him at the Genrich School, I assumed that Mander and Spire also arranged Fogg's transfer to the Museum.' Potts paused. Another player, hitherto unnoticed, had slipped into view. 'According to Fogg, a golden beetle led him from the school to the same craft which took Morag to the Museum. But Mander makes cocktails, not golden beetles. Which means . . .'

Crike nodded. 'Mander and Cassie Vane are in cahoots.'

This significant proposition evaded debate as the murk turned violent. The craft soared, somersaulted and plunged at breakneck speed.

'Jehu!' cried Potts, grasping Crike's hand to strengthen her grip on the joystick, which miraculously did not snap. Slithers of clear air accompanied the turbulence, until, after only minutes, dead air and the suffocating grasp of the murk returned. 'Like being spun in a kaleidoscope.'

'Silly man,' replied Crike. 'It's weather-watchers at play. I hope they haven't fouled our bearings.'

'They've certainly fouled mine,' muttered Potts, wiping his mouth with his shirt.

'We're going to hell in a handcart,' Crike said, removing Potts' hand from both her own and the joystick. 'And I mean all of us.'

9

Siege

'The Operations Room,' announced Fabius, 'formerly the Hall of Carvings.'

A collection of woodwork along one long wall confirmed the cavern's former role, but a huge circular pond with a wooden surround, filled to the rim, seized the eye. Beside it stood a much smaller pond, but otherwise identical. Tiny circles of glass dotted the ceiling. A row of desks dominated the other long wall, with racks of jars and tubes behind them.

'The messaging hub,' explained Fabius. 'Here, orders and information arrive and leave from the entire city. Jars carry messages via the tubes, vacuum driven. Environmentally clean as a whistle.'

'And the pond?' asked Morag.

'Water makes a better mirror. Glass steams, scratches and shatters.'

'War is the mother of invention,' added Hesper. 'Alas.'

A tube hissed. A woman at the message table reached behind her, opened the arriving tube and read the enclosed message.

'Balsas in position,' she said, 'wind negligible.'

'Activate them,' said Hesper without hesitation.

Another tube headed out. Minutes later, the glass eyes in the ceiling came to life, and so did the pond. No bigger than toys, held in place by tiny rotors, the balsas had released clouds of globe dust, as the images from their mirrors fed through to the main pool and a three-dimensional view of the mountain's exterior appeared in the water. The adjacent smaller pool showed only the night sky, for the moment mainly clear.

In a cavern below the Operations Room, Outrageous Fortune stood ready, all wheels, slings, shields and scopes. Huge boulders and iron bolts lined up on retractable racks, ready to feed the great war machine when the time came.

'Now we wait,' said Fabius, as Northerners distributed wine to their guests.

Cosmo Vane's fleet commander pored over a map. A severe but clever man, he styled himself Cytus, after Cocytus, one of the five rivers of the underworld. He had had dealings with Northerners and knew they were not the surrendering kind. The lack of any response to his master's ultimatum had been no surprise. His orders were to kill enough men and women to make an example. The map showed in detail the known portals to the mountain's interior. Three minutes to go to midnight and the expiry of his ultimatum. His finger hovered over his Morse machine.

'Sir,' cried the pilot of his craft.

Cytus walked a few paces to the cockpit. Hundreds of tiny motes of golden light, globestone dust, had been released from high above them. They had lost the protective shroud of night. He hurried back and stabbed out the Morse for *attack*.

His map proved accurate. Harpoons ripped open the three main portals like an old-world tin opener. As predicted, Outrageous Fortune trundled out.

'What idiots,' he muttered. 'No shields.'

Craft swooped. Synthetic balls of fire stuck to the wood like glue, reducing the fabled ballista to a blazing wreck in minutes.

'Welcome to grown-up warfare.' He turned to the co-pilot. 'Time for the troop carriers,' he said.

The co-pilot tapped out the message.

As the heavier craft lumbered in, Cytus had his first misgivings.

Outrageous Fortune had distintegrated with remarkable speed, and, through his telescope, he could see no sign of casualties.

'Shit!' he shouted. 'Get them out!'

Too late. Out of the shadows, in an area not caught by the globe dust, the true Outrageous Fortune emerged from its new home, arms flailing like a windmill. Three craft shattered in as many minutes, spewing their men on to the rocks below. A flaming bolt narrowly missed Cytus' own craft. The fireships returned to the fray, but Outrageous Fortune sprouted spiked shields, covered in damp turf, which impaled the fireballs before they could reach its core machinery.

Wiser now, the surviving landing craft veered away, their pilots unsure how to press home the attack.

Cytus sent in a smaller, more nimble craft to test the machine's range.

In response, Outrageous Fortune changed munitions, firing clouds of smaller stones instead of heavy single missiles. The attackers limped away.

Forcing it to use up its ordnance was the only strategy left. Cytus sent in another light craft.

But, then, inexplicably, after its first volley narrowly missed, Outrageous Fortune succumbed to mechanical failure. Its rate of fire slackened, and its mobility diminished.

Cytus raised his telescope. A shield arm snapped, and another, for no apparent reason. A rock from its ammunition racks levitated, without human assistance, and crashed into the superstructure. Blazing material lifted from the shield and slapped on to the superstructure. Outrageous Fortune's crew left their stations to fight this new menace, but their flailing weapons caught only air.

The invisible attacker finally acquired a semblance of a profile as it too caught fire. Oblivious to its own survival, the giant figure continued its demolition of the mountain's main defence like an enraged demon, until it too disintegrated in the heat.

'Good old Lord Sine,' cheered Cytus.

Emboldened, the troop carriers returned, landing soldiers close to each of the three ledges. Others held back in reserve. The nimbler escorts moved into the shelter of previously allotted gullies.

'Take me in,' said Cytus. 'They won't have a chance now.'

In the Operations Room, all present craned over the mirror pool and watched the swift reversal of their position in grim silence. To Fogg and Morag, the war paintings in the Museum, and the old-world horrors they portrayed, had come to vivid life.

'Can't you do something?' cried Niobe.

By way of response, Hesper moved to the smaller pool. She summoned Fabius and pointed to a tiny dot in the night sky.

'If it were late summer, that would be Saturn; but it isn't and it can't be. Nor is it a star. Stars twinkle.'

'What, then?'

'A craft.'

'But it's miles up and motionless.'

'Because it's watching – and waiting, just like us,' replied Hesper.

The message desk intervened: 'Report from the balsas: tranquil in the upper air, but a fast-building wind lower down, from the northwest.'

'In other words, towards us,' said Fabius.

'Figures,' replied Hesper.

To everyone else, her calmness was inexplicable.

The news of the northwesterly wind approaching from the valley below reached Cytus at about the same time. He had been warned by Cosmo about Jaggard, and an intervention by the weather-watchers had been factored in.

'Levelling off at Beaufort, scale six,' the pilot added. 'Calm air higher up.'

'Too little and too late,' said Cytus, as he descended a ladder to terra firma.

Almost all his troops had already landed and were now swarming up the slopes to the three exposed ledges, two of them well lit by the fire from the remains of the true and false Outrageous Fortune, now fanned by the strengthening breeze. His surviving craft, well sheltered by contours of the mountainside, had been fitted with additional protections against lightning. He felt confident that, once inside the mountain, his troops would have the edge in any hand-to-hand fighting against untrained pacifist Northerners. With the Postern Gate blocked, they could be starved out, if push came to shove. Despite the initial hitch, victory beckoned.

A View from the Gods

Jaggard had, for the most part, kept his word, as she had hers. The blindfold had been tight and effective, leaving other senses to compensate.

Hearing, touch of feet and hands, air pressure and temperature changes implied to Cassie the following journey: they had climbed to the top of Tiriel's Tower, with Jaggard leading the way; they had briefly stepped outside; she had then been guided to a seat on a floor which wobbled slightly. Her ears had then crackled and her stomach heaved, as if rising at speed. Jaggard had said nothing throughout and had been seated beside her. Her bag had not been searched.

Jaggard had gratuitously bumped his thigh against hers, but nothing more. Hours had passed with only a low-level hum for accompaniment. She resisted asking any question, considering it a sign of weakness.

On occasion, she felt him lean forward and back. When he did so, she sensed a change of direction. Straining for any sound which might indicate the presence of a third person, she detected none. Her hand found a convex surface on the side away from Jaggard. *We're in a small craft, which he is controlling*, she concluded.

The temperature remained constant, until her heightened senses reported a slight rise in Jaggard's body heat. Did he intend some act of intimacy? Or was it just the imminent excitement of impressing her?

After a click, a narrow tube flicked her left arm, which felt like a telescope, and Jaggard broke the silence.

'Ready to be impressed?' he asked in a voice dripping with anticipation.

Cassie turned the knot of the blindfold towards him.

He freed it with a cry of, 'Abracadabra!'

She yelped. They were miles up in the night sky, in a bubble with no apparent floor or ceiling. She fought a wave of nausea and clasped the arms of her seat.

'Look down, not up,' he counselled.

She steeled herself and followed the advice.

Below, a strange incandescence glowed not far beneath their craft and, further below, two fires blazed on the side of an imposing mountain.

Jaggard handed her the telescope. 'Watch the men,' he said.

She took the instrument, but examined the craft's interior before using it. The craft was made from glass or some similarly transparent material. They were seated side by side on identical seats, save that, in front of Jaggard, a joystick stood proud of a plethora of instruments. A Morse machine had been screwed to a panel to Jaggard's left. He tapped out a message, and the machine quickly responded.

Cassie peered down through the telescope. 'Where are we? Who's attacking whom?' she asked.

'Your brother is attacking the Northerners. That blazing wreck is their only weapon of note, so he seems to be winning.'

'Seems to be?'

'*Seems* to be,' he parroted.

Siege – The Second Act

Cytus was sharing his elation with a junior officer. It had been a weather-watcher's wind. The freakish stillness in the upper air confirmed that, but it had delivered nothing of concern, and there was no sign of any further resistance from the Northerners. He assumed they had learnt their lesson.

Another message, delivered from the furthest craft to the nearest and on to Cytus via a runner, induced a moment's hesitation.

'Low mist closing from the north,' said the runner, before adding words of reassurance: 'but no visible lightning or unusual turbulence.'

'You get side effects if you mess with the weather,' commented Cytus, as his men clambered up to the ledges which gave access to the Northerners' town.

A junior officer ventured a different view: 'You shouldn't get mist in a wind,' he said.

'You joining the weather-watchers?' barked Cytus, but the man had a point. He could just make out the mist, and it looked unnatural. 'Just get those fucking doors off!' he shouted.

Two craft closed and used harpoons on chains to prise open the doors. On the other ledge, gloomy without fire, the soldiers could see no door. They marched forward, only to meet resistance: a huge glass barrier on which hand weapons made no impact. More time passed as they retreated to allow the harpoons free access. The glass proved unusually thick. It fractured as deep ice does, but did not shatter. Identical barriers had descended to block the way in from the other two ledges.

'Silly bastards,' said Cytus. 'The more they fuck us around, the more they'll pay. Stoke fires by the glass and use heavier ordinance.'

Then he turned to look back, because his men had turned. The mist had reached the furthest support craft, and they appeared to be smoking; then, the next nearest. A ship, much closer, flashed a warning.

'Shrapnel of some kind and sudden turbulence!'

The two afflicted craft rose and attempted to bank away from the mist, but the grey cloud followed them and intensified. Their hulls began to disintegrate.

Cytus found a man with a signalling lamp. 'Avoid that fog!' he shouted.

But the mist was accelerating and spreading, its fingers seeking out craft with a hunter's eye. Closer now, it had an unnatural blueish tinge. Strips of chitin fell, themselves undamaged. Some craft dived into the mountain as if their steering were wrecked.

Behind this lethal fog, a second cloud, tinged red, raced towards them. Screams rent the air from men still on the lower slopes.

'Flies!' yelled someone nearby with a memory for old-world insects.

Seconds later, the swarm reached Cytus and the men on the platforms. They clawed at their faces to shield their eyes, or slapped their necks and legs, but to no avail. The insects did not pause to feed. Once a man was dead, they moved on.

High above, Cassie yelled 'Do something!' at Jaggard.

'In ten minutes or so, I will,' he replied. 'Prepare to be further impressed.' He tapped out another order.

Cassie watched the mysterious cloud roll back. She knew what made it: the same insects which had destroyed Fogg's beetle.

'You see, my dear, I control the winds,' Jaggard said. 'In a few minutes, you and I will pay our new subjects a visit.'

Those two words, *our* and *new*, came packed with meaning:

the end of her brother's reign, a betrothal and her succession on Jaggard's arm. It also meant an imminent sexual encounter. She pulled herself together. That's what her strategy entailed.

'I can't wait, *Lord* Jaggard,' she said huskily.

In the Operations Room, Hesper called the change in the wind before the message desk announced it – a remarkable turnabout from a northwesterly to a southeasterly, dragging the plague of flies back from whence they had come. The balsas, still stable in the calm upper air, showed two substantial craft approaching from the south. They landed close to the two ledges where fires still burnt, and disgorged a company of weather-watchers in their distinctive robes. Lightning rods in hand, they ascended to the ledges, ignoring the debris and the corpses.

'Open the barriers,' commanded Hesper. 'We've fought and we've been relieved.'

'I don't call weather-watchers relief,' shrilled an outraged Niobe.

'I rather agree,' added Morag. 'Out of the frying pan and into the fire.'

Hesper waved the protests aside. 'For the moment, we play along. I mean it, all of you.'

Fogg edged over to the small pool. 'That mysterious light is joining us too,' he said.

They watched the tiny ball grow into a bubble and become a remarkable craft, spherical and transparent.

'That's Jaggard, it's got to be,' muttered Niobe.

'And isn't that . . . ? It can't be . . .' stammered Fogg.

'It *is* . . . Cassie Vane,' confirmed Morag.

'But she wouldn't hurt a fly,' said Fogg, an unfortunate turn of phrase.

An evening of surprises delivered another.

Mander entered in full fig. 'I've rustled up a selection of cordials to greet their embassy.'

'Thank you, Mr Mander, we're obliged,' said Fabius.

'Miss Spire and Mr Fogg, you forever turn up like good pennies,' said Mander, with a bow.

'I could say the same of you,' said Morag, and she meant it. So many threads led back to the old retainer: Mander in the Amazon; Mander's postcards matching the Museum's paintings; Mander sending Fogg to Miss Baldwin and the White Circus; Mander the manservant to all the Vanes; Mander at Heorot and now Mander under the mountain at a time of crisis.

Mander ignored the remark and turned to the Elector. 'Maybe, ma'am, they best avoid Mr Jaggard. I suspect he still regards you three as renegades.'

Hesper nodded. 'Now is not the time to rock the boat. I'm sorry, but I'm with Mander. We're hiding you away until dawn, when we'll reassess. Trust me, something isn't quite right.'

'Let the enemy move?' said Fogg.

'You're a quick learner,' replied Hesper. 'Exactly that.'

Fogg, Niobe and Morag left with a guard. The ground shook beneath their feet as the Northerners' great horn bellowed out a blast of greeting to their rescuers. As the echo faded, the weather-watchers cheered the arrival of their Master.

With immaculate timing, the glass barrier rose, and a humbler fanfare announced the approach of Hesper and her entourage. Jaggard spoke first.

'Did I not keep my promise?'

'We're in your debt, Master.'

'May I introduce the Queen Consort.'

'Congratulations, Miss Vane, on the union of two great houses,' said Hesper.

Cassie spoke for the first time: 'The Master and I would like to tie the knot here, in the clear mountain air. Tomorrow morning, perhaps?'

'It's been a taxing day,' Jaggard interrupted, sounding a touch surprised by this initiative from his bride-to-be. 'I and my men require good quarters and the best provisions.'

'We have more than that,' replied Hesper. 'We have a banquet prepared and the most gifted mixologist in the wide world.'

'If it isn't the late Lord Vane's flunkey,' crowed Jaggard.

Mander hopped around the trays of drinks like a bird around an old-world bird table. 'These are in your honour, oh breaker of sieges, lord of the flies, ruler in the wings, cloud-maker . . .' he said, without a trace of irony.

'Master Jaggard hasn't all day,' said Hesper gently.

'First, we have a Strato Cirrus, an airy number for philosophical tastes: long in the finish, light and midly inconclusive. Next, an Incus, after the anvil cloud, for the sultry among us, who simmer but wish to come to the boil . . .'

'You try it, Lady Vane,' said Jaggard brusquely, as if suspecting poison.

'Delicious, as always,' said Cassie. 'You try it, dear.'

'Not bad, really not bad,' Jaggard acknowledged grudgingly.

'That's just the taste; its more pleasing effects are yet to come,' said Mander.

'Follow us, please,' said Hesper.

1 2

The Vorpal Blade

After the destruction of the Postern Gate, the Jabberwock retraced his steps through the abandoned chambers of the old Tempestas building, following the route they had taken earlier. He launched from a ruined balcony and landed on a sheltered slope on the southeastern side of the mountain. From there, he worked his way by foot down to the treeline.

As he feared, the shawl of trees, though not a perfect replica, had an ominous resemblance to the background to Tenniel's illustration of his fatal confrontation with Beamish. As in the illustration, he took up position between two pine trees.

He watched the balsas rise, stabilise and release their golden dust, and he caught the distant din of conflict, the acrid taste of woodsmoke and an unnatural change in the wind's direction. He ignored them all. They were human business, and, fond though he was of his new friends, he did not expect to see the outcome.

He consoled himself by singing a mournful ditty of his own invention, whose disordered lines drifted into his head with little rhyme and no reason.

> 'Listen to the tree-leaves,
> Heed the starlight's call;
> Count to seven,
> Talk to Heaven,
> And watch the blue blade fall.'

Fellow Wonderlanders had accused him of melancholia, a fair charge, but melancholy can be a positive creative force. Tonight, he felt merely hollow. On the second repeat, the barely broken voice he feared drifted back from the mountainside.

'My blade is true, but never blue – more a gilded silver,' it said.

Beamish swaggered into view, skipping over the rocks and kicking the snow off his shoes. The vorpal blade hung from a strap which ran from his right shoulder to behind his left knee.

'You've been avoiding me,' said Beamish, with a petulant point of the finger.

'I'm required to.'

'Nobody is required to keep me waiting.'

'You forget yourself and the text,' replied the Jabberwock, like a teacher irritated by a wayward pupil. *'Long time the manxome foe he sought . . .'*

'I hate pedants,' said Beamish. 'But, if you must be pedantic, you're meant to look fierce, not pathetic.'

'Not quite,' replied the Jabberwock, enjoying this brief moment of ascendancy.

> *'The Jabberwock, with eyes of flame,*
> *Came whiffling through the tulgey wood,*
> *And burbled as it came!'*

He hesitated. He had taken one word for granted. 'Whiffle?' he queried.

'You're the master of the text – do it! And look fearsome; I'm not here to behead a ninny.'

To his surprise, the Jabberwock was enjoying their verbal duel. He yearned to prolong it. 'That's a tumtum tree you're leaning on, by the way.'

Beamish unslung his sword. 'I couldn't give a toss what it is. Get whiffling.'

'What will you do when I'm dead?'

'Galumph back with your severed head.'

'After that?'

Testing question. Beamish had not thought beyond the literary climax of his existence. He pondered. 'I shall rule. I shall assassinate. I shall seduce.'

'You'll be busy, then.'

Beamish executed an extravagant sweep of the blade, inches from the Jabberwock's face. 'Stop playing for time.'

Time.

Tick-tock, tick-tock. The Jabberwock's hollowness dissipated. For all his affectations, the White Rabbit had been a lifelong friend.

'That's Rabbit's watch.'

'Was, was, was – spoils of war!'

'He wouldn't hurt a flea. He wouldn't know how to.'

'True, but he knows how to get beneath the skin. He irritated me once too often.'

'How?'

'He wouldn't tell me where you were.' Beamish demonstrated the Rabbit's demise with a flick of his free hand across the throat.

A restraining thread snapped in the Jabberwock's gentle psyche. The monster rose and settled some way back in the wood. 'I'll give you whiffle,' he muttered, and charged. Wings flapped, branches snapped, rocks scattered and his eyes were aflame.

'Good show,' cried Beamish. 'That's how we like it.'

He grasped his sword in both hands and struck at his adversary's neck. To his astonishment, the neck retracted and the right wing claw parried the blow.

'So you want it messy, do you? Death by a hundred cuts.'

This disrespect for the text, which envisaged a single fatal blow, enraged the Jabberwock. He ducked, he sidestepped, he blocked. The vorpal blade did get through, nonetheless. Green-ochre blood seeped from wounds to fingers, legs and a shoulder, but the quality of his evasive action kept the wounds shallow.

Belatedly, Beamish recognised his error. Imitate Teniel's illustration exactly – a double-handed blow, delivered from over the right shoulder – and the monster, obedient to the text, would abandon this tiresome defence. For a moment, Beamish held the pose, and – as on the *Aeolus* in his playfight with Morag – the Jabberwock froze, neck open and undefended. The concluding couplet of another of his verses tripped through his head:

> '*And all the fabled monsters tend*
> *To die to make a happy end.*'

But, this time, an intruder broke the spell.

Tick . . . tock; tick . . . tock; t-i-i-i-ck . . . t-o-o-o-ck . . .

The watch had abandoned its regular beat only once before, seconds before the White Rabbit's end. To the Jabberwock, it sounded a plea for justice, permission from the gods to counterstrike, though not physically. He raised his wings; he bared his jaws; he gaped his eyes; he raised his tail to point at Beamish like an accusing finger, whiffled a hideous scream as an anthem to the world's slaughtered innocents and inhaled every breath of air around him.

Beamish dropped his weapon, clutched his heart and toppled forward.

Tock.

Only then did the Jabberwock grasp the deeper meaning of his own verse. Beamish was the fabled monster, not him.

He clawed out a grave and buried the vorpal blade beside Beamish, who wore the startled expression of someone gifted a divine revelation. In different ways, they had both been released.

He flew back to an isolated crag on the eastern side of the

mountain. The urgency of battle had subsided. He needed time for contemplation and prayer.

Snug in his waistcoat pocket, the watch maintained a vigorous metronomic beat.

13

A Feast and its Aftermath

Hesper had ordered the Woodworker's Guild to entertain Fogg, Morag and Niobe elsewhere, and they were therefore absent when she settled down with the great and the good of the town to hear Jaggard's grandiloquent speech. 'I share with you tonight my brave new world,' Jaggard declared. 'We weather-watchers will refurbish the old Tempestas building, including the first Tiriel's Tower. *Tempestas* means "weather", and it is our birthright. Your craftsmen will have the honour of assisting this enterprise. Tomorrow, you and your people will all swear an oath of fealty. I require by noon the names of every adult, their skill and their home location, and by nightfall a comprehensive map of your tunnels and how they intersect with the old Tempestas building. My men will assume guard duties from tomorrow. In case you are unaware, their lightning rods are fully charged. They are as lethal outside as they are in.'

Nobody applauded, not a single clap, but Jaggard did not mind. Jaggard turned to Hesper. For the first time, she sensed anxiety.

'It almost slipped my mind,' said Jaggard. 'We know Miss Spire is here, and I'm told she has something which Lord Sine wants. If she does, and Lord Sine gets it, he'll keep out of our hair for the foreseeable. A concession worth having, I'm sure you'll agree.'

With the havoc wrought by Lord Sine's chameleon giant fresh in the memory, Hesper did agree.

'That's his envoy,' Jaggard continued, pointing out a woman in plain clothes. 'She's called Syphax and quite a looker. Lord Sine would like to have Miss Spire too, but never give an enemy all he wants first time round, eh?'

Jaggard poked Hesper in the ribs as if to emphasise her good fortune in sharing this nugget of wisdom.

'We wish you and Miss Vane a most enjoyable night,' was as far as Hesper could bring herself to go.

Cassie Vane, hitherto quiet, stood up to make her own speech. Hesper watched her closely. On Morag's account of the second Lord Vane's murder, Jaggard had been one of the conspirators. *Did Cassie know?* she wondered. Cassie's face exuded an odd mix of kindness and steel. According to Mander, he had delivered her to Winterdorf at her request. She must then have made a play for Jaggard, to whom the prospect of uniting the House of Vane with his own would have been irresistible. No one could miss the effort she had made to look alluring to Jaggard. The pieces in play were on unexpected squares. Hesper eyed the weather-watchers, clustered around their Master, lightning rods at the ready. The next Act, however it played out, would be testing.

'I have always appreciated craftsmanship and thank you for your hospitality, which I hope to repay,' Cassie opened in a soft but clear voice. 'My own humble efforts at the workbench kept me engaged through a testing childhood. I met your bretheren in the functionality shops in the Tempestas Dome and always enjoyed their company. To mark my future husband's rule, I have worked a small gift for him. His crown has not been fashioned yet.' She lifted a bag from her chair and took from it a golden necklace, which gleamed in the candlelight. 'It has many leitmotifs: lightning for his guild, a snowflake for the cold of Winterdorf and the cruel wastes of Deception Island, and a J and V for *Jaggard* and *Vane*.'

Hesper knew that Cassie had never visited Deception Island, and Morag's description had been of a place of wonder, not cruelty. Were those epithets, cold and cruel, a hidden description of her bridegroom to be?

Cassie placed the golden chain of office around Jaggard's neck, and this time the Northerners mustered a measure of appreciation, banging their carved wooden goblets on the table. Jaggard grinned and purred like a cat at the cream.

Jaggard and Cassie were led by torchbearers to a bedchamber which married simplicity with grandeur. The bed's four posts, with swollen centres in the form of bell-shaped beehives, supported a canopy embroidered with bees. The bedspread had been woven with a pattern of blayberry flowers. Here, electors-in-waiting slept on the night of their investiture, encased by these emblems of the work ethic and fruitfulness. Such symbolism was lost on Jaggard, who had eyes only for the bed and the imminent climax of his conquest of the Vane dynasty.

'Am I not a natural ruler?' he declared, cheeks flushed by drink.

'You were so strong, Master,' replied Cassie, imbuing the word *master* with a suitable ring of subservience. 'Should I let my hair down?'

'Only letting your hair down, Miss Vane, will impress me.'

Such a contrast, thought Jaggard. The daughter indulges her basic instincts, while the mother suppresses them. He unbuckled his belt, feeling sure the daughter would enjoy a little roughness.

'No, no, Master; me first,' purred Cassie. She kicked one shoe into the air and caught it, followed by the other. She arched her spine as she stretched her arms back to release her hair. She bent her head and flicked it back. Her fingers moved to the higher buttons of her dress.

Jaggard's throat tightened with anticipation.

She pointed at her gift, still draped around his neck. 'See beneath the lightning bolt, how J for *Jaggard* impales V for *Vane*.'

Cassie's bosom, more lush than he had expected, showed and unshowed as she played with the buttons and the widening gap at the front of her dress. Jaggard's fingers caressed the golden initials. He could not wait, but . . .

'It's on the tight side,' he said.

'Oh, yes,' she replied, spinning round, her back now naked to the waist.

The feeling of mild strangulation fuelled Jaggard's erotic energies. He lunged towards her. 'Turn around,' he shouted hoarsely.

She ignored him and skipped away, letting the dress fall.

Jaggard grasped his throat, tearing at the tightening chain. Beneath the ornate insignia, an elaborate clasp was slowly reeling in, like a gilded garotte.

Cassie, almost naked, stood over him, now on his knees.

'L-l-loosen for g . . . g . . .'

'Your fingermarks lingered on my mother's neck. Grey-blue, they must have been, the colour of slate. Mander says she wore a scarf for weeks. Compliments should be repaid.'

'P . . . p . . .'

'Why should you have what you did not give?' replied Cassie.

Jaggard gurgled and fell forward. Cassie waited until his neck snapped. She lifted the bedspread only to drop it, and covered his body with a sheet instead. Such a man was not deserving of flowers.

Almost in shock herself at an act so out of character, she refastened her dress, slid the door ajar and addressed the weather-watcher outside: 'Your Master is exhausted by his efforts,' she said, with a suggestive smile. 'Please find the Elector and tell her I wish to discuss tomorrow's arrangements.'

The weather-watcher scuttled away in search of a Northerner who knew the labyrinthine roads of this peculiar city.

A side door swung open. Mander emerged, hands clasped behind his back.

'It is done,' she said.

'A chrysalis breaks; a butterfly is born,' muttered the old retainer. His crabbed hands held two glasses. 'I call this *Imber Solis*, the bottled sunlight which follows a storm.' He handed her a glass. 'Toasting humdrum events is vulgar, but very occasionally . . .' He tipped his glass against hers.

Cassie felt the horror drain away, and in its place a sense of justice done. How could a mere drink be so clean and yet so intoxicating?

'To clearer skies,' added Mander.

14

A Rare Initiative

Sigurd had endured a day as troubling as it had been disturbing. He was a stranger to Winterdorf, the finished town. After their late-afternoon arrival, he had walked the streets and the river, and marvelled at Bruegel's vision brought to life. Yet the ghost of the man who had given him his chance in life haunted every step.

'I understand the second Lord Vane fell near here,' he said to an old woman crossing a pontoon bridge.

She ushered him along without a word to a nearby frozen pond. She seemed to read Sigurd, and voiced her memories with whispered candour. 'It were there. He was speared by mechanical men and then they lowered the beacons to freeze him in. He brought us peace, of a kind, you know, with self-respect and warmth, bless him.'

Sigurd thanked her and, though not a religious man, he muttered a brief prayer for his former master. He added a few words for the Spire girl and the Vane lookalike, Benedict, both of whom he admired for pluck and decency. He wondered where they might be now, and whether Benedict had recovered from his wounds.

'You're wanted,' said a voice. The man was young and visibly fearful of not delivering Sigurd as ordered.

'All right, but where?'

'The Town Hall.'

'To see?'

'His Lordship. Orders that cannot wait.'

You never escape, he thought. He had little choice but to obey the summons.

The second Lord Vane had encouraged democracy, subject only to his right to decide high policy. Winterdorf's Council Chamber had witnessed earnest debates and violent disagreements. Now, it housed one man, a despot, pacing the room, a picture of impatience and frustrated energy. And not entirely in control, Sigurd concluded. Unknowns must be at work.

'Where the hell have you been?' barked Cosmo, taking his seat behind an imposing oak desk.

'A bracing walk. I've been below ground for too long.'

'This place is like a curio shop, thanks to my father. All that tantalum wasted on mechanicals and beacons. It's time to resusicitate the old Tempestas building. Acheron's forces are besieging the mountain as we speak. Only . . .' Cosmo paused. 'Have you ever met Marcus Jaggard?'

'I know who he is, obviously. But he never came to Heorot.'

'He's a slippery bastard, and Tiriel's Tower has been unusually active in the last twenty-four hours. I know because we monitor their power usage, and they've used almost all their reserves. Jaggard has invested in craft in my absence, and they've all left. So I want you to go over there and report back.'

'Right.'

'Also, keep an eye out for my sister.'

'I thought—'

'You thought wrong. She's broken cover. Worse, she's been seen near Tiriel's Tower and hasn't returned. God knows what she's playing at. She hates Jaggard.'

'Right.'

Cosmo began to pace, as Sigurd debated whether to ask the obvious question. These developments surely militated in favour of Cosmo remaining in Winterdorf. 'And you, my Lord?'

'These are mere sideshows.'

'I see.'

'There are two places you know nothing about, Sigurd. One is an art museum in the middle of nowhere, which has never had a visitor. The other is a college which passes moral judgements on old-world inventions way past their sell-by date. It's murk-free, thanks to an otherwise useless tree which can't reproduce. But – and it's a big but – both buildings are far too elaborate to be as pointless as they seem. They must connect.' Cosmo tapped his nose as if to confirm the merit of this instinctive judgement. 'I'm trusting you, Sigurd.' He tossed an armband in Sigurd's direction. 'That's your authority to do the needful.'

Cosmo's priorities struck Sigurd as awry, and he sounded unnervingly skittish. The Northerners were proud and ingenious; the weather-watchers, on Cosmo's assessment, were devious and dangerous. And Jaggard would hardly expend his energy reserves without good reason. Cosmo was no fool, so why leave him in charge now?

'I'll do my best.'

'You better had.'

'How do I contact you?'

'You don't. I'll contact you. Just have someone on this Morse machine, day in, day out.'

Another oddity: had Cosmo lost interest in his subjects' fate?

'Right,' said Sigurd, repeating his stock reply. 'Anything else I need to know?'

A flicker of anxiety crossed Cosmo's face. 'The lith has gone missing. Everybody lets you down, sooner or later.'

'And Lady Vane?'

'She's where she should be. Don't worry about her.'

'Right.'

'And remember, a little brutality helps.'

This time, Sigurd ducked an acknowledgement. For a moment, he thought himself in trouble, as Cosmo pulled a peculiar face, contorted by extreme concentration.

'Are you all right, my Lord?'

He received no answer. The third Lord Vane vanished.

The point of disappearance yielded no clues. Sigurd shrugged. He saw no point in pursuing the inexplicable.

He tried the drawers of the desk. They contained nothing, save for a copy of *The Official History of Tempestas*. He thumbed through. Manuscript notes on the text read like possible updates, but not in Cosmo's writing. At the back, the last notes in part explained Cosmo's interest:

- *Museum: who built and why? Construction must be before its curators were born. Mander?*
- *College built by the first Lord Vane: tribute to his university days? Or something more? Built for the past or the future? Check the old Tempestas Library.*
- *Lord Vane's last words? 'Resurrection . . . remember Simul'?*

Sigurd turned to the frontispiece. Above the title, these words had been scribbled in ink: *Hilda Crike's copy. Do not remove.* Below it, in type, appeared the same name. Yet the book had been removed. What, he wondered, had happened to its author?

He opened the door to find six men and a woman lined up outside. Each wore a scarf with a distinctive insignia.

'We're here to guard you, sir,' said the nearest, a man with a full, silver beard.

A less military-looking troop would be hard to imagine. Silverbeard and two others, including the woman, had to be in their sixties; all of the men were on the corpulent side; none carried a serious weapon. Three held rustic spears; two, ice-hockey sticks; the woman, an admittedly wicked-looking trenching tool; and the last, a primitive bow with two arrows. Silverbeard struck a chord, but Sigurd could not make the connection.

'All arms were confiscated on the latest Lord Vane's accession,' said Silverbeard, following Sigurd's gaze. 'Except for these. Apart from the bow, they're in the paintings, so they're permitted.'

'Might I ask who chose you?' asked Sigurd.

'We're the town's leading guild masters, and Lord Vane selected us.'

'Hand picked,' added a fresh-faced young man.

They then identified themselves by guild, rather than name. It felt like an introduction to the seven dwarves.

'Cobblers.'

'Rearrangers.'

'Synthetic weavers.'

'Blacksmiths.'

'Synthetic thatchers.'

'Peat cutters,' said the one woman.

'Functionality,' said Silverbeard.

'Do you know Jinx?' Sigurd asked him.

'He's my brother, sir. Jinx and Jonah, the unwanted twins.'

'Right,' said Sigurd, smiling. Jonah and Jinx shared the most luxuriant eyebrows. 'I have some errands. First, I came with a man called Hengest. Find his billet and bring him here. Second, we need a key to Tiriel's Tower, if there is such a thing.'

Jonah, who appeared to carry most authority, allotted four men to these tasks.

'Third, what do you know about Hilda Crike?'

'She plays bats, but isn't,' replied Jonah.

'She's alive?'

'She's an old bird, but still wings it,' added the Cobbler. 'Rumour is, she stole a craft and went to Acheron. She ain't been seen since.' The young man blushed. 'That's obviously not for Lord Vane's hearing, if you don't mind.'

Sigurd nodded. Decent, the lot of them, he had already decided.

'Fourth, we need nine strips of chitin, say four feet by two, and, fifth, we need rope. Our ironmonger can then make us a primitive chitin shield each.'

'Shield?' asked the Rearranger nervously.

'We're paying Tiriel's Tower a visit. Orders are to investigate.'

'I get it,' said the Master Rearranger. 'Shields against lightning rods.'

'Something like that,' replied Sigurd. 'And, sixth, sharpen those spear ends until they gleam, Master Blacksmith.'

With Hengest's help, the shields were made and the spears sharpened. Miraculously, the Town Hall held a key to Tiriel's Tower, even though Sigurd had to flourish his armband to retrieve it.

Darkness had fallen by the time Sigurd and his motley troop set out over the bridges and ponds towards Tiriel's Tower. Conversation stilled as they entered the shadowy world of the snowfields beyond the town, until the synthetic thatcher suddenly pointed.

'Hey, that's old Crikey's house. I know, cos once a month it has a chimney fire and I have to repair it.'

'Excuse me?' asked Sigurd.

'It's called *Hunters in the Snow*, an old-world painting of a town in winter. The second Lord Vane modelled Winterdorf on it, and once a month we all dress up and stand as in the painting.'

'I see.' He had thought Heorot unusual, but Winterdorf sounded like a madhouse.

'Hey!' cried Jonah.

A tiny light at the back of the house winked and faded.

'Crikey's rooms,' Jonah said. 'But she hasn't been seen for days.'

'You all stay here,' Sigurd said. 'Don't move, and keep it quiet. Hengest, come with me.'

He and Hengest ran through the snow.

'We don't know the layout, but, if the thatcher's right, Crike lives in the rear section.'

'Knock or smash?' whispered Hengest, with characteristic bluntness.

'Knock. It may be a dying art, but we are courteous men, Hengest.'

During their approach, the rear windows held their darkness. Sigurd tapped firmly but gently on the back door, as might a friend caught in the cold and keen for warmth and company.

The door did not open, and no light reappeared. But a voice did respond.

'It's not locked, Sigurd.'

Hengest flung open the door and charged in. A tall man faced them in the gloom.

'Good evening, Sigurd,' he said.

A single candle flared. Hengest and Sigurd gaped at the face captured in the glow, the near-perfect features of the Vane lookalike they had known as Benedict. His face had changed – less perfect but more human – and his posture looked crooked. He sat behind Crike's table, surrounded by chaos. Papers strewed the floor. The room had been turned upside down.

'Stone the crows, you made it!' said Hengest.

'You must have a story to tell,' added Sigurd.

IV
DEATH & RESURRECTION

I

La Crescenza

A peculiar light, warm but not quite golden, as of dawn or dusk, washed over the trees and meadows surrounding Lady Vane's house. It had taken Tempestas' best technician a year to perfect the custom-built beacon which bestowed this effect throughout daylight hours. Lady Vane had been tempted by Claude Lorrain's *Enchanted Castle*, but the scale of the building and the ocean view had made it impractical. Miss Baldwin had found the solution in the same artist's *View of La Crescenza*, a generous mansion with a portico, red tiled roof and three towers, two of them crenellated. According to her, and she would know, the mansion had once existed on the outskirts of an old-world city called Rome.

Under Lady Vane's perfectionist eye, artificial trees in late-summer leaf had been a sterner challenge than the skeletal winter trees of Winterdorf, but the effect was more restorative.

Books, furniture and paintings purloined from outliers' homes adorned the walls. In construction, the Northerners had excelled themselves. Classical heads on plinths decorated hallways and landings, enhanced by mosaics set in the floor.

If Winterdorf, with its tangled mix of hovels and fine country houses, paid tribute to her husband's egalitarian spirit, this domain exuded an exclusive air. The bucolic setting, cleanliness and quiet made La Crescenza a perfect place for healing.

Jinx had deconstructed a titanium strut from his theatre to fashion new limbs for his patient: a steel claw for a hand, a shoulder and a knee, all on Benedict's right side.

Lady Vane had a bountiful supply of medicine and anaesthetics. Her maid sterilised and bandaged with skill. Sophisticated coagulants and intravenous support hastened recovery.

Four days in, and Benedict was speaking again. He first asked after Morag.

'Did Miss Spire survive?'

'We found no sign of her.'

'She is a survivor,' he declared, and thereafter let the subject be. 'I made an unforgiveable error,' he added. 'The tower was a severe test, but a fair one.'

Lady Vane caressed his good hand, more like a lover than a mother. 'Maybe,' she said, 'but the stakes were unreasonably high.'

'Lord Vane will know you rescued me. He will be most displeased. I was a conundrum; now, I'm a threat.'

'Better a living threat than a dead conundrum,' replied Lady Vane.

That evening, Benedict walked – a strange gait, robotic on one side, smooth on the other. Jinx made frequent adjustments, and also worked on the claw.

'Squeeze the tendon and the blade flicks out,' he explained. 'The loss of agility requires a compensating weapon.' With the blade sheathed, Benedict pushed his artificial wrist against the maid's braced arm, which buckled.

'Bravo,' cried the maid, earning a glare from her mistress, who expected distance from her servants, and especially this one. The maid had a full figure and a jolie-laide face, a combination which many men would find appealing, in Lady Vane's expert judgement.

'The blade has an épée's point and a sabre's edge, but, unlike them, it cannot be knocked from your hand,' announced Jinx with pride.

'You told Lord Vane you weren't a man of weapons,' said Lady Vane.

'I'm not, but Mr Benedict may need to be.'

'Now is the time,' said Lady Vane, with a smile, 'for your reward.' From her pocket, she handed Jinx the promised onyx.

'I did it for honour,' he said. 'This is a mere memento.' But the look in his eyes said otherwise. He polished the stone, he held it up to the light and even passed it across his lips.

Jinx's closeness to her daughter had never troubled Lady Vane. In her world view, Cassie had no future of note. But, if Benedict succeeded Cosmo, as she hoped he would, would he be beholden to Jinx as his lifesaver? Jinx's craving for fine jewels implied an interest in power. He would need watching. That thought soon gave way, as did all her anxieties on matters of state, to how to frustrate the hated figure who threatened them all: the Master of the Weather-Watchers.

That night, Benedict slept fitfully. The maid, Nesta, sat beside him, dabbing his head with a sponge from time to time and alert for any discolouration about the wounds. Only septicaemia in its various forms, Jinx had declared, could reverse the healing process.

'You often say *Noli* in your sleep,' she whispered.

'My downfall,' Benedict whispered back.

'Tell me, if it helps,' she said. 'Telling a good listener can ease the burdens.'

Benedict did so in snatches of narrative.

She interrupted only to say 'how clever' or 'I would never have thought of that'.

When he reached the shell, he said, 'Curiosity spoilt my concentration. You would not have made that mistake.'

On the floor below, the Heart of the Mountain tantalised Jinx in a dream. The stone turned in space like a planet. Two hands emerged from either side and toyed with the jewel, breaking its rotation. Smoke curled from the fingers, and the flesh burnt away, revealing the bone.

Jinx woke, spangled in sweat.

He reassured himself. He would not be breaking any promise by sending the coordinates. Cosmo must know already that Benedict had been rescued by his mother. He would have other means of locating them. *Surely*. Lady Vane would be well capable of appeasing her son. He resolved to provide only the bare information asked.

The fact that the Tower of No Return had been reconfigured as a killing ground for Benedict specifically, he conveniently left out of account.

Midnight, a good time to do the deed. He tapped out the coordinates. Nothing more, not even a sign off. The reply came within minutes.

I will send a messenger.

Jinx's flimsy reasoning collapsed. Cosmo was not coming. Cosmo would not be appeased. He knew the messenger, and what his mission would be. He, Jinx, could sing in the wind for his reward.

An old rage surfaced. He had been treated like a common conjuror by Cosmo Vane in front of his retinue. He would show them who wins when brain is set against brawn.

On the following morning, after another walk in the grounds, Benedict returned to his bed, where Lady Vane presented fragments of her life with appended moral judgements.

'Gilbert Spire was as irresistible to me as I was to him. Is it wrong to fit together pieces which match so exactly? We had no wish to cause pain, and would not have done, but for . . .' She left the name *Jaggard* unsaid.

And later:

'You might ask why I didn't save Gil on Deception Island. When we were discovered, he abandoned me without a word. I waited for twenty lonely years, bringing up a son with no true father. On

Deception Island, I shared Gil's bed, but he wouldn't settle down with me, even with my husband dead. He put his community and his wretched wanderlust first. So I put myself before him. I regret it now, although I think Gil wanted to atone. Do you believe in atonement, my dear?'

Benedict lay there, alert but impassive.

Lady Vane smiled and continued: 'I understand. You have to commit a great sin to answer that. Real atonement means a virtuous act with harsh consequences contrary to your own interests. Saving you from death, giving you a chance – that is my atoning act.'

'With what harsh consequences?' asked Benedict.

Lady Vane looked away. She loved life too much to contemplate its end with equanimity. 'You know what I miss here? Birdsong. Even in Winterdorf we had that. Mr Potts recommended orioles. I'm hoping Jinx can arrange it.'

As if on cue, Jinx entered with the maid, but he looked more haggard than usual. When he spoke, he looked nobody in the face.

'Please listen most carefully. In the event of a visitor, her Ladyship and her other servants must all hide and hide well. Benedict must do what I tell him to, as must you.' He nodded in the maid's direction. 'Forgive the secrecy, but it's best nobody knows everything.'

Ordinarily, Lady Vane would have rebuked Jinx for giving instructions without prior discussion. Such a reaction now seemed petty.

'I need a walk,' she said. 'Alone.'

For the rest of the day, nothing untoward occurred. Benedict's recuperation continued. Lady Vane's servants, rarely seen or heard, assembled in the late afternoon with a variety of musical instruments. They played old-world Renaissance music, and, on the square lawn of the villa's one formal garden, they danced until darkness fell, when they consumed the remains of the natural food from Deception Island. Jinx reconstructed his theatre and produced a light-hearted piece akin to old-world commedia dell'arte. If you had walked into Claude Lorrain's painting, the entertainment would

not have seemed out of place, although a sharp observer might
have caught in Lady Vane's face a sense of imminent farewell to
La Crescenza's arcadian peace.

On the following afternoon, a small Tempestas craft burst through
the murk and settled in the grounds, close to the tethered *Ceres*.
Lady Vane, Jinx, Benedict and the maid watched from Benedict's
bedroom window.

'Now, remember your roles,' said Jinx emphatically.

Lady Vane ignored him and strode to the door.

'No, your Ladyship, I beg you. Please.'

'I decide what I do in my own home, Mr Jinx, not you.'

They listened to the clack of her shoes descending the staircase.

Benedict rose from his bed and shouted at Jinx, 'Go after her!
Help her!'

Jinx floundered. He had the visitor right. The lith emerged from
the craft and walked towards the *Ceres*. Jinx felt a surge of hope.
Why not come straight to the house? The lith knew the *Ceres* from
aft to stern. He must intend to fly them all back. Why otherwise
take control of the vessel first?

Lady Vane felt similarly encouraged. Cosmo had sent his right-
hand man, and Benedict would, of course, be the issue. She rehearsed
the arguments, all based on Benedict's false narrative. Lord Sine
had surgically doctored his appearance to create a false Vane and
thereby dissension. As for explaining her devotion to this misfit,
outfoxing Lord Sine after Deception Island would be the line.

On she walked. The lith appeared to be carrying a staff. But,
closer to, she saw it was an unstrung bow with a single arrow. She
slowed and then resumed. Cosmo would not kill her or Benedict
with an arrow, let alone the same one.

The lith waited until Lady Vane was only fifty yards away, her
shadow elegant and thin on the close-cut grass. He strung the bow,
dipped the arrow in a bottle at his waist, nocked the arrow, raised

the bow high and fired towards the *Ceres*. A small gout of flame flared on the hull and quickly spread.

Lady Vane watched in horror as her beloved ship, a perfect meld of efficiency and style, blazed and disintegrated. The lith unstrung the bow, tossed the weapon aside and moved back towards her, away from the falling debris. The sails ignited, and, fleetingly, before the tumble of burning planks and spars, the *Ceres* resembled a galleon from hell.

The lith shortened the bow string by doubling it twice. He held an end in each hand, a strangling cord.

Lady Vane stood her ground. *I will not run. I will not run. Gil would not run. I will not run.*

'How dare you come here without my leave.'

'His Lordship's messenger goes where he pleases.'

'Well, messenger, what have you to say?'

'I'm here to carry out a sentence.' He paused. 'Without fuss.'

'On whom? For what?'

'You have both frustrated his Lordship's will. That is treason. The penalty you know.'

'I saved my and my husband's biological son, a Vane in all but name. Since when is that a crime?'

The lith gazed into Lady Vane's face, the impassive, merciless gaze of an executioner. 'You may choose: the rope or the blade.'

Lady Vane, aware she had no more cards to play, calmly weighed the choice: the garotte swinging from his hand, or the short dagger sheathed in his belt.

'Not my pretty neck,' she said gently.

The lith, acclimatised to desperate pleas for clemency from his victims, hesitated in the face of this gentle eloquence, only for Lady Vane to transform from ice to fire.

She yelled at the lith, 'And not by your filthy hand!'

She seized his dagger and plunged it into her breast. The last image, forced into her failing mind, was of her lover swimming out to sea, cradling his lethal cargo. *I come to join you.*

The lith retrieved the weapon and strode over Lady Vane's body without a downward glance, on towards the house. On the quarter deck of the *Ceres*, on Deception Island, the false pretender had worsted him in combat. *Lightning can strike twice*, the pretender had said when they met again. *I'll ram that insolence down your throat*, he thought to himself as he approached the main entrance, bowstring in one hand and the bloodied dagger restored to its sheath.

Jinx met him on the top outside step. 'Was that necessary?' he said.

The lith ignored the question. 'I bring justice and your reward,' he said, opening the palm of his hand, where the Heart of the Mountain rolled gently side to side.

Jinx picked up the stone. Reshuffle. The old greed surfaced. If the rest of his strategy worked, he could take it anyway. 'Lord Vane wishes you to eat it,' added the lith.

'*Eat it?*' mouthed Jinx.

'His Lordship's late mother deserves a day of mourning. Your delectation would be unbecoming. Those are his Lordship's orders.'

Jinx looked past the lith to Lady Vane's body. He swallowed the stone.

'Now, tell me where to find the young man.'

Jinx pointed up to Benedict's room. 'There,' he said, 'with his nurse.'

The lith pushed past him. Jinx stumbled out on to the lawn. The anchor of the *Ceres* ran along the ground like a metallic snake. It had nothing left to support. A sickly smell of smouldering synthetic grass puckered his nostrils. Then, his own breath coiled with smoke. He cried out and clasped his stomach as the acid burnt away his innards.

The lith ascended the central staircase to the top landing. A frightened Jinx would have told the truth. *No survivors* had been his master's orders – it was how the lith liked it, terse and straightforward. Without breaking step, he opened the door with a flick of his wrist. A bed, flanked by transparent tubes and trays of microtools, faced an ornate chimney piece. But the bed was empty, despite the imprint on the pillow of a resting head. A woman stood at the foot of the bed, unarmed. The lith upped his vigilance. The room did not feel right. His head swivelled round; no sign of his quarry.

'He has a message for you,' Nesta said.

The lith unsheathed the dagger. 'Bring it here.'

With a defiance worthy of her mistress, she replied firmly, 'Come and get it.'

Legs and arms splayed, both natural and artificial, Benedict hung between the exposed beams of his bedroom ceiling. He aimed his steel arm at the lith's cranium and released.

The wickedly sharp blade, propelled by the impetus of Benedict's fall, sliced through the bone and into the brain, killing the lith instantly. The titanium joints adjusted to the impact without breaking. Benedict rose from his knees, raised the lith's cloven head and extracted his hand with surgical precision. Nesta stared open-mouthed, her white apron spattered with gore.

'That was for them,' said Benedict calmly. 'Please assemble the servants on the lawn, while I clean up.'

Nesta gathered her wits. She removed her apron and cleaned Benedict's arm and hand with it. 'You were a true warrior,' she said.

'The lith had a design fault. He could not look above his head – too thick a neck. From above, he was defenceless,' replied Benedict.

'You should send a message saying *Mission accomplished* – to lower their guard.'

'That would be a lie.'

'A lie in your own defence is merely a stratagem,' she replied..

I intend to serve you in any way I can. No doubt you have a journey to pack for.'

'You must stay here. For now, at least.'

On the lawn, Benedict gave his address to Lady Vane's household. Lady Vane lay within their view, in the shade of the villa's most commanding tree, as if in rest, head propped on the trunk and her body covered in a coloured quilt. Her expression was one of calm resignation. Jinx's body had been covered in a blanket and placed well away from hers. His corpse was malodorous and his stomach burnt away. For the moment, the lith's body remained in Benedict's bedroom.

'You are triply bereaved. You have lost your second home . . .' Here, Benedict pointed to the smouldering remnants of the *Ceres*. 'You have lost your mistress. You have lost Mr Jinx, a guest, a man of talent and my rescuer. Their destroyer, the third Lord Vane's messenger, otherwise known as the lith, acting on Lord Vane's orders, is dead. I killed him before he could kill me. Those are the facts. What matters now is restoring order and decency. We bury Mr Jinx beneath the beacon; he liked machinery that works. Her Ladyship will be laid to rest by the woodland walk, in view of the house. The lith will be buried in quicklime and wiped from the earth. I shall take his craft and go in search of justice. You'll be marooned here for a while, but, rest assured, you'll not be forgotten and I'll be back.'

They watched and listened in awe of this Vane lookalike. He had arrived crippled and within reach of death. Now, he sounded like a king.

2

Tiriel's Tower

Benedict's narrative of these events, as presented to Sigurd and Hengest in the gloom of Crike's cottage, was a masterpiece of precis. He omitted details of the violence, downplayed his own contribution and said little of his reconstruction. He dealt with the Tower of No Return in one sentence: 'I made a mistake at the end and paid for it.'

As Benedict talked, Hengest, a surprisingly fastidious man, cleared the debris into tidy piles.

In his own way, Sigurd too adopted a businesslike approach. 'I have men outside – seven, to be exact. One is Jinx's twin brother. He should be told privately, so not now, please.'

'Where is Cosmo Vane?' asked Benedict.

'He disappeared,' replied Sigurd, 'literally, into thin air. I'm to deal with the weather-watchers in his absence. They're up to no good, apparently.'

'It's a pity about this place,' said Benedict, a homeless person who had found Crike's homely cottage appealing on his previous visit, when Fogg, Morag and Niobe had also been there.

Sigurd delved into his pocket. 'Cosmo found what he was looking for: Crike's *History of Tempestas*. There are jottings about a Museum Dome and a college of some kind.'

As Benedict's right hand took the book, Sigurd and Hengest caught a glint of steel through the small finger of his glove. Benedict gave the book no more than a glance.

'I've learnt,' he said, 'to concentrate on what's immediately in front of me. But, if I may break that rule just the once – any news of Morag Spire?'

'Cosmo arranged an ambush at the top of the tower. Someone unknown enabled her to escape. But otherwise nothing.'

Benedict nodded. 'Now, introduce me to your men.'

Benedict had changed, Sigurd decided, for better and worse. He had lost that know-it-all quality, but the appealing innocence which went with it had dissipated too. In short, he had grown up since their first meeting at Heorot.

As they reached the door, Benedict lifted a floorboard and produced an odd metal staff. 'A friend stole this from the weather-watchers on my last visit to Tiriel's Tower. Who knows? It may prove useful.'

'It's a pity he didn't steal a costume too,' added Hengest.

'She, actually.'

The seven guild masters greeted Benedict as a welcome reminder of better days, when the second Lord Vane had ruled Winterdorf.

By the time they left, night had descended, the gloom leavened by a waxing moon. In the distance, a vertical string of lights marked Tiriel's Tower. A scattering of high clouds, shaped like spiral nebulae, drifted overhead.

'Not a recognised formation,' whispered Benedict. 'Cosmo is right. They have been playing with the air.'

All heads peered up, save Hengest, who pointed behind them.

'Look at those shapes. They're following us.'

Jonah, the Master of Functionality, instantly recognised them. 'We're in trouble. They're the mechanicals from *The Hunt in the Forest*, and they're programmed to hunt down people like us. They're also near unkillable.'

'Whatever next?' said Hengest.

Sigurd gauged the distance. The horsemen and the men on foot held together, the former at a trot and the latter with a loping stride. 'We've fifteen minutes, at best,' he said.

'Get to the tower before they do,' Benedict shouted. 'It's our only hope.'

Sigurd could not see how, but, having no strategy himself, he adopted the order. 'Do what the man says, quick as you can. They've narrow bridges to cross, which might help.'

The first bridge did help. The mechanicals had no clear sense of priority between them. They milled around while they worked out an order of march.

'What now?' gasped the Master Cobbler as they reached the tower gate.

'We use the key,' said the Master Blacksmith.

'We'll be toast if we do,' replied Hengest calmly.

'Toast if we do and toast if we don't,' moaned the Master Weaver.

'We're not going in *yet*,' said Benedict. 'We gamble on the weather-watchers coming out. Retreat to the wall of the tower, but not too close to the door.'

'Do what he says,' added Sigurd.

The mechanicals crossed the next two bridges without fuss, quick learners. Three hundred metres from the tower, they levelled their spears, horsemen and footmen alike, and broke into a ghostly charge.

'I hope you've a gift for magic among your many talents,' said Sigurd, drawing his sword.

'Sort of,' replied Benedict.

He produced the lightning rod which Niobe had removed from Tiriel's Tower on their first visit there and then left in Crike's cottage. He adjusted it to focus its stored energy into a single charge. He directed it, not at the door, but at the spike at the tower's summit. The charge lanced down the spike with a roar. Benedict knew what these rods could do. Jaggard had destroyed Winterdorf's bell tower with a single strike.

The effect was immediate. The tower door opened, and a dozen weather-watchers poured out. The mechanicals switched their attack to this new enemy. Jags of silver arced among them. At least half came to a halt, twitching like demented dancers. But the others reached the armourless weather-watchers to deal their own cruder damage.

'Now!' cried Sigurd, darting through the still-open doorway.

The guild masters needed no encouragement. Hand-to-hand combat was not their forte. They hurried in and Sigurd locked the door. Two weather-watchers stumbled down the spiral staircase towards them. One, middle-aged, wore richly embroidered robes; the other, younger, was more plainly dressed. The Master Weaver, seeking safety at the rear, suddenly found himself at the front. A jag of lightning from the nearest hurled him backwards, but the bolt bounced back off the chitin shield and stunned the attackers. Sigurd and Hengest overpowered them with ease. The guild masters' scarves served as gags and bindings. No other weather-watchers revealed themselves, and a deathly quiet descended on the tower.

Sigurd said what all were thinking: 'I fear Lord Vane set us up.'

Jonah spoke, sounding anxious: 'And we may have a traitor among us.'

Sigurd quietened the cries of outrage with a raised hand.

'Why do you say that?' he asked calmly.

'Those mechanicals need programming. They were at the perfect place, at the perfect time to intercept us. Lord Vane had long gone. We left after the curfew, and I saw nobody on the way. Mechanicals, however, can be triggered from a modest distance.'

'They usually patrol in town,' added the Master Rearranger.

'If they came from Winterdorf,' said Benedict, 'we'd have seen them.'

Sigurd went to the window. The ground outside was strewn with dead weather-watchers and disabled mechanicals. But two horsemen, having survived the battle intact, were now heading for the door to the tower. He looked at the guild masters, one by one, face to face. Even allowing for threats to their families, common currency in Cosmo's armoury, he did not see them as betrayers. A different explanation, true to the Cosmo he knew, came to him.

'Give me your bow and arrow,' he said.

The Master Rearranger obliged.

Sigurd hurried up to the first floor and opened the window. He removed his armband, tied it round the shaft of the arrow and fired as far as he could. The horsemen turned and followed the arrow with levelled spears.

'Ingenious,' acknowledged Benedict. 'He hid an activator of some kind in the armband. Get close enough, and they come for you. But it leaves a bigger puzzle. He wants me dead, but he didn't know I was here. Why turn against you?'

Sigurd suspected that Cosmo had now lost faith in everyone but himself. His chosen few had shown little enthusiasm for further mock-heroic contests with creatures devised by Lord Sine. Nonetheless, he felt a keen sense of personal betrayal. He had served Cosmo as a loyal subject. He had held Heorot for him and fought by his side against the Stymphalian birds. On hearing of Lady Vane's savage death, he had resolved to leave Cosmo's employ, but this pre-emptive strike against himself and the guild masters confirmed the need for more positive action.

Benedict exchanged glances with Sigurd. It was time.

Sigurd walked up a few steps. 'While we explore the tower, Benedict needs a private word with Jonah. Nothing which need concern you. Off we go.'

Sigurd and the other guild masters ascended the tower, eager to uncover the hidden secrets of the one guild which never shared.

Benedict removed his glove and exposed the claw beneath.

'Your brother made this. He also rebuilt my legs and my ribs. His quick thinking saved my life. But then Cosmo sent an assassin to kill us all. Again, thanks to Jinx's quick thinking, I survived, but your brother and Lady Vane did not.'

Jonah sat down on a lower step. His cheeks caved, his eyes lost their inner light and he played with the wild silver hair which he and Jinx shared. 'He said he was going to an underground town and that Mander would meet him there. He also said it would be dangerous. I advised against it, but he's headstrong. In good and bad ways.'

'I'm sorry.'

'You don't need to say. We're twins, Mr Benedict. It's not a surprise, and I don't want the details. But I do hope he died defending Lady Vane?'

'He died defending Lady Vane, and his killer is dead too.'

Jonah stood up and shook Benedict's hand. 'Thank you. I'll have to carry the torch now, won't I? And, don't worry, I'm not the moping kind.'

An exclamation from high above them, in the Master Cobbler's distinctive voice, dragged both back to the present emergency.

'Look at this!'

They bounded up the stairs. The Master Cobbler had found the tower's Operations Room. A huge screen portrayed a weather map dominated by murk, but with a clear narrow corridor running to a mountainous area. Tiny arrows marked a returning wind back from the mountain.

'There's only one mountain clear of the murk that I know of,' said Hengest, 'and it's where the Northerners live.'

'They're under siege by Cosmo's forces. He told me. He also suspected the weather-watchers were interfering somehow.'

Jonah, Master of Functionality, true to his word, did not mope. He concentrated on the instruments. He darted from wire to cylinders to a crate of spheres protected by chitin, all the while throwing up his hands and crying, 'Clever!' or 'Ingenious!' or 'Why didn't we think of that?' He ended up by a wall studded with dials. 'Watch this!' he said, turning one of them slowly.

The image on the screen moved into close-up. Jonah played with another dial until the mountain filled the screen. It was a bird's-eye view from high up, but close enough to show a blazing fire and the carnage littering the slopes.

'Those are our craft,' said the Master Weaver.

'Were, I'm afraid – were,' intoned Hengest.

'And aren't they bodies?' asked the Master Rearranger anxiously, pointing at specks among the darker shadows of ravaged craft.

Benedict could not fathom the cause of this destruction.

'There was a rumour,' said a melodious contralto voice. Hitherto, the Master Peat-Cutter had not said a word beyond declaring her expertise at the outset. She spoke as if each word had been chiselled from granite. She had worked her way through life at a snail's pace, measuring every step in advance of taking it. 'A plant out there clears the air, but unleashes flying insects which destroy all in their path. Like old-world locusts, only these ones are said to feast on steel and flesh.'

'You never told us that,' protested the Master Blacksmith, with approving nods from the others.

'I don't peddle rumours,' said the Master Peat-Cutter solemnly. 'But, when I see a possible proof, and rumour turns into information of value, then I do.' She paused. 'We're looking at the present. Shouldn't we focus on the future?'

The Master Rearranger interrupted with his own suggestion: 'We could question the prisoner in the fancy dress.'

The proposal proved unnecessary. The Master Weaver's knots had held, but not the Master Cobbler's. The weather-watcher burst into the room, arms still tied, but hands and face free.

'How dare you fuckers barge in here?' he hissed. He paused and stared at Benedict. 'Not another bloody Vane.' He pointed at the screen. 'Enjoying the show? That's what we do to your kind. You patronising bastards. You're toast, when the Master gets back.' His gaze moved to the winking bulbs in front of Jonah.

Hengest intercepted the weather-watcher before he could reach the panel and hauled him back.

Sigurd pointed at the door. 'We've had enough of this fellow's foul mouth. Master Weaver, do the needful.'

Hengest ushered the weather-watcher out. On his return, he closed the door. 'Trussed up good and proper, this time,' he said.

Benedict turned to the Master Peat-Cutter. 'You said we should look to the future. What did you mean?'

'If the rumour is true, as it seems to be, don't we want to know where these lethal insects are heading next? It seems the tower can no longer direct them. Power is almost out, and our little bolt can't have helped.'

Benedict turned to Jonah. 'Can you do that?'

'I can try.'

Jonah played with the dials and widened the field of view, tracking west, following the channel of clear air before turning in a southerly direction.

Benedict stared at the channel of air, which was now running in a straight line. The screen scrolled on until the corridor ended in a bank of murk on the left-hand side of the screen.

'Hold it there,' said Hengest.

They all came close to the screen.

Very slowly, the murk was being eroded, as if by an unseen hand.

'Intelligent plant life?' the Master Peat-Cutter whispered to herself.

The Master Blacksmith, keen to show he was up to speed, joined the debate: 'Such a straight line of march suggests a destination in mind.'

Benedict nodded and tried a hunch. He recalled the coordinates from Cézanne's *Card Players*, which the *Fram* had followed after their departure from Deception Island.

'Would this path eventually lead to 57.75 degrees north and 1.25 degrees west, or thereabouts?' he asked Jonah.

Jonah tapped a series of figures into a keyboard beneath the dial. The screen became a blur as the view continued the corridor's

trajectory, but through the murk. After several minutes – so uni-
formly yellow, they barely noticed the screen changing – a tiny
island of clear air appeared.

'Stop!' cried Benedict. 'Now, zoom in.'

'Brilliant!' exclaimed Jonah.

All, save Benedict, looked in wonder at the magnificent ensemble
of mottled yellow stone buildings and spires.

'The College of Novelties, home to the Boojum tree,' announced
Benedict to the bewildered company, before explaining his visit
there with Morag, their interception by Lady Vane's vessel and the
onward journey to Heorot.

'Why would they go there?' asked Sigurd.

'I've no idea,' replied Benedict, 'but the College is in serious peril.'

At that moment, a Morse machine at the back of the room
sputtered into life. The message was brutally short.

*Acheron army destroyed. Northerners surrender. But the Master is
dead. Instructions urgently please.*

'Talk about our lucky day,' said Hengest with a grin. 'We have
the new Master, and that rat Jaggard is dead.'

Sigurd and Benedict exchanged glances.

'We need a quick reply or they'll smell a rat,' said Sigurd.

'How about a wild goose chase?' suggested the Master Peat-Cutter.

Sigurd scribbled a message and shared it.

*Alliance with northerners secured. Take your craft and men to the White
Circus beyond the mountain and await my arrival. Do not attack locals.*

'It's a little polite for our foul-mouthed friend,' said Benedict,
nodding at the door. 'I'd amend the third sentence. Say: *Leave the
local bastards alone, I have plans for them.*'

The proposal won a round of grins and unanimous agreement. Sigurd tapped out the message. The reply was immediate.

Orders received. Thank you, Master.

Moments later, the lights dimmed and the screen went blank. Tiriel's Tower was powerless.

'What now?' Hengest asked Sigurd.

'We gather whatever lightning rods we can find. We put our two captives in the town clink.'

They found a rack of lightning rods. Outside, the ground was covered with twitching mechanicals and slick with the blood of dead weather-watchers, who, once at close quarters, stood little chance. The two surviving mechanicals abandoned the armband and charged at them, but two well-directed bolts scrambled their functionality. Jonah wandered the battlefield immobilising all of them.

Sigurd called everyone together. 'We have an obvious priority,' he said. 'To warn this college somehow.'

'I've a craft,' said Benedict, 'some way from town. But it's only a two-seater.'

'Your choice,' said Sigurd bluntly. 'I best stay here and liberate whatever remains of Cosmo Vane's rule.'

'Amen to that,' said Jonah.

Benedict had toyed with taking Jonah or the Master Peat-Cutter, but he did not want to risk the lives of his new friends.

'Thanks, all. I've decided. I go alone.'

With that, he strode off over the snowfields.

'Snap into it,' said Sigurd, as he led his troop back to Winterdorf and hopefully freedom. In his head danced the image of Morag Spire following Benedict into the Tower of No Return. He hoped to see her again, for she had spirit, but he shrugged off the thought. Military men cannot afford to deal in dreams.

3

A College Reunion

Morag emerged through the portrait of the first Lord Vane in the library of the College of Novelties. Ahead of her, a maze of passages and bookshelves stretched away, but the narrow side aisle to the lobby remained as before.

She had waited until dusk in the hope of scouting the ground before declaring herself. She hastened through the main quad to the cloister and was reassured to find the Boojum tree still in good health. But there beneath it, on the single bench, sat Benedict, head in hands, deep in thought. He looked different, with his right side twisted and out of true. A large glove, like a falconer's gauntlet, encased his right hand.

'Benedict?' she whispered.

He lifted his head and mustered a wan smile, but did not get up. 'Morag.'

She bent down and kissed him on the cheek. 'This is wonderful. Who rescued you? How did you—?'

'Both dead.' His gaze returned to the ground.

'Who?'

'My mother and Jinx.'

'Your mother?'

'The lith killed them both. The lith is dead too.'

Benedict had never referred to Lady Vane as his mother before. There must have been a reconciliation of a kind.

'But you're alive, and that's what matters most.'

'Does it?' mumbled Benedict. 'I didn't save them, they saved me.'

Morag recalled how Benedict had given much to repair her grief on her father's death. She suspected he had witnessed the deaths of Lady Vane and Jinx. This would take time.

'I'm so pleased to see you.'

'It was here, right here, that she found out the truth.'

Morag remembered the evening well. Cosmo and his minions had invaded the tranquillity of the cloister. Lady Vane had been oddly radiant; Benedict, confused.

'Yes,' she said.

Benedict rose to his feet with the stiffness of an arthritic. She took his arm.

'Once I get moving, I'm fine.' For the first time, he looked into her face. 'You must have had adventures too,' he added, more an observation of fact than a question.

'Not quite as a violent as yours, although . . .' She stopped. Now was not the time to relate Beamish's feats of swordmanship.

'Polychronis is giving dinner in his lodgings,' Benedict said. 'He'll be pleased to see you.'

'No puzzles to solve, I hope.'

'Plenty, I'm afraid.'

'I meant no puzzles to get to the lodgings. You know, not like the tower.' She squeezed his good arm and felt the tension in his body ease.

'Let's go via the gardens,' he said.

As they walked, and Benedict's stride showed no obvious handicap, their respective stories were exchanged.

While relating the occupation of Tiriel's Tower, Benedict added an aside: 'Remember Sigurd? He asked after you.'

'I liked him. He didn't join in when they humiliated poor Mander.'

'Nor did my mother,' said Benedict.

Morag nodded. She could not fully articulate her present feelings for Benedict. Tenderness and affection remained intact, but something deeper had been either lost or diluted. He was no longer the innocent she had met in the snowfields of Winterdorf on the day of the first Lord Vane's death. Time will clarify, she reassured herself, as they headed up the stairs to the Warden's lodgings and a babble of familiar voices.

4

A College Conclave

Polychronis eyed the place names round the meeting table. The college had never received so many guests in so short a time. In no particular order: Crike and Potts, in Crike's stolen craft; Fogg and Niobe, in Jaggard's glass craft (at Hesper's insistence); Benedict, in the lith's craft; and Morag Spire by her own unexplained devices. Dinner the previous evening had been the time for reminiscences, but the serious business could wait no longer.

Polychronis invited the newcomers and Piety to a morning meeting in his private quarters, with college representation confined to himself and Platchet. He wanted reason, not panic, and, in his experience, academe did not always excel in a crisis.

He opened with his usual conciseness and self-deprecation, as Platchet moved around the circular table like the minute hand on a clock, charging glasses and offering a variety of pastes from the Matter-Rearranger.

'A mortal threat confronts us all. By our calculations, this plague of flies is fifty hours away and closing. Recent data suggests the flies are now active day and night. Before inviting your thoughts, I want to offer my doubtless unimaginative assessment of our resources and weaknesses. Resources first: two beacons, one craft of glass and wood, *Simul*, which may prove immune to the insects. Master Jaggard's craft is glass only, but we doubt it'd hold against sustained attack. All other craft are fitted together with struts and screws. Useless, in other words. We have forty-seven academics and supporting staff, who will do whatever I ask them to. And we have your collective wisdom and first-hand experience.'

Across the table, Piety self-consciously raised her hand over the scar on her cheek. Polychronis took a swig of Platchet's special brew and cleared his throat.

'As to our weaknesses, the college's doors and latches are of metal, as are our window bars and frames. We have no prospect of keeping them out. Our knowledge of their biology is limited. We have no conventional weapons, save for those held by Piety's men, and they are not designed to fight insects. Protective suits would take too long to make and would not last anyway; sustenance and hygiene would be problematic.' Potts paused, aware the debit column far outweighed the positives. 'The flies appear to be intelligent and have a guiding mind,' he continued. 'We found several secreted on the fuselage of our returning craft, surviving the murk by hiding beneath the dead bodies of their fellows. They appear to have come to reconnoitre.'

Platchet paused at the window overlooking the quad. 'We have a visitor,' he said neutrally.

Piety blushed, stood up and joined Platchet. 'I invited him,' she said.

Walking down the library steps and into the quad strode Cosmo Vane, his step jaunty and his expression one of wry amusement.

'Why?' Polychronis asked Piety gently.

'He happens to be the incumbent ruler.'

'A parricide and a torturer,' hissed Niobe.

'Now, now,' said Polychronis, 'recrimination helps nobody with time so short. It's my fault. I shouldn't have asked the question. We are where we are.' He turned to Platchet. 'Let his Lordship in. I'll fetch a chair.'

Morag watched the Professor with interest. He looked disappointed in Piety, but why? What did he expect? She served Cosmo. She had been at the Black Circus and was chosen to manage his men at the college. Maybe he had tried to change her, and people can change. Take Benedict.

Fogg leant over and whispered in her ear, 'She's not all bad. Piety, I mean. She tried to save Miss Baldwin.'

Cosmo entered. He faced the silent table with that familiar sardonic grin.

'Dear me, not a single word of welcome. I'm up to speed, I'm alone, unarmed and all ears.'

Polychronis returned from an adjacent room. 'A glass for our new guest, please, Platchet. And everyone move round.'

'Ah, Pollycock, I see you've started without me.'

'That rather implies we knew you were coming, when, Piety apart, we didn't. But the more the merrier and maybe the wiser. I was just listing our strengths and weaknesses, by way of an introduction.'

Platchet placed Cosmo beside Piety. They both took their seats.

'Put it to the floor, Pollycock; this lot should come up with something.'

Polychronis, everyone noticed, had not called Cosmo 'my Lord' since his entry. He now followed Cosmo's suggestion, without acknowledging it.

'Mr Potts.'

'There is a single master tree, according to Fogg and Niobe. It dwarfs the rest of the borogrove.'

'I've seen it too,' chipped in Morag. 'It walks on its roots, as from a fairy tale.'

'Attacking it might give us a chance?' continued Potts. 'On the other hand, trees when injured tend to throw seed, so I have my doubts. It could make matters worse.'

'Benedict?'

'I'm no naturalist, but this tree is clearly used to clear air. Snow might confuse it.'

Polychronis made a note. 'We're not weather-watchers, I'm afraid.

But we were given a couple of beacons, so they might stir up a local blizzard.' He looked up. 'Miss Spire?'

'I think the rotten fruit on the master tree holds the key. Cure that, and who knows? But I've no idea how.'

'Miss Crike?'

'Pass,' said Tempestas' historian, with an intensity which suggested holding back.

'Niobe?'

'We're getting what we deserve.'

'Up to a point,' said Polychronis, 'but you've seen what those flies do. Nobody deserves *that*.'

'I'm up for it,' Niobe hurriedly added.

'But what is *it*?' said Morag tetchily.

They were getting nowhere, and the clock on the Professor's mantlepiece continued to swing its pendulum.

'Piety?'

'How do they breed?' she asked.

Cosmo gave a simple clap. 'Best question so far,' he said.

Niobe recalled the sudden attack by the flies in the clearing by the master tree. 'They emerged from the rotten fruit. We saw no nest.'

'They're asexual,' added Potts. 'So, Morag is right. This rogue fruit is key. We don't know the lifespan of the flies, but, to judge from what happened on the mountainside, they're fast on the increase.'

'Burn the tree?' suggested Piety.

'I share Mr Potts' misgivings,' replied Polychronis. 'Also, it's clearing the air. Win this battle and we could start again.' He moved on. 'Lord Vane?'

Cosmo sank casually back into his chair. 'I want to hear Mr Fogg.'

Polychronis betrayed a flicker of surprise. Fogg, the art curator, had seemed the most peripheral of his visitors for this particular challenge, and he was no friend of Cosmo's.

Fogg had been striving so intently to connect the photographs in the Tempestas library, of the Amazon expedition, with the current crisis, he had barely been listening. 'There was a dustpan in the Museum. I used it weekly, mostly in the same place,' he mumbled to himself.

This innocuous, even vacuous observation galvanised two of those present and puzzled everyone else.

Crike leant forward with a look of fierce concentration, and Cosmo's smug smile vanished in an instant.

'Go on,' said Polychronis gently.

'When you're alone ...' Fogg looked at Morag with a smile. 'When you think you're alone, you don't always ask the obvious questions. I mean, the dust was always by one of the totem poles, the one in the photographs in the Tempestas library. It was always fresh dust.' He paused. 'I mean the totem pole Potts' father brought back from the Amazon.'

Now, Potts too sprung to life. 'Dust – or at least regular fresh dust – means insect activity.'

Crike gazed hard at Cosmo Vane, a look bordering on hatred. Miss Baldwin and the second Lord Vane had been intimate friends.

'I'm doubtful we should be sharing all this so freely,' she said, 'but, as we are, there's also the question of the seed. Old Jaggard poisoned the native's one fertile tree before taking its seed. Only his weather-watchers must manipulate the murk, so the tree had to go. But the seed was damaged too, which is why the Boojum tree is infertile. But there's a deeper issue. We've assumed these flies come from Lord Sine's experiments on the Boojum tree's genetic material. That always struck me as unlikely. Suppose they were always a feature of a fertile tree, good fruit and bad. Suppose that there is a third insect which destroys the rotten fruit and leaves only the good. A golden fly.'

'Hooey,' said Cosmo aggressively, but nobody missed the excitement in his voice.

'Listen to your betters for once. Golden flies were tattoed on the native chief's body,' continued Crike. 'You can see them in the photographs Potts senior took. Their equivalent of angels, I imagine.'

Fogg saw another truth. 'Potts senior was a friend of Mander. He created the Museum. For its art, perhaps, but why not also as a safe repository for the totem pole? Just in case.'

Cosmo sprang to his feet. 'Brilliant,' he said. 'My weavers showed me your pile of dust, Fogg. Now, I see its significance, and it's too late for you lot, I'm afraid. You've had your chance.'

Benedict pointed an accusing finger. 'You murdered your mother. You murdered Lord Vane. You murdered Miss Baldwin. You tried to murder your loyal lieutenants. And I think you deliberately sent your own men to their doom on the mountain slopes.'

Cosmo smirked. 'Pigmies all,' he said.

'And now you have nobody but yourself,' replied Benedict.

'I have to say, that silver claw suits you rather well. But, yes, the real question is who's to manage this second chance. Not you no-hopers. You're carrion.' With that parting shot, the third Lord Vane pulled a face, so contorted as to suggest he was in the grip of poison.

'Stop him!' cried Morag. 'Hold him!'

But they moved too late.

The third Lord Vane disappeared.

'Dear me,' said Platchet, 'he's taken his knife with him. It's one of a set.'

For the first time in living memory, Polychronis lost his composure. 'For God's sake, Platchet . . .' But not for long. He closed and opened his eyes, and calmed down. 'Apologies, Platchet. But where's the man gone? And how?'

They all looked at Morag.

'He's gone to the Museum,' she said.

'And we can all guess what the knife is for,' added Potts.

'How on earth can he . . . ?' stammered Polychronis.

'It's how I got here and how he got here – via the painting of the first Lord Vane in the college library. Cosmo has a jar of momenticons. He'll have studied them and practised.'

Piety hung her head. Her shoulders shook. 'I'm terribly sorry. I thought ...' She paused. 'No, I didn't think. How can I make amends?'

'Give me a momenticon, and I'll sort him out,' said Niobe through gritted teeth.

Morag shook her head. 'Momenticons only take you to fantasy worlds,' she explained. 'He and I share this travelling gift. It's related, but different. You think of a picture whose energy you can catch, and ... off you go.' She pulled no face. She merely closed her eyes.

'Miss Spire, do take a knife,' said Platchet.

But, too late, she had gone.

5

Einstein Redux

'Did you sit her down and ask my questions?'

'Lord Sine, have I ever not done what you ask?'

'What did she say sits between the two windows of his sitting room?'

'A wall clock.'

'What colour is the rug on the floor?'

'Red.'

'Excellent!'

'A chest with a glass cabinet occupies the right-hand wall. I think that's the lot.'

'Miss Spire was with the Northerners?'

'We met in the Elector's rooms.'

'Nobody was prompting her?'

'Lord Sine, nobody knows these things any more. Who cares about the layout of Einstein's house?'

'Someone who wants to be sure she went there.'

'Well, she did. She's an outlier like me, and I can spot a deceiver.'

Now convinced, Lord Sine beamed like a schoolboy. 'In that case, let's get on with it.'

'She brought two hairs. Shall I use both?'

'One should do. But you never know. Yes, use both.'

'It'll be another week before we have an organism to release.'

'Accelerate. This is the future, Syphax. Do you know what a noocracy is? The rule of the wise. The brave new world will be run by me and history's finest. Next up, I have Isaac Newton's spectacles with a captive eyelash, and Marie Curie's comb. But Albert had to be first.'

Three days later, Syphax stood with Lord Sine alongside the birthing pool. A hoist raised a bulging grey sac dripping with viscous water on to a platform above them.

'How did the mind-loading go?' Lord Sine asked.

'It was extraordinary. Not only did Albert absorb all the data, he's been working on it – *in ventro!*'

'Well, let's have him. No, hold on, we don't want him prancing around starkers.'

Syphax pointed out a tailor's dummy on the back wall, fitted out with a brown three-piece worsted suit, a white shirt, a monochrome tie in a similar brown and, beneath it, dark socks tucked into a pair of brogues. 'We've put together a wardrobe based on the photographs in your Museum. He'll feel quite at home.'

Lord Sine glanced at Syphax. Usually a model of calmness, she seemed on edge.

'He's lively, all right,' she added.

New life forms tended to emerge from the pool subdued and confused. This sac danced and shook, as if its occupant were engaged in a brawl.

'He'll damage himself at this rate.' Lord Sine moved forward to the controls and activated a thin blade, which ran towards the sac. 'Easy, Albert, easy, we're here for you.'

The cutting edge was not needed. A scything five-fingered slash from within slit the sac vertically in half and released Albert. The physicist of immortal memory was discernible in the high forehead, electrified hair on the head and reflective happy-sad eyes, but little else. Dark fur, damp with fluid, matted his skin, and his contorted face had a feral, feline look. Splayed fingers and toes had long bladelike claws. The creature's stoop was so deep, its pose came close to all fours. A half-hearted disjointed tail dangled between the legs.

Syphax looked on in horror, but also satisfaction. Revenge, of a kind, for her murdered family had been achieved.

'How? What?' stammered Lord Sine in outrage.

'You said to use both hairs,' said Syphax.

Lord Sine put his head in his hands, as the half-human, half-animal let out a piercing mew.

'She brought back Einstein *and* his fucking cat . . .'

Lord Sine's last words.

The creature leapt from the platform, glared for a moment into his creator's face, as if in admonishment for his mangled being, and, with a swish of his right hand, severed Lord Sine's throat. Then the creature itself bulged and flailed as its disparate parts struggled for coherence, only to disintegrate into a ghastly pool of misshapen bones and offal.

At the top of the stairs, the Red Queen appeared.

'Curiosity killed the cat?' she shrieked.

Syphax hurtled up the stairs, past the Queen and into the garden, realising at last that she had devoted years of her life to a madhouse. She ran and ran, and clambered into the first available craft. She did not mind where it took her. Anywhere but here.

6

The Museum Dome Revisited

In her haste, Morag had forgotten that she and Fogg had left the Museum Dome in lockdown. She arrived in pitch darkness beside Bruegel the Elder's *The Harvest*, chosen not only because she loved the painting as a counterpoint to *Hunters in the Snow*, but also because its sunny spirit would not appeal to Cosmo. She did not relish arriving beside him when he had a knife in his hand, even a table knife.

The air, though cold, felt fresh on the cheek, and the painting's frame felt right, as did those of its immediate neighbours. All as before, so Fogg at least would be relieved.

A beam from a torch below her danced across the roof girders, and she cursed her stupidity. She should have chosen a painting at ground level, not halfway up the Museum's many floors. At least, with the escalators immobilised, she could run down them. The torch beam shrunk to a tiny spot hovering in mid-air over the central atrium. She strained her eyes.

Cosmo held the torch, face caught in the glow, high up the totem pole with the flower motifs, working away with the knife.

Locating the escalators in the Stygian gloom slowed her descent.

'Four to go,' cried Cosmo's mocking voice.

Morag knew she had to distract and delay. She played her only card. 'You don't know who I really am.'

'Oh, come on – it's Morag Spire. Miss Always-one-move-behind.'

'And you don't know who *you* are either.'

'You don't fool me ... spouting nonsense ... and playing for time.' His words came in split phrases, such was his concentration on the work at hand.

'This gift we share. You should ask yourself where it comes from.'

Morag found the last escalator as the spotlight resumed its life as a dancing beam. Cosmo descended the pole and leapt to the floor with feline grace.

'One floor to go,' he cried, extinguishing the light as he landed. 'Catch me if you can.' His footsteps faded away.

On reaching ground level, Morag fumbled forward, arms extended like a sleep walker. Fingertips met wood. She felt the contours of the carving. It was the other totem pole, but the familiar bird face at head height helped her orientate herself.

But where to find light?

The Tower of No Return had responded to the word *illuminate*, like a puzzle in a children's book. *Think laterally, as you did then*, she chided herself.

She rummaged through Fogg's rituals, set firmly in her memory by their precision and repetition. One caught her attention. Every morning, he had laid out visual aids for visitors on a table by Reception; and, every evening, he had put them away in drawers below the green faux-leather Visitors' Book.

Starting from the totem pole, her outstretched hands found the flat shelf of Reception and the hinged section which gave Fogg access to the drawers behind. Her fingers ferreted through badges like so many tin coins, guide books and plans, until she found the objects she sought, with their smooth surface and plastic surround. She had seen Fogg use one once – a magnifying glass with a light attached.

Mercifully, the energy source had lasted. She flicked a tiny switch on the side and recruited a second magnifying glass. With a light in each hand, she returned to the atrium. The totem pole now stood at a precarious angle. The base support had buckled, but held. High up, a painted carving of blossom had swung open.

Morag saw no point in risking an ascent herself. Whatever had been there was now in Cosmo's possession, and he had vanished. Whorls of dust marked the floor around the base of the totem pole. The magnifying glass revealed tiny flakes of cellular material, as from an old-world wasps' nest, which went some way to vindicating Crike's theory about the origins of the Museum: as much a hiding place as for art preservation. She searched for a trail, but Cosmo had been careful to leave none. The imprint of his shoes and the dust faded to nothing after a few yards. But she felt sure he had not left this level of the museum.

So where had he gone?

Surely not to the college, where destruction threatened. The annihilation of Acheron's forces, the death of Jaggard, and Cosmo's failed attempt to eliminate his own lieutenants suggested he retained no interest in Winterdorf or Acheron. Moreover, the plague of flies would presumably strike there too before long. A rendezvous with Lord Sine, perhaps? Yet Lord Sine had no art on his walls.

A bizarre possibility struck her. He could have taken refuge in a painting, to throw her off the scent. But Cosmo would only enter a painting which intrigued him. He had no interest in other people, so portraits were out; nor in the past, so old-world views were also out; likewise any work related to religious worship. An alluring nude, perhaps, or a beggar to mock, but this level had neither.

She tried a different tack. Might a particular artist draw him in? Cosmo had her jar of favourite momenticons and would have visited some already, but, now in the Museum itself, he had a wider choice. Leonardo's conceptual brilliance or Caravaggio's dissolute amorality might appeal – but, again, not on this level.

She wandered from wall to wall. Three years in their company, but so many events had blurred her recollection as to precisely what painting hung where. Yet, she knew, as soon as the light picked it out, that this would be the one, if any were.

A self-taught genius who had no regard for rules.

A man who thought his art unrecognised and his person unloved.

A landscape as troubled as it was beautiful.

A man whose demons were transferred by brush and oil into image.

A man on the brink of suicide.

The painting she had tipped askew in the night to annoy Fogg on the third anniversary of his curatorship.

Vincent van Gogh's *Wheatfield with Crows*, a painting which throbbed with light and dark energies, from the weeks before his death.

She had been in once, uplifted by the beauty of the place and its rendering, but had left bereft at the artist's incurable despair. She had not made a momenticon. The scene was too dangerous for that, but Cosmo would have picked up these contrasting forces and found them irresistible.

Fear and Morag were relative strangers, but she entered the world of *Wheatfield with Crows* with deep foreboding.

Warmth, sunlight, swirls of cloud and the rich tang of herbs assailed her senses. A playful breeze jostled the wheat this way and that. The rough farm road in front of her split three ways. Hooves and cartwheels had turned the umber earth, with lines of grass vivid between their tracks. The middle way twisted into the wheat field; the other two flanked it, to left and right.

She could make out no human presence. An easel stood facing the middle way, beside a canvas stool on which rested the artist's palette, smeared with greens, browns, blues and yellows, and a bundle of brushes tied together with a rag. The work appeared complete, and true to the scene, save for its peculiar inner turbulence and one striking absentee: the crows.

She stooped to examine the palette more closely, and there, nestling in the grass, was a single bullet, but no gun.

Looking up, she saw Cosmo rise to his feet in the wheat some forty metres away and walk towards her. His left hand held his jacket; his right hand levelled an old-world revolver at her head.

'What did you mean when you said I didn't know who I was?' he shouted.

Morag, as on their first meeting in the Genrich Dome, felt an urge not to cooperate. 'Where's the painter?'

'Not here. Talk about a let-down. Now, answer my question, unless you want a third eye.'

'You don't listen. I *said*: ask yourself where our shared gift comes from.'

'I do, frequently. It passes comprehension.'

'Think who else had it.'

A flicker of doubt crossed Cosmo's face. He halted his advance. 'Your father misused it in his various treasonable pursuits. My father, artistic but lazy, never bothered.'

'If you're referring to the second Lord Vane, he did not have the gift. He'd have mentioned it, if he had. That's your weakness, Cosmo. You don't trouble to understand people. He loved fine paintings.' She paused. 'Your father was not the second Lord Vane.'

'How dare you!' He jiggled the revolver.

Morag did not flinch. 'Lady Vane and my father were lovers. We share the gift because we share a father.'

Cosmo looked appalled at the discovery. Was it his sense of entitlement, the old-world stain of the bastard son, hatred of Morag's father and her, or the fact the Spires were commoners and, in his book, troublemakers?

At that moment, the atmosphere changed. Down the central farm road walked a middle-aged man with a grizzled face, a weather-beaten hat, old leather lace-up boots, loose-fitting trousers and an open shirt flecked with paint. With him came his thoughts, a maelstrom of contradictions – light and dark, joyous and despairing – so potent that Morag and Cosmo sank to their knees, fighting to guard their own sanity.

The artist could not see them or even sense them, that much was clear. He moved to the easel and peered at the painting and then at the view. Fleetingly, the mood lifted; he had done justice to the scene, or had he? Doubt crept in. He walked up to the stalks of wheat, still bowing this way and that, clapped his hands and shouted, 'Corbeaux, corbeaux!'

They rose, the crows, and with them came van Gogh's personal demons: such certainty on the canvas, such turmoil beneath it. Morag wanted to comfort him, to say he and his art would be revered forever, but she could not reach him.

Cosmo stood up once more, and the crows swirled about him. For the first time, Morag saw terror in his face, and realised that this jet-black flock was exposing the void at the heart of his being: lack of love, given or received. She did not see him raise the revolver, such was the swirl of birds, but she heard the shot and saw Cosmo fall.

The crack broke the spell. As she left that desolate scene, she glimpsed the revolver back beside the stool, where, in another reality, it must always have been.

Restored to the Museum's darkness, she stepped back, only to stumble over Cosmo's prostrate body. She found one of the magnifying glasses and switched it on. The body was quite untouched, the face oddly peaceful. Panic seized her. The drama of the experience had obscured the purpose of her visit. Had she lost what she came for?

Cosmo's left hand still clasped his jacket. She unwrapped it and there, within a dark hexagonal frame, no more than a foot across, was what looked like an old-world bees' nest, row on row of cells sealed with a waxy substance.

The Museum had one more unexpected card to play. Its lights came up, the ventilation fans resumed their hum, the temperature began to rise and the roof to open. Morag belatedly realised that the darkness had protected her from Cosmo, more than him from her. Someone had been remotely watching these events unfold.

She could not leave his body to moulder. With the aid of the now-functioning escalators, she manoeuvred it down to the airlock with its chitin walls. Here lay the remains of Tweddledum and Tweedledee, now no more than greyish dust and rags.

She laid Cosmo down, with hands across his chest, and knelt to reflect on his short but brutal life. He had good looks and talent in abundance, but not an ounce of warmth. Nature or nurture? Her father, for all his faults, had generosity in abundance. Lady Vane, perhaps, did not. Somehow, he had inherited the worst of them both. The second Lord Vane, father to children who were not his, could not have been a natural stand-in parent, and Lady Vane had indulged him until Benedict's arrival. My half-brother, she reminded herself, as she closed his eyes, withdrew and let in the murk.

Looking round, she vowed never to return to this place. She clasped the totem pole's secret, concentrated hard on the college's fine but severe portrait of the first Lord Vane, and disappeared.

Time's tricks. The meeting had hardly moved on, and she returned direct to her chair between Benedict and Crike. Every head turned, first to her and then to the object she held.

'Here it is,' she said, placing the hexagon on the table. 'From a concealed compartment, high on the totem pole.'

Polychronis halted a flurry of questions with a firm slap on the tabletop. 'Attend to Mr Potts,' he said.

'What is the Museum's temperature?' asked Potts.

'Seventy degrees Fahrenheit, when not in lockdown,' responded Fogg. 'It's more about moisture, really.'

Morag updated the position: 'It was a little cooler, but not much. Some ventilation was maintained.'

Polychronis turned to Platchet as the safest pair of hands in the room. 'Get this to Professor Blenkiron. Quick as you can, and keep it wrapped. Give her the temperature. She'll know what to do.'

Now came the less welcome questions.

For example, Niobe: 'You outfought Cosmo! Bravo! But how?'

'My half-brother is dead. But as to the how and the why, I'd rather not . . . really. Not now, if ever.'

Polychronis, whose people-management skills had already impressed, stepped in. 'Morag, do go with Platchet. I find Museum visits are best followed by a dose of fresh air, and it's your find, after all.'

Morag smiled and accepted the invitation. Polychronis turned to the next affected party.

'Piety?'

Cosmo's occasional lover and doubting servant rubbed her eyes with her sleeve. 'I'd rather stay. I . . . I wish to make amends.'

'We believe you,' replied Polychronis gently. 'And, as you know what these flies can do, please join me and Mr Potts for some investigative work. In my experience, the layman's eye has value too. Woods and trees, if you get my meaning.'

Polychronis paused, allowing the insistent tick of the clock to speak.

'Meeting adjourned. All depends on what this new find reveals. Meantime, I suggest we prime the beacons – Benedict? And choose a room to fortify as a refuge – Fogg? My staff will assist in any way they can.'

Nobody demurred, as the clock ticked on.

Hilda Crike lingered. 'Mr Polychronis, do you happen to have a small bottle of that magical green liquid we had last night?'

'Warden's privilege,' replied Polychronis, opening a slim drawer in his desk to reveal a row of miniature bottles filled with mint julep. He gave her one, deciding not to probe her reasons for this odd request. Her insightful performance during the meeting and their other exchanges had suggested a resourceful loner who worked best when left to her own devices.

7

A Gift from the Amazon

In the hidden cubicle at the heart of the college library, scene of the red fly's attack on Piety, Potts, Polychronis and Professor Blenkiron peered intently through microscopes at the hexagonal cells within their wooden hexagonal frame. Morag and Piety watched on.

'Not dead, I would say,' observed Potts.

'Pupae waiting to hatch,' agreed Professor Blenkiron. 'And they're very advanced.'

'So it's the trigger we need,' said Polychronis.

'Maybe a seasonal increase in temperature or humidity? They come from the Amazon rainforest, according to Crike,' said Professor Blenkiron.

'No question about that,' said Morag. 'But . . .'

Her caveat did not need stating. The risks of playing with different temperatures were obvious to all.

Piety, hitherto silent, offered a thought. 'Miss Crike suggested the golden flies destroyed the rotten fruit somehow. Might that waken them? Somehow?'

Potts nodded. Odder things had happened in old-world nature. Odour, chemical reaction, even vibration could trigger remarkable changes. 'There's no harm in trying, if we have the material,' he said.

'As Miss Spire observed, the flies emerge from the rotten fruit, so, yes, we have harvested a small quantity from the corpses we've gathered – but, by small, I mean *small*.'

Polychronis went to a sideboard, which concealed a small cold store, from which he extracted a petri dish. 'Hold your noses,' he said.

They did, but, even so, the odour left them nauseous.

Polychronis produced a paintbrush with a long, thin handle, as for oil painting – not unlike those on van Gogh's stool. Potts, with painstaking exactness, dipped the brush in the fruit's residue and smeared it over the central cell in the hexagon.

Morag and Piety could not see the others' expressions as they returned to their microscopes, but the excitement was evident from the way they hunched and pressed down their faces. In minutes, the naked eye took over.

From the central cell, a golden fly with long legs emerged, breaking the waxy seal. It bore no resemblance to the rotten fruit's progeny. A thin thorax ended in a swelling at the rear and a head with bulbous eyes and strong mandibles at the front, with, in addition, what appeared to be a rigid proboscis. It whirred its wings, as if to dry them, before stalking from cell to cell.

'What's it doing?' asked Professor Blenkiron.

'Killing its rivals,' replied Potts.

They watched in horror as the insect tore open each waxy seal and stabbed the dormant occupier.

'Can't we stop it?' exclaimed Morag.

'It's nature's way,' said Potts. 'Old-world queen bees killed their rivals and their mother too.' He turned to Professor Blenkiron. 'I need a jar, please, with room for a little water and some more of this paste.'

The container arrived in Potts' hands just as the golden fly finished its macabre business. With a nimble scooping motion, Potts captured the insect and added a small section from the nest. 'In case he lives off his relations,' he explained with a grin, always amused when the uninitiated realised Nature had its cruelties too.

'Or she,' added Morag.

'Good spot,' said Potts. 'That bump on the back is an ovipositor.'

'Yuk,' muttered Piety.

A young academic burst in.

'Warden,' he said, 'our steel drones are disappearing faster and faster. The tree must be closing in.'

'You mean it's accelerating?' said Polychronis gently, more by way of correction than question.

'She and all she carries,' Morag added anxiously.

'No time to lose,' said Polychronis, hurrying out with the jar. 'And that means no time for democratic process. I suggest Morag and Potts take our golden friend and release her near the master tree. There's only one craft which is fly-proof, and that's *Simul*. Jaggard's glass one won't do because you can't release anything from it. If we can get the golden fly close enough to smell the fruit, it might do the rest unaided, though what "the rest" is, is anyone's guess. Meantime, we need to get those beacons going, and a refuge set up.'

Polychronis, looking like an insect in flight himself with his gown billowing behind, took to a bicycle and headed across the meadow to the nearest beacon, where Benedict was preparing to inflict winter on the college.

'Bring it forward, please. They'll be here by late afternoon, if not before,' Polychronis instructed.

'Did you find what you were looking for?'

'A single golden insect holds our hopes,' replied Polychronis.

'Ah,' said Benedict, 'so old Crikey was right. When Tempestas brought back the seed of your tree, their Amazon host was tattooed all over with them. So, maybe the golden wonder can do the business.'

'Hopefully, or we're flyblown.'

'I always wondered who took the expedition photographs,' added Benedict.

'Was Peregrine Mander there?'

'He was.'

'Then it's him. He has an old-world box camera and almost as many photographs as postcards, according to Platchet.'

Nearby, Morag and Potts, who had also taken bicycles, examined *Simul*. Small and sleek, it had been fashioned entirely of wood and glass, all held in place by dovetail joints rather than metal. It had a double cockpit – the main one in front, a smaller one in the rear – and behind that a modest cargo space for storage of specimens, eggs, seeds and the like. Both cockpits had the same simple controls. If one pilot were lost, the other could take over.

Potts placed the jar with the golden insect in the hold and patted the hull. 'Northerner workmanship,' he said admiringly, 'so at least it won't fall apart.'

'How do we release our little bomb?'

'Releasing her from the craft should be easy enough.'

Potts spoke breezily, as if to reassure her, but Morag was not fooled.

'And from the jar, with perfect timing, with flesh-eaters waiting to pounce?'

Potts grimaced. 'We'll find a way.'

As they talked, the temperature plummeted and snow began to drift across, first like confetti, then heavier flakes. In time, the college buildings lost their contours. Let the enemy work.

The weight and variety of the challenges confronting Polychronis had prevented Piety from delivering a personal apology for her terrible misjudgement. Only with Cosmo's death had she seen how in thrall she had been to his corrupting influence. She hated herself for her supine deference, hence the urge for a dynamic contribution by way of amends.

She slipped away from the upstairs room on the south side of the main quad, where a refuge was in preparation under the Warden's supervision. Windows were being boarded up and the fireplace sealed with a glass panel. She left by the main gate, snow squeaking beneath the soles of her shoes, and headed to another craft, held together by rivets and shielded with chitin, made to resist the murk, not metal-eating insects.

Piety opened the passenger door to be greeted by a puff of vapour with an aroma like liquorice. She slipped into unconsciousness so quickly that her journey in the arms of her attacker to the nearby garden shed did not register.

Meanwhile, Polychronis surveyed his defences with little optimism, feeling regret at his own lack of talent for physical action. He might have weighed the pros and cons of a thousand inventions, but he could not fly any of the craft in the college grounds. He wondered if, when the moment came, fear would paralyse or inspire him. For the moment, at least, he felt impelled by affection for his staff and his visitors to give his all.

The refuge had been built with an eye to short-term survival. He commandeered Matter-Rearrangers from Platchet's scullery, and fresh water. The coming contest might turn on holding out long enough to allow the golden insect to work its wonders.

Fogg surprised him with an eye for detail. 'They're intelligent,' he said. 'We must assume they operate by smell when we are hidden. So why not a decoy room, to buy time?'

'Excellent idea,' said Polychronis. 'Fill the Long Room above the arch to the garden quad with coats, gowns, and anything that smells of humans. It has many windows and might hold them up. As for ourselves, we need a disguising odour. Platchet! Your call!'

'I'd go for a herbal tang with an undercurrent of old-world manure,' replied Platchet.

Fogg smiled. Platchet's speech and diction sounded uncommonly similar to his uncle, Peregrine Mander.

The butler never ran, but he had a range of walks, and this variety slid across floor, staircase and quad like an ice skater on blades.

8

The Master Tree

Potts took the controls.

'You have young eyes, I have old hands,' he had said to Morag when appointing her lookout.

The convex cockpit would give a generous all-round view, when they broke from the murk. Just before take-off, Potts had removed the lid of the jar and replaced it with a thick paper cover, fastened to the edges with glue and pierced with tiny holes, gambling that the golden insect would break free, once close to the rotten fruit. He had also, with Professor Blenkiron's help, fashioned a miniature parachute to facilitate a gentle descent. The insect's shadow still moved from time to time. It seemed unflustered.

'We'll have to get it close,' said Potts, 'that's the challenge.'

'What do you think it does?'

'I used to study termites. A queen could lay thirty-six thousand eggs in a day. There must be a queen or two inside that fruit.'

'But suppose it kills the queens; what about the swarm already out there?'

'What indeed,' said Potts, and, for once, he looked grim. 'At least *Simul* is a damn sight easier to steer than those gyro jobs,' he added, as they lifted off and cruised into the murk.

The craft had a simple intercom linking the two cockpits. Potts asked for the bearing for the tree's line of march, taken at Tiriel's Tower, and Morag obliged. Then Potts turned garrulous, as if out on a Sunday stroll.

'What do you make of the Warden?' he asked.

'He's rather a star. A leader who leads without your noticing.'

'Agreed.' A pause. 'Just to let you know, I'm tapping my old tuberous nose. It's ugly as sin, but sometimes catches what others miss. Polly is holding something back. For the common good, no doubt, but I wish I knew what it was.'

Conversations in a restricted space surrounded by murk had an intensity all their own, and Potts, too, was a stimulant.

Morag added a tangent to his observation. 'The first Lord Vane was a very dynamic man. I could feel it in his portrait.'

'Huge energy,' confirmed Potts, 'even in old age, when I first met him.'

'The black-and-white library is the college's raison d'être. It seems genuine, but isn't it rather backward-looking for him?'

'It's to avoid future mistakes,' countered Potts.

'Yes, but does that really fit? What future? There's so little nature left, and he must have known that.'

'Right,' said Potts, in a tone of voice which suggested the small talk was over. 'You take the controls.'

The joystick in front of Morag, previously loose, firmed up. She eased it left, right, up and down, but initial results were jerky.

'Gently does it,' said Potts. 'It's more sensitive than it looks. Use the floor pedal for speed, but don't press hard.'

She tried again – better, this time. A dial on Morag's control panel lit up, showing the points of the compass and the craft's current direction as a luminous arrow.

'Bank and come back the way we came,' ordered Potts, 'as tight a circle as you can.'

She did so.

'Then, a right-hand turn.'

She did so, imperfectly.

'Once again,' said Potts, 'and slow the speed a little.'

She did so, more smoothly this time.

'You pass – with flying colours!'

The joystick went loose once more, and Potts resumed control. But Morag's rest was short-lived.

Brilliant sunlight, as if filtered through holes in dark glass, flashed across their faces, only to disappear seconds later as they re-entered the murk.

'That's why it's accelerating,' said Potts. 'The path has been narrowed to get to us quicker.'

'A plant with strategy?'

'Or an insect with strategy.'

'They'll have seen us.'

'For sure. We'll re-enter further back. Keep your eyes skinned.'

The craft banked round, reversed course, and turned sharp right, as in her training session. They followed the clear way briefly, but still with no sign of the tree. They swerved back into the murk as a cloud of flies closed.

'Damn,' said Potts. 'We must have flown right past it on the way out, which means it's close to the college grounds by now. Third time lucky!'

And it was.

'Jehu!' he cried as they burst back into the corridor of clean air, straight through the branches of the master tree, which had doubled in size since Morag's encounter with Beamish.

In height and girth, it far exceeded the Boojum tree, and the rotten fruit and the branch supporting it had similarly expanded, to such an extent that it gave the whole a mis-shapen appearance. By some genetic quirk, the long aerial roots appeared to be mus-cled, as the tree strutted forward like a clown on stilts. Runners ran ahead, breaking the earth. The blossom from the lesser trees cleared the air in its wake.

Such was its speed that the master tree always led the way. Flies in their thousands, red and blue, swarmed around the trunk and at the front edge of the opening way. Their high-pitched whine conveyed anger and hostility.

Potts passed judgement as they rejoined the murk's protective shroud. 'Good news: we know where we have to be, and a larger fruit makes an easier target. Bad news: we're going to have to approach through the clear air and then hold steady so I can launch our little hero.'

'Heroine,' whispered Morag.

Potts ignored the remark. 'This is where you take over,' he said, clambering from his seat into the cargo hold. 'I can't see a sausage back here, so yell when we're in position.'

'Consider it done,' replied Morag without conviction.

Sometimes, seconds play out like minutes, and minutes like hours. This was one of those extended moments – enough time for Morag to decide to go with instinct rather than careful calculation.

She swung *Simul* round and started her right-hand turn just before meeting the open pathway. The master tree lay directly ahead. She slowed right down as she closed in on the fruit.

'Get ready!' she shouted.

By now, the flies had worked out that this intruder had no metal they could attack, but also that the two glass bubbles served as its eyes. Flies swarmed all over both cockpits, which turned dark, and Morag lost all sense of direction.

'Shake them off!' yelled Potts, but it was easier said than done.

Morag could see nothing. Worse, acceleration and evasive action left her even more disorientated. For once, she panicked. 'We're going to bloody crash!' she shouted.

Unseen, above them, Hilda Crike steered her metal-made craft into the clear air and headed towards the college. Insofar as she held anyone dear, Potts and Morag Spire were in pride of place: he for shared memories and mutual affection bordering on love; the other for her bloody-minded pluck. The mission could never have been as simple as Potts had thought. These flies had the honed instinct of born hunters, and that was their weakness. She watched in consternation as *Simul*, blinded by flies, soared and swerved, high and dangerously low, in a desperate but fruitless attempt to recover its bearings. Diversion, the oldest strategy in the book, had to be the way. She pulled from her pocket the bottle of mint julep and downed the contents in a single swallow.

Fortified, she came in low and released the cockpit. The blue flies would come for her craft and the red for her body; and they duly did. She had several causes for satisfaction in that fleeting moment. Potts' pursuers had abandoned him for her, so giving them a chance, and, if the chance were taken, she might have earned the chapter she craved in her own *History*. She had no intention of being torn to pieces by insects. She clambered out and, as the swarm struck, let herself fall into space.

To Morag, the sudden lift of flies and the restoration of vision was inexplicable, but she had no time to investigate the cause. She righted the craft, brought it above the huge dark fruit and yelled down the intercom, 'Now!' She watched the tiny parachute float down and snag in a branch close to the rotten fruit. Ahead, the college's grounds loomed through the murk like a garden emerging from mist, and the master tree came to a halt.

Potts returned to his seat and looked up rather than down.

'Oh no!' he cried.

A solitary figure smudged in blood and the red of its attackers tumbled to earth through the outer branches of the tree, like Icarus.

9

Death Match

The golden insect caught the odour of its ancient enemy, similar to, but more pungent than the tang of the blackened fruit. It gnawed through the jar's paper ceiling, flew down and began to burrow. It followed the scent through the labyrinth of spongey tunnels like a bloodhound, shortening its legs and straightening its neck in the interests of speed.

The wall of the nest demanded harder work. It chewed its way through the outer covering and the comb until it reached a rounded passageway where the scent strengthened yet further. Glands in its abdomen secreted a similarly malodorous chemical by way of disguise. The passage led the golden insect to the brood chamber, a large domed space hemmed in with hexagonal cells containing grubs and food supplies.

No need to wait. A bloated half-luminous monstrosity with multiple eyes and staglike antlers lumbered towards it. It loosed a spray of acid, usually fatal to friend and foe, but with no effect on this gilded carapace.

The golden insect extended its legs, raised its neck and began to dance. Its hideous opponent followed suit, a different step, the thorax waggling from side to side.

The opening ritual played out, they locked together in a fight to the death, an ancient fight refought in each generation, a fight between the intruder's agility and the resident's physical power.

10

The Refuge

The door to the refuge had been refitted with oak hinges and its keyhole blocked with melted glass.

The room was almost too small. Sixty academics, guests and a few children squeezed in. The lucky ones, selected by ballot, had the benefit of beekeepers' suits. The rest wore makeshift veils and masks to protect their faces, and an assortment of gardening and laboratory gloves. Weaponry comprised a miscellany of mallets, hammers and other implements assembled on a table in the centre of the room.

'Wouldn't hurt a fly,' one wag had said.

Next to this amateur arsenal, a tin bowl steamed, imbuing the room with the aroma of a old-world farmyard.

Opposite, across the quad, Fogg, with two young members of staff, set up the Long Room as a diversion. Tailor's dummies from a display of academic dress now held dirty clothing, with an emphasis on gardeners' wear. Papier-mâché masks from the Warden's party had been added for visiual deception.

Polychronis sat at the only table, with a Morse machine beside him linked to Professor Blenkiron, who was stationed in Jaggard's glass bubble in the college meadow as an advance observer, and to Fogg in the Long Room. Blenkiron had been instructed to keep words to a minimum. With windows boarded, the refuge was all but blind to events outside. The door remained ajar to admit Fogg and his assistants when the moment came.

Tension mounted as Blenkiron's pithy reports described the

tree's approach. Not all knew the code. As the short and long clicks echoed around the room, the knowledgeable translated for the ignorant.

Grey above . . . snow now falling . . . sunlight beyond the meadow . . . tree moving towards us . . . mist in the upper branches . . .

Silence. Polychronis messaged Fogg:

Get out of there. Now.

Fogg peered through the Long Room window. He could see only grey sky and snow, but the hum of the approaching swarm was unmistakable.

'Run!' yelled Fogg.

They rushed down the staircase and sprinted across the quad towards the attackers, who now appeared as a plume of smoke swirling across the college meadow.

The Morse machine stuttered:

Flies . . . thousands . . . red and blue . . .

'Here they come!' cried Polychronis.

Fogg and his companions slid into the refuge with seconds to spare. Around them, most were keeping their composure, but a few uttered unhelpful platitudes.

'This can't be happening.'

'Why us?'

Benedict joined Polychronis at the table. 'Any thoughts?' he asked.

'I know how the dinosaurs felt,' replied Polychronis.

The Morse machine resumed its tapping.

Swarm splitting . . . beacons under attack . . .

'Blenkiron can see the meadow and above the college,' advised Polychronis.

A crash of glass, loud enough to be audible in the refuge, announced the collapse of the Long Room windows into the quad below.

A warning came in from Blenkiron:

. . . chimney . . . your chimney . . .

'Check the chimney,' Polychronis asked Benedict, judging him the most reliable lieutenant. Fogg looked exhausted by his efforts.

Benedict crouched in the hearth with a torch. The glass panel across the flue remained in place, with no sign of flies on the other side. He did not catch the expected whine or hum of wings. He was wondering whether the glass panel was proof against noise, when a scissory swish emanated from the brickwork, like a jazz drummer working wire brushes. He emerged from the hearth and discreetly bent his ear to the chimney breast: same sound. He hastened around the room. The wall panelling yielded nothing.

He returned to Polychronis. 'They're attacking the render. I can hear them, and I doubt we have long.'

Outside, the last window in the Long Room crashed to the ground.

Polychronis whispered to Benedict, anxious not to create panic: 'That leaves a nasty dilemma. If we attack the render to get at the flies beneath, we'll only accelerate their entry. Do nothing and they break through anyway.'

'Time,' said Benedict, 'that's what we're playing for.'

Polychronis opened his arms, theatrically, to bring the room to attentive silence.

'As predicted, we're under siege, and they're mining away.' He pointed at the chimney breast, where tiny puffs of dust were now rising between the bricks. 'It's tempting to play whack-a-mole, but do that and we're toast. When they emerge, use the nets. Beekeepers to the fore.'

Precious minutes passed before flies were poking their heads through the brickwork, mostly on the lower part of the chimney breast. The nets were surprisingly effective. Flies, red and blue, raged against the mesh. But a weak point had been overlooked. The glass panel above the hearth fell. The supports had been destroyed from within the brickwork. Seconds later, the room was engulfed with flies, both red and blue – so many that nobody thought to attack them. Everyone crouched, as coached by Polychronis, and covered their eyes with gloved hands.

The hostile whine of their wings abruptly changed to a chaotic dissonance. Polychronis, feeling nothing, peeped up. The entire ceiling had turned to a moving blue-red, as if it were a floor and two vast buckets had been emptied over it, one of each colour, and allowed to flow freely.

Fogg, beside him, looked up too. 'What the hell are they doing?'

Polychronis did not answer. He stood up and watched intently. They were climbing over each other as if in panic, as if seeking a solution to an insoluble problem. Suddenly, with an explosion of sound, the swarm disappeared up the chimney like a malign spell.

None remained. Everyone listened in silence, fearing it was a feint. The Morse machine sputtered back into life.

Read me . . . read me . . . the whole cloud . . . heading into the murk . . . lemmings . . .

Benedict, tapping out the reply, brought the rest of the room to their feet. Slowly and cautiously, face masks and gloves were removed. Then someone cheered, then everybody did. On everyone's lips, the same question: what *had* happened?

Polychronis supplied the answer.

'Their queen is dead. We've been saved by the golden belle.'

11

A Place in History

Morag's joystick turned lifeless. Potts had seized control, though 'control' was hardly the word. The craft hurtled through the murk in a crazy parabola.

'We have to get back to the college,' she shouted, but Potts ignored her.

So many memories: Crike sending her to Potts' library at the time of the Tempestas party; she and Crike entering Winterdorf as aged sisters; their meeting at Crike's house when she had visited Vermeer in his studio and found the bearings for Deception Island; her own disguise as Crike at the Town Hall meeting; Crike's insights in the Tempestas library under the mountain; Crike the historian and Crike the humourist. Morag's eyes moistened, but she did not weep. Over time, reflection on her father's death had educated her in the art of grief. Crike would not have welcomed losing her faculties or fading away in some airless bedroom. She would have preferred a heroic place in history, the one she had penned herself.

Potts, however, was overcome by a more conventional grief. Without thought for their safety, he landed the craft in clear air on the approach to the master tree.

Morag peered through her cockpit: not a fly in sight, here or ahead. The tree was shivering like a child in the cold. The stilt-like aerial roots were sinking slowly into the earth.

'She's settling,' she cried, but Potts had already clambered out and was quartering the ground. She followed suit and ran to join him.

Crike's body lay face down, near the debris of her craft. Potts stooped.

'No,' said Morag firmly. 'Leave her as she is; remember her as she was. This is a task for others, not for you.'

Potts stood up. His shoulders shook as tears coursed down his cracked cheeks. Morag waited before holding the old man close and walking him slowly back to the college meadow. They had reached the grass when a loud crack turned their heads back. The tree's misshapen branch, the bearer of the rotten fruit, had snapped where it joined the trunk.

Ahead of them, the door of a garden shed opened and Piety stumbled out.

'That craft was mine. Who took it? Someone used chloroform. They stopped me.'

'Stopped you doing what?' asked Morag.

'What the craft did. A diversion. It was obviously needed. Polychronis is far too nice.'

Morag gave Piety a hard look. 'This is Oblivious Potts. He has just lost a lifelong friend.'

'Oh. Sorry.'

'And you should be grateful. Crike did you a favour. It was her time, not yours. I'm a student of self-sacrifice, believe me. Now, help me help him.'

'Sorry,' said Piety again, taking Potts' other arm. 'You did see?'

'I saw the tree drop anchor.'

'The flies, thousands of them, self-destructed in the murk.'

'A mother's love lost, I guess,' said Morag.

They walked on towards a mill of familiar faces caught in the sun as the artificial grey of the beacon-fashioned sky unravelled into blue.

Mint Julep with a Twist

Polychronis' second party took over a month to organise, for a variety of reasons: remedial time for architectural damage, arrival time for guests from far-flung places, time to restore the library to its former role as a refectory, time to study and understand the borogrove's changed nature, time for mourning, and time for political decision-making which could not wait. A temporary Council was appointed. The Guild of Weather-Watchers was disbanded and their technologies brought under the Council's control. Acheron's ruling body, all Cosmo's placemen, was also disbanded without resistance. Cosmo's death and the destruction of their fleet had left them leaderless and powerless.

Time for burials, too: Crike, in the shade of the Boojum tree, and the second Lord Vane, his body recovered from the ice, on a bank with a commanding view of his beloved Winterdorf.

Polychronis sought a back seat in these developments, but nobody else would permit it. He chaired the Council, which unanimously decided that the invitation should come from the college and bear its arms of a book with facing black and white pages inscribed with the College motto.

Every visitor brought at least one reunion. Indeed, looking around the Great Hall as it filled, panelling aglow in the candlelight, Fogg saw the guests as a visual index of the company's often separate adventures: Lomax and Tamasin from the White Circus; the Knight, the White Queen and Mr J; Carlo and his wife from Deception Island; the other guild masters from Winterdorf; Hesper and Fabius from the Northerners' town under the mountain; Hengest and Horsa from Heorot; Syphax, with news of Lord Sine's demise; and Spire's crew from the *Fram*.

Mander's arrival brought a bizarre pas de deux between him and his nephew.

'You're senior to me, Mr Mander,' said Platchet.

'It's a question of etiquette. I'm retired. You're on active service, Mr Platchet,' replied Mander.

'That's not what I hear, Mr Mander. You've always been Master of Ceremonies.'

And so it went on, until Polychronis intervened with a complex compromise. Placement, place settings and drink to Mander; everything else to Platchet; joint head waiters, in name and in fact.

Fogg watched new relationships blossom too: Polychronis and Piety; and maybe even Potts and Hesper.

Cassie had brought the large wooden pieces from the board in her cottage, whose physical likeness to their subjects reflected the carver's skill and Cassie's gift for observation and description.

These statues of the fallen were spread around the tables: Hernia, Gilbert Spire, Miss Baldwin, the second Lord Vane, Lady Vane, Jinx, Beamish and Crike. Cosmo Vane, her half-brother, Cassie placed on her own table. She gave Jinx to his twin as a memento. Morag insisted on Hernia for hers. Only one character was absent. Cassie had burnt Jaggard's piece to a cinder.

Mander's placement had Jinx's brother on one side of Morag, with an empty place on the other. Mander sidled up with two glasses of *Imber Solis*, the all-restoring cocktail he had given to Cassie after her eventful night with Jaggard.

'We don't like to disappoint, Miss Spire, and I feared he might not make it with so much restoration work in Winterdorf. But he has arrived – so I thought a special for you and a special for him.'

Sigurd entered. He wore his working clothes and looked slightly out of place. He strode in unperturbed, with a soldier's gait, only to turn gauche on finding his seat.

'Miss Spire, you're alive, you're well. That's . . . that's . . .'

He gave up on words and hugged her close.

'Yes, you two, drink to that,' suggested Mander.

In Sigurd's face, Morag read something new to her. His mouth was taut, his eyes glassy. He hugged her again.

Across the table, she watched Benedict watching. His nurse, Nesta, sat beside him, animated and undeniably attractive. New threads had entered the tapestry. How they would mix and where they might lead, she could not tell. Nor did she know where she wanted them to lead. Lady Vane had her complexities, and Benedict's true nature had, she felt, yet to settle. For the moment, she would enjoy Sigurd's company. His first report was to compliment Benedict on his role in liberating Winterdorf, and the second to say that the town's streets were once again full of the bustle of life. He was explaining Cosmo's stratagem with the armband and the mechanicals, when Cassie approached with Syphax in tow.

'My new friend,' said Cassie. 'I believe you've met. She witnessed Lord Sine's demise, courtesy of one feline hair delivered by you.'

'It wasn't intentional. The second hair was meant as an insurance,' replied Morag.

'Well, it delivered,' said Syphax. 'You lost your grandmother; I lost my family. Justice was done.'

'You knew?'

'I let the fates decide. I asked the question: use one hair or two?'

Morag did not dispute that justice had been done, but she felt uneasy. Cassie had eliminated Jaggard; Syphax had disposed of Lord Sine. She wondered where this budding friendship might lead in time.

Syphax pointed. 'Talking of cats,' she said.

The Cheshire Cat had appeared on the gallery above Mander and Platchet.

'Is he the after-dinner entertainment?' asked a puzzled Platchet.

'There's no need for that,' replied the Cat. 'They're all crackers.'

'Cat litter,' muttered Mander. 'You get used to it.'

The Cat burst into a mellifluous baritone: '*But you'd go a million miles for one of my smiles.*' He then grinned from ear to ear and disappeared.

Above their heads, a golden beetle criss-crossed between the ceiling joists, observing and recording all the while.

Polychronis' speech at the end of the feast struck a cautionary note. Mankind had made a mess of things before the Fall, during the Fall and after it. He spoke of the new problems they faced. The growth of the borogrove had slowed to a normal pace. It would take skilful husbandry to propagate. The effect of any thaw on the huge ice wall near Deception Island exemplified the challenges of restoration. The human frailties – greed, bigotry and ambition – so evident since the Fall, would have to be curbed. But he talked also of the excitement of repair and a new age of exploration.

He ended with an upbeat toast – 'To our second chance, to wise choices with an eye to the black books as well as the white, and to love and friendship as the key to all' – followed by an unexpected invitation.

'It's a fine night. As you leave, please take a mortar board. Admission to honorary membership of the college has to be earned. Run up the forty-seven Mound steps, jumping over the primes, and only the primes, without losing your academic hat – and your gown awaits you. You've a time limit of 107 seconds, which incidentally is also a prime. Professors Blenkiron and Scherbel will demonstrate.'

They filed out to the gardens like a new generation of students.

Morag found herself next to Potts and the Jabberwock.

'I found the toast well meant, but a tad optimistic, with so much extinction,' she said.

What little she could make of Mr J's reply suggested he agreed:

'No voice in the Chamber
No feet upon the stair.
No time to kill
Lost minutes fill
The dodo's secretaire . . .

But,' Mr J added, 'I did like the julep.'

They stood in a semicircle, facing the Mound, on the garden side of the iron gates. Torchbearers stood on either side.

'Why do we need a demonstration?' complained Benedict. 'We all know our primes.'

'It's so you can show off,' Morag replied.

'Well, I don't know mine,' said Sigurd, 'let alone in under two minutes.'

'We'll do it together,' replied Morag.

'Sorry, not allowed,' said a student. 'It has to be one at a time. Otherwise, it confuses the referee.'

Polychronis stood beside one of the torchbearers with a red flag.

'This is all very pointless,' said Niobe. 'Party bloody games.'

Fogg alone held his peace. A keen observer, he had already worked out that Polychronis did nothing without purpose.

Professor Blenkiron skipped up, sure-footed, mathematically accurate and quick. She disappeared and, two minutes later, reappeared on the summit with a wave.

'So,' said Benedict, 'the point, please?'

Sigurd spoke. He might not know his primes, but he had a soldier's eye. 'That's not Professor Blenkiron. It's the other one. Similar build, but . . .'

'Now, there's a thought,' said Morag. 'Whenever we see one go down the other side, another appears at the top. What are you up to, Pollycock?'

'Time for a recce,' said Sigurd. He sidled down the gravel path beside the garden's enclosing stone wall.

'There's no sign of our Professor,' he reported back. 'In fact, there's nobody on the far side at all.'

They joined the queue of guests. Climbing the Mound in 107 seconds, missing the second, third, fifth, seventh, eleventh, thirteenth, seventeenth, nineteenth, twenty-third and twenty-ninth, thirty-first and thirty-seventh, forty-first and forty-third, and top step of all, without a mistake and with mint julep in their veins, proved too steep a challenge. The college members cheered every misstep. To universal surprise, Benedict failed, unaware that one is not a prime number, only to greet his defeat with delight.

'I'm wrong!' he cried, with a broad grin. 'I'm wrong!'

'Anyone else to go?' asked Polychronis.

The White Knight stepped forward. 'Enemy minefield ahead,' he said in the clipped speech of his military mode, 'but we have the map.' He turned to his audience, saluted, turned back and made his ascent, calling the steps as he went. 'One, mine, mine, four, mine, six, mine, eight, nine, ten, mine . . .' And so on, with spurs jingling and white hair flying.

The red flag stayed down. The Knight passed over the summit and did not return.

'Bravo!' cried Polychronis.

Stung by their own failure and the Knight's success, the guests, now allowed two consecutive attempts, succeeded. None returned, leaving only Morag, Sigurd and Fogg.

Morag had a sense of journey's end. She turned to Sigurd. 'You go first. I feel I should do this with Fogg. We started out together.'

'Of course,' said Sigurd.

Soon, only she and Fogg remained.

'After you,' said Fogg.

'I'll wait on the other side,' she said, 'whatever happens.'

She danced up, counting as she went, to find empty lawn on the other side, but, as she descended towards it, bluish lines ran out from the Mound's base, enlarging into the shape of light which a doorway throws. She hurried down, but, mindful of her promise to Fogg, waited. The opening closed and near darkness returned.

Next came Polychronis.

'Very considerate of you, Miss Spire. We'll wait for young Fogg,' he said.

Fogg did not appear for some minutes, having missed a step on his first attempt. Once together, Polychronis ushered his guests through the open door and into a glass atrium, bathed in a ghostly luminescence. An escalator ran down from a stone floor.

Fogg and Morag had half anticipated what awaited them. So much had been invested in the entrance, this subterranean installation had to hold something of immense value, and the meaning of value had radically changed since the Fall.

They descended the escalator into a vast chamber subdivided into disparate areas enclosed in transparent bubbles of varying size, with walkways between them. Some bubbles held racks, others vertical lockers, and, in the two largest, whose surfaces were pockmarked with frost, a multitude of embryos hung like sleeping bats. Mobile ladders reached high into the ceiling. On a few, gowned figures moved up and down.

'The Chamber of Mammals,' explained Polychronis.

Morag grasped the strategy. Nobody builds a Mound for nothing. So you create a college ritual as the disguise. At changeover time, one worker would go out and depart via the Mound's summit as soon as the replacement arrived. To judge from Professor Blenkiron's deception, they were paired by similarity in physical build.

Walking on, smaller escalators and side passages came into view.

Polychronis pointed as they passed. 'Flying insects. Birds' eggs. Seeds. Reptile eggs. Marine animals. Fish. Separate bubbles are necessary to maintain the apposite temperature.'

He led them down a passage to another chamber, bathed in the same cloying bluish light, but with a different layout. Glass trays, stacked level on level, occupied the side walls, with subdivisions like a fisherman's fly box. Each housed a tiny pile of fine particles, varying from white to ochre to dark umber in colour. The central space displayed an array of small bags, suspended from the ceiling, but the shapes inside were not embryonic. On one side, dark, straggling filaments pressed against the outer surface of the bags; on the other, patterned sections dominated.

The other guests were wandering nearby, awestruck at the sheer scope of this underground ark. Polychronis remained with Fogg and Morag.

'We inherited a garden, and we poisoned it. Here, we nurture the wherewithal for our second chance.' He strolled around the perimeter. 'Seeds, large and small, from the double coconut to mustard seed. Up there, rootstocks and tubers. One day, we hope to reintroduce the world to the full palette of Nature's colours.'

'So this place is Simul?' Fogg asked.

Polychronis nodded.

'My father came here?' asked Morag.

'He did. One of the few we could trust with such a secret.'

'He set the college's bearings in our Airlugger,' replied Morag.

'Stands to reason,' replied Polychronis, with a grin.

'And Mr Potts? Does he know?' asked Fogg.

'Potts senior must have done. But Potts junior, no. Lovely man, but . . .' Polychronis left unsaid the words *not a model of discretion.*

They did not ask about Mander, whose instant mastery of the college's geography testified to long acquaintance.

'Isn't there a darker side to all this?' said Fogg. 'You wouldn't prepare such a place unless total destruction was expected. And I'd say the same for our Museum.'

'But it was expected. Mankind created the murk, not Tempestas.'

Fogg reflected. Not everyone knew everything. Polychronis could have little knowledge of the weather-watchers and the likes of Mr Venbar.

Morag added yet another perspective: 'I always wondered why the second Lord Vane went along with the slaughter at the Tempestas party. Maybe he feared Lord Sine's workforce of human automatons would get hold of all this, sooner or later.'

Polychronis shrugged, as if such political niceties were outside his brief.

'I'd really like to show you the butterflies,' he said.

Morag looked around her. Euphoria dominated, but she felt the dead weight of responsibility. She sensed that Fogg did too. They walked past predators and their potential victims, seeds dependent on specific conditions for germination, sea creatures awaiting new oceans. Work on a giant scale lay ahead.

The Jabberwock was the first to leave the Mound. He made his way to the cloister, where, seated on the roof like an oversize gargoyle, he prayed for the soul of Hilda Crike, a kindred spirit and the only human to have tousled his antennae. A flicker of movement high in the Boojum tree caught his eye. A golden insect was prospecting among the flowers.

'They'll never understand us,' he said to the insect, 'but a little respect might pull us all through.'

'I'd put it differently,' said a voice from the shadows.

The Jabberwock peered through the branches. Just discernible in the low light from the chapel windows, a stooped figure in a white tie and tailcoat stood stock-still alongside the tree trunk.

'You would?' queried the Jabberwock.

'Lasting good has to be earned,' said Mander, before slipping back into the shadows.

The Jabberwock pondered.

'Trite but true,' he replied.

The Solution to the Stepping-Stone Puzzle

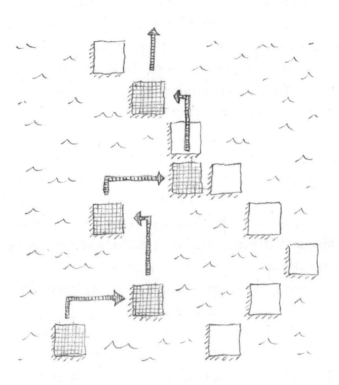

GLOSSARY, PLACES & PEOPLE

GLOSSARY

Airluggers: A form of airship equipped with chitin shields and, by reason of their energy efficiency, used for research by Tempestas shortly before the Fall. At the end of *Momenticon*, the following craft of this type still exist, and flee Deception Island at the climax of the battle (with those on board in parentheses): the *Aeolus* (Morag and Benedict) and the *Ceres* (Lady Vane, Cosmo Vane and the lith). A third, the *Fram*, Gilbert Spire's vessel, is wrecked during the battle.

Arbor spirantia: A mysterious unstable natural organism studied by Gilbert Spire when working for Genrich. At the end of *Momenticon*, Lord Sine buries it in an armoured chest, far from the Genrich Dome.

Beacons: Installations which can clear the murk in their immediate locality, but which are dependent on tantalum. They enabled the construction and maintenance of Winterdorf, Acheron and other habitations. Designed by Tempestas under the second Lord Vane.

Chitin: Material based on the protective skin of many insects, and resistant to the murk.

The Fall: The ecological catastrophe which destroyed most life on Earth, save for the humans employed by Tempestas and Genrich and a few outliers.

Functionality: The science which allows mechanical constructs (e.g. of birds and animals) to move, call, etc.

Genrich: Lord Sine's company, which sees genetic engineering as the only way forward for the human race and which employs genetically modified humans alongside a few outliers (such as the Spires).

Golden beetles: Manufactured by Cassie Vane in the functionality shops of the Tempestas Dome. She assigns one to watch over Fogg and another Morag. Another keeps an eye on her mother, Lady Vane.

Momenticons: Pills containing visual thoughts captured by weavers, enabling their takers to share the experience. The ability to generate such visual intensity is an extremely rare inherited gift. Only Gilbert Spire and his daughter Morag Spire, and her half-brother, Cosmo Vane, are known to possess it. Momenticons were deployed in an attempt by Genrich to cure the mental afflictions of a generation of Lord Sine's human constructs, and later to destroy them.

Murk: The poisonous cloud enveloping the Earth after the Fall.

The old world: The world before the Fall.

Outliers: Natural humans protected from the murk by Tempestas or Genrich, with a view to later employment. Selected only for talent.

Tantalum: A rare chemical element, essential to power in the post-Fall era and in increasing demand as supplies run low.

Tempestas: Founded by the first Lord Vane, this is the other great company which, alongside Genrich, survives the Fall. It warned the world of imminent ecological disaster to little effect.

Toves: Disfigured humanoids of low intelligence, created by Lord Sine and used as crude scavengers, mainly for tantalum. They alone are resistant to the murk.

Weather-watchers: A secretive guild within Tempestas which can control the weather. Headed by a guild master (*see* Marcus Jaggard).

Weavers: Instruments designed by Cosmo Vane to capture intense visual thoughts (his and, later, Morag's; *see* Momenticons).

Places

The Tempestas building

The first home of Tempestas, the company founded by the first Lord Vane, which warned against the dangers of climate change before ecological disaster struck. It was embedded in a mountain, whose air uniquely resisted the murk. Later abandoned, it is overrun by toves and visited as a ruin by Fogg on his journeys in *Momenticon*. Old Tempestas records remain there.

The Tempestas Dome

Tempestas' second home, built by the second Lord Vane, in the form of a dome, protected from the poisonous murk by a chitin shield. The surrounding landscape is peopled by plants, birds and animals which are mechanical constructs. Scene of the Tempestas party (*see below*) and later abandoned for towns and other habitations constructed to imitate famous paintings (*see below*).

The Genrich Dome

Home to Genrich, Lord Sine's company, which sees genetic engineering as the only way forward for the human race. Built before the Fall and protected by a chitin shield. It is Lord Sine's home in *Momenticon*. The Vanes have private quarters here.

The Museum Dome

Built in mysterious circumstances at the time of the Fall to house Man's best art and artefacts. At the beginning of *Momenticon*, Fogg is its curator. It has never had a visitor.

Winterdorf

A town built by, and home to, the second Lord Vane, it is a replica of two paintings by Bruegel the Elder: *Hunters in the Snow* and *The Bird Trap*.

Acheron

A town and a replica of Bosch's *Garden of Earthly Delights*. Home to Cosmo Vane.

The Cottage

A replica of Constable's *Cottage in a Hayfield*, where Cassie Vane lives alone after her family's move to Winterdorf.

Deception Island

A real old-world island in the Antarctic, which is, by a freak of nature, immune to the murk. Its climate becomes more temperate after the Fall. Home to a vast tantalum deposit. Unsuccessfully attacked by Lord Sine and Cosmo Vane at the end of *Momenticon*.

Tiriel's Tower

Home to the weather-watchers. First located in the original Tempestas building under the mountain, then in the Tempestas Dome, and finally in Winterdorf.

People
in no particular order

The first Lord Vane

Founder of Tempestas, implicated in the Fall, father of the second Lord Vane.

The second Lord Vane

Builder of the Tempestas Dome and Winterdorf, where he is murdered by Cosmo Vane in league with Marcus Jaggard. A decent, artistic man, save for his involvement in the Tempestas party.

Lady Vane

Wife of the second Lord Vane and mother of Cosmo Vane (following her affair with Gilbert Spire) and Cassie Vane. Beautiful, ruthless, but not without warmth. The location of her home remains a mystery.

The third Lord Vane / Cosmo Vane

Takes control of Tempestas after murdering the second Lord Vane. He is in fact the bastard son of Lady Vane and Gilbert Spire, though few know this, and the few do not include Cosmo. Clever but cruel. He shares the gift of entering paintings with his half-sister, Morag Spire, and, also like her, can make momenticons.

Cassie Vane

Daughter of Lady Vane, by whom she is neglected. She has a genius for constructing miniature creatures (*see* golden beetles, above). She befriends both Fogg and Morag, but later withdraws from public life (*see* the Cottage, above).

The first Lord Sine

A master geneticist, founder of Genrich, contemporary of the first Lord Vane and father of the second Lord Sine.

The second Lord Sine

Rough contemporary of the second Lord Vane. Like his father, amoral and convinced of Genrich's long-term agenda, despite the setbacks (*see* Manuals, below). He suspects that Gilbert and Morag Spire have special gifts, which he is interested to exploit.

Marcus Jaggard

Master of the Weather-Watchers, ally of Cosmo Vane. His father had been Master under the first Lord Vane. A lascivious and ambitious man, biding his time.

Gilbert Spire

An outsider and adventurer, and father of Morag Spire, he came to the Genrich Dome to work for Lord Sine. There, he met Lady Vane, but is exiled after their affair is discovered. He then leads a community on Deception Island, home to various forms of natural life, including birds and trees. The origin of the seeds and eggs behind this success is a mystery. At the end of *Momenticon*, he repels the attack on Deception Island by Lord Sine and Cosmo Vane at the cost of his life.

Morag Spire

Daughter of Gilbert Spire. She lives in a hidden attic in the Museum Dome before escaping its shutdown, and has many adventures before and after, as recorded in *Momenticon*. Her mother commits suicide when she is young, after Gilbert Spire's failure to return home. She can create momenticons and, like her father, works for a time in the Genrich Dome. She is present at the Tempestas party and the attack on Deception Island. Attached to Benedict. At the end of *Momenticon*, she escapes with Benedict in the Airlugger, *Aeolus*.

Fogg

A child survivor of an Antarctic expedition. Rescued at the Fall by Gilbert Spire. Finds himself Curator of the Museum Dome, and for years is unaware that Morag also lives there in rooms above the ceiling. With Morag, and later Benedict and Niobe, he has many adventures as recorded in *Momenticon*. He is a brilliant copyist and lover of Niobe. At the end of *Momenticon*, he is stranded on Deception Island with Niobe.

Benedict

A Vane lookalike of obscure origins with a remarkable memory and intellectual gifts. Attached to Morag, but platonically. He escapes the siege of Deception Island with her in the *Aeolus*.

Niobe

Daughter of a miner, with a gift for detecting tantalum deposits from geological maps. Lover of Fogg, whom she meets at a Genrich school for talented outliers. Warm-hearted, fiercely loyal, brave, but impulsive.

Peregrine Mander

Manservant to the first and second Lord Vane and an associate of Potts, Spire and Crike. His deference is misleading. He is a master of manipulation and long-term designs, with a gift for appearing when you least expect him.

Oblivious Potts

Naturalist and advisor to the second Lord Vane. After running the library at the Tempestas Dome, he lives alone in a discrete valley close to Winterdorf. He assists Fogg, Morag, Benedict and Niobe in their endeavours to frustrate Cosmo Vane, as recorded in *Momenticon*. A friend of Crike. At the end of *Momenticon*, he flees his home, pursued by Cosmo Vane's forces.

Hilda Crike

A friend of Potts, who sees herself as a secret agent for the forces of good. She lives in Winterdorf. Resourceful, peppery, fiercely loyal.

The lith

A giant humanoid made by Lord Sine, and Cosmo's enforcer.

Piety

Companion and occasional lover of Cosmo Vane. Corrupted by him, but not without some underlying decency.

Mr Venbar

A senior weather-watcher who alone stayed on in the original Tiriel's Tower (*see* the Tempestas building). In *Momenticon*, he is killed there by toves, while assisting Fogg to escape.

Miscellaneous

(1) The **Northerners** are craftsmen who inhabit an underground town in the same mountain as the original Tempestas building (*see above*), where they worked for Tempestas before the Fall. They remain there and continue to work for the two great companies, but at arm's length.

(2) **Wonderlanders** are human constructs made by Lord Sine to showcase his talents. They resemble and act like characters in Lewis Carroll's Alice books. The Hatter, Tweedledum and Tweedledee died in *Momenticon*, but others remain.

(3) **Manuals** (Morag's word for them) were hyperintelligent humanoids created by Lord Sine to carry out his various projects at Genrich, but they suffered from mental illness. They were eliminated at the Tempestas party on the second Lord Sine's initiative, with the second Lord Vane's connivance, having been lured by momenticons into entering the murk.

(4) **AIPT** An automated physical trainer widely used in Tempestas buildings and vessels. Fogg has one in the Museum Dome, which joins him on his travels.